Advance pr

From Drying Lakes is fi
capture the innocer
hood. What's more, James Mossman
storyteller who knows how to lure the reader into the very pages of this book until Boy's story becomes your story. Hidden in these stories is a powerful message that will change the way you look at life and relationships. Once you start reading this book you won't be able to put it down.

—Daniel S. Hanson, author of *Room for J*, *A Place to Shine* and *Cultivating Common Ground*

I highly recommend *From Drying Lakes*. It is a journey back into the soul of America, fraught with passion, humor, and surprise. A memoir of growing up during the Great Depression that rivals Huck Finn and Tom Sawyer, it reveals with extraordinary honesty the mysterious passages of the human heart.

—Stan West author of *Until They Bring the Streetcars Back*

It is challenging to put into mere words the wonderful range of emotions I experienced while reading *From Drying Lakes*. The stories conjured up strong, powerful images that felt familiar. I sense a deep kinship with the character of Boy. The idea of family is crucial to the survival of our society and our world. The first chapter of James Mossman's book clearly demonstrates how family strength and unity were able to save a life and ensure the creation of families to come.

The subsequent chapters expound on these themes by providing examples of how important inner strength and self-reflection are to our own, personal survival. And I found that some of the greatest truths in this book are those events that provoke laughter, where the humor is born by identification with the experience rather than by mocking or derision.

From Drying Lakes may be set in the period of its author, but its message speaks to the people of any era. In one of the most enlightening and artfully written sections, the Epilogue, James Mossman, in a few pages successfully brings together the soul of his work and how it relates to these times. Bravo!

—Mark Copenhaver, Playwright for the Mystery Theatre and former musical director and playwright for Dudley Riggs Brave New Workshop Comedy Theatre of Minneapolis, Minnesota.

From Drying Lakes presents an impressive first book. I'm enchanted and curious about the contents, and admiring of the author who has endeavored to take on the huge task of his own history (long before his birth) and ever-so-gradual rise into manhood (and what that means). His thoughtful Epilogue, alone, gives a reader much to think about. The memoir, history, and stories that follow promise to be useful and memorable for any reader, perhaps especially men and "boys" who wish to have a clearer handle on their own place in both their pasts and in contemporary times.

—Cindy Rogers, Editing Services

FROM DRYING LAKES

A NOVEL BY

JAMES F. MOSSMAN

Beaver's Pond Press, Inc.
Edina, Minnesota

FROM DRYING LAKES © copyright 2005 by James F. Mossman. All rights reserved. No part of this book may be reproduced in any form whatsoever, by photography or xerography or by any other means, by broadcast or transmission, by translation into any kind of language, nor by recording electronically or otherwise, without permission in writing from the author, except by a reviewer, who may quote brief passages in critical articles or reviews.

ISBN 1-59298-091-0

Library of Congress Catalog Number: 2004116969

Book design and typesetting by Mori Studio
Cover Photograph by Jim Gindorff
Trying to Save Piggy Sneed Used with permission from John Irving.

Printed in the United States of America

First Printing: January 2005

08 07 06 05 04 5 4 3 2 1

Beaver's Pond Press, Inc.

7104 Ohms Lane, Suite 216
Edina, MN 55439
(952) 829-8818
www.beaverspondpress.com

to order, visit www.BookHouseFulfillment.com
or call 1-800-901-3480. Reseller discounts available.

From Drying Lakes is dedicated to the men and women who, at an early age, were dealt lives that had to emerge from a drying lake created by the loss, through death, divorce, war, poverty, or abandonment, of an important loved one's time, energy or life.

It is also dedicated to the many mentors and wise ones who helped those who survived fill again the *drying lake of their life* by guiding them in learning to love and laugh and grow.

ACKNOWLEDGMENTS

There is a long list of benefactors I would like to and need to acknowledge for their help in the writing of this book. First, I would like to acknowledge the individuals I know consciously who have been of immeasurable help to me.

At the top of this list is my wife, Jacque Bieber. She has endured my intensity as I have struggled to put my thoughts on paper in a somewhat understandable manner. Beyond being my mentor, Jacque also was my proofreader. She spent many long hours in these endeavors. Also, Jacque's skills in networking and promoting are now coming to the foreground as first, we worked to find a publisher, and were fortunate to find Beaver's Pond Press in order to make this manuscript a book.

For all that Jacque has contributed and continues to contribute to this endeavor, I can but say a very humble, "Thank You."

Secondly, I acknowledge Joe Kaufert for the many hours he has taken from a very busy teaching schedule to read and reread this manuscript and make many very helpful suggestions regarding content, organization and flow. Without Joe's help I am afraid much of my creativity would have been lost in a mumble jumble of over-intellectualization and obsessiveness with minutia at the expense of either an individual story or how the story fit with the fabric of the whole manuscript.

Further, I want to acknowledge my sister, Jeanne M. Wiger. She is integral to many of the chapters inasmuch as she lived the times and places with me. Jeanne's willingness to read some of the chapters and to engage in lively discourse, always stating with, "I don't remember it that way," has been of immeasurable help in sharpening my skills and dialogue projections onto characters that had died before we were born. Thanks, Jeanne.

Among many, some others I want to call out to acknowledge are:

Dan Hanson, who gave me a wonderful compliment by publishing the chapter titled "The Harvest" in his book. This was just the encouragement I needed in order to persevere in completing my project. Also, Dan imparted a valuable piece of wisdom when he said to me one day, "To write you have to love words." Thanks Dan.

My friend, Jim Gindorff, graciously agreed to provide both the pictures for the front and back covers of the book, advise me on photo inclusions and lend his professional expertise in consultation with the design studio. Thanks, Jim, for your fine artistry.

I want to thank Bonnie Lind for both reading and commenting on the manuscript when it was in its earliest form, rough and incomplete and for her tireless work on the final edit. Thanks Bonnie.

I want to thank my friend, Jack Leonard, for his help in organizing the "Cavalry" chapter. Jack and I have been friends for 56 years. In my way of thinking and being, that is a gift of the gods all on its own. Thanks Jack, and also Elisa A. Titus, in the Alumni Office at Breck School, for sending me materials from the Breck Archives.

Finally, if this book finds light of day in the literary world, I want to thank anyone who reads it, for I firmly believe that the audience of any work, whether it is seen, heard or written, is as much a part of the meaning of the work as is the author, artist, composer or musician. Thanks, Who Ever You Are.

—*james f. mossman*

"A fiction writer's memory is an especially imperfect provider of detail; we can always imagine a better detail than the one we can remember. The correct detail is rarely, exactly, what happened; the most truthful detail is what could have happened, or what should have. Half my life is an act of revision; more than half the act is performed with small changes."

From *Trying to Save Piggy Sneed*
by John Irving

PREFACE

This is a book about a boy and his family, living and growing and sometimes dying, in Minnesota, the Dakotas and Montana Indian country, where they tried to survive and grow during the dust and depression years of the 1930s and 1940s. Some of the stories are set in the years prior to the "dust years" and some of them happened when rains and war returned. I have not tried to make the book historical in detail and yet it does reflect the histories of some of the ancestors.

The pivotal perceptions and experiences emanate from a character merely known as Boy, who is deliberately not given more than the generic name "Boy" as he is given the opportunity, by fate, to walk and discover his unique path. This, perhaps, is a gift of freedom, in some form, one that every boy of the future must be given if he is to become a man helping with the survival of a crowded and over-crowding world. Besides, and perhaps primarily, the boy is just Boy because life threw him into a journey where he needed to discover his identity, without the traditional parental and cultural guidance. In this way Boy is not unlike many children, where conquest, abuse, poverty, war or oppression cast them into refugee situations devoid of the usual structures of guidance, who must discover wise ones and mentors on their own.

From Drying Lakes is presented this way because there was the one thing Boy knew about his identity—that he didn't know anything. He didn't know anything about what a boy growing into manhood should look like, feel like or be like. Therefore, this book is about his soul's path of discovery as he tries to find some answers, or at least, the real questions. Boy's quest takes him to his history within a unique family and to a listening point within himself where he can be both observer and actor as he lives these years. Even in Lou's early death, Boy is set free to hunt for a new way of becoming a man guided, of course, in untraditional ways, by his goddesses of the hunt, Sophia, Inga, Elizabeth, Frieda, Ione and even by the stories of the Grandmothers, Anne Elise and Ann Eliza.

Most people start life with a name carefully chosen by parents, or at least the mother. Boy was named by happenstance, or perhaps you could say by mistake, as you will see later in the second chapter, "Louis."

Most names carry energy and the energy of the name is defined in loving or abusive ways by the parents. Boy's name also carried energy, but he had no idea what it meant until much later in life after many of the episodes of his life had unfolded; so too, for his parents, especially Boy's mother. Because his parents had not chosen Boy's name, they did not know or recognize what he was and was to become.

The conflict within Boy's baptized name, James Francis, was as much a mystery and challenge of discovery for his parents and parent figures as it was for Boy himself. This "Son of Thunder," as Holy Script described disciple James, (the name boy adopted for use later in life), versus the Franciscan gentleness of Francis (Boy's middle name), provided Boy with the lifelong mystery and challenge of "what's in a name?" This challenge of understanding one's name should be an opportunity for every child, as it can be the key to one's identify and self-worth.

While all of the events are set in actual locations, the characters are caricatures and fictitious representations. Any resemblance to an actual person is incidental.

FAMILY MIRAGE

GRANDPARENTS

Bolette Helgesdatter = = = = = Magnus Nelson

Bjorn Lie = = = = = Ingeborg Andersdotter

GRANDPARENTS

Emma Jett = = = = = William Truax

Joseph Lewis Mosman = = = = = Evaline Adams

Anne Elise Nelson = = = = = = Andrew B. Lee

Ann Eliza Truax = = = = = = = = = = Beal Turner Mossman

Bertrum Marcus Cora Inga Matty Elizabeth Julius Magnus Martin Rudy **Sophia** = = = = = = = = = **Louis** Emmy James Francis Ike Fred

Jeanne **Boy** (John Marshal)

LEGEND

= = = = = Married to

••••••• Offspring of

——— Siblings

(   ) Died shortly after birth

PART ONE

To Chuck and Sharon
and
Perks - The Best
COFFEE HOUSE

with a bit of
Caffein One can
over Come ANYTHING

James Mossman

THE DRYING LAKE

It was cold in his room as his eyes opened to the low light of a mid January morning. He shivered as he looked over to the bed across the room where his sister slept. All he could see was a hump under the heavy quilt Aunt Emmy had made. One of her long brown curls crept out from beneath the quilt into the frost-chilled room. The hump raised and lowered rhythmically in cadence with her breathing.

Boy snuggled down beneath his quilt, but still he shivered. His room felt dry and cold like the world outside. The snow, little that there was, covered the brown fields, dried pot holes and empty lakes. While Boy didn't know anything about droughts and great depressions, he knew he was cold and thirsty and needed to be held in the warm, strong arms of his mother and father, there to be given water and warmth that would green again his little four-year-old life on this wearisome winter morning.

Boy struggled out of bed, bringing Suzy, his stuffed dog, with him, and began the trek down the corridor that would lead to his parents' room. The door to their room was closed but he knew he could open it, and so he did. He stopped. He was not sure what to do next. They were in each other's arms, gently moving, his father on top, his mother softly moaning. Moments passed and then Boy said, "I'm cold. Hold me, rock-a-bye me."

He could have just as well have fired a gun. His father jumped; tangling in the bed clothes he fell to the floor. He cursed and gathered himself. Throwing on a robe, he headed out the door and down the stairs.

Sophia gathered her nightgown about her and Boy into her arms. Through his sobs of fear and shame Boy could hear the man he loved, more than any in the world, banging on the coal-fired furnace in the basement below. When the furnace noises stopped he heard his father's footsteps coming up the stairs.

Then there was a scream and a deadly crash as the 6-foot, 6-inch man tumbled back to the bottom of the stairs. Boy, in Sophia's arms, looked down from the top of the stairs at the paralyzed, crumpled body of his father there below.

In that moment the drought, the drying lakes, came inside the heart and mind of Boy, his mother and sister. From here their life would need to start again. The emptiness of their beings would need to fill and green.

THE GUN

Sophia's grandparents were born in Sweden and Norway. Her grandfather, Magnus Nelson was born in Varmland, Sweden. He was a court jeweler and had served in the king's army. He also was a self-ordained preacher. In other words, he thought well of himself. He went to Norway where he married Bolette Inga Helgesdatter. Bolette was born in 1832. In the 1850s Magnus and Bolette immigrated with their oldest child, a girl, Anne Elise. Relatives said it was so Magnus could avoid conscription into the Norwegian Army. Anne Elise was about six years old when she came to the new world. She was to become Sophia's mother.

Andres Bjornson Lie was born in Valdres, Norway, May 31, 1840. He immigrated to the United States in early 1862 and settled briefly in Wisconsin. By April he had joined the Union Army, enlisting in the 13th Wisconsin Infantry, Company D. He fought in the battles of Vicksburg, Lookout Mountain, and with General Sherman on his famous March to the Sea. He was wounded and imprisoned in the infamous Andersonville prison. He and one other man were the only ones to escape and make their way back up north. Nonetheless, his experience in the Andersonville prison left him with terrible nightmares for the rest of his life.

Andres Bjornson Lie changed his name to Andrew B. Lee after the Civil War, partly because he wanted to simplify his name and partly because of his deep admiration for the great Confederate General Robert E. Lee, whom he considered to be a far superior person to either General Ulysses S. Grant or General William T. Sherman, under whose commands he had fought.

By the time Sophia was born on May 28, 1891, Andrew and Anne Elise already had ten children to feed, raise and love. Later, Cora Elvine, their second daughter, born in 1885, would die in June 1907 at the age of twenty-two. Andrew and Anne Elise did not take death lightly. They put all of their combined energies into raising and educating healthy, creative, independent offspring. When death or catastrophic illness intervened in their lives, they saw it not as a punishment from God, but as a challenge to take whatever radical steps needed in order to preserve the gift of life that had been entrusted to their care.

Now it was spring 1913. Sophia slowly descended from the train to the platform at the little depot in Farwell, Minnesota, as the wind caught her hair. The breeze was warm but dirty with the cinders from the train's belching, coal-powered steam engine. She coughed, and the pain and rattle in her chest reminded her why she had taken this journey back to this tiny west central Minnesota village where her parents had homesteaded and where she had been born.

Anne Elise and Andrew were there on the platform to escort her to the buggy for the ride back to the farm in Nora Township where she had grown up. She was the eleventh child. Sophia had been out of college but a year, having graduated from Augustana College in 1912. She was now 22 and a failure in the eyes of some. As they bounced along in the buggy, smelling the fertile springtime earth of Nora Township, the three of them were quiet and lost, each in their own thoughts.

Andrew was questioning if he had been right in his belief that each of his five daughters should have the opportunity of an education. He and Anne Elise had offered the same to their seven sons. They had both been adamant that daughters should be college-educated, if they chose, and sons should have the opportunity of college, but more importantly should have a trade. All five of their daughters, but none of their sons, had taken them up on their challenge of college education. The boys seemed to be doing all right, but not his girls.

Cora, considered the most beautiful of the girls, had died of tuberculosis. Anne Elise had taken the death very hard, as had Andrew, but in true Norwegian style his eyes had remained dry, even as his heart bled and nightmares invaded his sleep.

Andrew feared what the death of another daughter would do to Anne Elise, especially if Sophia had tuberculosis as the doctors feared. Opportunity and education always seemed to take his daughters away from the fresh air and good food of the farm and place them in high-stress situations within uncaring and sometimes angry cities.

But then each of the children was different in many ways including health and temperament. While all the girls had followed in Anne Elise's footsteps and had become teachers, they each had different talents and approached life in their own unique ways.

Matty, tenth in line and the third oldest daughter, graduated from St. Cloud Teacher's College after attending Augustana College for a time. Her interest was in music and in teaching music. After a time she moved to Kensington, the nearest village to the home village of Farwell, to teach music. Matty was stubborn and rigidly opinionated. As the buggy rocked along, Andrew's thoughts and musings flowed in pace with the clop, clop of the horses' hooves on the freshly graded NoraTownship road.

There was Magnus. He had stayed home and was now running the farm. He had never been in robust health. On the other hand, Rudy and Martin had gone west to Montana. Rudy and Martin seemed well and happy running their general store in Nashua. Julius had married Lena and they had gone to Fergus Falls where Julius plied his trade as a master carpenter. He was certainly healthy, but then he was always so angry, no bug would dare survive in him.

Inga, the oldest daughter, was like her mother. In fact Inga was the long-awaited daughter. Her mother had almost despaired of ever having a girl, since her first six babies were boys. Inga demonstrated such talent that as a girl of twelve, she was sent to live with Anne Elise's wealthy sister, Jen Houseman, in St. Paul. While living there, Inga attended and graduated from St. Paul Central High School. Life with Aunt Jen, while it had its privileges, was like living in a very strict finishing school. When Inga returned from St. Paul, she attended St. Cloud Teacher's College. She was a teacher and a musician at the time Sophia returned from Wisconsin. Inga had the robust nature of her mother, nothing would ever get her down. These traits of toughness, mingled with compassion and clear headedness, were a great support and resource for Sophia in this difficult time. Elizabeth, the youngest, was still in school at the college in St. Cloud, also learning to be a teacher.

Andrew continued to let his mind wander as the buggy bumped along. "No, it's bad luck," Andrew mused. Just bad luck, that Sophia got sick while working in the Lutheran orphanage in Stoughton, Wisconsin. He recalled the letters he and Anne Elise had received. He knew, from her letters, that she'd stood up to the administrative powers in the orphanage. Andrew thought Sophia's sense of injustice caused her to become ill. Mr. Olson, the superintendent at the orphanage, believed that the charges he was burdened with were guilty of some kind of sin for being orphans and needed strict confinement and discipline if they were to be saved.

Sophia defended the teenage girls who were in her care at the orphanage. Andrew was proud of her for that, even if the price was the sacrifice of her health, which in turn was the challenge they would all have to face together. Hard times had a way of opening new doors, forming new relationships and creating new solutions. What these hard times were going to birth he did not know. This is where he thought God came in, at least his God. His God never worked with major miracles any more than He indulged in major punishments. His God opened doors a little at a time and trusted people to make their way the best they could, with the help of one another.

"Well, God, here we go," he thought as the buggy bumped over yet another rut, and he felt Anne Elise firmly wrap her fingers around his arm as she always seemed to do when she knew what he was thinking.

God had blessed him and Anne Elise with these children, and certainly they shared the common value of believing in a God of equity and equality. If the practice of those values led any one of them into a place of exhaustion and disease, then all of them would need to rally 'round the flag of family and unity', thought Andrew.

He looked at Anne Elise out of the corner of his eye. God, how he loved her! He had never figured out how someone of her refinement could put up with someone of his stubbornness and determined ways. He knew he couldn't change. Who he was had gotten him from Norway to this country and then had gotten him through the War, wounds and all, and then had gotten him out of that damnable Andersonville prison.

What he couldn't understand was why God had blessed him and let him find Anne Elise. He didn't believe in miracles, but meeting her was awful close to a miracle.

Andrew recalled how he had met Anne Elise:

It was April 24,1865, and he had just mustered out of the Union Army. He didn't want to go back to Wisconsin. He had had enough of rocky soil in the south and in Wisconsin, where he had first landed, when he came from Norway.

That was partly why he had enlisted in the 13th Wisconsin Regiment. Sure! Part of it was because he thought it was the right thing to do. But a larger reason was he believed what his cousins had told him, which was that there was better land to the northwest.

Now, with the war over, he wanted better land, more fertile land, than the rocks and stones that northeastern

Wisconsin had to offer.He determined he would go northwest and file a homestead claim. He took his few belongings and headed for La Crosse. From there he could catch a steamboat to Hastings, Minnesota, and then it would be but a short way to St. Paul. There he could figure out where the best homesteading acreage was still available.

Union soldiers were being welcomed home. Parties were abundant and Andrew was invited to one hosted by Mr. Magnus Nelson, an interesting soul. Magnus had served as a court jeweler and had been in the King of Sweden's army. He had left Sweden and gone to Norway to escape the army. There he met Bolette Marie Helgesdatter, married her and had his first two children. His oldest was a daughter born in 1851. Then a son was born two years later. He took his family and left for the United States when Norway threatened to induct him into their army.

Magnus joined his brother in Wisconsin. They decided there was nothing there for them and so went by river boat up the Mississippi from La Crosse to St. Paul, looking for work. Finding none, Magnus settled for a time in St. Anthony Falls where he got a job cutting hay for Mr. Fridley. Magnus was also a self-ordained preacher, so the hay-cutting job didn't appeal to him that much. He wanted to be captain of his own soul and, some thought, also the souls of others.

In October 1864 he loaded up his belongings and headed for a half section of land where he had filed a homesteader's claim in Gilcrist Township, Pope County, Minnesota. He found his plot, built a primitive house dug into a hillside and roofed-over with rough hewn boards, but soon found that farming was not for him. He wanted something a bit more grand and less tiresome, so he sold his acreage to his brother for $300. He returned to St. Paul where he had left Bolette with their four children in a frame house a bit north of St. Anthony Falls, a house that had been provided by Mr. Fridley.

Shortly after he was reunited with his family, he opened his house to welcome some of the returning soldiers home, especially if they were Norwegian boys. He took pride in his self-appointed status, believing himself to be better than most others.

While Andrew, who attended the party, was not taken with Mr. Nelson's attitude, he was taken with Mr. Nelson's oldest daughter. She was beautiful and, luckily, less shy than Andrew. At the party she came and sat by him. They danced. They talked. She asked about the war. He told her the story about the Norwegian women he had met in the South, who while they were devout Southern ladies, were more devout toward their Norwegian womanhood.

"This encounter," Andrew told Anne Elise, "happened in Georgia when I was in General Sherman's army on the March to the Sea. We had run out of food and milk. My lieutenant asked me to go with him to a nearby farmhouse to inquire about getting some milk. As we walked through a pasture we noticed some cows, but when we asked the old woman and her two daughters for some milk, they told us that they had none. The three women, however, excused themselves and stepped into the house. The lieutenant and I overheard them talking in a strange language. The lieutenant asked me, 'Isn't that Norwegian?' I replied, 'Yes, and she is abusing us Northerners horribly.' When they came back outside to where we were, I addressed her in Norwegian and in the same dialect as used in Nordre Aurdal, the valley in Norway where I was from."

Andrew took a breath and went on, "Well! You should have seen the confusion, and then embarrassment, and then pleasure on their faces. They couldn't believe they were hearing the language of their childhood, a language they hadn't heard for thirty years! We not only got all the milk we wanted, but were invited in for a chicken dinner. Southern fried, of course! They invited us back the next morning to get more milk and chickens, as much as we needed."

Andrew softly chuckled to himself as he retold this story. Then his face went serious and sad. "The next day, late in the afternoon, I was wounded and captured and taken to the Andersonville prison." Andrew almost whispered.

When he got his composure back, he didn't want to talk about the War anymore. What he wanted was to hear the lilt of Anne Elise's voice and feel the warmth of her energy as she sat beside him and told about her schooling at the Normal Teacher's Training School in Glenwood.

Anne Elise said, "I'm glad my father gave into mother's insistence that we girls are just as important as boys and should be educated." The next two hours excited Andrew as he had never been excited before. Not only was Anne Elise beautiful, but she thought as he thought. They talked and talked about their dreams and values and what they thought the world could be if everybody had a chance that depended not on skin color, or culture, or gender but on who they were and what they believed.

Finally, Mr. Nelson came into the parlor. In a stern voice he said to Anne Elise, "You shouldn't talk to just one man. Besides, it is time for the guests to leave." With that he dismissed the young, enamored soldier.

Two days later Andrew was on a train heading northwest. He would take it 70 miles to St. Cloud, where the tracks ended, then, he would walk another 70 miles, if his map was right, to Glenwood, in Pope County. The Land Bank man said that if he went to the courthouse there, somebody could direct him to the land claim he had filed. Andrew was certain it would work out because somebody would know his cousin, Tolef Tolefson, who had come to homestead in this area the year before and had the claim adjoining his in Nora Township.

The man was right. Andrew found his way and then his land. The next two years were hard, but he settled in. Using carpentry skills learned in Norway, he and his cousins and neighbors built a school, a church, his barn and his house, in that order. Once the school and church were finished they needed a teacher for the school and a preacher for the church.

Andrew declared, "I will find the teacher." Then he instructed his cousin, "Tolef, you find the preacher for the church."

That autumn, Andrew walked back to St. Cloud where he bought a team of horses and a buggy, stabled the horses at the local livery, and paid the man to feed them and watch his buggy. Then, he got on the train headed for St. Paul. Once in St. Paul, he went directly to the Nelson house.

"Is Anne Elise home?" he asked a foreboding Mr. Nelson. "You probably don't remember me, but I was at a party you had in April, right after the War. I remember talking with your daughter and she was training to be a teacher. I have been in Nora Township the last two years. I have a farm there and we just built a school. We need to find a teacher," Andrew stammered on.

Mr. Nelson grudgingly swung the door open a bit more. "Come in. You can talk to my wife and daughter if you want," Mr. Nelson said, "but it won't do you any good because I don't approve of her teaching in some godforsaken place." With that he left the room and Andrew stood, hat in hand, and waited.

As Mr. Nelson knew and learned yet again, his wife was a force to be reckoned with. A week later Andrew and Anne

Elise, with her trunks and books, were on the train headed for St. Cloud. There he picked up his team of horses and his wagon for the rest of the trip to Nora Township.

Andrew had been confident that he could convince Anne Elise to come and teach—so confident that he had bought the team and buggy and had rented a room from the Tolefsons, who had the farm next to his. There Anne Elise would have board and room with plenty of quiet to do her study.

In the two years that followed, Andrew and Anne Elise spent many hours together. He reshaped some of the space at the school to make it more comfortable and to fit her desires. He picked her up for church and escorted her to all the socials. Everybody in the township knew he was sweet on her and she on him. He increasingly liked her for her mind and who she was. She increasingly liked him for his gentleness and strength. Both of them acknowledged it was much more than mutual admiration and more than just their minds that they wanted to share and merge.

In the early spring of 1870 they made the trek back to St. Paul to announce their engagement and to be married before they would return to Nora Township. Bolette was pleased, but Magnus was infuriated. He forbade his daughter to marry this commoner named Andrew. He ranted on and on in his best self-ordained preacher style but, alas, to no avail.

When the day of the wedding was set, he declared, "I will not attend!" No matter how much Anne Elise pleaded her case with him and told him of her love for Andrew, all he would do was scowl at her. Then, in a stern voice that could be heard throughout the house, he said, "I am very disappointed in you! I thought we had given you better morals and values than you display. I do not see or understand how you can do this to your mother and me. Have you not learned the Fourth Commandment? Will you not honor your father and mother as the Lord demands?" On and on he scolded her for her disobedience.

But Bolette Nelson did not agree with her husband. Privately she said to Anne Elise, "You are not only pleasing me, but I think God is pleased with your choice of Andrew for a life mate. I think it's God who brought Andrew into our house and into your life. Don't waver in your love and choice! Your father will calm down and come to understand. I will see to that!"

The day of the wedding, Magnus Nelson sat groomed and trimmed in the front pew of the church. When the service was over, Magnus stood, with the prompting of Bolette's elbow, and gave his blessing to the young couple in a strong and loving voice.

Magnus went to work two days after the wedding, which was a Monday. He now worked as a federal grain inspector. This day he was inspecting the grain in a boxcar that was on a siding to the main rail line, between Swede Hollow and Railroad Hill. The siding where the boxcar rested was directly alongside the main line going west.

Magnus had finished his inspection of a load of North Dakota wheat and was about to leave when his foot slipped on some loose grain and he lost his balance, tumbling out of the boxcar and into the path of a large locomotive rumbling west. For just an instant Magnus heard the shrill steam whistle of the engine. That's the last he ever heard. He died instantly! Anne Elise and Andrew delayed their departure for Nora Township for several weeks while they and Bolette helped each other grieve. When they did leave, they again took a train to St. Cloud, picked up their horses and buggy from the livery stable and continued their journey, stopping for the night in Sauk Centre. In the morning they bought and loaded all the supplies in their little buggy and continued on through Glenwood to Nora Township and their new home.

Nora Township was located eight miles north and a bit west of Glenwood, the county seat, which nestled on the shores of Lake Minnewaska. Nora Township was hilly, rolling land dotted with prairie potholes. Andrew and Anne Elise's homestead had a large shallow lake surrounded by cottonwood trees and black maples. The house that Andrew had built was a square frame building with two floors. He had placed the house a little ways from the barn and the barn close enough to the lake so the cows could easily drink.

Anne Elise and Andrew's was a loving relationship. They had found the fulfillment of each of their dreams in one another, albeit Andrew was a bit more stubborn and direct than Anne Elise had figured him to be. In due course, the children were conceived as they snuggled and talked and loved on the long, cold fall and winter nights. They added to the population of the township and the school. Anne Elise was their teacher.

Sophia, the fourth girl, was conceived on a late August night in 1891. It had been a hot wet summer so harvest was delayed, and worry was that the grain would spoil in the field. Andrew and Anne Elise would hold and comfort one another, pushing away the worries as they always had. The potency of their love reigned even now, when Andrew was fifty-one and Anne Elise was forty-one.

Sophia was a good-looking, sensitive child, endowed with a flair for the uncommon and the unreal. This latter trait led her to many places that others could often not even imagine. It also helped her become a source of great entertainment and pleasure to relatives and friends. Sophia's ability to step outside the usual way of seeing things was, perhaps, her greatest survival trait.

Shaking the memories from his mind, Andrew looked at Sophia, pale and leaning on Anne Elise's breast, turned the horses, and headed up the dirt path to the familiar house where she had been born and, as a girl sitting in the tree behind the house, had dreamed and schemed what her life would be. Now the script would change. She had dreamed of becoming a teacher because of her love for children. Later, as she entered womanhood, she dreamt of teaching religion, perhaps because of the influence of her mother, but more likely it was because of the crush she had on the young Reverend Gornson, her pastor. She also had dreamed of a career in nursing, but that was not as strong and was discarded altogether when she spent a few months studying nursing and emptying bed pans at Lutheran Hospital in La Crosse, Wisconsin. She finally settled in, studying teaching and religion at Augustana College.

When Andrew and Anne Elise had gone to Farwell, the little village with one main dirt street which led away from the railroad tracks, the grain elevator and the slaughter house, to meet the train and bring Sophia home, Magnus, Sophia's older brother, had been busy. The doctor had been summoned for Sophia's consultation, as had Reverend Thaddeus Philios, pastor of the church.

Magnus had not married, but had stayed on the farm to help run it and he would continue on in that role as his parents aged. Magnus was of a gentle nature, with a slender build and fine features. Soft lines formed his face and accented the firmness of his jaw. His eyes were deep blue pools that reflected his sensitive, artistic soul. His long fingers fit with his talent as a self-taught, accomplished violinist. Only his stooped shoulders told of the heaviness of his work and his propensity to bear the burdens of other people. Among his other skills, he was a maker of fine wine and he knew how to organize things.

By the time the horse and buggy returned, the girls—Matty, Inga, and Elizabeth, already had put together the *sacred* lunch, which was a necessity if Norwegians were to gather for any significant reason that had to do with life or death, such as baptisms or funerals, or now a consultation regarding Sophia's illness. Inga, Matty, and Elizabeth had left their various responsibilities and come home to the farm so they could be there when Sophia arrived.

Sophia gingerly climbed down from the buggy and made her way up the steps, around the cats and into the parlor where she was suddenly embraced by Inga and Elizabeth. Matty, always the aloof one, stood to the side.

The room was heavy with silence and yet much was being communicated. Tears streamed, leaving trails through the dust as they cascaded down Sophia's and Anne Elise's cheeks. Tears also left a wax-like shine on Inga, Elizabeth, and Matty's rose-colored faces. They embraced. Holding one another, they found strength and Sophia's fear seemed to ease.

Sophia was first to find her voice and softly said, "I don't know what to do. I just don't. The doctor in Madison didn't say so, but he acted like I would probably die!"

Inga exploded, "You are not going to die! Just put that idea out of your head right now!"

Then, as if magically, the doctor and the reverend appeared, standing uncomfortably next to Andrew and Magnus. Elizabeth and the neighbor lady, Christina Tolefson, had retreated to the kitchen to bring the sandwiches, Jello and hotdish into the dining area. Everybody ate in silence. With food, the feeling of comfort was restored and they began to talk.

Doctor Bernt Halvorson reviewed the notes that Sophia had brought with her from the doctors in Wisconsin. The notes described her fever and the cough. They painted a picture of the color of Sophia's sputum, told of the symphony of the sounds the stethoscope had revealed in Sophia's lungs, and finally listed the medicines Sophia had received.

Anne Elise, firm and strong of face, listened attentively. Andrew sat by her side with his hand on her knee. His face was masked with determination that he hoped would will health to his almost-youngest daughter. This child, more than any of the others, was the one with whom he shared a spirit of adventure—the spirit that was driven by the belief to trust in the Lord but take risks when you have to, a belief that brought him from the old world to the shores of Canada and on to Wisconsin and then to the fields of battle in the enslaved South. Most importantly, it had led him into the arms and heart of Anne Elise, his "Lizzie"!

Now, in this moment, they shared the depth of their fierce determination to find justice and wholeness in God's created world. In the deepest recesses of their hearts, they were prepared to do whatever was necessary to help Sophia get well.

Doctor Halvorson looked up from the notes and saw the human drama of fear and stubborn strength before him. His shoulders slumped and with a pleading look he turned to Pastor Thadeus.

"You tell them what the recommendations are, Thadeus," he said.

Reverend Thadeus began in his quiet, gentle, but firm voice, "They say Sophia should go to a sanitarium."

"You need to know, if she goes there, she may not come out alive," he said under his breath. "Or, they say, they can try one more thing. It's experimental, but some have been helped. There's not much else to do," he painfully concluded.

"What is the treatment?" Anne Elise demanded.

Now it was the doctor's turn."It's a form of creosote like they use on telephone poles so they won't rot in the ground. They refine it and boil it in water and the steam is inhaled into the lungs. Sometimes it helps but often it destroys the lungs and the person suffocates," the doctor informed the shocked little group before him.

They had hoped he would have better news for them. They wanted something to hang onto, something to hope for. And now, what this respected member of their community had told them was just about the opposite. It seemed there was no hope!

Anne Elise was on her feet."You will not choke my Sophia with these inhumane medicines. I know what they do. I watched Cora die. They create suffering and they do not help," Anne Elise softly but firmly asserted, with a look of vengeance, ready to do battle with any and all seen or unseen evil foes.

"I do not know what to do, but we will think of something. Good is stronger than evil. Health is stronger than illness. God is stronger than Satan. We will think of something," she proclaimed. Anne Elise was on a roll and nothing was going to stop her.

Andrew knew her nature as completely as his own, and he knew her fierce determination. Andrew turned to Magnus and told him, "Get the buggy and go into Farwell and telegraph your brothers. Tell them to get back here by Sunday, a week from the day after tomorrow. Tell them Sophia is sick and their mother is going to have a family conference to think of something to make her well. Now get going."

With those instructions Magnus left in his usual quiet way to do what was asked of him. But he would do it with a flair that was a closely guarded secret part of his nature. The doctor and the reverend looked on. They weren't about to try to remind Anne Elise that her plan might not work. They knew better. They had heard how Anne Elise and Andrew had stubbornly loved, willed and carried the whole Nora Township back to health from the hell of the plague of the mid `70s.

Anne Elise had cooked the food in her kitchen and Andrew carried it to the homes of the ill. He bathed the feverish and buried those who died throughout the entire township and sometimes beyond. When he came home from his rounds each night, he left his clothes in the barn and bathed in the warm water Lizzie had left in the tub outside the door so he would not bring the plague into their home. When his clothes got dirty he burned them and began again.

No! The doctor and the reverend were not about to challenge Andrew and Lizzie's determination in their quest to find a way to heal Sophia.

Now the doctor and the reverend stood and looked helplessly at each other. Dr. Halvorson broke the silence. He shrugged and said, "Miracles aren't my business, but I sure hope there is one. I would really like to see my knowledge pushed beyond its boundaries."

Reverend Thadeus nodded agreement and then said, "I suppose miracles are supposed to be my business, but I honestly don't know if my faith is strong enough to believe in them. I guess my faith will be tested this day and tomorrow and in the days to come." He looked at the ground, hands folded.

He said then, almost to himself, "O God, don't let me or my doubt get in Anne Elise's way." He added, like an afterthought, "Or yours either, God."

He would tell of this moment to the classes he would teach years later, when he was president of the seminary in St. Paul. He would say to his students, "You must be careful lest you become proud and arrogant in your faith, for sometimes the faith of those you lead is truer and stronger than the faith of those of us who would pastor. Sometimes God works in mysterious ways, in ways that don't seem to be limited to the Christian way. You must remember God knows what he is doing."

Magnus had sent the telegram as he had been instructed to. He had worded it very strongly:

Come quickly stop Be here by a week from Sunday stop Sophia is dying stop We must do something to help her live—mother says stop Get here stop I will meet you at the depot in Farwell stop Magnus stop

Rudy and Martin arrive first, from Montana. Rudy, like his older brothers, was of slender build. He had a quick smile and a physical energy that kept him always on the move. His enthusiasm spilled over in all directions. Word was, "Rudy can sell anything to anybody any time."

Martin, while of a similar build to Rudy and the other brothers, was more deliberate. His attitude was usually pensive and reflective. He was like a slow moving river, running deep.

Rudy and Martin came to Fargo from Nashua, Montana, the little town where they had their general store. They had boarded the Northern Pacific rail line in Glasgow, the larger neighboring town in eastern Montana. They had transferred to the Soo Line in Fargo to take them to Farwell. They came on Wednesday. Magnus met them as he had promised.

Julius arrived late that evening from Fergus Falls, in western Minnesota. Magnus dutifully made whatever trips were needed to get his brothers from the Farwell depot. By Thursday all the "Lee boys" had arrived. To look at any one of them was to know that they were indeed a band of brothers.

Inga and Elizabeth came back to the farm on Friday, arriving late in the evening on the Soo Line train. Inga had waited in Glenwood for Elizabeth to come from St. Cloud Teacher's college and they would travel back to Farwell on the train together.

The trip was light and easy in spite of the task that awaited them. Elizabeth admired Inga as only a younger sister can. "I don't care what it is that Mother wants us to do in order to help Sophia, but I don't think it will be near as hard as the stuff old Mr. Holden makes us do in geometry," Elizabeth offered.

"Well, I don't know. What Sophia has sounds pretty bad," Inga replied, and then continued, "I guess, I think, that the best chance for Sophia to get well lies with her. She has always been pretty stubborn and yet creative. She always looks at things differently from the rest of us. I think it will help her if she knows that we agree with how she stood up to that Mr. Olson, you know, the man who was superintendent at the orphanage. I think it's terrible what he did to Sophia all last year! According to her letters, he was always yelling at her and scolding her for not punishing the teenage girls she was in charge of. All she was trying to do was to help them have a life." Inga rambled on as if thinking aloud.

Elizabeth had been quiet while Inga was talking. Now all that broke the silence was the sound of the steel train wheels on the steel tracks. Then Elizabeth spoke. "I didn't intend to be casual when I said I didn't think it would be hard to find a way to help Sophia, I just meant that I think Sophia is the smartest of us, and that if we listen to her she will have the right ideas. I'm sorry, Inga, if I didn't seem serious enough. I'm just scared. I don't want Sophia to die! O God, what are we going to do, Inga?"

Now Elizabeth's oldest sister slipped across the compartment to sit beside her little sister. Her arms went about her and she was still holding Elizabeth when the little local train rumbled into the Farwell station, there to be met by Magnus.

Saturday was a day of more conversations, some happy, celebrating a family reunion for the first time since Cora's death. In twos and threes the family met that day. The conversations eventually turned serious and got around to Sophia and what could be done to bring her back to health.

Julius said, "Well, I think the situation is hopeless and the reason I'm here is to support Mother and Father. I don't want them to think I don't care about the burdens God puts on them." He continued, "I know I shouldn't think this way, but I don't think God's very fair, what with willing a young, talented girl like Sophia to be sick and maybe die."

Matty chimed in, "I don't think God's unfair at all. I think Sophia brought this on herself by going against the rules Mr. Olson set up for the illegitimate girls and boys at his orphanage." Inga couldn't let that go unanswered, so with an audible edge responded to Matty, "You don't know what God thinks! Besides, there is no such thing as an illegitimate child, there are only irresponsible parents. If you were just half as compassionate and fair-minded as Sophia. . ."

"Young ladies!" Anne Elise broke in. "There will be no more of that kind of talk in this house. Sophia is sick and we do not know the mind of God, but we do know that our job is to try to help her back to health. I want no more blaming or loose tongues in this house! Do you understand?"

Now the room was deathly silent. Julius sneaked out the door, quietly closing it as he left.

Inga, Matty, Elizabeth, and Magnus stayed close to Anne Elise, wordlessly doing the chores and cooking the meals. Inga and Elizabeth waited until they could go out by the tree behind the house where they could privately share the stories of Sophia's work in the orphanage—stories she had told them in the letters she had written.

Inga couldn't let go of the thought that anybody would think a child "illegitimate." She openly admired her sister. "I admire anybody like Sophia, who will stand up to a nasty old superintendent who would whip young girls for being evil just because they were born to parents who weren't married. Somebody like Sophia, with that kind of gumption, isn't going to back down from this little illness. Besides, God doesn't punish good," Inga said with an edge again shaping her voice.

Inga recalled how Sophia had battled, and finally succeeded, in getting permission for the teenage girls to form a group of their own, instead of being split up and scattered throughout the orphanage. Sophia persuaded Superintendent Olson, "It would be a kind of punishment for these girls to be removed from the other children. Why not house them in the attic?" Mr. Olson, without thinking, agreed.

Once together "her little flock" in their own space, Sophia could relate to them in a loving way not based on punishment for sins undone. Here she could sit with them late into the night and listen to their worries, joys, dreams and aspirations. Here they could laugh together, cry together, play together, think together and pray for liberation. Here she could protect them from the rules of the superintendent and his institution.

Anne Elise had quietly come around the corner of the house and overheard Inga and Elizabeth's conversation. Anne Elise, containing herself no longer, added to the story, "Why, Sophia would sit up most nights by the door to smuggle in her teenage charges so they could get by the old grouch. You know, all she tried to do was help them have a normal life so they could go to town and see the pretty clothes in the windows of the stores. Once in awhile, Sophia wrote, she would get caught and have to take the superintendent's self-righteous wrath. It was almost like being whipped on the girls' behalf. No matter what happens, even if God takes her now, I'm proud of her," Anne Elise concluded.

Elizabeth added, "The reverend even accused Sophia of leading these girls down the road to perdition. He said she was causing these urchins to become just like their mothers, unfit."

Now Matty appeared at the gathering. She had been listening and could be still no longer. "Well, I think Sophia brought this illness on herself. She had no business interfering with the rules this good man set. After all, these girls are bastards. We all have to live by rules and he was just trying to do his best. I know I shouldn't say this, but I think God is punishing Sophia. We all know that you can't change a bad seed, any more than you can change a Jew into a Gentile. A bad seed produces bad fruit. These girls were bad girls and so were their mothers. Sophia is getting her just deserts for interfering in their treatment." With that Matty walked away.

Anne Elise began to cry. She did not want any of her children to have such prejudices. "I wanted you all to believe in the goodness and equality of everybody and have tried to teach that," she said.

Magnus, who at some point had quietly come around the corner to sit down on a chopping block to listen, now stood and went to where his mother was standing. Then, he put his arm around her. Softly he spoke. "I think Sophia did the right thing. She's like you. You taught us all well. I think tomorrow when Doctor Halvorson comes and Reverend Thadeus is here, we'll figure out something that will help Sophia—something where the cure isn't worse than the disease. I think Matty will realize what she has done and come around," said Magnus in his usual mediating manner.

"Remember how Matty told Sophia to kick the cow that had swatted its dirty tail across Sophia's face? Remember how she had said, 'I wouldn't let a cow do that to me. Why, I would just kick it!' Sophia did and broke her toe and couldn't go to the ice cream social?"

"Matty doesn't have very good advice when she talks before she thinks. I think Matty sometimes is jealous of Sophia and speaks out of jealousy or anger. She and Julius sometimes have a lot of anger. But I still think they're both good people. I'm glad to have them as brother and sister," Magnus concluded.

When Magnus looked up, because he was looking at the ground when he spoke, Anne Elise was smiling as she recalled the broken toe and the rivalry between her two girls.

Sunday the church bell rang and they all went to sit in the church Andrew had built to listen to Thadeus preach about the wisdom of God and the mercy of Jesus. After church they all gathered in the parlor at the Lee farm.

It was a parlor built with care and Anne Elise had decorated it with equal parts of tender love and practical functionality. The parlor, which was both a family and a community gathering place, extended the entire length of the south-facing side of the two-story frame farm house. Its large windows kept the room cheery even on the darkest days of winter or the rainy days of summer. Across from the windows that looked out on the rolling landscape that changed with the seasons sat the coal-burning stove that heated the room and much of the rest of the house. Above the double doors leading into the room from the hallway that connected it to the kitchen, the dining room and the rest of the house was an open transom decorated with spindles hand carved by Andrew.

Andrew also had made the chairs, the tables, the little desk and the bookcases that furnished the room. The only furnishings in the parlor that Andrew had not made were the spindle rocking chair, the hope chest, and the upright piano that Anne Elise had brought with her when they married. Rag rugs that Anne Elise had made covered the polished, wide-board oak floors. She also had made the lace doilies that adorned the tables and rested beneath the fancy kerosene lamps. There was a table and lamp by the piano, the rocker and Andrew's large high-backed chair. On the table next to Andrew's chair rested the family Bible and a copy of the Farmer's Almanac. Magnus' violin hung by the piano.

Unknown to the others who gathered Sunday afternoon, Rudy and Martin had been hard at work on their private plan for helping Sophia. Martin had started working on the idea already on Thursday. He awakened early, aware he had been dreaming, but was unable to remember the details of the dream. But the thoughts the dream stimulated were there almost like a script.

On Thursday, Martin had taken Rudy aside and shared his dream-driven thoughts. "It seems to me," he said, "what

Dr. Halvorson was implying was the more traditional treatment for Sophia's condition is for the patient to go to an asylum. What I think the purpose is, as far as the patient is concerned, is to get as much fresh air as possible in a quiet and peaceful surrounding. Are you following me so far, Rudy?"

Rudy had been thoughtfully nodding his head and now said, "Of course. My own experience, you know, was that I was never as robust as you and the other boys, especially not as strong as Julius. But you well know I got stronger when you and I went into business out there in Montana, in the drier climate. God only knows we got plenty of fresh air and the only thing that disturbs the peace is the wind and the cowboys when they get drunk and shoot their pistols in the air on Saturday nights."

"Yeah, you and I are thinking the same way, I believe," Martin observed and then continued. "What usually gets talked about is how the community thinks it benefits by getting sick people outside of its confines. Now it seems to me," Martin continued to reflect in his usual way, "that the drawback in the asylum thing is that you got this whole bunch of sick people all lumped together so they keep spreading the germs around, and in that way they keep each other sick."

Since childhood, Martin always had been a sensitive soul and as the sixth-born son without any girls, his gentle, thoughtful demeanor had been a particular blessing for Anne Elise who very much wanted a daughter. His present thinking about a plan to help Sophia was probably driven as much by his desire to support and help his mother as it was to help Sophia.

Rudy and Martin's lumber, hardware and implement business in Nashua, on the edge of the Indian reservation in the Missouri river bottoms had flourished because of the balance struck between its owners' personalities.

Rudy really could promote anything and was a super salesman who could convince anybody that he needed whatever he was selling. What Martin brought to the table were in-depth observations and thoughtful plans identifying what a person or situation needed. What they shared in common was a sense of fairness, compassion and generosity. The frontier community of Nashua, both white and red, trusted and loved them.

"So," Martin now continued, "What if we located a quarter of land and filed it as a homestead parcel in Sophia's name?"

Rudy's excitement exploded! This kind of idea stimulated all his systems. His brain whirled as he thought of the freshness of it, the risks it involved and how he could sell Sophia and the family on its merits.

"Great!" Rudy exclaimed. "I'm sure there is still land available. We can check on that even from here by telegram. We can donate the materials from the lumber yard and store for a cabin for Sophia and. . ."

Martin interrupted, "We've got a lot of thinking yet to do. Let's see, what's the first step we have to take now?"

For many hours, into the next two days, Rudy and Martin continued their private scheming. On Sunday, they wanted to present their plan to the whole group.

It had been late afternoon on Thursday when Andrew realized he hadn't seen Rudy and Martin for a number of hours. Magnus came and reported to Andrew that one of the teams and a buggy were missing. That evening, when Rudy and Martin had driven the horse and buggy up the drive and into the yard Magnus asked, "Where have you been?"

"We went to Glenwood to the courthouse. We wanted to get some information for the meeting on Sunday," they answered, almost in unison.

"We don't want to say anything unless we know what we are talking about," practical Martin said.

"But we think we got a good idea that could really help Sophia get well," Rudy, the enthusiast, blurted out. "Now all we have to do is sell the others on it. And Sophia too, of course," he said.

Martin fidgeted, obviously uncomfortable with Rudy's impetuousness.

"What's the idea?" Magnus asked.

"We haven't completely worked it out, but. . ." Martin began.

Rudy interrupted him.

"Out near Nashua there's still some land left to be homesteaded. It's in the Missouri River bottoms, but it's only about eight miles from where we live and have our general store. We checked at the courthouse in town and it's still available. You tell him, Martin, what the idea is."

Martin looked irritated, but felt trapped so he continued, "What we were talking about was the idea of sanitariums that makes the most sense is that people get lots of fresh air and peace and quiet. So we thought if Sophia got that without having to be around a lot of other people who were real sick she might just get well," Martin said, now looking at Rudy for approval.

Rudy looked at Magnus and saw he was nodding his head. Magnus always did believe God was in charge of healing and He did the healing in his own time and in natural ways.

"Sounds like a good idea to me," Magnus said

"I wonder if the others will agree," Martin wondered.

"From what I heard yesterday afternoon, nobody else seems to have a better idea. We'll just have to see if Sophia's willing to go that far away and if she's willing to live alone," Magnus added.

"How long would she have to live out there?" he asked.

Rudy was quick to respond. "She just has to live there six months a year for five years."

Magnus let out a slow whistle. "That's a long time."

"But she'll have us there," Martin said. "We're only a few miles away. Besides, we can build the cabin for her. Some of our friends, both in town and the Indians that live down there, would be glad to help out, I'm sure. They also would keep an eye out. "

Rudy added, "We've given the Indians credit at the store and they also have helped us out many times before. They've even invited us to some of their gatherings for a meal."

"That's not what most people think about Indians," Magnus said. "Most people are scared of them and think they're savage."

Rudy, not wanting the conversation to go in this direction, interrupted. "I know she'd be OK. Besides, it beats dying."

Then the conversation changed to other topics, but Martin knew in his heart they had Magnus' cooperation and they had laid a solid foundation for the talk and planning for the get-together on Sunday.

The Reverend Thadeus and Doctor Halvorson arrived in separate buggies. Christina and Tolef Tollefson had come over from their farm across the section. Now they were gathering in the parlor. Magnus had moved the furniture to the side so he could set up some benches for extra seating.

Reverend Thadeus opened with prayer for guidance. Sophia sat next to Anne Elise. She looked drawn and exhausted.

Doctor Halvorson began, "I have been thinking and I think the best bet would be for you to go to a sanitarium for a while," he said looking directly at Sophia.

"No, no," Sophia softly protested.

"I don't know what else there is. Anne Elise here doesn't want the creosote treatment and I think she's right," the doctor said.

Then Rudy spoke up in a loud, commanding voice. "We have an idea that we think might just work."

He then began to discuss the idea he and Martin had come up with and had shared with Magnus. Everyone in the room listened attentively and the mood that had been heavy seemed to become more hopeful with the new option for helping Sophia.

Suddenly the mood of concern and fragile hope was broken.

Matty cleared her throat and stood up. Then, in a loud voice she said, "I believe Reverend Thadeus will agree with me. I think Sophia is being punished for taking matters in her own hands with regards to the girls at the orphanage. I think she's sick because she disobeyed God's way of justice and we shouldn't interfere with God's punishment."

She continued, "We have all been taught the basic things we need in life like honoring authority, how to follow rules and how to do things as they were intended to be done. For example, when I have studied music, I have learned that what I must do to have it sound right is to play it according to the way the composer wanted it played and according to the general rules for music. If I go off on my own and just play a piece any way I want or according to what I think sounds good to me, I am a disgrace to my music teacher, the composer and the people I'm playing for because I'm fooling them, because they think I am doing things in a right way and I'm not!"

"I think Sophia just went off on her own, didn't follow Mr. Olson's good rules of discipline for these bastard girls, which would have given them their only chance to learn to find their place in life and maybe get along. If they learn to do what is asked of them and follow what's set out for them, why, they might at least become cleaning ladies or something useful to somebody else. But no! Sophia taught them to dream and to break rules and to talk to each other about these things they thought and dreamt and thus learned bad habits from one another."

"I think Sophia was just too weak, a daydreamer, and doesn't know how to be strong in the real world, to live where things are not always like fairy tales. I think she gave in to the girls, and now is getting her just desserts by God making her sick, and I don't think we should intervene in the *will of God*."

Magnus' face was flushed. He didn't say anything, but he was angry or as close to anger as he would ever get. Everybody in the room knew that he had taught himself music and was good at the violin. He didn't know many of the rules of music, though Anne Elise had taught him what she knew. He had learned to play by intuition. He was so good, much to Matty's secret envy, that he was always asked to play at weddings, receptions, anniversaries, church socials and almost any event that took place in Nora Township. It wasn't in his nature to get in a fight, but he felt Matty was judging him even as she took God's place and judged Sophia.

Anne Elise sat in shock, just staring at her middle daughter. She couldn't believe what she had just heard. After long moments of deadly silence, Anne Elise gasped and began to cry.

Sophia sat, hands limp in her lap, staring at the floor. She wasn't even aware that Inga had come and stood by her and put her hand on her shoulder and with the other hand was gently stroking her hair.

Martin had come and sat by his mother and put an arm around her shoulder and now her head rested on his shoulder, muffling her sobs.

Andrew was on his feet. He shot an angry look in the direction of his third oldest daughter. His eyes were riveted on her eyes. There was no question that he did not approve of her attitude or her interpretations.

But it was Reverend Thadeus who spoke up. His neck arched. His strong face was highlighted by his fancy clerical collar. His voice was deep and resonating.

"God does not work that way. God does not disapprove of compassion or intuition that leads to acts of love. He does NOT give us rules to make us into puppets or take away our courage to do what is right even if it means doing that which is different. And most certainly, God did not create people to judge one another. Judgment is left to the Lord. Sophia did what was loving and right. This is most certainly true," he concluded, forgetting he was not teaching a confirmation class.

Matty went silent and wilted. But she dared not leave. Julius broke the silence and brought the conversation back to the task at hand. "I like Rudy and Martin's idea. It has all of the advantages of a sanitarium, but none of the illness dangers. But the important thing is what Sophia thinks. It's hard to be that far away, especially if you're sick. What do you think, Sophia?" he asked.

Sophia sat, shoulders stooped and eyes focused on the floor. She was deep in thought, puzzling over what she had just been hearing. When she looked up it was obvious that she had been crying, but now the tears had stopped. Sophia took a deep breath and imperceptibly her shoulders relaxed. She seemed glad to finally have an open invitation to speak after having spent days listening to others' concerns, plans and arguments over and about her. Finally a faint smile lit her face for the first time the whole weekend. Then, with a firmer voice than she had been able to muster before, replied, "I like the idea. It sounds like an adventure, and I wouldn't just stay focused on my sick feelings. I would get to meet some people I have always admired from the reading I've done. I would like to get to know some Indians. Besides, I know Rudy and Martin would be there for me. Most important my deepest belief tells me I think it would help me get well. I think what Martin and Rudy have done in looking into this is kind of like being used by God to help me."

Most everyone in the room was nodding their heads in agreement. They looked at Martin and Rudy, who were blushing a bit, but the little grin on their faces told it all. They were happy that most of the family and friends appreciated what they were trying to do.

Sophia spoke. Her voice was lowered as were her eyes. She again looked sad and defeated. "I just don't know how I could afford it. I'd have to have a cabin to live in. I would have to have money to file a claim. I would have to have a ticket for the train. I would have to have money for. . ."

Magnus interrupted, "We could all help out. Rudy and Martin have already been to the courthouse and they know how to file a homestead claim."

Inga chimed in, "I have some money saved I could put in."

Rudy said, "Our store could give the nails and we could get the boards, tar paper and window glass from the lumber yard to build the cabin. I know lots of the people out there would be eager to help you. They were already worried about you and wanted to know what they could do to help out when they learned we were coming out here for this meeting."

Doctor Halvorson interrupted Rudy and volunteered, "I can get the money for the train ticket. Thadeus here can get the church to give some money for groceries and for you to live on. He can call it mission money for you to work with Indians."

Reverend Thadeus coughed, not liking to be volunteered by someone else, but putting ego aside, he nodded in agreement.

Andrew and Anne Elise had tears in their eyes. They didn't like the thought of Sophia going so far away, but they liked the plan because it just might work. They didn't know how sure they were about the Indians. They had never really known an Indian up close and had heard all the horror stories and lies the same as everybody else had. Andrew knew from his war experience that prejudice is an insidious cancer of the soul that spreads like wild fire feeding a vociferous appetite on myth and lie and partial truth.

Anne Elise and Andrew had retreated to a corner of the room where they talked quietly. "What are we worried about, Lizzie?" Andrew questioned. "Martin and Rudy have been out there now for several years and nothing bad has happened to them. Lizzie, do you think, that in spite of ourselves, we have inner secrets that make us believe boys are better and stronger than girls and therefore more protected both by themselves and God? I sure hope we don't believe that!"

"I hope we don't believe that either, and here is God's challenge to test us, to see if we truly believe our girls and boys, and you and I, are of the same strength and worth," Lizzie concluded.

With that she squeezed his hand and they turned and went back to the others in the room.It was settled: Homesteading would be the treatment for tuberculosis.

Early Monday morning, Magnus took Rudy and Martin in the buggy to catch the morning train in Farwell. They would change trains in Fargo and board the Northern Pacific for Glasgow arriving in Montana on Wednesday.

When Magnus got back to the farm he saw Elizabeth and her father in deep conversation out by the tree behind the house. He approached them to tell them that Rudy and Martin had made the train in good time. He stopped when he overheard their conversation.

Elizabeth was saying, "But I'm still worried about Sophia. What if she gets really sick out there and there aren't any doctors to take care of her? Father, you know it's still the frontier. It isn't civilized like we are here. From what Rudy told me they have only trails, they don't even have roads and people ride all over on horseback. The cowboys come into town and shoot guns and get drunk and. . ."

Andrew was smiling. He dearly loved this youngest daughter. If she had anything she thought or believed or worried about, she would come and tell him. He was her confidant. He knew that. He didn't always know what to do with the things she shared with him, however.

Now he was baffled. He didn't know what to say to reassure her. He knew what she said was true. Yet he knew she wasn't asking him to stop Sophia from going, nor did she want Sophia not to go. She seemed to just want him to tell Sophia that she was worried about her, but she didn't think Sophia would want to hear that from her younger sister.

Andrew held up a hand cautioning Magnus not to interrupt and then said, "Oh, Elizabeth—you know Sophia will be all right, but you want her to know that you worry about her, even while you're proud of her and maybe even envy her a little. Am I right?" he asked with a hint of a smile.

Elizabeth looked at the ground and nodded. "What I really was supposed to tell you was that Mother said lunch is ready."

Six weeks later an official envelope arrived with the homestead claim enclosed. Andrew looked it over and then took it to Thadeus to review. When he got home he showed it to Sophia and she signed it immediately. The next morning Magnus took it by buggy to Glenwood to post it off to Washington. Sophia now had a homestead claim filed for 160 acres along the Missouri River in Montana Teton Sioux Indian country.

The following weeks were busy for Sophia and Anne Elise packing Sophia's trunk. There were constant interruptions as they were asked to listen to all kinds of words of encouragement and caution. The words were spoken by neighbors and friends and family. Sometimes the words were written and posted by mail. Gossip and reports of Sophia's pain and plans spread further, not only in the township, but beyond. When letters would arrive packing would stop and time was taken to read them. Not one person's concerns were discounted or put off.

Not only did everyone in the family have an opinion as to what Sophia would face, but so did the whole community. Dangers were expounded by most everyone. Everyone in Nora Township had an opinion or a fear to express.

The Indian stories came in for the most recitations and most were about savagery. Everyone knew someone, or had heard a story about someone, who had been raped or killed. Reverend Lindeman, a kindly former pastor, came all the way from Moorhead to tell about his brother-in-law who had been scalped by the Indians but had lived to tell about it.

Inga and Andrew politely smiled but then would return to fantasizing with Sophia about the adventure and not about savagery and the cultivation of prejudice. Most, including some in the family, had lost track of the reason Sophia was going west.

Anne Elise kept the most level head. First she would remind Sophia that she was going there to get well, not to be a missionary or to get killed. Then she and Andrew kept reminding Sophia that God created people in all colors, forms and fashion and had said that it was good. "You have nothing to fear in any way if you take God with you," Anne Elise would say.

Usually at that point Inga, if she was home, would remind her sister that "God helps them that help themselves." Then Inga would tease Sophia that maybe she could find an Indian who would have her as his bride.

Finally, the day came for Magnus to take Sophia to the train for the trip west. Sophia was still pale, gaunt and weak, so Anne Elise hid her tears and Andrew coughed often to mask his feelings and concerns as they rode with their daughter into Farwell to stand together on the depot platform until the train arrived.

Sophia boarded while Andrew settled her suitcase on the overhead rack and Magnus got her trunk safely stowed in the baggage car. The tearful goodbyes followed, accompanied by an extra long embrace between mother and daughter, broken only by a gentle tap on the shoulder as the train conductor, whom they all knew, quietly said, "Time to board." Then, more loudly so the engineer would hear, he cried, "All aboard." The train was gone, a puff of smoke between parallel rails disappearing into the distance.

Two days later Sophia stepped onto the platform at the Glasgow, Montana, depot. Her body was stiff from three days of jolting at the mercy of the train as its wheels clickety-clacked past the barren landscape outside the grimy window of the Pullman car in which she rode to her new life.

First the green fields of eastern North Dakota gave way to the brown prairie grasses, waving in the wind, sometime during the second night after they had stopped in Minot, North Dakota to feed the locomotive its ration of coal and water. The change was imperceptible as to when they entered eastern Montana and would have gone unnoticed had the train not stopped at Wolf Point, where Sophia got out to stretch her legs and see the sign, Wolf Point Montana, on the depot wall.

Now standing on the Glasgow platform, her eyes adjusted to the bright sunlight and her body shivered in the brisk wind of the freshening air which was following the path of the thunder and lightening that had rattled and pelted the Pullman's windows with rain and hail the night before. Perhaps the shivering was as much from fear as it was from the coolness of the air. The sky was big, the town's buildings unpainted, and the gumbo mud streets uninviting. Sophia thought, as she surveyed her surroundings, "If this is the 'big town' out here, what will Nashua be like? Or worse yet, what will my homestead be like?"

As she was lost in her thoughts Rudy touched her on her shoulder. He was there to meet her and take her to Nashua.

"You look real tuckered out, scared and tired," he said. "Let's get you a bite of breakfast and then we'll head for home where you can get a bit of rest." With that he took her by the arm and helped her balance on the wooden plank which lay across the muddy street. Once across, they went into the little brightly lit café where Sophia finally was able to catch her breath again.

On the way back to the General Store, twelve miles to the east in Nashua, where Martin and Rudy lived, Rudy told her about the cabin they had built down on the river bottoms where her claim was located. Apparently Rudy, in his excitement, had forgotten that all of this had been written and detailed step by step, board by board, in the numerous letters that had gone back to Farwell in the past several weeks. Clara, Martin's wife, was the one who was given the task of writing all the progress reports on the homestead preparations.

There had been so many letters and so much curiosity among the neighbors and town folk in Farwell that Andrew had taken to opening the letters when he and Lizzie picked them up at the post office. Once they had read the letter they would post it for others to read. Andrew would exchange the earlier letter with the next installment, when it arrived, so everybody in the Nora community was kept up to date on the progress of the preparation of the homestead cabin awaiting Sophia's arrival.

When Rudy began to tell Sophia how he and Martin had plenty of help, Sophia intervened, "I know, you sent us all of this in all your letters. I really liked getting the letters and reading about all the volunteer help you got from some of the men in town and from some of the Indians who lived in the bottoms, now that the soldiers at Fort Peck have driven them away from the higher ground at the fort. I liked that you told me that the Indians were of the Sioux Nation and that they were Teton Sioux and spoke Lakota. I feel like I have been a part of this whole thing because of the letters–like I'm not a stranger, even though I'm just getting here," Sophia concluded.

They fell silent as the buggy bumped along the rutted road. When they arrived at the R & M General Store, Martin rushed out to meet them. Soon the conversation turned to sharing the plans that had been made for Sophia to actually take over her homestead.

Martin first inspected her clothing and her footwear. He obviously disapproved and disappeared into the back supply room where he found some high leather boots. He handed these to his sister and said, "Put these on. They will protect you from snake bites. Where you're going there are plenty of rattlers." He began to go through her trunk to be sure she had all the right clothing and equipment she would need in her new lodgings. When he had added a few things, like Lava soap and an extra wool shirt for the cool mornings, he was satisfied. He took a deep breath, looked at Sophia and smiled, "Well, Annie Oakley, I think you're ready!"

"We'll leave tomorrow morning at seven," Rudy informed her. "That way Martin and I can be back here to tend the store when it gets busy in the afternoon."

The next morning the team of horses with the buckboard rumbled out of town heading south. Rudy and Martin had chosen to take the team and buckboard rather than the little Model T Ford truck because the horses and wagon were more dependable. That little truck could get its self stuck in almost anything, they had found out the hard way. Finally the rain the night before had settled it. It would be the horses and wagon that would transport Sophia to her new place of residence along the river Missouri. Rudy drove the team and Sophia sat by his side. Her trunk and suitcase, some last minute provisions and Martin were in the wagon box in back.

The eight miles seemed endless. The scenery was beautiful, but Sophia's endurance was taxed to the limit. She had managed to keep both her spirits and her energy up, but now she was losing the battle. At high noon they arrived. They had bounced and bumped along following a rutted trail across a barren, lonely prairie. Then suddenly they had descended a hill down into a wide green valley. Sophia noticed the wide brownish river in the distance. The great Missouri, of which she had read. Here in the valley the grasses were taller but the sky was just as big and the elevation beyond the river seemed like a sentinel watching over all.

Martin, noticing where Sophia was looking, said "Up there is where Fort Peck is. The Indians used to live up in those high lands but when they built the fort they forced the Indians to come down here to the river bottoms to live."

"I know. Rudy told me on the ride from Glasgow," Sophia said as she nodded in recognition of what Martin was saying, but her eyes had already turned to look at the simple one room cabin with its two windows, one in front and one in back.

Sophia, without a word, carefully climbed down from the wagon and went inside to look the cabin over.

There was a single built-in bunk with a honey pot beneath. No spring, just a horsehair-filled mattress. There was a chair. A table. Two kerosene lamps. A kerosene stove. Some cupboards and a place to store food. No refrigerator. There was a sideboard with a water bucket. The river was a hundred yards away. It would provide both water for cleaning and drinking, but she would have to boil it if she drank it. Also, she could keep things cool by putting them in emptied sugar or flour sacks and submerging them in the cool, mountain-fed, snow-melt water along the river bank. She would have to hold everything in place with stones.

Rudy proudly pointed out that the door had brass metal hinges and a brass handle with a latch.

After the inspection of the cabin was complete, Martin prompted that they needed to get back to town but that they would be back in a few days with more food and a few more blankets. They promised to bring her a better mattress as soon as one came in from the east. They promised it would not be made of horsehair.

Goodbyes were said and Rudy and Martin climbed in the buckboard and bounced down the rutted trail, heading back toward town. Sophia turned her back. She didn't want them to see her tears nor hear her sobs as they disappeared in the distance. In that moment, Sophia's loneliness was more overwhelming than she had ever experienced.

"God, why did I ever choose to do this? Why?" Only the wind heard her words. She went inside and began sorting about the cabin, putting things away. About an hour later she heard voices and the hoof sounds of several horses. She looked out the window and there was a band of Indians milling about. They seemed to be putting up a camp or something.

Fascinated, she watched the circle of poles with the skins and canvas laid on top, being pulled in a circle until it was upright and put in place. First there was one tepee and then two and when they were done there were six. Women and children were setting up cooking pots and tramping down grass in a kind of dance and to the beat of a drum. They sang as they danced, but their singing was weird and eerie.

She had never seen nor heard anything like this before. And then, fear swept over her—bone chilling fear. She remembered the story of the scalping as told by Reverend Lindeman. The rape stories . . . the kidnapping stories. She began to cry. Her knees became weak. She sat down and put her head in her hands. She lost track of time and didn't know how long she sat there.

When she looked up she saw an older Indian man walking toward her cabin. Momentarily she panicked. Her stomach turned to knots. She felt faint. She told herself to be strong. Could this man be any worse than the Reverend Olson from the orphanage? She answered her own question. "Yes, probably he could be worse, if the stories told by the neighbors at home were true. But things have always worked out before—even in the worst of times," she thought.

She remembered her mother's words about God creating good. She remembered that she had been told that God would protect her. She remembered Inga's words that "God helps them that help themselves."

With that she got up from where she sat and opened the cabin door so the Indian man would know he was welcomed. Now she noticed that he was leading a dog on the end of a rope. It was the ugliest dog she had ever seen. Its legs were short and bowed. Its face was all pushed in. Its jowls hung down and drool hung from them. It panted and its tongue hung out to one side. It was an English bulldog somehow out here in the middle of nowhere!

In his other hand the man held a gun, it was a little .22 caliber rifle, the kind the Remington Gun Company made for general stores and mail order houses back east and cheap enough so anybody could buy them—anybody, that is, who had a mind to use guns!

Sophia stood frozen in fear. She had no place to run, no place to hide. The reddish-skinned man now stood directly in front of her.

He cleared his throat. He had a speech he had prepared, the best he could, in English. "Your brothers are good men. They told us you were coming here to live because you are sick. We helped them build your house. Your brothers are *kola*." It was evident that this was hard for him and he couldn't think of the English word for "friend" so he used the Lakota word, "*kola*." "They have given us food and ways to buy things when we had no money."

He paused and looked her deeply in the eye. His gaze did not waver. "I have brought you a dog to keep you company because it gets lonely here sometimes."

He handed Sophia the rope. Dumbfounded, she took it.

The man continued, "I have brought you a gun to protect yourself from snakes and cowboys who sometimes get drunk and rowdy," he said. He handed Sophia the gun, which she took as though in a trance.

"My people will come here each year. We will come and camp here. You are welcome to come and eat with us sometimes. You can come to our ceremonies for doctoring and healing for your lungs." He put a hand, palm down, over his chest. "I will bring you medicine from Mother Earth."

Again, for a long moment, the Elder Man of reddish skin looked intently into Sophia's eyes. "My people will camp here each year when you come. You can come and eat with us sometimes," he repeated as if for emphasis. He had finished his speech and with that he turned and left, walking back toward his camp.

Sophia stood looking after him as he retreated to the little tepee village. It was as though she was rooted to the ground. Almost anything else this reddish-hued man might have said or done would not have surprised her so much. He could have screamed at her or come to scalp her, or shot her so the dog could lick her blood, or raped her! But to come with a speech and a gift? Myth and story, told in Minnesota, had not prepared her for this welcome, this gift of love.

Sophia felt numb and lost for words. She looked at the rope in her hand and her eyes followed it to the neck of the dog who sat gazing up at her, smiling and drooling, eyes happy, waiting to play. God he was ugly, but, oh, so beautiful!

The empty space of her isolated cabin in this lonely land by the muddy river was being transformed. Suddenly aware of the weight in her other hand she looked down and saw the gun and tied to its barrel was a leather pouch filled with .22 caliber shells. That arm suddenly felt heavy and out of place. She slowly and carefully lowered it to the ground and as she leaned to put it down, the dog in his best bow-legged waddle came to her and used his long, wet tongue to plant a kiss of welcome on Sophia's face as his drool ran down her dress. She laughed—the first sound her voice had made. As her hand left the gun, she wrapped her arms about the compact and chunky English bulldog body. She pulled him into her lap and rocked back and forth as she sat cross-legged on the prairie grass.

How long she sat and rocked and wept tears that washed away the months of fear and tension, she did not know. Maybe God didn't even know. What she knew in that moment was that the fear of death had faded, shrunk and then disappeared. She would live!

The dog licked the salty tears from her cheeks as she listened to the drums, sounding like a heartbeat, bringing life as the sound wafted through the air and engulfed her little cabin. Now the Indian voices, raised in song and chant, acted like a lullaby and her mind drifted to a new and deeper place of inner peace.

The touch on her shoulder startled her. She looked up—directly into the round Indian woman's smiling face.

Dog, soon to be named Buster, had wandered off to pee and now sat, tongue hanging from the side of his mouth, waiting to hear what the women wanted.

"Come. It is late. The sun is almost gone. We will feed you," the Indian woman said quietly as she reached for Sophia's hand.

"What about the gun and the dog?" Sophia protested.

"Put them in your house. They will be there when you have filled your belly."

The kind, soft-spoken Indian grandmother led Sophia by the hand back toward her camp. When she got to the little group of tepees, she was invited to sit in the circle with the women. No one spoke for some time, but Sophia knew they were all looking at her and deciding what kind of a woman she was.

Nor did Sophia speak. The moment was magical and she yearned for them to like her. After a time, one of the women handed Sophia a bowl filled with some kind of stew and said, "Eat. Your sickness has taken your roundness. Our food will help you get it back."

When she had finished eating, several of the women walked with her back to her cabin. When they got there, one of them handed her a bowl filled with assorted scraps of meat. "This is for Dog so he doesn't get skinny like you." They all laughed, including Sophia.

As she watched the women fade into the shadows as they returned to their camp, Sophia felt more tired, but happier than she had for months and months—maybe ever.

She was brought back to reality when dog pushed his cold wet nose against her leg and another strand of drool ran down to her foot, now covered with the moccasins the women had given her at supper.

Sophia looked at the dog and said, "I'm going to name you Buster, because you are always busting in on my thoughts." Buster merely panted and drooled some more until she put the bowl down. He gobbled it down. Afterwards when he had finished, Sophia gathered him in her arms and carried him into bed to sleep the night with her in her little bunk bed with the horsehair mattress.

This night Sophia didn't even undress. She just drifted off to dream of little people-beings touching her with eagle feathers by her heart and lungs and on her head. When she would become restless and surface to a conscious state, she still heard the heart beat of the drum crossing the night-shrouded space from the Indian village to her little cabin and she would follow the heart beat back to that deepest place of healing rest.

In the morning, Buster was still on the little bed, but pulling on her arm ready to go meet the day and find its prizes. Sophia chided him, "All right now, out with you," and with that she opened the door and Buster bounded out.

Before returning to the little kerosene stove to prepare her breakfast, Sophia looked across to the tepee village where she saw thin smoke plumes rising from each of the tepees. The women seemed to be busy dragging willow bows up from the river bank. Later Sophia would learn that these were to build a shade under which the men and women could sit in the heat of the day. There they would talk or sew or make tobacco ties.

Sophia would be invited to sit under the shade with the women and would learn their way of sewing and making the prayer ties (tobacco ties) for the ceremonies and sweat lodges that would happen on some of the evenings. These ceremonies and sweat lodges were for help and healing and she was encouraged to attend.

One of the older women, an elder, who knew some English, explained, "Our people know how sickness comes when things are not in balance. In our ceremonies, the grandfathers and grandmothers come back from the other world to help us restore balance in our lives. They will come and help you, too."

Sophia listened a lot in the days that followed. Often the ones that knew a little English would help her understand. Sometimes they even tried to teach her to speak a bit of their Lakota language. She and they together laughed at her sometimes awkward attempts. Little by little, she was accepted.

One day one of the younger women said "*Kola*, come here. I want you to teach my boy your speech." Sophia was overwhelmed. She had learned that *kola* meant "friend." She was now accepted. She was one of them and they were part of her. From that time on, as long as she came each year to live on the land and prove the homestead, she called them kola. Privately, in her heart she thought of them as her *oyate*, her people, but she did not say that, even to her closest friends, for she knew that to be *oyate*, she needed to be born to the tribe, the Lakota Indian nation. She told only Buster of the knowledge of her inner heart.

Sophia did go to many of their ceremonies for healing and for help. Deep friendships formed with the women. The Medicine Man doctored her.

The women ministered to her in their sweat lodges. And her body and lungs were purged of the spirits of evil, illness, and death.

She ate many meals by their fires and learned to love the taste of their food. The smell of sage and sweet grass were like perfume for her soul and she liked the way it clung to her clothes so that it could go with her all the day. She listened to their songs and drums that no longer sounded frightening or eerie, but friendly and welcoming.

They gave her clothes the women friends had made especially for her. They said she needed more of Grandfather Sun. They teased her that she had hidden from him so long that her skin did not have Grandfather's touch of red.

In return she taught their children English when they wanted to learn English. They, in turn, tried to teach her the proper language of the *oyate*.

When Rudy and Martin would come from Nashua to visit and bring supplies, they were quick to notice the friendships Sophia had made and soon began bringing supplies for the tepee village as well. Sometimes these supplies included bolts of cloth that the women were able to quickly convert into beautiful dresses and clothes for all in the village.

Rudy said to Martin one evening, as they bounced in the Model T Ford truck, on the way back to Nashua, "You know, I maybe shouldn't think this way and I probably shouldn't say it, but I'm really proud that we instigated this journey of healing for Sophia. I'm sure if old Reverend Thadeus heard me say this he would scold me and tell me, 'You know my boy, pride comes before the fall.' But I don't really give a damn! I think we did a good thing. What do you think, Martin?"

"I'm with you. I couldn't agree more, Rudy. And, you know, I believe Mother and Father would say the same thing. Father, in particular, really likes Sophia's spirit and watching her with the folks out there. I can understand why."

True to their word the Indians came each year, for five years, while Sophia proved the homestead. At the end of the five years she was one with them and they with her.

She believed to the day she died that the Indian spirits had healed her with the love she had experienced in the community of tepees and Buster's warmth when he slept at the end of her little bed.

The dog traveled with her each time she returned home to Farwell and when she came back each year to the little homestead cabin and the tepee village. When the time came that the homestead claim was fulfilled and secure in Sophia's name, and the government had no more claim on the land, Sophia began the painful process of saying a final farewell to her dear *kola*.

On her final night, a feast was held in her honor. There were tears and laughter, stories and remembrances. The Elder who had brought Buster and the gun to her that first day when she had arrived at the cabin stood and said, "We did not know you when we met you. We knew only your brothers and we trusted them. Now we know you and we love you. Wopala to Tinkasila—in your talk 'thank you to God'—that you came to live among us. Now I sing this honoring song for you." He sang a song in Lakota and sat down. Sophia wept. Rudy and Martin, who had come to be a part of the evening, wept as well.

A final ceremony was held and when it broke up well after midnight, Sophia and her women friends sat and talked until Grandfather Sun raised his head above the horizon and cast a soft aurora light, like a halo, about this special group of the people, the *oyate*. Then the other women quietly left to return to their tepees and their lives. Finally, only Sophia and the grandmother who had first led her to the camp those many years before were left. With effort, Grandmother arose, reached down and took Sophia's hand and together they walked back to her cabin where Rudy and Martin were waiting in the buggy packed with her things, Buster sitting on top. They would take Sophia back to her other life.

The next day Sophia boarded a train that took her to St. Paul. Buster was left behind to live with Rudy, even though Rudy's wife didn't appreciate Buster's looks nor his drool nearly as much as Sophia had. Well, maybe not the drool–none of us is perfect.

On the long train ride east, Sophia mused about all her experiences and worried what the future might bring. The Great War was coming to an end in Europe and soon the doughboys would be leaving the trenches of the Argonne Forest in France and coming home. There would be so many that jobs would be hard to find. This worried Sophia. She had decided what she would do as she thought about it during her solitary time on the prairie.

She wanted to be a storekeeper. She had observed the life that Rudy and Martin had and she knew she had skills similar to theirs. She wanted a store where she could sell fine clothing made and fitted with care, like the Indian women had taught her. The problem was she didn't know a thing about selling or running a business. She would need to find a mentor, somebody who could tutor her in these skills. Where would she find such a person? She didn't know, but believed the way would open as it had on the plains when the Elder had brought her the dog and the gun.

As if for reassurance, she looked up at the overhead rack above her seat and stared, for several minutes, at the little gun, wrapped in oilskin that rested there. Sophia drifted into sleep as the train rumbled on, making its way to St. Paul, Minnesota, where she would live with her austere Aunt Jen Houseman, her mother's sister.

LOUIS

Watertown, South Dakota, 1931. The Depression was in full swing. The land was a dust bowl from Oklahoma to the Arctic Circle. Farmers' eyes were blinded and their throats choked on dust as they struggled to hang on to what was left of their land and their lives as they watched the dark wind blow away the rich topsoil of farm and soul alike.

Louis Marshall Mossman, sales manager and poet, was sandwiched between the corporate John Deere giant and the customer-farmer whom he loved. Already he had lost one job with McCormick Deering-International Harvester—a job he had held for 23 years but lost because he could not bring himself to foreclose on the debt-ridden, indentured stewards of the land. He could not bring himself to take homes and land just to satisfy the gluttonous appetite of the big red giant, International Harvester.

Now, John Deere, the hungry green monster of the plains, was asking him to do the same. At home, in the little bungalow where they had recently settled, Sophia had Boy at her breast. She was beleaguered. This was a child she did not want and now it was sucking the milk of life from her. From the next room she heard the pain-laden cries of her one-year-old who was very sick. Sophia was burdened by life itself. She had little left to give to a husband struggling with his passionate, occasionally impractical and sometimes depressed poetic soul.

Louis was a big man. At six-foot-six, 240 pounds, he would have been a good candidate for foundry work. Instead, his soul was that of a poet and an artist placed in a package others could not understand.

He had been born on a gloomy October day in 1885. He was the youngest of the children born to Beal Turner Mossman, a rugged Scotsman, and Ann Eliza Truax, his Scots-Irish wife. Together they had came from Indiana to West Bend, Minnesota, and then to a homestead on Birch Lake near Grey Eagle. Their first child had been a boy, born in Coesse, Indiana, and then a girl was born, followed by three more boys, all in Indiana. When they arrived at Birch Lake in Todd County, Minnesota, on April 1, 1880, Ann Eliza felt her family was complete. Besides, she was tired of children, boys in particular. Then Louis Marshall came into the world. She recalled the night he was conceived. She had feigned sleep as Beal moved and grunted on top of her. Her lack of passion had not protected her. Beal was 49 and she was 45 when she bore her last son.

Louis Marshall Mossman was born into a world that wanted its men to be rugged individualists. It was not a world that valued males who liked butterflies and trees and quiet afternoons dedicated to daydreams about the sting of the cold from the first snowflake of winter or the smell and taste of earth after the lightening and thunder of a male rain, as the Indians called it.

A fortunate turning of the stars brought Emmy Evaline, Louis Marshall's only sister, back to Birch Lake shortly after he was born. Emmy was twenty years old when she returned. At eighteen, she had eloped with Mr. James Gilbert and had run off to join the circus. James Gilbert, at 7 feet, 4 inches, was the "tall man" in the circus. Emmy, herself, was over six feet tall but her claim to fame was her auburn hair. In its natural state, Emmy's hair would touch the ground. With a little help from a hairpiece, she could sit astride a horse while her hair reached the ground as she embraced Mr. Gilbert standing by her side.

For two years they had lived in New York during the winter. Their apartment on Elizabeth Street on Manhattan's Lower East Side was home. It was but a stone's throw from the Dime Museum where Gilbert earned a few dollars as the giant—the freak—while waiting for the spring's warmth and the circus to travel again. For two seasons they traveled with Barnum & Bailey. The spring and summers were exciting and fun, but the winters were harsh and taxing in the tiny, sparsely furnished, barely-heated tenement.

When Emmy left home to elope with James Gilbert and follow the elephants and lion tamers from one town to the next, she left behind a worried mother and an angry father.

Beal, in his anger, forbade his wife to even think of Emmy as their daughter. Her name was not to be spoken. Ann Eliza said nothing, but in her heart she did not agree with disowning Emmy. Intuitively, she knew her daughter would contact her.

Ann Eliza would wait until Beal went to the fields or barn to work before she would gather in the mail. And as she knew it would be, the letters and cards soon began arriving from Emmy. They came from many places: Dearborn, Michigan; Macon, Georgia; Anderson, Indiana; Scranton, Pennsylvania. The list of places went on and on. Most of the messages were hopeful and happy while they were on the road, away from the tiny tenement in New York City. However, in the winter, the ones from Elizabeth Street often were sad. They had the feeling of gloom and seemed to be gray, almost black, and lacking in hope. Ann Eliza learned to fear the New York postmark.

Nonetheless, Ann took each card and letter to the black walnut dresser in the bedroom she and Beal shared. Carefully she hid them under her camisoles, petticoats, and drawers. She knew Beal would not touch her personal, private things.

Ann Eliza never answered any of the letters. She feared Beal's wrath. In Grey Eagle a letter posted to New York would be an event not unnoticed. She feared what the postmaster might say to Beal when he went to town on his creamery run. She knew as well that letters arriving from New York and all kinds of other distant places were fodder for the wagging tongues wandering up and down the streets of Grey Eagle. She had figured that if Pete, who brought the mail, ever said anything about the letters coming from Emmy, she would tell Beal she had not read them and had burned them in accordance with his wishes. That's the best she could do since Pete was duty-bound to deliver the letters or lose his job. She trusted that Beal would believe her. He always did. Ann Eliza hated having to choose between her daughter and her husband, but choose she did, and lie she would, since Beal had demanded it.

One day in May, 1885, a letter arrived from Chicago. It read:

> *It's good to be on the road again. James and I so enjoy each other when we travel. He is such a good showman and I am learning how to act as well. You will not believe this, but in June we will be in Minnesota at the fairgrounds in St. Cloud for a five-day run. I so wish you could come and see us.*

Ann Eliza was three months pregnant with the child she did not want. She knew the wisdom of the day said she should not travel. She also knew that Beal would never agree to her seeing Emmy, much less Mr. Gilbert. Yet that night she schemed how she could make an excuse to take the train from Ward Springs to Sauk Centre and then somehow get the train from Sauk Centre to St. Cloud, and to the circus, without being found out.

At four a.m. she awoke with a brilliant plan in her mind. She lay very still. She dared not even think about the plan for fear the prospect would excite her and she would become restless and awaken Beal, who snored beside her. But at five, when Beal awakened, got up and took the honey pot to empty on his way to the barn for milking time, she let her thoughts flow free. The excitement was overwhelming.

She decided she would take the two youngest boys, Fredrick and Beal Jr., Ike, with the excuse of going to Sauk Centre to spend a few days with her friends, the VanCamps. Ann knew in her heart that she could tell Maude of her plan for the clandestine meeting with Emmy and James. Maude would keep her secret. She also knew that the promise of the circus would keep the boys within her circle of conspiracy. Besides, little Fredrick always lied, so even if he told, no one would believe him.

Once her plan was firmly in place, Ann Eliza talked to Beal about her proposed visit with the VanCamps, and he was all in favor. June 18 dawned bright and clear as Beal harnessed the team and loaded Ann Eliza, the boys, and their suitcases, into the buggy. At Ward Springs he put them all on the local train for the twelve-mile ride to Sauk Centre.

Looking at Ann, he said, "Have a good visit, but be careful and don't get too tired from all your talking and gadding about. You know you're in the child way." With that he turned the buggy and drove away.

When they arrived at the Northern Pacific depot in Sauk Centre, Ann grabbed little Fred with one hand and a suitcase with the other, and in a firm voice she instructed Ike, "Take the other case and hurry on now. Follow me across the tracks."

They settled on the east bound platform to await the Main Line eastbound train that would take them to St. Cloud. A two-hour wait and then they were on the train heading for the circus and the rendezvous with Emmy Evaline and James Gilbert.

The circus was fabulous. The boys' eyes were like saucers as they watched the high wire, the trapeze, the clowns, the elephants and the lion tamer as he drove the beasts through the circle of fire.

Ann Eliza and Emmy didn't sleep for two days. There was so much to say and so much catching up to do. "Did you hear. . . ? What ever happened to. . . ? How is old Mr. . . ? Is daddy taking good care of my horse Jiggs? How is daddy? Is he still mad? Do you think he'll ever talk to me again?" Emmy's tears and questions spilled like a waterfall.

James Gilbert smiled fondly at Emmy as she rambled on. It was a look that Ann Eliza did not miss and it pleased her. When Ann Eliza and the boys went back to Sauk Centre two days later for her visit with Maude VanCamp, she felt that the only weight left for her to bear was the pregnancy and the unwanted baby. Her daughter was well and deeply loved. Emmy had returned, and that space in Ann Eliza's heart was filled once more.

Back home, sitting in her favorite rocker on her front porch listening to the mosquito-and-cricket evening concert while watching the sun sink into Little Birch Lake, Ann Eliza rocked back and forth. She silently reflected on how good it had been to see Emmy.

October came and Louis Marshall was born.

On March 30, 1886, Henry brought the telegram from the depot in Grey Eagle. Beal tore it open and read in silence. Without a word he handed it to Ann Eliza and turned his back. He stared beyond the window at the ice-covered lake with its ghost-like birch trees. He coughed, his breathing became shallow and his shoulders shook as he struggled for composure. He felt Ann Eliza's hand on his arm and he heard her sobs choking her. He took her hand in his and they stood looking at the lake as if asking it to wash away the shame and pain of choices made in haste and the walls of alienation erected by the choices. It appeared as though they were imploring the dormant water lilies, hidden beneath the ice, rooted deeply within the lake's watery bowels, to blossom forth with the wisdom they would need. The little lake had always been the source of God's creative solace.

Beal broke the heavy meditative silence saying, in a voice still gruff but filled with tears, "Joe and Frank will go to New York to help Emmy bring Gilbert home. I want him buried in Greenwood cemetery, on our ground, where one day we will rest."

Ann Eliza heard the healing begin. Beal, once again, welcomed Emmy into his heart and embraced her within his family.A fortnight later, a flag-draped, extra long coffin was lifted off the baggage car of the Northern Pacific westbound train. It rested on the platform awaiting its ride in the buck-board wagon to Sauk Centre Methodist Church and then on to the Mossman plot in Greenwood Cemetery. Frank and Joe, their task completed, watched as the casket was loaded on the back of Beal's wagon.

Late in the winter of 1886 Gilbert had taken ill. First he had coughed. Then his fever had risen and his breathing had become labored. The third night, Emmy awakened, aware the rattling breath had seized. She checked on James; she found that he had died. James Gilbert, Tall Man of the Circus, had died of pneumonia born in the damp and cold of their little flat.

Now Emmy stood and watched as the casket was lowered into the earth. Sobbing, she was led by the arm of her father to return to Birch Lake farm to grieve her empty life. However, there she met Louis Marshall, not yet six months old, for the first time. Emmy stared a moment, then stared again. Softly, she said, "Oh! My!" She blinked back her tears, then blinked again, and then was ready for her next adventure.

Much to Ann Eliza's delight, Emmy put her grieving aside and plunged headlong into mothering the infant. By common consent, Louis Marshall became hers to bond with and rear. She protected him well—even too well according to some relatives.

It was not that Ann Eliza and Beal rejected this son. The Birch Lake pioneer farm was home, as it had been for all his older siblings, but Louis Marshall did not grow up as his brothers had. His circus-sister-turned Methodist and organist had a profound influence on him as she seemed to understand his poet lover's soul.

This early welding led in later life to deep valleys of ambivalence for Louis. In one moment Louis could love her as though she were his mother. In another, he could also hate her with a vengeance for the control she exercised over his soul and being.

Louis Marshall, the adult, was not like other men. He was not cold, distant, nor one who hid his feelings. He was a complex man who brought delight to those he loved. He was partly clown, part poet, part businessman, part dreamer, part warrior, part playboy, part lover—maybe mostly lover.

He had learned, perhaps absorbed, maybe grown, all of these dimensions when he inadvertently landed in Emmy's broken life and filled the breach of love caused by Mr. Gilbert's death. He left home and moved with Emmy to Sauk Centre and later, following the Sauk River to Sauk Rapids and then back to Sauk Centre. He was living with her when she married Mr. Miller and he was with her two years later when she buried Mr. Miller.

Because of Emmy, Louis had gone to high school in Sauk Centre and there, as a classmate of Sinclair Lewis, had learned to express his inner thoughts and feelings through poetry and drawing. Their creative souls had fed each other and their imaginations had stimulated lives that learned to explore new levels of creativity and experience. They sailed together on Birch Lake as they matured into young men. Sinclair became more inward and morose, while as Lou grew into manhood, the admiration he elicited from others grew to even greater dimensions.

While he liked the compliments he got from his sister Em, his teachers, relatives, and parents of his friends, he liked even more the attention he got from his friends, especially the girls. He didn't like admitting, even to himself, how much he liked it and how warm it made him feel inside. Hours were spent pouring over his poetry often thinking as he wrote of a particular girl. And then the next day or week it would be another. Sometimes the poems that flowed from his pen were sensual, even verging on sexual.

But more often, they were what he called his "show-off" thoughts. He saw himself rescuing "damsels in distress" or gliding with the grace of a gazelle, as he waltzed the girls of his dreams across the floor. Some of these thoughts and feelings he shared with his friend, Sinclair, when Sinclair was in a buoyant and happy mood, which wasn't often. More often, Lou kept these thoughts and feelings to himself and let them flow out on paper and in fantasy. Always, though, they manifested in reality when he sailed or danced, played tennis or golfed.

Lou, with Emmy's encouragement, became a first-class tennis player, golfer, and dancer. The Hesitation Waltz and the Castle Walk became his specialties. He sampled the meaning of manhood and dreamed of romance in the moonlight.

Once he had tried to share his feelings in a moment of intimate confession with Irene, a girl from Grey Eagle that he liked. She giggled, looked shy and then, he thought, she laughed at him. From that moment on, he became less talkative about his inner self and he kept his conversations with others light and humorous. He liked being seen as the life of the party.

With Emmy, he became increasingly superficial in his sharing. When he lived with her alone, and later with Will DeLaurier on Main Street in Sauk Centre, he was always upbeat when she questioned him after a date or a day in the sail boat on Little Birch Lake.

"Who were you with?" Em would ask.

"Some of the boys," Lou answered. If she pressed him about the girls, he always felt like he was blushing, but with vibrato would answer, "Yes, dear, Irene was there." Or it might be Mary, or Ann, or Rose, or whatever girl he knew was familiar to Em.

It was a real relief to Lou when he turned eighteen, finished high school, and got a job as a teller at the Grey Eagle State Bank. He moved back to the family farm on Birch Lake because it was only five miles to drive the buggy to work in Grey Eagle. However, the real relief was that he did not have to face Emmy when he would get home from an evening or day of fun. His confidants became his older brothers, Ike and Frank, when they would come home to the farm. They just listened and didn't pry and always told him, "Have some fun!" They liked their "little brother" and while they didn't say it in words, their mannerisms told him so. He felt like a man in their sight, which pleased him and helped him keep at bay the self-doubt that lay buried deep within.

Two years later, when Lou was twenty, he was offered a sales job in the western sales district with International Harvester. Frank and Ike encouraged him and promised him that they would deal with Emmy and her worries.

For Lou, the job, the travel, the praise his bosses gave him was like a breath of fresh air. He could be himself. He was debonair. He was dashing. He was funny and lively. Lou golfed, sailed, played tennis, and danced with an air of confidence. The look on his face suggested mystery and intrigue. He cultivated "that look" as he stood before countless mirrors in the many hotels where he spent the nights during his sale's travels. He had many girlfriends, who he liked and who liked him. They lived in Idaho, the Cascade Mountains of Washington, in Montana, and on the plains of

Saskatchewan. The wind blew through his hair as he drove the endless miles of his district and his mind blossomed with creative thoughts and perfect harmony, as golden as the fields of ripening wheat through which he passed. He had come to a place in his life where he felt happiness. Lou was pleased with himself!

Lou's friendship with Sinclair continued, even after he moved back to the farm and then, still later, when he took the traveling job. Lou was the explorer, and while Sinclair chafed under the restrictions laid on him at home, in secrecy Lou shared both Emmy's stories of circus days and his own experiences of life, but to no avail. The friendship began to fray. Lou seemed to have it all. Sinclair delved deeper into his writing, venting his anger on paper that was to become his legacy.

For Lou what blanks were left in his imagination and experience, Emmy helped fill—for an emotional price, however. It was a toll born of her own experiences with abandonment, first by her father, then James Gilbert, and finally Mr. Miller. Her pledge to herself was that another man would not leave her. She told Lou in tones and in ways not to be challenged, "You will not leave me. You will not go away." This was the price for providing love, for after all her motivation was love, love of Lou for truly she loved him as her own.

She had loved Lou throughout her seamy courtship with Will DeLaurier, a French-Canadian version of Walter Mitty, a gentleman of great propensity whom she had met while with the circus. They met after a performance in Dearborn, Michigan. Letters from Will followed, but Emmy was faithful, first to James Gilbert, then to Mr. Miller. For Mr. DeLaurier was, after all, married and the father of several children. Besides, he was coroner for the city of Detroit, Michigan. No matter that he was not yet a citizen.

Emmy wasn't that sure, either, if she thought well of the five notches carved into the handle of Mr. DeLaurier's .38 caliber revolver. These were the ones he bragged about as trophies from his coroner days in Detroit. While Emmy liked symbols and symbolism, these notches were symbols of "kills" and death and that she did not like.

However, five years after that fateful circus performance and the deaths of Mr. Gilbert and Mr. Miller, a courtship with Mr. DeLauier began. Will had been recently defeated in his bid for election as mayor of Detroit. This occurred when his opponent discovered and advertised the week before election that Brother Bill (as Will called himself during the campaign) was not a United States citizen.

Will needed comforting and solace. Licking his wounds and bandaging his injured pride with solitude was not sufficient. Will turned again to Emmy Evaline, whom he had not forgotten. In fact, he had kept her memory alive and well by periodically gazing at the picture that he had secretly taken of her in her circus tent dressing quarters. There she stood, long auburn hair touching the floor, camisole tossed in the corner, breasts exposed, nude to the waist, looking intently at the clothes rack for her next costume. Emmy was unaware of the camera's gazing lens, but Will obviously treasured this image for it was still in his trunk at the time of his death sixty years later.

Steamy, mournful letters to Emmy followed in rapid succession after his mayoral defeat, arriving in Sauk Centre shortly after Mr. Miller's death. The letters became epistles of unrequited, passionate, devoted love as only a Frenchman could articulate.

Emmy was vulnerable and, after a time, Will's unrequited love was no longer unrequited. The courtship of Emmy Evaline led to Mr. DeLaurier's divorce and Emmy's third marriage.

But for all her following of her spirit and her heart, Louis was still her love. When it came time for Louis to leave Emmy and their home, he was already a hurting and conflicted young man. Emmy's double messages caught Lou full force, like a hurricane, slamming ashore each time he would return from his travels in the west. His feelings of lightless, pleasure, and confidence would erode, blown away by the winds of Emmy's expectations. Though the excitement of his travel and the company he kept helped him hide the burden of his pain, Emmy's emotional boundary-leaping left its mark.

Outwardly Lou displayed a handsome profile and was tall and graceful. His humor, sensitivity, athleticism and creativity made him a favorite. He was a romantic and women loved him. His appeal did not stop with outward appearance. He was inventive and creative. Together with his brother Ike he co-invented a new plow shear. With his brother Frank, he imported Black Angus cattle and Hampshire sheep from Scotland and together they developed a Scottish showplace farm in the highlands of west central Minnesota along the shores of Little Birch Lake.

But, inwardly he struggled. There was a black hole deep within that he did not understand. The confidence of self was fickle and in quiet lonely time betrayed him. He felt himself different from other men. He did not understand them. At times he envied their commanding ways. He felt himself too soft. He felt the tears within. He thought, "I would be manly if only I could dominate . . . somebody! Something! Maybe women?" He didn't know what.

He did know what he must do, but it was not within his nature. His inner voice screamed out, "You are a failure as a man, too sensitive, too soft. Damn the poet deep within. Damn the shame and guilt of being. Damn Emmy!"

If only he could escape the responsibility he felt to care for Emmy, and his mother and father, and all those around him! In these dark moments his self-pity swallowed him. He forgot the moments of freedom and light, as his inner voices screamed, "I only want to enjoy myself and who I am. I only want to enjoy my friends who value my way of living." But he knew that if he did, it would surely hurt Emmy and all the others in his family. He was trapped in the prison of his soul.

Sophia was twenty-seven when she met Lou. She and Josephine had gone to the dance at the Lakeside Pavilion, not far from their cabin on the shores of Lake Minnewaska. They both liked the big name bands that Tooty Callahan brought in to play for the dances at his Pavilion by the lake. Some nights the bands were local, but often they were patterned after the likes of Ben Bevhi's or Isham Jones' Orchestras. This night is was Isham Jones and his Orchestra that had traveled up from Chicago. Sophia knew the night would be special because, while she liked to foxtrot and two step, her favorite dance was the Castle Waltz and no one played it better than Isham.

Lou, between selling trips to the west, had driven the twenty-eight miles from Sauk Centre to the Pavilion. He loved to waltz and wanted to hear the band and also to get away from Emmy. Lou saw Josephine and Sophia across the dance floor and was drawn to them as though by a magnet. First, he asked Josephine to dance. She refused, saying she preferred to watch. Lou was fine with this inasmuch as asking Josephine had been a ploy. His real attraction was to Sophia.

Turning to Sophia, he asked, "Will you dance with me?"

"I'd love to," Sophia replied.

At first there was an awkward silence as they glided across the floor. Sophia thought, I have never danced with anyone who dances as well as this man. Then, she became aware that Lou was looking at her. Sophia blushed, as the words of Isham's composition "It Had to Be You" filled the air.

"So, do you come here often?" Sophia asked, aware that she was blushing, which was a thing she never did. She wanted him to focus on something other than her.

"As often as I can when I'm not traveling or meeting with my brother, Frank, about the farm," Lou replied, then fell silent.

Grasping the moment for conversation, Sophia asked, "Tell me about your travels?"

And so Lou began telling stories. Soon they were laughing.

They danced the rest of the dances with no one else that night. When the announcer proclaimed the last dance, Lou asked, "May I drive you home?"

"I'd like that but I had better check with Josephine first since we came together," Sophia responded.

"Josephine, would you mind if I rode home with Lou?"

"No, not at all," Jossey replied, in a somewhat hurt and angry tone, "but how will I get home? You know I do not drive and that I came with you."

Sophia had completely forgotten that Josephine had never learned to drive. "Oh, oh yes! I guess I just was not thinking," Sophia stammered. Josephine smiled. She knew what was happening to her friend, and she wanted to put a stop to it. Sophia reluctantly acquiesced and went to explain to Lou why he could not drive her home. She did make sure, however, that she gave Lou the phone number for the cabin she and Josephine called home. Sophia also gave him directions to the cabin and a standing invitation to come and visit whenever he wanted. From that time on, he was a regular caller at their cottage on the shore.

Sophia loved his stories about the West. She listened closely to the tales of his travels through the Cascade Mountains in Washington. She felt she had been to Fourth of July Hill in Idaho and to the wheat fields in Saskatchewan.

Lou knew he loved Sophia from that first moment he had been drawn to her from across the floor at the Pavilion. When he danced with her, his body responded with a rhythm born in heaven. He tried to analyze his feelings. She was like no woman he had ever met. He tried to tell her and the more he tried the more confused it all became. His poetry could only scratch the surface of his soul.

Finally, he vowed to give up trying. But on his solitary journeys across the Dakotas and the Canadian plains, his mind ruminated beyond control. Still he tried to put her from his mind, yet each time he returned home, his first sortie was from the Gray Eagle farm to the Minnewaska cottage where Sophia lived with Josephine.

In the end, his resolve never to marry because he dared not expose others to his dark, depressive demons was defeated. When he asked Sophia to marry him, and she said, "Yes, of course," he panicked.

"But we have to wait. I do not have enough money saved. Besides, Emmy would never approve!" Lou stammered.

After a lengthy pause and with disappointment in her voice, Sophia responded. "We can wait, if you think that it is best."

Now, standing awkwardly before Sophia, he recalled how he hated Emmy! Then he hated himself for hating her. And the hate would not go away. Now the question burning deep within his belly was, would he come to feel the same fear and hate if he were to again get that close to another woman? What if he married Sophia and felt these feelings toward her? He never wanted that! And yet the question burned.

The engagement would last eight years as Lou constantly struggled with himself and never did resolve the worries that ate away his inner love of self. In private conversations with himself, Lou acknowledged that the real reasons he could not bring himself to marry was his fear of Emmy's rejection and his fear of the rage he felt toward her. But yet, that day, deep inside, the cancer of repressed hatred stirred.

A psychiatrist would have had a wonderful time with Louis Marshall, had he been a patient. The psychiatrist would have perhaps diagnosed Lou as bipolar, or passive-aggressive, or a misogynist. Certainly as ambivalent and, if nothing else fit, he would have been seen as a female dependent male suffering from dysthymia, a recurrent pattern of lengthy periods of emotional highs and lows.

Lou would have told his psychiatrist, had he had seen one, of the time when he tried to enlist in Officer's School during the Great War of 1917. Lou would have told him how years before he had tried to enlist, he had broken his leg in five places while supervising the unloading of steel tractor wheels from a train's flatbed car for International Harvester tractors. One of the wheels had slipped from the grasp of the workmen, rolled down the loading ramp, knocked Lou down and run over his leg. The leg healed, eventually, but that injury was the reason he was rejected when he attempted to join up.

Lou would have continued his story about how he had aggressively persisted in his attempt to enlist. "But," he might have said, "the more I persisted the more Emmy disapproved." Lou would have explained that his anger came from Emmy blocking his opportunity to escape his poet prison and demonstrate to himself and others that he was a courageous man. Proudly, he would have pointed out to the psychiatrist that he had succeeded in getting the Army to let him enlist. The commander of enlistments, himself, had listened to his case. Then he would pull from his pocket the letter in which the commander of the Minnesota Division had written:

"We can use you as support staff and your injury will be no problem. We'll get the paperwork to you soon and all you need to do is sign and get it back to us," the commander concluded.

Lou then would tell the quietly listening doctor, "It was a matter of waiting for the Letter of Appointment, signing it, and returning it, if I just had been home the day the letter arrived. Unfortunately, I was not."

He would have continued, "You see, Emmy took in the mail that day and promptly hid the letter." Lou's face then would have turned red with rage, but he quietly would have continued, "She steamed it open, read it, resealed it, hid it from me and then gave it to me days after the deadline for my acceptance had passed. I had even missed the day I was to report for assignment!"

"Did you tell Emmy you were angry with her?" the psychiatrist would have asked.

"No, of course not," Lou would have replied.

"Were you angry with her?" came the question.

"Of course not! She was just trying to protect me, take care of me, you know," would come Lou's answer.

"I think you were angry with her. I would have been, and I believe you were—angry with her," the psychiatrist gently would nudge.

"It's not good to keep your anger inside. Someday it could even kill you. What harm could it do to say you were angry even if she deceived you because she loved you?"

"No! Absolutely not! I am not angry! She just wanted what was best for me!" Lou would blurt it out and then look at the floor because he had been caught and his private rage was laid bare.

Lou knew he would hate himself until death if he ever felt such dark feelings for Sophia. In the end, however, Sophia convinced him it was time, and they were married on December 28, 1928.

On their marriage day, Lou was heard by Sophia's sister Inga to say, "This is easy! This is great! Why did I wait so long?"

Lou would find that it was not that easy. The Great Crash of 1929 was about to happen. Following their marriage, the depths of their struggles with the Great Depression, both universal and personal, would emerge. At these times Lou and Sophia would often hold each other as they waited for sleep to rescue them and save them from another day.

There was a night in 1932 when they held one another and talked in soft voices, longing for a better time. The children had been born. Moves had taken them from Fargo to St. Paul to Watertown and back to Fargo. Now they talked of the day and its events. They talked of Jeanne and their fears for her health. They talked of Boy and their hopes and prayers for him. They puzzled over what to do.

Sophia was quiet a while, then said, "Remember the story I told you about the fortune teller? The gypsy? Remember how she told me life would be like this?" Then Sophia became pensive and quiet. She was remembering. Like picture frames in a film, the memories of the years before Lou's presence in her life rushed before her mind's eyes.

Sophia, following her years of homesteading in Montana, had returned to St. Paul and gotten a job in sales at Glemaker's Fine Furs for Women. After her apprenticeship, she and her friend, Josephine, decided to launch out on their own and open a ladies-ready-to-wear store in Glenwood. Sophia and Josephine were dear friends. Not only were they business partners, but they also lived together in a handsome little cabin on the shores of Lake Minnewaska.

In many ways they complemented each other and were inseparable. Josephine liked and relied on Sophia's independent and adventuresome spirit, for she was a shy and private person. Her shyness was hidden by her acquiescent and kind personality and by her meticulous grooming.

On the other hand, Sophia relied on Josephine's cautious ways to be a balance for her more impetuous nature. The intimacy of their relationship was closely guarded and for some time was the only satisfaction either of them needed. They socialized together in every way, even as they worked together. Their relationship was not of short duration.

The scenes of the lake and hills outside the window of their cozy cabin shifted several times with the changing seasons of the year. It was almost as though in a moment of time the scene across the lake could go from gray and frozen tundra to lush hills of tender green and air filled with the melodies of a thousand birds. Then it would transform again to the dark greens of a plentiful summer accented with golden fields of ripe grain. And then again the change would come and the V-shape of ducks, geese, and swans flying south would fill the skies while the trees ripened to full color of gold and red, orange and brown.

Then, it would all begin again as Sophia and Josephine luxuriated in their pleasure and the beauty of yet another turning of the seasons. When their store required replenishing for the turn of the seasons, they would make buying trips to Minneapolis together. There they would mix business and pleasure away from the scrutinizing eyes and waggling tongues of the women who patronized their little shop and talked on the street corners in the small mid-western town they called home.

Sophia had been reluctant to tell Lou about the frivolous choice she and Josephine had made one day years before on one such buying trip. She had been afraid that Lou would suspect the true nature of the friendship between Josephine and herself. She was afraid he would judge her harshly and expose her to ridicule, and worse. Finally, though, her trust for Lou had grown to where she told him all the stories of her life and now, snuggled in his arms, she asked him to recall the Gypsy story.

She and Josephine went out to dinner. They drank some wine and on their way back to the hotel passed a Gypsy troupe camped across from Loring Park. One of them, a woman, came out and asked in broken English, "Tell your fortune? Read your palms?"

Sophia said, "Why not?" Josephine quickly agreed thinking the Gypsy might tell her something good about her friendship with Sophia. Sophia, on the other hand, hoped the woman would discourage Josephine's intense interest in her, for she was tiring of the dependent relationship.

When Sophia's turn came to talk to the Gypsy woman, she was a little afraid and uncertain about what she was supposed to do or say.

"Ohhhh, I see," the Gypsy had said, looking at Sophia's palm. Then she was quiet for some time. She continued, "You vill be married two times. Yes, two times. Two times it vill be hard. You vill lose much money. You vill live where the air is dirty. Your first man he vill lose his job two times. No! Three times. You vill have three childs. One vill die. Two you vill vant and one you vill not vant, at first."

Having gotten over her fear, Sophia asked, "Which one will die?"

"Oh, yes, the first one, of course," came the reply.

"Your man, he vill live seven years and then he dies. Your second man too, he lives seven years and then he dies too."

"Oh no!" Sophia murmured and then was quiet. She composed herself and asked, "What about the child I don't want at first?"

"That vill be your last baby. He likes animals and space. And now I see a spirit animal. It comes and makes a rope around you, your daughter and your son. I see the animal as very important helping you get through times of loss and broken bones and broken hearts," the Gypsy continued. Abruptly she got up and walked away.

"Tell me more," Sophia pleaded.

"There is no more. I vill tell you nothing any more!" And the Gypsy disappeared behind the door that divided the little wagon.

When Sophia returned to Josephine, she had tried to laugh it off. She had called the Gypsy crazy. However, in the months and years that followed, she thought often about the Gypsy's message. When the memory came it was often after a dream, or in the tiredness late at night, or in times of doubt and stress.

Another time, in the silence of his thoughts, Lou recalled the night shortly after they married when he returned from a western trip to the little house in the heart of Fargo along the Red River of the North. Sophia had met him at the door. At first, he could not read the look on her face.

Then she spoke. "Lou, I think I am pregnant!" she whispered.

"Oh, my God!" Lou responded as he swept her into his arms.

In that moment he recalled the warmth that had wafted through his being like a warm summer breeze. It had eased away all the doubts that he had about his manhood. In the days that followed, the prison of fear and hate was replaced by light and warmth. He tried hard to convince

Sophia that she should rest. He wanted her to quit working at the Nash Motor Car Agency they bought with Sophia's brother, Rudy.

They had gone into partnership when Lou was fired from International Harvester for not foreclosing on the beleaguered farmers. Rudy convinced Lou that all he needed was to be his own boss. Times were good! It was spring of 1929 and Lou's savings would multiply if he would but invest in this partnership selling fine autos.Lou did not listen to his inner cautious voice and there would go his savings come Black Friday that October.

By summer Sophia had tired of Lou's solicitous concern about her burgeoning belly. She looked at him and laughed. "Nonsense! You know it's good for me to get out and not to die of boredom sitting in this house alone. Besides, I am good at selling—maybe even better than you," she chided.

Lou smiled and nodded. He thought that maybe was true. But even more, he liked her spunk.

Secretly, Sophia brooded. Somehow the pregnancy made her feelings more acute. And the memory of the Gypsy was never far away. She loved the nights when she and Lou would snuggle, and he would put his hand on her belly to feel the baby move and kick. Lou's poems and "Andy Gump" cartoons increased in number and everything seemed to be about a father and a son.

The pregnancy was almost full-term when Dr. Marvin Johnson of Valley City Hospital and Clinic called and asked if a touring car could be driven over for him to see. He was sure he wanted to buy, but he did not have the time to leave his practice and come to Fargo to shop. Certainly, Lou would understand.

Sophia, who had taken the call, replied, "Of course!" and she made arrangements to drive the demonstrator car to Valley City, sixty miles away.

Lou was furious! He did not want her to go, but there was no alternative. He already had customers he had scheduled.

Sophia left at seven o'clock the next morning. The sun was bright and warm; the wind blew tumbleweeds and dust across the graveled highway. The dust rolled behind the Nash. Through the opened windows, above the engine's hum, Sophia could hear the meadowlarks and the gentle cooing of mourning doves. Occasionally she would slow to let a pheasant safely fly across the road. Sixty dusty, washboard miles was a long and tiresome way, but then she crossed the hill's brow and looked down into the valley below. Valley City emerged like an oasis from the plain.

Dr. Johnson's office was not hard to find. The large mansion on the edge of downtown proudly sported a sign on the corner of the lot that read, *Memorial Hospital and Medical and Surgical Clinic, Marvin Johnson, M.D.*

The dust-coated Nash stopped before the clinic. Suddenly Sophia became aware of how tired and dirty she felt and how badly she needed to pee. Stiffly she emerged from behind the steering wheel, stretched, and made her way hastily up the sidewalk to the front door of the clinic.

"May I help you?" inquired the nurse dressed in a stiffly starched white uniform crowned by a small white cap covering her auburn and white hair wound into a tight bun.

"No, thank you, just tell me where the bathroom is," Sophia replied.

"Are you sure you are all right?" the nurse asked as she surveyed Sophia's very large belly.

"Yes, of course, I just need a bathroom."

"Of course," the nurse replied. "It is right down the hall. Second door on the right," she added quickly, suddenly realizing Sophia's urgent need.

Once the toilet flushed and Sophia stood and faced the mirror above the sink, she muttered aloud, "Oh my God! What a mess I am. I am surprised that I did not frighten that poor nurse!"

When she emerged from the bathroom, the dust was gone from her face and clothes, and her hair was neatly combed into her familiar pompadour. Turning to her left to return to the desk, she found herself face to face with Dr. Johnson.

"My, you're a brave and determined woman to drive this far this late in your time just to show me a car," he said in a soft and gentle baritone. Then he chuckled. "I think it means I'll have to buy the car, no matter what, or my wife will never speak to me again."

They went out to look at the car together. After the doctor looked closely over the car, noticing every feature from the spare tire mounted on the running board to the buckles on the trunk, from the engine, to the windshield wipers, to the ornament atop the radiator cap, he murmured his approval. "Oh, my, what a beautiful automobile!"

He turned to face Sophia. "It is a fine automobile, but there are some things I would like to change. You know, things like color choice and engine size. I have always wanted a twelve-cylinder engine and this one has only eight. Can I special order?"

"Yes, of course!" Sophia answered, scarcely concealing her pleasure. Inwardly she felt the excitement build. Top of the line! The biggest sale we have ever had and our biggest profit yet! Wait until Lou hears this. He will get over his jitters about my pregnancy and know this trip was just right and worth it. Her enthusiasm pushed her to want to start for home immediately. Nonetheless, appearing calm on the outside, she produced the purchase agreements, filled them in, waited while Dr. Johnson read them in his most somber and precise manner and then signed them.

"Do you want some tea before you leave? Or maybe you would like to rest a bit? It is a long trip in the heat of the day—um, well, it is a long trip any time." There was caring and concern in Dr. Johnson's voice as he spoke to Sophia.

"No. No. I'll be fine," she assured him and herself as well.

She was anxious to get home as quickly as possible to share the good news with Lou.

"At least drive slowly and use care. They have rebuilt portions of the road to get rid of some frost boils. There's fresh loose gravel in places and it sneaks up on you," Dr. Johnson advised. "We don't want anything to happen to your bundle, do we?"

She heard his parting words as she started down the street, but she already knew about the loose gravel. She had driven that stretch of road just this morning. On the outskirts of town, she accelerated. She was glad the car had as much power as it did.

Clouds rolled in and it was threatening rain. She could hear the sound of thunder in the distance. As her sense of urgency increased, so her speed increased as well. When Sophia quickly glanced at the speedometer, it read sixty miles per hour.

Just at that moment there was a deafening blast of an air horn, and her head jerked up in time to see the Wells Fargo Overland truck bearing down on her. She had drifted across into the lane for the oncoming traffic. She pulled the wheel strongly to the right. The Nash responded and the Overland roared on by, but the Nash's tires caught in the newly laid gravel, gripping them like quicksand and hurtling the Nash toward the ditch.

Feverishly, Sophia wrestled the steering wheel to the left. The car responded, but the speed and momentum rocked the car and amidst flying stone and dirt, over it went. Once—twice—three times, almost. When the dust cleared, the Nash was on its roof.

Forty miles away, in Fargo, Lou broke out in a cold sweat. His heart raced. He could not breathe. Involuntarily, he sobbed, "Oh, no!"

Rudy, Sophia's brother, looked up from his desk next to Lou's. "You all right?" he asked.

"She's hurt!" Lou exclaimed.

"Who's hurt?" Rudy asked.

"Sophia," Lou said.

"But she's over in Valley City," Rudy protested, not understanding Lou's intuitive awareness of Sophia's predicament.

Lou did not answer, instead he ran for the door leading to where his car was parked by the curb in front of the garage. Close on his heels was Rudy, still talking but blindly following. Lou got into his car and had the engine roaring to life at the turn of the key as Rudy scrambled into the passenger seat.

"Where are we going?" Rudy asked again.

Lou still did not answer. The car lurched ahead, gaining momentum, heading west toward Valley City. Lou was like a man possessed. The gas pedal of the little Lafayette Nash was pressed hard to the floor and the car was going as fast as it was ever meant to.

Rudy sat gripping the dashboard so hard that his knuckles turned white. "Where are we going?" this time he demanded to know.

Just then they rounded the curve and crossed the bridge, and there in the distance was the police car with its blue lights flashing in a circle. The ambulance was parked just beyond.

Then, Rudy knew.

Lou braked the little car to a skidding stop and jumped out into a cloud of dust and gravel.

"Is—is—she alive?" Lou blindly asked.

"Yes!" came the response.

"Thank God! And the baby? And the baby?" Lou demanded.

"We don't know," George Ostby, policeman and a friend of Lou's, replied.

Lou grabbed Sophia's hand. "Oh, God—why did I let you go?"

"I sold the best car we have," Sophia said through puffy but smiling lips while looking at her husband through blackened eyes.

Without hearing, Lou continued, "I'm such an ass! I shouldn't have let you go!"

"Don't worry, Lou. I will be all right. I'll be just fine," she reassured him.

"And the baby? My boy?" Lou demanded yet again.

"We will see—we will see. Right now I am very tired," Sophia whispered.

But Sophia already knew something was different. The baby was in trouble. Lou knew it too.

That night at St. Luke's hospital in Fargo, John Marshall Mossman was born. He struggled for breath and life but his little heart was not up to the task. Three days later his struggle ended.

Lou sobbed and was beyond consolation. He withdrew into himself. In his heart he knew that he had killed his son. Lou believed that it was he who was not strong enough. It was he who was not aggressive enough to put a stop to Sophia's trip to Valley City.

No other man would have let Sophia go to Valley City by herself as far along in her pregnancy as she was and to do the work that he should have been doing. Why, the morning she left he had not even told her that he loved her. She could have died too. What an ass he was! His self-loathing burrowed even deeper. Lou felt the shame and guilt consume his heart. It ate away the very juice of life, like a death beetle destroying a magnificent tree.

Finally, after many days of this, Sophia had had all she could take of Lou's self-pity and his self-loathing. Six weeks had passed since the accident. Her health and energy had returned, but Lou was still like a zombie. To be in his presence was like being in a dark, underwater chasm where one's very breath was being sucked away.

Undaunted by the death of John Marshall, Sophia wanted to get pregnant again. At thirty-eight, she felt that time for her to become pregnant was running out. But how was she to get Lou interested in life and love again?

One night, watching the pale silver light of the October harvest moon streaming through the window, she found herself overwhelmed by wave after wave of loneliness. "Lou, I need you to hold me. I need to know that we and our love have not died along with John Marshall," Sophia pleaded.

Lou did not move, nor did he speak.

"Lou, I need you to hold me!" Sophia sobbed.

Then she felt his large, cumbersome body roll toward her and his arms enfolded her. First their breathing deepened and then assumed a common rhythm. She felt his hand tenderly caress her breasts and belly and then her hair below. By dawn's light the single streams of their love had joined to form a powerful common river flowing into the sea, conceiving new life.

Lou's self-esteem expanded in concert with Sophia's belly. He was convinced that this time, his son, this John Marshall, would not die. He would do all in his power—he would be supernatural. His very being would protect Sophia and keep her safe and the child—the boy he wanted to much—within her as well.

Sophia felt stifled, as though she were in prison. Lou would not let her drive. He would not let her climb stairs. He had hired Beatrice, a local maid, to do the housework, even though they had no money for such a luxury.

At first Sophia thought Lou's concern was cute and humored him. She, the prairie homesteader, the orphanage reformer, the entrepreneur of women's clothes, Gypsy at heart, was being treated, pampered, and over-protected like a hothouse plant. But soon the humor left and the cuteness got tiresome.

One day she had finally had enough. "Lou, stop it! You are killing me with your so-called kindness and your arrogance about fear. This is more than I can stomach. First of all, we do not know if this child I am carrying is a boy or a girl. Secondly, you will love whichever it is! Now do not give me any Methodist confession about how sorry you are and how you failed in trying to care for me. I am not staying cooped up in this house any more! If the child dies, it dies. But I am going to live!"

With that, Sophia flashed a car key in his face, walked out, got into her car and drove away. It was minutes, maybe longer, after Sophia's car had left that Lou came out of his shock and said to his departed love,

"You can not do that! You might get hurt again!"

Sophia, of course, did not hear him. She was already at the edge of town heading for her favorite secluded spot by the Buffalo River. This was an oasis in the drought, a place with enough moisture remaining for the spring wildflowers to grow and bloom.

Lou, on the other hand, heard every word he uttered to the wind and realized how stupid he sounded. His career as the "warden of the Fargo Seventh Street prison" ended that day. He vowed he would trust Sophia to care for herself, the baby, and even him. God, he loved her spirit. He wished his were like hers. No longer would he try to break that tensile steel strand of life.

The Buffalo River flowers absorbed Sophia's anger. Their colors transformed its energy into passion and compassion, painting her aura a golden hue, which radiated from her as she walked into the house. She found Lou ready to embrace her, to restrain her no longer.

He championed her freedom.

He was sure God had spoken to him in the darkness of his despair the afternoon Sophia left. He knew that if he just let go of his fear and let Sophia do as she wished, that God would bless him with a son and all would be well. He knew if he let God be God, his prayers would be answered. After all, is that not what Emmy had taught him as he grew up? Is that not what Methodists believed—if you let God lead you, your prayers will be answered? Certainly God would understand that a boy was important, and this boy was particularly important for it would mean he was forgiven for his negligence and inability to keep Sophia from harm before.

On July 17, 1930, at St. Luke's Hospital in Fargo, North Dakota the baby crowned, then shouldered its way out of the narrow passage into the light of day. While the midwife spanked her on the butt, she howled. The theory of the day proclaimed that this was done to help the lungs start working, but one wonders if the baby's crying was not more from anger, embarrassment, and pain.

Nonetheless, here she was, a beautiful little girl.

Then Sophia drifted off to sleep. When she awakened, Lou was leaning over her, kissing her cheek.

"Did you talk to the doctor? Did he tell you?" Sophia wondered.

"No, I just got here. I called and Rudy said he brought you to the hospital," Lou replied.

"Now where is he? Where is our boy?"

"She's beautiful, Lou. You will just love her. I know you will!" Sophia answered.

Lou's smile disappeared. His shoulders slumped. This was not as it should be. Where was the boy? Where was John Marshall? Lou left the room.

He heard Sophia call, "Please, please just look at her."

He wandered off in a daze. Once in the parking lot next to the hospital, he cursed God, screaming in his loudest voice, "Why, God? Why? Can nothing ever work for me? Why do you hate me, God?"

He screamed even more loudly, but no one heard because all the screaming was deep within his heart and mind. Finally, the anger subsided and the fiery rage cooled. His composure returned. With his reason returning to him, he thought, "Yes, I will go and see her. At least I will be there for Sophia and help share her disappointment."

However, when he opened the door to Sophia's room, he was not greeted by an atmosphere of disappointment. Tiny Jeanne Elizabeth was lustily feeding at Sophia's breast. The look on Sophia's face was one of pure bliss.

Lou was taken aback. How could this be? Did Sophia and he not share the deepest connection of feelings and spirit? Had they not both deeply wanted a son? He did not understand.

Dutifully, he went to her side. He pulled the pink blanket away from the baby's face and looked at her with scorn. No, not scorn—wonder. A moment later Jeanne released Sophia's nipple and turned her face upward, as though looking at her father. At that instant, Lou's heart melted, heralded by the sound of Jeanne Elizabeth's resoundingly loud burp.

The poet of Lou's soul greeted and merged with the goddess artist living deep within the baby's being. In that moment, through the portals of their souls, they created the imaginary characters of creativity and humor, characters they would later share in the short years they would have together before Lou's death. The imaginary characters spawned names, first in baby chatter and then as she grew to a little girl.

Lou would come to tuck her into bed each night when he returned from traveling the dusty Dakota roads. Jeanne would tell of the adventures that day of Goggenbush and Beanie. Lou would play along for he liked her imagination and loved her creativity.

Goggenbush was the first to show. He was talkative and playful, full of life and fun, but still a prankster. He would take, then hide things, and then the game of "find it" would begin.

Beanie came later. Beanie was shy and loved to be held, but would never ask. Her's was a winner's smile, a winner's way. When tiredness reigned, Beanie reached out with her touch, "her" arms would embrace Lou's and they would hold each other and wash away the cares and hurts. Lou always felt his spirit and strength renewed by the game. He wondered to himself how he ever could have thought he didn't want a daughter.

One day in the car, when Jeanne Elizabeth was four, they were driving along a Dakota road, cornfields were scorched by the heat and the drought. Jeanne yelled, "Stop! Stop!"

Lou, startled and frightened, hit the brakes hard, the Nash skidding and twisting, finally coming to a stop.

"There he is! There he is!" Jeanne screamed in her small voice.

"Who?" Lou yelled back.

"See? Goggenbush," Jeanne calmly stated.

Lou's face turned red. He could not decide whether to laugh or spank her, so he sat and held the wheel for what seemed like a long time. When he reached to turn the key, it was gone.

"Where is the key?" Lou demanded.

"Why, Goggenbush took it and gave it to Beanie," Jeanne announced.

"What?" Lou exploded.

Jeanne continued, "Then Beanie took it and gave it to Goggenbush—out there," and she pointed to the cornfield on the right.

Only Sophia's restraining hand on Lou's arm saved Jeanne from a trouncing. Then both parents began to laugh. And then they laughed harder and harder. It was almost dusk when they finally found the key lying by a cornstalk three rows in.

When they got back to the car, Jeanne announced, "I knew he would leave it for us. He said he would. Besides, Beanie would not let him keep it." Lou said nothing, but glumly turned the car around and headed back to Fargo as Jeanne nestled happily in Sophia's arms.

In the months between Jeanne's birth and her first birthday, times were not easy in Fargo. In that first year, Jeanne had had pneumonia twice and an illness the doctors could not then diagnose. The mysterious illness left her lungs and legs weak. Years later, Dr. Chatterton diagnosed the mystery disease as polio.

Jeanne's health, the country's deepening economic depression, and the years' long drought all began to take their toll on Lou and Sophia. Jeanne was not yet a one-year-old when Lou announced one evening, "Sophia, the doctor wants me to check into St. Luke's Hospital in St. Paul. He thinks that a Dr. Fritchie there may be able to help me with my ulcers and all this acid my body seems to produce."

He paused, then said, "I just do not know how we can afford it, though."

"Nonsense!" Sophia retorted. "Your health has to come first, or else we have nothing."

That night Sophia laid awake, but pretended sleep so that Lou would not know how worried she was. The car business was not doing well and now their savings were almost gone. But, most of all, the broken English of the Gypsy woman rang in her ears: "Your husband—he vill die."

The next day Sophia sat and wrote a letter to her sister Inga. She poured out her heart, her fears and her desperation regarding Lou's and Jeanne's health, their finances, and her general feelings of hopelessness. She felt trapped and angry with God for the hand that had been dealt her.

Ten days later, when Sophia retrieved the mail, there was a letter from her wealthy but austere Aunt Jen who lived in luxury at 516 Summit Street on the corner of Summit and Heather Drive in St. Paul. Sophia tore open the letter and read:

Dear Sophia,

I hear from your sister, Inga, that you are now nearly destitute after having squandered your money on an ill-advised business selling cheap automobiles. Inga also tells me that your husband, Lou, is not well and should be treated here in St. Paul by Dr. Fritchie. As you may know, Dr. Fritchie is my personal physician. He is not cheap, but he is good.

While I cannot approve of your bad judgment regarding business and child bearing, neither can I let my poor departed sister's destitute daughter go without help. Therefore, I am enclosing a check for $1000, which should cover Mr. Moss-
xpenses for two months.

hter, Jeanne, will need a place
wait for Mr. Mossman to get
hina on an extended trip of four
you the use of some rooms in my
y servants will adequately see to
ep your daughter disciplined so
my precious belongings.

your earliest convenience. Also
n will arrive so that Elmer, my

hie to check Mr. Mossman into
our arrival.

tter. She put it down, picked
ugh she were going to spit on
.

"Damn her! Damn that presumptuous, arrogant bitch!" Sophia began to cry. She knew she was trapped. She knew she had to accept the offer because of Lou's health and their financial situation. She also knew that to accept the offer was to accept Jen Houseman's unfair judgment, which she hated even more than taking the money. Sophia sat and held herself and rocked as one in a trance. The afternoon wore on. She mused: How could this woman—this aunt—her mother's sister—be so totally different from her mother. Sophia's mother had been humble, strong, and sensitive. She had been a woman of compassion, a loving person.

This aunt was arrogant, haughty, and mean . . . and yet had outlived her mother by several years already. "This is not fair! God is not fair!" she thought angrily to herself. "I hope Aunt Jen rots in hell!" she said in a stage whisper. Sophia put the letter aside to await Lou's return home.

After supper, when Lou had folded himself into the overstuffed mohair living room chair and was smoking his daily cigar with Jeanne snuggled on his lap, Sophia handed him the letter without comment.

"What's this?" Lou questioned.

"It's from Jen Houseman. Read it," Sophia replied with a slight, unintended edge to her voice.

Lou read it and put it down. He sat in silence for some time. Only when Jeanne squirmed trying to escape the cigar ash that had fallen on her sleeper did Lou come out of his trance. His face showed defeat and resignation. "I suppose we will have to accept her offer. We do not have any other options that I can see," he shared. Then almost to himself, he whispered, "God, I'm such a failure. I cannot even take care of myself much less my family."

He lapsed into silence for a time. Finally, gathering energy, he proclaimed, "But we will not take her damn train and have her chauffeur meet us. We will drive!"

Lou was in St. Luke's Hospital in St. Paul for three weeks. Sophia walked down Ramsey Hill Street each day to see him while the maids, both upstairs and downstairs, competed over entertaining Jeanne. It was like having two full time nannies and not a care in the world. Aunt Jen might be a witch and a bitch, but even witches do some good, Sophia mused, even if they do not know it. The mile walk down Ramsey Hill to St. Luke's was easy. The walk back up to Summit was hard.

When it came time for Lou to be discharged, Dr. Fritchie sat across the desk from Lou. In his serious and professional manner, he said, "You must learn to relax. Do things that are enjoyable. Learn to play again. If you do, the ulcer will heal and the acid in your system will return to normal. If you do not do your part, the tension will kill you. Now, you must stay in town for a few weeks so I can examine you to determine if the ulcer is healing and the medicine I am prescribing is working."

Lou agreed. "I will stay," he said. "And I will try to learn how to be a little lighter and easier." They shook hands and Lou left the hospital. Waiting for him in front was Jen Houseman's chauffeur and Packard limousine. Sophia had sent the chauffeur for him.

It was all very convenient and well timed. Just that morning Sophia had brought in the mail and found a letter addressed to Lou informing him that his application for the district manager's job with the John Deere Corporation had been received and accepted. The job was his! He was to report to the district office in Watertown, South Dakota, on the Monday after Thanksgiving.

Lou read the letter, then reread it and read it yet again a third time, this time aloud. He exploded with excitement. "This is great, is it not? This is just wonderful—too wonderful!"

To himself, he thought, "I can now take care of myself as the good doctor advised me and I can take care of my family as I should. Sister Emmy and brother Frank will be proud of me." Besides, he mused, "I have two months, two glorious autumn months to enjoy with Sophia and little Jeanne."

To Sophia he proclaimed, "Life is great. It could not be better, except I believe it will become better and better. The Mossman motto on my ancestors' coat of arms is really true: *Me Melioria Manent*, meaning 'Better things await me.' Ah, so true."

"Simmer down, now, Lou. There is still a lot ahead of us, but this is good right now. I am just happy to have you out of the hospital, on the mend, and home with us again. I do not think I could be happier or more relaxed either, but I believe we have to be moderate in our celebration. I do know that this is the happiest I have been for months and months," Sophia said.

"Well, I think we should take full advantage of Aunt Jen's generosity and learn to play again! Her personal doctor says that is what I'm supposed to do!" Lou exuded.

Sophia agreed with her husband. "We do have the opportunity right now. The maids want to have Jeanne as much as they can. They even fight over whose turn it is to care for her. So, we are as free as larks to do whatever we want!"

In the weeks that followed, they played. They golfed at the Town and Country Club. The tennis courts there were a regular haunt as well. Some evenings they danced the night away at the Coliseum Ballroom. Often, in the wee hours of the morning, they nestled in each others' arms in the cozy confines of the softly luxurious bed in the Blue Room on the second floor of Aunt Jen's Summit House.

Many nights they made love with newfound freedom and abandon. Sophia felt her family was complete and knew in her heart that she could not get pregnant as long as she was still nursing Jeanne. After all, this was common women's knowledge that had been passed on to her by some very wise old women who knew about these things from experience.

Sophia believed that as long as her milk flowed freely she could enjoy her body; she could relish the erotic caressing touch of her lover. She could enjoy the elation of orgasm then relax and rest securely in the arms of her man as they drifted into sleep. There would be no more responsibility to shoulder.

In time, the late November day came when they were ready to head west into the dust and wind of the Dakotas and to their new home in the dusty land called South Dakota and the lonesome town called Watertown.

Sophia was sick to her stomach and pregnant. Sometimes, the body does not recognize the wisdom of a myth or prove what the mind wishes to believe. "Lou, I hate it! I hate leaving the city! I hate going to this Godforsaken place! I most of all hate this child in my belly!" Sophia cried. Sobbing, head held in her hands, she pulled at her hair as the Nash rumbled west.

Lou listened. Tears rolled down his cheeks. He wiped them with his sleeve, struggling to stay focused on the road.

"Oh God, and I did it to you. Why can I not do something right? Why can I not make things better?" The words of self-hatred and derision spewed from his mouth. His knuckles turned white as he gripped the steering wheel.

"My sister Mat thinks I should get rid of this," Sophia said darkly as she angrily clutched her belly. "I tried! This morning I beat myself as hard as I could. I was hoping I would bleed. Hoping it would come out! Hoping it would die or that I would die!"

Lou turned his head and looked at her. He was stunned. He had not suspected the depth of her despair. He was jolted back to reality by the blowing of the truck's air horn as the car drifted across the center. He jerked the wheel to the right, gravel kicked on the shoulder, but he missed the truck.

"Oh God, Sophia! Do not do it! We'll find a way," Lou pleaded.

"Maybe it is a boy," he said to himself, beneath his breath.

Sophia heard him. "Well, if it is a boy—then maybe you will be satisfied!" she spewed back angrily. "We can call it John Marshall if you want. Maybe it will make up for that little bastard that died and brought us all this pain."

Lou said nothing but stared straight ahead. The silence deepened.

Softly Sophia began to weep. Then her whole body began to heave with wrenching sobs. "Oh, Lou! I did not mean that. God forgive me. It is just that . . . It is just that. . ." Her voice trailed off into silence.

Lou stopped the car. Then even as Jeanne awakened and began to cry in the back seat, Lou went to the passenger door, opened it, took Sophia by the hand and pulled her from the car and into his arms. He held her for a long time as the howling wind and the howling child accompanied the whirling dust that covered them. Rivulets of tears ran down their cheeks and left clean streaks where the dust had been.

Five minutes and an eternity later, resolve returned. Lou helped Sophia back into the car. She opened her blouse and gently placed the unhappy Jeanne to her breast. The remaining miles to Watertown were wrapped in a blanket of silence covering the pain and doubt within each of them.

The days that followed were not happy. The unrelenting wind and dust blackened the noon sky so that day and night became the same. The evil wind brought illness and deepening degrees of dark despair.

Pneumonia, then whooping cough, found Jeanne again. Night after night, to help her sick child rest, Sophia sleepily and softly sang the words and melody to "Little Baby Bunting" and "Jesus Loves Me."

When Lou was home from the road and away from the despair of the farmers watching their soil blow away, he sat by Sophia's side as she sang, sometimes dozing off as he tried to let her know he loved them both. At the same time he tried to hide his fear.

"God damn it, God! You dirty bastard, God!" he screamed at the wind as he drove from one Dakota farm to the next. He was unable to bring himself to foreclose on the land to satisfy the debt owed the great green monster, John Deere. Lou knew he compounded his and Sophia's problems for soon he would be without a job, but he could not bring himself to kill the spirit of those who worked the land.

He was a poet, not a businessman.

Night after night Sophia pleaded with him. "You have to do what you have been hired to do. We need the money. We need the money!"

But this time Lou stood up to her, and she knew he was right. In the early hours, when the arguing was done, they assured each other that they would find a way.

Once again Sophia thought about the Gypsy woman as she lay in Lou's arms. "You know," she said, "The Gypsy said a spirit animal could change things and help us. Maybe we should get a dog."

Lou was quiet for quite a while. While he was lost in thought, Sophia lay looking at him secretly, wondering if he would die before his time and leave her with her daughter and this baby she did not want.

"Well, if we get one, I want it to be a Scotch collie. A collie would go with the Scottish farm on Little Birch Lake."

Sophia shared his dream. "If we get it soon, the dog and children could grow up together. They would not be afraid, and it would guard them."

Toward dawn, when sleep finally came, the decision had been made. They would get a Scotch collie, white if possible. His name would be Scottie.

On the morning of August 13, 1931, Lou groaned when Sophia poked him in the ribs with her elbow. "It is coming! I have got the contractions. Call Dr. MacGee."

Lou was standing by the bed even before he opened his eyes. He was fumbling to put on his pants and when he succeeded, they were on backwards.

"Where's the darn fly?" Lou exploded.

"You have them on the wrong way!" Sophia doubled over with pain and laughter. "You are supposed to help me. Big help you are!"

Soon what had been wrong was righted, and they were on their way for the short ride to Watertown's Methodist Hospital.

10:30: Lou paced the father's waiting room just outside the labor and delivery rooms. For almost five hours he had heard the periodic screams of the three women in labor. He knew Sophia's voice like his own. When she screamed in her pain, tears flowed from his eyes and nausea flooded his body.

10:33: He realized that all had been quiet for more than twenty minutes. Had . . . had she died? Had his Sophia died? What would become of Jeanne? What would he do? Had this baby died with her, too? Panic washed through his mind and body. He was convinced that the worst of all possibilities had happened. Where was Dr. MacGee?

10:40: Lou started toward the double doors marked NO ADMITTANCE. LABOR AND DELIVERY ROOMS. Just as he reached the doors, they swung back, almost hitting him. His outstretched hand had reached to push open the door and had pushed it into Dr. MacGee's chest instead.

"Oh, there you are! A little scared, are we?" smiled Dr. MacGee. "Well, it is a scary thing—this business of having a son. You never know what they are going to get into."

"A . . . a son?" Lou said as if he could not comprehend.

"Yes! A 10-pound, 8-ounce boy and he is damned angry about having to be out here in the world by himself. Better lungs I have not heard in a long time," the doctor enthused.

"He is alive?" Lou stammered.

"Oh, yes! And how!" Doctor MacGee responded.

"And Sophia? Will she live?" Lou demanded.

"Oh, yes, she's as healthy as a horse! She did a great job. She is some fine woman," said MacGee admiringly. Then he added, "But looking at you, I am not sure you will make it." The doctor chuckled, began to whistle, and then walked away.

Lou, like melting wax, slid slowly down the wall on which he had been leaning until his 6-foot, 6-inch frame was like a puddle on the floor. After holding Sophia and bringing her roses and pestering the nurses about everything under the sun between making trips to the nursery at least every half hour, Lou was told by the nurses to leave. "Go home," they had said. Everything is fine! You need to sleep and so does Sophia!" Before he left, he went to look once more through the window at his newly born son because he couldn't quite comprehend that such a miracle, such a blessing had really happened.

When Lou finally got home, he collapsed into his overstuffed mohair chair and mused. "John Marshall—hmm. John Marshall, my son. Nice name. Solid ring to it. Old Beal would be real happy to know I have a son and he has a grandson. I bet he's looking down from heaven right now and stroking his mutton chop beard the way he always did. I only wish he and Ann Eliza were alive to see him. Oh well, I guess sister Emmy seemed pleased enough, maybe even a little jealous."

He continued, lost in his thoughts.

"I want everybody to know! I know what I will do. I will send a telegram to brother Frank—that craggy old billy goat will not know what to think or say. All he said when Jeanne was born was 'Harrumph! Just a girl, is it?' and that was all. I do not think brother Joe even told Frank when Ione was born."

"I know," thought Lou, "I will tell him the kid is named for him! I will tell him that James Francis Junior arrived at 10:30 this morning!

"I can hear him now saying, 'I do not want any damned kid named after me!' That cranky Scotsman might be the practical one of us, but it is time for him to be the butt of a little joke, instead of the one dishing it out. Then after he has gotten all flustered, I will send him another telegram and tell him the boy's real name." Louis Marshall Mossman chuckled to himself as his mind's eye pictured his brother in his far-from-usual state of consternation.

Lou yawned and murmured to himself, "John Marshall, a good name!" Then he called the Western Union office and sent the telegram. Finally, he drifted off to sleep. Too tired to undress, he slept in his chair with his feet resting on the ottoman.

On August 14, supper was interrupted by the doorbell. It was the Western Union boy who greeted Lou when he answered the door. He brought a night letter from J.F. Mossman in St. Paul.

With great glee, Lou tore it open.

It was four pages long! Lou began to read. His smile melted from his face and a puzzled look replaced it. Lou read:

> *This is the finest thing that has ever happened to me—to have your son named for me is the most wondrous gift that could ever be offered. I do not know what to say. Everyone else has always bought my rough exterior and I was just as happy to have them do so. I did not want people to see my tears or to be able to hurt my sensitive soul again as Kathryn did. I thought my heart would break that time, when she left—then too many times after that. Now you have touched my inner soul and you have not scarred it or trampled on it, but gifted me with the naming of your son.*

And so the night letter went on for three more pages. The pouring out of the dammed-up river of love and gratitude flowing from the heart of one James Francis (Frank) Mossman, older brother of Louis Marshall Mossman, whom he now used as his Father Confessor.

When Lou finished reading the four pages, he slumped in his chair and the telegram slipped to the floor from his numb fingers.

He heard his voice echoing in the empty room.

"Well, John Marshall is dead and James Francis Junior has just come alive and been named. How am I going to tell Sophia about her son's new name?"

The boy's birth was like an oasis in a bleak and forlorn desert. The wind-born dust continued so thick that the noonday sun disappeared and the sky turned black. Jeanne and now "Boy" were easy prey for the airborne diseases that were having a field-day spreading whooping cough and pneumonia and who knew what else.

Nights were once again sleepless for Sophia and Lou. They could not escape the wheezing sounds of death. By day Lou became more depressed than the day before as he drove the Dakota roads to foreclose on farmers and take their land to satisfy the John Deere Company.

In the night Sophia and Lou held each other and prayed for better times to a God who seemed to be more like a John Deere stockholder than a gracious, listening deity.

The better times did not come. They felt their hope had been served with a divine foreclosure.

The boy, despite the vicious germs, had grown strong and stubborn. He walked at nine months, ran at ten. He spoke real words at sixteen and a half months.

One day, when he was eighteen months old, he climbed the steps at Mrs. Goodall's house next door. She made the best and sweetest cookies he had ever tasted. The six-year-old boy across the street knew this as well.

This day he came across the street and faced Boy. No little kid with curly blond hair was going to invade his territory. He swung his fist and hit Boy square in the mouth. Boy tumbled down the porch steps, blood running from his nose and mouth.

He climbed the steps again.

The older boy hit him again, and down the steps he fell once more.

He started climbing again, this time wailing loudly. The other boy hit him yet again and laughed as Boy fell down again. Boy began climbing the steps for the fourth time and then Mrs. Goodall was on the porch, broom in hand. She swung the broom at the same time the older boy squealed and threw his punch. The broom was a fraction quicker and the six year old crumbled to the floor.

"Out! Out now!" Mrs. Goodall yelled as he gained his footing and scrambled back across the street.

She scooped Boy up in her arms. He looked at her and through puffy lips and with pleading eyes said, "Cookies?" Mrs. Goodall laughed and took him in. She called Sophia, then washed his face and hands and comforted him with cookies and milk.

Late in November 1933, Lou answered the phone. The railway express man was excited and talking rapidly. "There is a white Scotch collie puppy here and he seems very unhappy and hungry." Would Lou come right away and get him?

"Yes, yes of course. I will be right down. Just hang on to him. He will be all right," Lou prattled into the phone's receiver.

So Scottie came to find his family, his flock. And strange looking sheep they were!

Scottie was two months old when he arrived in Watertown. Boy was two years and Jeanne was three.

May 1934 was a warm, bright, sunny time. It was a month just as all of the other drought bearing months had been. When the wind was not blowing and you could see the landscape, it already looked parched, thirsty, and brown.

At the edge of town, where the local John Deere implement mogul lived, there was an oasis of green. His was the only family in town who could afford to pour precious water on their lawn.

Several times Boy and Jeanne had gone with Lou when he had had business dealings with the mogul. As he and Lou talked, Jeanne and Boy rolled and played on the sweet-smelling grass. Tears and pleas to stay were always shared when business was done and the time came to go. This spring day in May, Sophia came up the basement stairs with her basket filled with wet clothes. The day was clear and still, so she could hang the clothes on the lines in the backyard.

"Jeanne! Boy! Come and help. You can hand me the clothes while I hang them. Jeanne! Jeanne, where are you?" Sophia called.

Neither child came, no matter how loudly she called. Then she sensed that Scottie was gone, too. She called again and whistled, but to no avail.

Scared, Sophia left the clothes basket and ran for the phone. Hopefully, Lou would be in the office. He was.

"The children are missing! So is the dog! Please come. Please!" Sophia was not used to pleading, but she was scared, more scared than she had ever been. In this situation she was not the one in control.

"Yes, I will be right there. Please, just wait. I love you. We will find them!" Lou reassured her.

In what seemed like an eternity to Sophia, but in reality was only ten minutes, Lou burst into the house.

"What direction did they go?" he wanted to know.

"I don't know!" Sophia angrily retorted. "I was in the basement. I wish we could afford to have someone do the wash, then I could watch the children the way I should. Damn!"

"I know." Lou said. "I do not do for you what I should."

"Be quiet! I can't deal with your self-pity!" When she looked at Lou's worried face, her anger cooled.

"Let us just try to find them," said Sophia in a soft and defeated voice.

They began walking from their house toward the edge of town. They had gone two blocks when they saw the toddlers coming toward them, herded by the collie. Each of the children had a handful of dandelions.

That night Scottie was given an extra portion of food. When the collie finished and licked his jowls, Lou produced the meaty soup bone the butcher had given him "to reward that dog who found the kids."

Sophia sat quietly and recalled the Gypsy's words once more: "The spirit animal—he vill rescue you."

Lou could not take it any longer. He quit the John Deere juggernaut. He would have no more of perpetrating their greed at the expense of well-meaning farmers who were caught in a cosmic situation not of their making.

He and Sophia and the children would move back to Fargo, there to work once again with Sophia's brother Rudy, but this time as a salesman for the Sioux Falls Insurance Company. Rudy had worked there for several years and had his own small agency serving the Fargo area. Of course, because it was Rudy's agency, it was the best insurance agency in all of North Dakota. All you had to do was ask Rudy and he would tell you.

It had been three years since Jeanne was born. Rudy had divorced May, much to the dismay of the family. Then he had remarried. Shortly after his divorce, Rudy had been in a severe car accident. It was a miracle that he lived. He had been hurled from his car near the place where Sophia had had her accident years before. The months of recuperation in the hospital brought him into daily contact with his primary nurse, Joan. They had fallen in love and then married. His health had returned, and he eagerly welcomed Lou and Sophia back as his partners in the insurance business.

In December, 1935, Lou sat repentantly in his mohair chair in his home office. He had just come in from working with Scottie. He had had a harness made so the dog could pull a sled and Jeanne and Boy could ride. But this day the dog in his harness and the kids on the sled had come near death because of Scottie's obsession with chasing cars. Lou had screamed, but to no avail. Charging blindly down the street after them, Lou had finally managed to catch the collie. Then he had totally lost control.

He cursed and pummeled the dog in a way and with a rage of which he never thought himself capable. God! How could he be so angry? His face felt hot and flushed; his heart raced and his ears rang. The dog was just being a dog, and yet Lou felt that he should be in control. He should be able to control the animal, or was he a failure even at that? It was the same old thing. Had he not learned anything through the years, through his living?

He was such a failure, he felt, as his inner voices lashed away at his very soul. His inner rage and anger were never far away. He knew this. He also believed that one day it probably would kill him. That thought was buried deep in Lou's subconscious that December 24, 1935.

Lou sat in his favorite chair, Jeanne on one knee, comfortably clad in only her little shirt. Boy sat on his other knee, playing with his father's ear. Boy felt as he always did when he was cradled in his father's arms, or was sitting on his knee, or romping with him in the yard, or sitting on the sled being pulled by Scottie while his dad ran alongside encouraging and directing the ghostly white dog.

"Tell me a story! Tell me what it was like when you were little," Boy pleaded. "What did you get for Christmas?"

"Yes! Yes! Tell us a story. Did you have a Christmas tree, like we do?" Jeanne chimed in.

Lou cleared his throat and began. Sophia paused to listen, standing in the archway that led to the living room, all decorated, the large brightly lit Christmas tree replete with ornaments and the little plastic golfer squarely in the center. The tree had the prominent place in the room sitting in front of the bay window. Sophia had been clearing dishes and cleaning up from the meal of roasted lamb.

"I do not remember much from when I was real young like you," Lou said. "But when I got to be about ten or eleven, your uncle Beal and uncle Fred would take me with them when they harnessed the team to the sleigh and headed across Little Birch Lake. The horses were up to their bellies in snow, but I can't remember that it seemed to bother them at all they were so big and powerful. They seemed to sense the special excitement of what we all were doing. When we had crossed the lake we came to a woods between the lakes, right on the shore of Big Birch Lake. There stood a copse of pine trees. Many of them were B-I-G, tall and wide." Lou held his arms stretched open wide, a span of eight feet between his hands as only a 6-foot, 6-inch giant could achieve.

"I stood there in awe, looking up to the tops of the giant pines mirrored against the crystal blue sky. It looked to me as though they were protecting the smaller trees.

"Brother Beal would look and look for just the right smaller tree to be our Christmas tree. It seemed to me that Fred only complained and wanted to go home. He said the horses were getting cold, but I think it was Fred wanting to go home.

"After a while I would quit looking at the giant guardians of the forest and would follow Beal. I kept trying to step in his footprints in the snow. I could always tell when Beal saw and found the right tree. He would start to run toward it, and if he turned so I could see his face, he had a special kind of gleaming smile. If he said anything, it was only ahh, ahh, yes!

"We cut the tree down being careful not to hurt any of the branches. While Beal and sometimes Fred worked cutting the tree, I would look up at the giant pines and thanked them for taking care of this little one and for giving it to us for Christmas."

Lou looked down at the children on his knees. Jeanne was fast asleep and Boy was struggling to keep his eyes open.

"That was a lovely story," Sophia said. "I have never heard you tell that one before."

Lou looked at her with his eyes filled with love. "Thank you," was all he said. But his eyes said so much more.

When he looked back at Boy, he was sound asleep. Lou stood up, Boy under one arm and Jeanne under the other. He started up the stairs leading to the bedrooms. Sophia followed him up. They would tuck the children into their beds, kiss them goodnight, and turn off the light, just as they always did.

This night, this holy eve, Lou and Sophia retreated back to the tree to hold and snuggle, to talk and love. Life was good as Scottie lay curled at their feet, waiting for Christmas morning.

At 8:00 on January 19, 1936, the northern sky was pink, basking in the winter morning auroral light. Boy awakened. He was lonely and restless. He wanted to be "rock-a-byed" and sung to. He was thirsty too. He crawled out of the warm nest of his bed and started down the hall. Surely Mom would help!

Down the corridor he opened the closed door. He was greeted by the vision of his father lying on top of his mother. They were rocking back and forth. His mother was softly moaning and his father was grunting.

They heard the door open. All movement ceased. Lou raised himself. Sophia was left open and abandoned.

Boy heard his father's curse as he pulled his robe on and covered the erect vivid beauty of his nakedness. Boy turned his eyes and then his body as his father jumped out of bed and headed for the corridor and down the stairs to the furnace room in the basement.

Sophia, who had managed to straighten her gown, reached for her son to hold and comfort him in her arms. They heard Lou shoveling coal and banging on the furnace hopper. Then the noise stopped.

After a while, Sophia could hear him climbing the basement steps. Then the basement door closed and she could hear Lou climbing the stairs to the second floor where the bedrooms were.

"Oh, my head!" Sophia heard Lou cry.

There was a horrible crash as she heard Lou fall. The sound of his massive body tumbling down the stairs was agonizing. Grabbing Boy in her arms, Sophia ran to the stairs. She stopped at the top of the stairs; looking down she was unable to believe what she saw. Then with a sound she did not recognize, her voice cried out, "No! No! No!"

She ran down to where Lou lay. Sitting at the bottom of the stairs, she held Lou's head in her lap. Listening to his moans, she watched the light of consciousness depart from his eyes and the ashen gray of death descend.

At first Sophia just sat there, not believing what was happening. She was in a daze. Then she began to sob and her sobs turned into a scream, unintelligible, and animal-like. She did not hear Boy's cry, nor his words as he stood at the top of the stairs. "Mommy! Mommy!" he cried. He hurtled down the steps and threw himself on his daddy's chest.

Jeanne's appearance broke the scene. When she appeared at the top of the stairs, Sophia screamed, "Do not come down! Do not!"

As though Jeanne's presence gave her strength, Sophia gathered herself and went to the phone. She told the operator to connect her with the hospital. After what seemed like an eternity, Boy stood at the bay window and peered out at the circling, flashing lights atop the ambulance. Jeanne had her arms around her brother and neither of them said a thing or knew what to think. Their world had died. The world they had known had crashed in upon their heads. Their hearts and very beings joined the drying lakes.

Sophia sat beside Lou in the ambulance as it made its way to St. Luke's Hospital. She held his hand, now limp and damp and cool. Outwardly she appeared numb; inwardly she was enraged.

"Damn that Gypsy! God damn that Gypsy!" was all she could mutter under her breath over and over again. She knew she should pray to the God she had been taught to believe in and know—but she could not—not now.

Lou was pronounced dead that afternoon at two. The blood clot in his brain confirmed what he had always believed.

He was not like other men. He was not strong enough to help himself nor those he loved. He died as he lived.

In the front parlor of the house on 7th Street in Fargo, people gathered to join the wake for Lou. Boy watched as one and then another walked up to the casket, shook their heads, and cried. Scottie lay beside the casket, head between his paws. Boy walked to the casket. In time, he felt Uncle Rudy's hands lifting him to look at the man he loved.

Rage stormed in every cell of his being. This man had left him. The one who loved him slept the sleep of eternity. He wailed and he cried. He did not know yet how to curse. He kicked the casket again and again. He felt Rudy throw him down and then he was imprisoned beneath the casket by legs and feet. He tried to get out but was pushed back.

He lay beneath the casket and cried. It seemed forever, but maybe it was only time measured in minutes—long enough to watch Scottie stand on his two hind legs and place his front paws on the edge of the casket.

Everybody praised the dog and Emmy Mae said, "Look how much he loved Lou!"

Boy thought: Did they not know? Did they not? Boy loved him too.

PART TWO

AUNT INGA'S DONUTS

Glenwood! The Pope County seat nestled in a valley surrounded by the glacial ridge Agassiz. This barrier ridge was formed when the glacier Agassiz melted and retreated and rested on its journey northward many millennia ago.

Glenwood is located at the head of a lake bearing the Indian name Minnewaska, which means "white water." Certainly, it was when the stormy winds would churn its shallow depth and leave dangerous waves, "white tails," dancing on its surface. It seemed a natural place to go when you came out of the turbulent storms of life.

The town of Starbuck nestled at the foot of the lake, ten miles south and west of Glenwood. Starbuck was named for a matched pair of oxen that died pulling their master's ox-cart loaded with furs on its way south from Winnipeg, Manitoba, to St. Paul, Minnesota. Later Starbuck became the Mecca of the Norwegians who had come to settle and farm the glacial soil of west-central Minnesota. These hearty northern folk had come to this stormy western valley about the time the Civil War had ended. In the end, Starbuck was so Norwegian even the dogs spoke it and the horses danced to it.

Glenwood was a bit more cosmopolitan. It boasted a fine flavoring of Bohemian to go with its Norwegian. Regardless of which end of the lake you lived on, or whether you were Norwegian or Bohemian, all the fine cooks had brought their recipes from the old countries. They were passed down from generation to generation and covered every food from rulle polse and lefse to the finest Bohemian stew.

There was, however, one food that stood out above all others in its influence and importance. That food was the lowly donut! The donut was present at every major decision for town and country. It mattered not whether the decision was made at morning or afternoon coffee or in the chambers of the highest commissioners' council, the donut was there.

Donuts played a major part in the healing of illnesses such as colds, bruised knees, skinned elbows, or hurt feelings. Wise people duly prescribed them along with aspirin, poultices, and chicken soup. Donuts made their way to every threshing season and quilting bee. Donuts found their way to practically every wedding and, of course, to every funeral. Occasionally donuts were invited to baptisms and often to confirmations and first communions.

In short, donuts were the staff of life!

While there were minor variations between Bohemian and Norwegian donuts, or so the judges at the Pope County Fair would solemnly maintain, the donuts were often more compatible than the humans who midwived them from their wombs of hot rendered lard. Small wonder then that those special healers and leaders who were called to midwife the donut took their task very seriously and displayed extraordinary respect.

So it was with Inga Phair, the greatest donut maker of all time, or so Boy, who was five years old, believed his aunt to be. Boy knew it was not just personal bias. Aunt Inga's donuts had won the ribbons at the county fair, so obviously the judges agreed. The gods had smiled kindly on Aunt Inga and bestowed on her a part in the story of creation—at least in Pope County.

However, none of the larger issues concerning donutry and its pivotal role in the psychological, physical, and political development of Pope County and its inhabitants were of much concern to Boy as he encountered Aunt Inga and her donuts. What he did know was that he liked her and he liked her donuts.

Boy's first encounter with the love, humor, and benign deceptiveness woven into the recipe of Inga's donuts happened on a gray December day in 1936. It was cold and blustery outside the Minton Hotel. The snow was moving horizontally and spinning in tight dervish swirls, dancing across the intersection of Glenwood Avenue and Main Street. The smell inside the room on the second floor was almost unbearable. It was a miasma blended from a combination of diarrhea and vomit produced by two little kids sick with God knows what. Dr. Elder thought that it was significant enough that it should have a long name so that it would warrant putting up a quarantine sign. That meant Boy and sister Jeanne were imprisoned in the little room. The only diversion was to press your nose against the frosty window and watch the horizontal snow while trying to forget the horrible smell and many happenings of the past eleven months.

A few weeks before, Sophia Mossman had moved her family from the little cottage refuge by the lake, where she had settled with her children when she had left Fargo. Winter's wind-and-snow demons had caused the move after proving they were too tough to endure. The winter demons laughed as they blocked the roads and made the daily seven mile journey into town impossible. Jeanne needed to go to first grade, and Sophia needed to get to her fledgling shoe store across the street from the Minton Hotel. Boy did not need to go anywhere because he was too little. Single parenting was hard, almost unto death, but it was not an option; it was Sophia's fate.

Now, at that very moment, as Sophia stood in the window of her shoe store, looking up at the second floor of the three story red brick hotel, she could not know that there was a knock at the door of the smelly room. Boy slid the door bolt back and there stood Aunt Inga. There was a bundle of blankets in her arms and a glint in her eye. She had come to rescue Boy—if only for a time.

Soon Boy was bundled in the blankets and hustled out the door, down the back steps, out into the alley behind the hotel, and into the old Essex automobile. For some reason, known only to Inga, Jeanne was left behind—alone!

Once in the car they headed for the little stucco house Inga shared with Jaspar just on the edge of town. Jaspar had been introduced to Boy as Uncle Phair, for some reason Boy never figured out.

As they drove away from the hotel Inga's comment was, "What the good doctor does not know will not cause him to lose any sleep. And it will not hurt you," she said, looking at Boy.

The back door of Aunt Inga's house on Green Street opened onto a little entryway that led directly to the kitchen. A table stood to the left in the little kitchen and the sink rested beneath the window to the right. Next to the sink was the stove, still supporting a large vat full of hot lard. Boy could have been blind and still found the donuts on the table.

This magic would happen many times in the years ahead. Sometimes the rescuing magic occurred late at night in the midst of one of Sophia's stress and hysteria-induced heart attacks. Boy thought the threat of death was real, and he pleaded with the gods to spare his mother and make her well. The gods did not listen, but Aunt Inga would throw open the door, take him by the hand, hustle him into the car and take him home to be with Uncle Phair for a few days. Those few days sometimes lasted months.

He would leave his mother's home feeling scared and shamed and hurt and then the door would open and the aroma of fresh donuts would greet him. He was ushered to the little kitchen table with its yellow enameled top and there would be the donut and the glass of milk waiting for him. The world was then somehow secure.

For Boy, the magic of Inga's donuts not only rescued him but nurtured his learning of life's lessons. Sometimes the donuts were on the table at four in the morning when Boy made the two block trek from home to meet Uncle Phair for the day's hunt.

When he would arrive at the brightly lit, donut-scented kitchen, Inga would already have packed the lunch and put the pups in the back of the Oldsmobile, which had replaced the Essex. She would then usher Boy, with his gun, into the car with the pups. Finally she was ready to set off on the journey with Phair at her side. She would drive her entourage to the duck marsh in the backwaters of Lake Emily, south of Starbuck, sixteen miles away.

Always donuts were present at times of play and work, healing and learning. They filled Boy and taught him to listen for and anticipate the small inner voice of love that filled the internal chambers of his heart with messages of strength and hope and sounds of joy.

FRIEDA

The little girl, vibrant and full of life, was on the paved playground behind the Cyrus School. It was spring, recess time, warm breezes blowing from the west. All the energy, stored in every cell of the six and seven year olds collected from the winter and the morning and from the sun and from the wind, needed release or they would explode.

The big boys from grade six cried, "Let's play Crack the Whip!" A chorus of agreement echoed in the valley.

The big kids were in front. The little kids were at the line's end. Faster and faster the big boys pulled and ran. Frieda, small for her age and only six, was at the very end and could hardly keep up.

Then the leaders stopped. The human whip cracked!

Frieda lost her grip on the child's hand that held her to the line. She went flying, crashing against a post in the schoolyard fence. She caromed off and slid across the pavement of the schoolyard.

Her spine was broken. Her skin was torn.

In time, both her skin and back would heal, but she would spend the rest of her life as a humpback. Others would scorn her. She would be seen as too ugly to have a love and family of her own.

The weeks and months of healing had also been weeks and months of penance and forced confession. She had been told that certainly God had seen her irresponsible play and now was punishing her so she would learn only to do right and to be more serious.

God was now, and forever more, a God who watched your every move and kept score. If your score was not perfect, He would punish. Life was a serious business, lived before an ever-watchful, vengeful God who would even break your back to get you to obey.

Nonetheless, in the deepest recesses of her soul, a part of Frieda's playful, loving spirit remained unbroken. Even a vengeful God was not strong enough to crush it altogether. However, the struggle was waged in the underground spaces of her soul between her inner playful self and the shame of being punished; it would last a lifetime.

This battle would be waged upon Shakespeare's stage of life, empowering the actors as they took their parts in her tragic play, "The Battle of Shame and Life."

It was dark and raining when Sophia, in a gray Lafayette Nash, pulled up in front of the little white frame house two doors down the street from the Morris Swedish Covenant Church.

Recently widowed, Sophia in desperate need of help with her children, who were six and seven, had been told that this woman in Morris, twenty-some miles to the west, might be available. She was thirty or thirty-two, never married, and a good Christian woman. She lived with her sister and her husband, but wanted somewhere else to live because her sister's husband drank too much. Sophia thought that this alone was a good recommendation. Besides, Frieda had another sister who was a missionary in Africa.

Sophia had always admired those who did mission work, especially in mysterious, exotic foreign countries. In the quiet recesses of her soul, she had fantasies about the inner goodness of those who would leave all to go to strange, exotic, scary places to do good.

She, herself, had done a little of it when she had worked with the girls at the orphanage in Stoughton and lived and worked with the Indians in the Missouri River bottoms of Montana. But she had never lived and done well in a foreign country, like "Dark Africa," as it was called in the books that always fanned her passion for the different and the exotic.

In the parlor of the white framed house, Jeanne and Boy sat quietly and stiffly as Sophia asked Frieda questions about how much money she would need, when she could start, and what day off she would want.

Frieda's questions came back like a tennis volley. "Could she discipline the children if they needed it? Would they be expected to help her with the housework? After all, she couldn't lift much with her back and all."

She would definitely want every Thursday and one weekend every month off. "Would that be acceptable?"

Her needs were not great, but she would want $25.00 a week plus board and room. She said she thought she was worth it. Sophia said she thought so, too.

While this verbal volley was going on, Jeanne and Boy began to fidget and squirm on their respective chairs where they had been told to sit—quietly! Nobody talked to them or seemed to care what they thought or what questions they might have of this strange-looking woman. The questions served and questions returned were boring.

The rainy night, the house with its stale beer and baking odors, the hunchbacked woman—all were scary as far as

Boy was concerned. He just wanted to leave. He did not know why they needed Frieda anyway.

He had gotten a job when he turned six sweeping out the Coast to Coast store behind Sophia's little shoe shop. He could make a lot of money. He got paid five cents every time he swept the floor. Besides that, he knew how to do the laundry. He could cut up the Fels Naptha soap bars without cutting himself—at least not very often. He could even manage the wringer on the old Maytag without getting his hand eaten by it. He silently thought, "My sister, mom, and I can manage just fine—thank you." He thought of saying to the lady, 'We don't need you!' But, then, he thought better of it. He knew that when they got home the wooden spoon would be taken from its drawer and he would be spanked for being rude. Then Mother would probably have another "heart attack." Dr. MacIver would be called. Boy would be blamed for causing it all and then he would be sent away to stay at Aunt Inga's. No. He would just sit and wait. He would try to count the keys on the pump organ that sat across the room.

Jeanne seemed to have a better time of it. Hope, Frieda's sister, was showing her all the interesting things that Greta, the missionary sister, had brought back from Africa. They were laughing and playing and Jeanne had even gotten to hold some of the precious stuff from the Dark Continent.

Then Hope disappeared into the kitchen and came back with sugar cookies and milk. After Jeanne had been served, Boy was invited to cross the room and have some cookies and milk. When he had finished his first cookie, he heard Sophia say, "Well then, you can move your things in on Saturday and start work on Monday." Boy and his sister were hustled out into the rain and into the cold Lafayette for the sixteen-mile trip home to Glenwood. So Frieda came to live with them.

After Frieda came to be their nanny, life in the little bungalow on the shores of Lake Minnewaska changed. Organization and expectations ran high. While Frieda was no Mary Poppins, she did have her playful side as well as her stern, disciplined, life-is-serious side.

Saturday mornings were dedicated to washing, waxing and polishing the hard wood floors in the kitchen, hall, and dinette. This procedure quickly assumed the status of ritual and sacred act. A potion made of boiling water and lye soap was used to cut the wax applied the week before. It left the floors white and sterile. Boy hated this part because it fell to him to apply the potion and left his knees sore and his hands red and burning. He wondered why this always ended up as his job. Frieda's answer was consistently the same: "You are the man of the house and you should not complain but just do your job. Besides I told you to do it."

Jeanne's job was to smear the paste wax on the freshly washed boards. That seemed like it would be so much more fun. Jeanne would laugh and make pictures with the wax as she put it on the boards.

Secretly Boy wondered if Frieda liked girls better than boys. But the thought of favoritism soon vanished when the wax was on and had dried a bit and Frieda's voice intruded into his private world with, "Time to put on the socks and polish the floor."

Boy and Jeanne ran to the drawer where the thick, white cotton socks were kept and then raced one another to see who could get them on first. They slid and skated back and forth across the kitchen floor. They raced up and down the hallway, seeing who could slide the farthest. Finally, they would end up in the dinette, often amidst screams of delight and bumps of joy, which punctuated the play. Laughter ruled in the kitchen playground. Then, before the job was done, the corners and edges had to be polished too. The laughter ebbed, but the warm, good feelings took a new direction, for about this time the air filled with the sweet aroma of freshly baked sugar cookies and bread about to come out of the oven. Frieda had been busy too.

Saturday morning life seemed good as they sat on the polished floor and watched the butter melt into the still-warm bread.

THE SWIMMING LESSON

It was late June 1938. Boy was six, almost seven, and life was beginning to be almost normal once again. At least it seemed much different and better than it had been. They had moved into the house on the shore of Lake Minnewaska the previous fall. It felt good to escape the Minton Hotel where his mother, sister, and he had lived cramped for months while the little house was being built.

In the months after Lou's death, Sophia had relocated her family to Glenwood where she had sisters and other relatives for support. She had started a business and now built a house. As a result, Sophia had little time or energy to spend as a mother and parent. Both Jeanne and Boy were adrift in a world of worried adults.

The world was changing. The clouds of war were forming once again. The poverty, hunger and depression following the thunderous crash of the stock market were not yet a memory but an ever-present villain lurking just around the corners of consciousness.

How would the mortgage be paid? Would the shoe store fold? Sophia fretted, "Will I live to see my children grow?" Her nights were sleepless as the questions bumped into one another and ricocheted off into the black hole of inner space, creating new questions.

And as for Jeanne and Boy? They were left to fend for themselves emotionally. Fortunately, they had each other and became best friends. But sister and brother can never fully help each other. They each needed a teacher and protector. Jeanne wandered the shores along the lake and found first in her mind, and then later in reality, mentors and protectors. There was Uncle Joe, Lou's older brother who gently consoled and counseled her. There was Myrtle Olson, a wise teacher and friend of Sophia's, and her sisters, Elizabeth and Inga. There was even Uncle Rudy, at times, when he was in town. Mostly Jeanne watched and identified with Sophia and learned the lessons of survival.

But Boy got angry deep, deep inside. Then he just got sad and scared. He would wander the hills by himself. Much later in life, he could capture the feelings in poetry that came from deep within.

Before his mother's house
Wind moved the lake with white-tipped vengeance.
To the child-boy it was like his soul,
Powerful, troubled, turbulent,
Gnawing at the edges,
Promising something more.
But What?
He was lonely.
But no one came, and no one stayed.
Behind his mother's house
The hills rose high.
There he could go and peace would follow.
No one seemed to miss him.
He wondered why.
His mother asked

What he had learned when he returned.
He wondered if she cared.
In the hills Scottie dog and he could be
Whatever he chose to see.
He could be a hero, an explorer, royalty, or pauper.
The clouds above them formed castles,
And mountains.
Faces and warriors
And haunted houses.
Rain washed away the tears.
At night the stars stood watch
And dreams were filled with wonder and with magic.
At dawn sun warmed the chill of being.
As his soul nursed and sucked the milk of knowing
The gift of life which flowed freely from the hills,
He could be alone, but not lonely,
For there were no broken promises
Of being loved and wanted
And then rejected by the sayer.
Instead, the fragrance of the flowers
And the gossamer wings of moths
Bore his fantasies and prayers
Of hope for love and safe belonging.
When he came home from the hills,
As he always would,
The angry winds within his soul would start again.
Silently he felt the chill of shame.
He came to believe the turmoil of life's storms
Emanated from his being.
He came to believe he was the cause
Of all rejection by the other.
The more he desired, the greater the empty void became.
Then his eyes and steps would again

Turn to the hills,
Where aloneness was not lonely.
Where his dreams of love
Were guarded by the stars
And Creator Grandmother of the hills
Held him to her breast.

In the recognition and knowing of one spirit by another that is often born of sensitivity to issues of being that reside in levels of consciousness beneath the surface of the obvious, links are formed and survival becomes an option and beyond survival—love.

So it was with Boy. Aunt Inga, his mother's sister, his fairy godmother in the flesh, and Mr. Phair, her husband of later life, came bounding into his life. Inga had more the persona of Tug Boat Annie, but Boy didn't mind.

Aunt Inga was there whenever Boy needed a protector, a loving word, or a kick in his pants. One of her favorite sayings was, "The Lord helps them that help themselves!" Sometimes this was recited when Boy needed to be reminded that he was not helpless and could do things he never thought he could do.

There were special times when her voice would come to him when he was in a tight spot and he needed to try a little harder to dismiss the fear-born demons. Other times, Aunt Inga would recite "the Lord helps them that help themselves" when she would stop the car by a cornfield. After she recited the canticle, the car doors would open and she and Boy would get out and disappear into the field to get some of the tender corn for supper. Inga, the respected, successful businesswoman, church and community leader, appeared, skirt held out like a basket, filling with the succulent ears that Boy picked. As the corn dropped into the skirt-basket the world became right and good again.

Inga and Jaspar Phair had married as a matter of mutual need and convenience. Inga was forty-four and "Phair" was fifty-nine. Inga wanted a companion and helper who would not be offended by her sometimes brusque and different ways. She also liked the fact that he was a good businessman who could help her with the books and as a buyer of fine women's clothes for her successful ladies' ready-to-wear shop. As it turned out, he also was able to help her start a chain of beauty shops in rural, west central Minnesota. He did this at a time when the world was reeling from dust, depression, and war. Yet, he could sell the idea of the need for beauty and self-esteem.

For Phair the marriage was a way of escaping loneliness. Long before, after an unsuccessful first marriage, he had discovered that his attraction and orientation was not like that of other men. His soul was sensitive and he saw beauty in the male form.

For a time he had tried to live a lifestyle that let him have relationships with other men as he vocationally functioned as a professional hunter for the Canadian Government. He was a good hunter, but soon he gave this up because he felt it was too violent. It was against his nature to kill birds just so they could be shipped to markets in the East where their flesh would satiate the vociferous appetites of the wealthy looking for exotic tastes to fill their corpulent bellies.

He also discovered that at times when he was hired as "the fine gentleman guide from England," some of the hunters who were homosexual had the same vociferous sexual appetite for exotic/exploitive experiences without value or meaning. This was as much against his nature as was killing birds just for the sake of sport and fun.

When he left the ranks of the professional hunter to become manager extraordinaire of fine British Columbia hotels owned by the Canadian Pacific Railway System, Phair had resigned himself to a life of celibacy and loneliness.

Then he met Inga. She had come west by train to visit friends homesteading on the plains of Alberta. When her visit ended, she decided to go on to see British Columbia, a place she had never been. She had heard about its mountains and its beauty and wanted to see them for herself. She stayed at a Canadian Railway Hotel in Vancouver. There, Inga met Phair.

They talked and talked. He told her all about himself. It was as though a dam had broken and the waters of isolation and loneliness spilled out. She told him about her life and store and how she was different, too.

When she returned to Glenwood, plans were made for Phair to follow when he could. They were married in 1935 and moved to an apartment above the Greek Cafe on the corner of Main and Glenwood Streets.

The first thing Phair did, after settling in and balancing the books for Inga's shop and laying plans for the beauty shop in Appleton to open, was to buy a sixteen-foot cedar-strip fishing boat. And then he bought a duck boat. And then he bought decoys. And then some more decoys. He had all the fishing poles and baits and hunting guns that had come with him from the west.

Because Phair did not drive, Inga was his chauffeur. By the time they had located and acquired the boat from the boat works in Alexandria, the decoys from Herter's in Waseca, and all the other clothing and paraphernalia from St. Paul, St. Cloud, and God knows where else, Inga's appetite for the blood sports had been awakened. She would spend the rest of the time until Phair's death as his closest companion in the field or driving to the duck blind or to the harbor at Halvorson Point where the boat was kept.

Phair always looked the dignified English gentleman as he rode beside Inga in the Essex, and later the Oldsmobile, whether to blind or boat, boutique or beauty parlor.

When Sophia came to town with Jeanne and Boy in tow, Inga, childless, rejected Jeanne but adopted Boy like a hen bluebill with an abandoned redhead duckling. Boy loved it. He had found a home. Phair became Boy's teacher, mentor, and disciplinarian. He was Boy's father. He was open and honest about how others thought him different and how he indeed may be. But, never once did his boundaries waver when he was with Boy. It mattered not whether they were alone or in a group of other men. He always ensured that Boy was safe in every way. Boy was to learn to be responsible in the ways of the hunt, the world, and life. He was to become his own person and not an object for another. He was to develop courage and skill and to learn how all these bits of knowledge, attributes, and skills fit together in life.

This day in June of 1938 broke clear and warm. The phone rang. Inga's voice came over the wire and into Boy's ear, "Phair wants to go fishing. I'll pick you up in half an hour."

Boy's response, as always, was "OK."

He liked to go with Uncle Phair. He trusted him. Uncle Phair had always treated him like he was important and somebody to be proud of. Phair introduced him by name and as a friend to the other fishermen at Halvorson Point when they launched the boat. Boy was never "my wife's sister's little boy." Boy liked that.

In Phair's eyes, Boy seemed to have some stature of his own. Maybe Phair did that because he knew what it was like to be used, pigeonholed, and treated like an object. Whatever it was, Boy liked the respect and the expectation that he could hold his own. It made him want to try all the harder to learn the lessons of the day.

Some days those lessons had been about launching or rowing a boat. Other days they had been about fishing and casting, bait selection and minnow mounting. Sometimes when he was bored and the fish were not biting, the lesson had been about whistling and singing, so a breeze would come up and the walleyes would bite. Phair said he learned that in England. Or was it Canada?

Boy wondered why whistling would make the wind blow. Yet, sometimes it seemed to work. Phair seemed to have mystical powers that always made things good. He would sit in the stern of the boat, his white fishing hat with its narrow brim filled with favorite hooks and lures, resting squarely on his head. The fishing poles that he wasn't using always lay along the gunnel to the left and the large, oversized, long handled landing net was propped along the gunnel to the right.

This day, Inga, as usual, helped Boy and Phair put the poles and gear in the boat. She said goodbye and retreated to the Essex for her trip back to town to tend the store. She would pick them up at six.

They pushed away from the dock and Boy began to row them out to their favorite fishing hole. However, Boy noticed that this day was a little different. Phair, instead of fiddling with some hooks or lures or rearranging his tackle box, merely sat with his hands folded in his lap and was kind of humming a little tune. Boy thought he was trying to get the wind to blow because the lake was like a mirror.

When they had gone about two hundred yards, which was only about half the distance to the favorite fishing hole, Phair stopped humming and told Boy to drop the anchor. Boy did as he was told and down went the anchor. When it hit bottom Phair said, "Pull it up. Let's see how deep it is here."

Boy pulled it up. He looked for the water line on the rope and measured it with his eye. Then he reported, "It's about eight feet, Uncle Phair."

"Good!" said Phair.

Boy wondered why he said "good" because they almost always fished in ten feet of water. Phair had always said that that was the best depth for fishing walleyes this time of year. Now he seemed to be changing.

Next, Phair said, "You don't swim yet, do you?"

"No, sir," Boy replied.

Phair said, "Well it's time to learn."

Boy said, "Yes sir."

Phair said, "Take your clothes off. Down to your under shorts."

Boy looked at him. His eyes said "What!?"

"Hurry on now," said Phair.

Boy did, but inwardly he began to feel butterflies and other little critters that were harbingers of fear. He heard Inga's voice ringing in his ears, "The Lord helps those who helps themselves. Now get on with it!"

He stood in his underwear looking at the water.

Phair said, "Get in the water!"

Boy said, "Now?"

Phair said, "Yes, you'll be all right." He picked up the big landing net and held it firmly in both hands. He said, "You see, if you begin to sink, I'll land you like a fish. You know how that is."

Boy said, "Oh!"

Phair said, "Now get on with it. Over the side you go."

Boy crawled up on the gunwale. He was really scared now. Inga's voice kept ringing in his head. "The Lord helps them that help themselves!"

Slowly, like slow motion that he had seen in the movie at the theater on Main Street, he moved one leg and then the other. He pulled himself up on the edge of the boat and pushed one leg and then the other over the edge into the water.

He moved with the stiffness of cold syrup. He poured himself over the edge and into the water. The water was warm and so was the sun. Boy hung onto the edge of the boat for dear life.

Phair sat, still holding the landing net. He smiled and said, "Good! Good Boy! Good first step. I knew you could do it." He kept nodding his head in approval.

Boy began to breathe again. It felt good to know that he still could.

Phair's voice sounded far away as it floated over the boat's edge and down to him, "Hang on to the boat, but start to move your legs. Start to kick. That's what's goin' to give you power when you really start to swim."

Boy kicked!

Phair sat there with the landing net, peering over the side, nodding his head and smiling. Then he held up his hand in a signal to stop kicking and splashing. Boy stopped and the splashing quieted.

"Now let go with one hand and begin to move it in the water while you kick," Phair instructed. The butterflies returned. Boy looked up at him with a look that was like "You must be kidding. Please, sir, be kidding."

But instead, Phair said, "Now let go!"

He wasn't kidding!

Boy closed his eyes, swallowed hard, and did as he was told.

Phair again grasped the landing net with both hands. Boy waved and kicked and waved and kicked. One hand

and then the other and suddenly both his hands were off the boat and in the water frantically waving and flailing about. He was floating away from the boat and going in circles. He was beginning to sink beneath the water's surface. Fear had taken over and his body no longer had the buoyant energy to let it float. It acted more like a rock and was headed for the bottom to join its friends, the clam and snail shells.

Just as he disappeared beneath the surface, he looked up. Phair was still there, but now he was standing, still nodding and smiling but he was reaching out with the landing net. He scooped it under Boy and lifted him up and back to the edge of the boat.

He must have seen Boy's eyes as big as saucers. He said, "That last part was scary, wasn't it? But you did good. Let's try again. We'll make it work better next time."

Boy wanted to say, "What's this 'we' business?" But, he didn't.

Instead he tried again. Boy learned to kick and move both hands without sinking or needing the landing net.

Phair said he was learning to tread water. Whatever it was called it seemed to work, and Boy's confidence grew.

The lesson lasted twenty minutes, which Boy thought was as long as eternity. At the end of the twenty minutes Phair said, "Time!" in true English fashion. The pub had closed. He lowered the net for Boy to grab and scooped Boy out of the water, depositing him in the bottom of the boat. Next Phair reached in his tackle box and produced a towel. Boy had never seen him keep a towel in his tackle box before. He handed it to Boy, and reached in again and came up with a dry pair of under shorts. He knew Boy was going to begin to learn to swim that day and he was prepared.

Next, he reached in his lunch bucket and found the thermos and the cup and the donut. He poured the hot chocolate that Inga had made and handed it, along with the donut, to Boy.

When Boy had dressed and finished the hot chocolate and donut, Phair said, "'Pull the anchor! Row us out to our fishing hole. Let's see if they're biting."

The weather that summer stayed clear and warm the rest of June and through July. By the end of two weeks, Boy was swimming around the boat, while Phair paraded up and down the center of the boat, net held high, ready to pull him out if he needed help.

The third week Boy learned to dive, sort of. Mostly, it was Phair pushing his behind while he knelt on the edge with his hands over his head, as Phair had instructed him. Anyway, it was a quicker way into the water than the cold syrup method.

The fourth week Boy would swim away from the boat about twenty-five feet and then back again. Phair was always there, landing net held high, smiling and nodding, unless Boy swam too far. Then, he would yell at Boy and remind him in no gentle terms that this was a lesson and he wasn't yet done learning how to swim. There was more yet to master before he was safe to swim the waters on his own.

As Boy and Phair fished after each lesson, Phair kept talking about how swimming through the waters, and how to do it well and safe, was like learning how to get through life, well and safe, by knowing what to do. Boy didn't understand then, but Boy came to understand that the lessons learned were more than just about the water and the strokes and ways of swimming.

Inga always came at six o'clock, and they met her at the dock. When the boat was secured in its anchorage for the night and the gear was loaded in the car, they started back to Phair's and Inga's new little stucco house on Green Street. They had bought it and moved there to get away from the cramped, hot, smelly apartment above the Greek restaurant.

On the way back to the house, Inga always talked about supper.

Sometimes on the way she would stop the Essex along side a cornfield and then recite: "The Lord helps those who help themselves!" Phair would chuckle as the car doors opened and Boy and Inga disappeared into the field.

THE PAPER ROUTE

Boy came home. He was excited as only a seven-year-old can be when he thinks he has done something good. He burst in the door. His voice was loud. He forgot about the muddy boots and the kitchen floor. He even forgot to shut the door.

"I got it! I got it! He said I could! All I have to. . ."

Frieda's voice was loud and sharp, "Stop it! Look what you've done to the floor! Shame on you!" The firm staccato continued, "Now go back and shut the door and be quiet!"

Boy closed the door and went down to the basement. After a while, Scottie, the white collie, came down and licked his face. He sat down and put his head in Boy's lap.

About 6:30 Boy heard the back door open and close as Sophia came home from her shoe shop. He started up the steps to tell her about his new job and how he was going to earn lots of money and how he could help her buy things. But at the top of the steps he overheard Frieda talking to Sophia. "I don't know what I'm going to do with that boy! He parades in here with dirty boots yelling at the top of his lungs—not even shutting the door. I think he just needs a good sound spanking. And, I maybe shouldn't say so, but I think you should give it to him."

"Where is he now?" Sophia asked.

Frieda replied, "Somewhere around here, I guess. He better be home for supper is all I can say."

This last of the conversation was not heard, for Boy and the collie had sneaked out the back door into the early spring twilight. They headed across the front lawn, across the road, and down to the shore of Lake Minnewaska.

Tears rolled down his face. He was hurt and angry. He picked up a stone and threw it as hard as he could. It skipped across the water and sank just before it reached the edge of the ice that was receding out into the lake as the spring thaw warmed the water.

Boy cursed and screamed and cried. Scottie, his dog, looked on and then nuzzled the hand that hung down from the young lad's weighted shoulders. Boy sat down and stared out at the lake as the shadows lengthened and then dark descended. In the dark a cacophony of migrating ducks could be heard as they fed and rested in the open water near the shore. As the sounds of night surrounded Boy a peaceful mood crept in. He told Scottie about his paper route and how he would be the best paperboy in town. "Why," he told the dog, "I will get enough new customers that they will have to let me have the prize of a trip to Minneapolis to see the headquarters of the Minneapolis *Journal* and the Minnesota Gophers football game."

How long Boy daydreamed, he could not tell. When finally he did get up and head for the house, the sounds of quacking ducks had been replaced by his mother's angry voice shouting for him to come home.

When he entered the back door, the kitchen light was on and around the corner he could see Frieda sitting with her arms folded across her chest. The look on her face was not pleasant, nor welcoming.

When he rounded the corner and entered the kitchen, he quickly noticed that the large wooden spoon that usually resided in the top kitchen utensil drawer was now firmly held in Sophia's hand. First she glared at him for what seemed like hours as Boy shifted his weight from one foot to the other and Scottie emitted a soft whine.

In a very angry, firm voice she asked, "Where have you been? You angered Frieda with your muddy feet and impolite and raucous ways and you have scared me half to death. Can't you ever learn to make life easier for Frieda? She'll leave us if you don't! Then where will we be?" She paused to take a breath and went on, "I have to work so we have food to eat, so I need her here and I need you to listen to her and not carry on like you do, always excited about something or other. You are going to be punished because that's the only way Frieda thinks you'll learn!"

Sophia grabbed him by the arm and began to spank him. One—two—three—

Suddenly, she stopped. She stood straight, breathing hard. Her face was a mask of fear and pain. Sophia clutched her hands over her left breast. "I . . . I . . . Oh God! My heart!"

She half staggered down the hallway to her bedroom "Call Dr. MacIver!" she cried. Her voice and breath were short and choppy.

Boy, still crying, stayed in the kitchen. He was alone. Jeanne was in the bedroom with Sophia.

Frieda was running about looking for the good doctor's phone number. Finally, she called the operator for it. The operator replied loud enough so Frieda had to hold the phone away from her ear and Boy, halfway across the room, could hear the operator's voice. "Well, his number is 290 up in Lowry, but it won't do you no good, because I hear from Mable that he's down in the Cities right now going to a convention or something. Do you want me to ring up his partner, Dr. Jarvis?"

Frieda's affirmative response got that job done. Now it was time to call Sophia's sisters Inga and Elizabeth and tell them to come over, because Sophia was having a "heart attack" again. Once more, Frieda reported how Boy had misbehaved and Sophia had had to spank him. "That's what set it off!" she authoritatively declared. "I have called the doctor, but maybe you should come over anyway," she told each of them.

Fear overwhelmed Boy as he sat alone in the kitchen looking at the floor. Boy didn't know what he was scared of. If Sophia died he would be the cause, Frieda said, and he would be all alone. That scared him! If she didn't die, he would still get blamed for making her sick. That scared him, too!

What he did know was Aunt Inga wouldn't blame him. She would probably come and get him and take him home with her and Phair. What Boy didn't know, because it never dawned on him, was that it was Frieda's choice that he was spanked and not Sophia's.

It was two weeks later when Frieda, claiming she was following the doctor's orders, permitted Boy to come visit Sophia. Sophia, smiling and propped up in bed with the sun streaming in through the east window, asked what job he had gotten. He told her about the paper route.

"They said I'm too young to get a regular route, but Mr. Benson said I could deliver to any new customers I could get and call that my route. But Mom, I don't know what to do. I got forty-three new customers and now I can't carry all the papers. And—and . . . Mom, I asked God to please not let you die. I told Him I'd never be bad again and that you can have all the money I make," Boy said, looking out the window at the sun and shadows playing hide and seek around the light green, newly formed leaves on the tree beyond.

THE PHEASANT HUNT

Boy was nine years old and Uncle Phair had determined that it was time he began hunting in earnest. From the time Boy was seven he would disappear into the hills behind the house with his dog and little .22 rifle given to his mother by the Indians. He had gotten good at shooting rodents and tree stumps, but still knew nothing of what it was to be a hunter.

Uncle Phair understood well the soul of the hunter and what it took to grow that soul. He was long both on discipline and details, both prerequisites if one were to enter the inner world of respect that bound the hunter and the hunted in a dance of life and death. But Phair also knew that the inner fabric of the hunter formed the tapestry of the stories of creation, nurture, courage, and death. It was the balance of the feminine that saw and knew and lived the full circle of life and death and balance. One being gives its full essence for the life and health of another. Predator chases prey only to become prey chased by predator.

Perhaps it was because of his English heritage, steeped in Celtic ways, that Phair understood the ancient message given by the goddess of the hunt. Or, perhaps it was because of his inborn sensitive soul that set him off as different from other rough-hewn men who understood only the violence of killing and not the balance of life and death. Or, perhaps, it was the many years of conditioning from being the executive manager for the Canadian Pacific Railway's hotel and fine dining room in Vancouver, British Columbia. Whatever gave rise to his nature, it found its focus in imparting his wisdom of the "hunter's soul" and his hunting skills to Boy, whom he had come to think of as his own child. His wisdom and skills as hunter, follower of the Goddess of the Hunt, were extensive, honed by the years he had been a professional hunter and guide in British Columbia, before he had become hotel manager for the Canadian Pacific. Now he welcomed his opportunity to teach Boy.

The six weeks before the opening of the pheasant season in September were tightly scheduled by Phair and arduous for Boy. The weather was hot and made the specially fitted 12-gauge shotgun, that Phair had bought and insisted the lad use, seem twice as heavy as its 8 pounds.

Phair's explanation for so large a gun had been that no one he would train would use a smaller bore than 12 gauge. The chances of wounding a bird with a smaller bore were too great. A clean kill was what counted. The rule was this—anything you pointed the gun at you intended to kill, clean, cook, and eat.

Cooking was as much a part of the training as was learning to point the gun, and equally important was becoming knowledgeable in the habits and habitat of the birds. The overriding lesson, however, was ethics and safety. Cheating on the rules just would not be tolerated. The rules of the hunt were learned so well they could be recited while one slept. Any lapse of attention or careless act came under the eagle-like scrutiny of Phair's watchful eye. When he noted a lapse of mindfulness, the ever-present ruler grasped in his right hand, Phair was quick to bring a forceful, if not painful, reminder of the constant need for watchfulness and attention. "I forgot" was not an acceptable excuse. Neither was "I'm sorry," a loophole to escape responsibility.

For six weeks, including Sundays, there was a lesson every day. Frieda thought that the inclusion of Sundays was a defilement of the Sabbath, if not of God. However, she had learned early on not to tempt Phair to give his lecture on the topic that "the only reasonable religion was the practice of Masonry." So, she kept her silence and prayed that God would bring His righteous wrath down on teacher and student alike.

Each lesson lasted an hour. By the hour's end, Boy was reduced to rage and tears. As he walked the two blocks home from Phair's house, he sputtered and fumed and cursed and cried. He vowed he would not go back again.

Perhaps that vow was not kept, but repeated daily, as much because of Frieda as anything. She would greet him as he entered the kitchen, which was her domain with, "Why are you crying? You asked for it. I thought you were more of a man than that."

Then his anger turned away from Phair and on to her. Boy thought, "She doesn't know what it really is like and doesn't care. Besides, she is right. I had asked for it." And underneath he knew he really liked Phair and knew that Phair really liked him.

Boy knew he was the son Phair had never had and wanted him to be successful. Mostly he wanted Boy to be proud of himself. He wanted to be proud of Boy as well.

Frieda got the silent treatment. In fact, Boy had learned not to say anything to anyone. He went inside his heart and mind and learned to hone his imagination. His dreams, both waking and sleeping, were of birds flying, his gun swinging, the bird falling. His dreams always ended with Phair's proud smile and with him handing a pheasant to Frieda to clean and cook. In his mind story, she always had to ask him how to do it. Then Boy's smile burst forth within.

Finally, the training was over and the beginning of the hunting season had arrived. At 4 a.m., Saturday promised a clear cool dawn and a sunny day as Boy walked over to Phair's with his gun slung over his shoulder. Inga, clad in her hunting garb, drove them south of town to the farm where they had permission to hunt.

Buddy, Phair's water spaniel, bounded out of the car, his rat-like tail whipping at the air in a show of total excitement and anticipation. Boy looked at the dog and the dog looked at him and they understood each other. They shared the same feeling.

Phair chose a field and instructed that they begin the walk down the field toward the fence line a quarter mile distant. Buddy ran, nose to the ground, back and forth in an easy rhythm. He knew the birds were running ahead, but he patiently stayed within range of Boy and his Uncle knowing from past hunts that when they got to the fence they would catch up. The birds would fly. The guns would sound. And, then, he could retrieve.

It all happened just as Buddy knew it would, except Boy missed his shot and only Phair's bird was there to retrieve. At day's end, there had been four more shots Boy had missed. Phair had his limit, four roosters and two hens and Inga had two roosters.

Boy was crestfallen. All the work and all the training and he had failed. He feared Phair's criticism as he walked alone back to the car. At the car, Phair came over. He said nothing at first but just put a hand on Boy's shoulder. He took off his glasses and produced a kerchief with which to mop his forehead. Phair's gray hair was matted with sweat and he looked tired.

He was not too tired, though, to say to Boy, "It was a good day. I was real proud of the way you walked in line and worked the birds today. You watched yourself and didn't shoot that time when you would have had to shoot across me. Yes, I was real proud of you. Tomorrow or another day, you'll get your birds. You're a good hunter!"

He turned and walked to the car where Inga was impatiently waiting. She hadn't walked the last field but had taken her two birds and gone back to the car. Once Phair and Boy were in earshot she called, "Come on! Hurry it up! Get in the car, we got to go home and clean these birds and get something to eat!"

The next day was Sunday. Both Sophia and Frieda insisted that Boy and his sister be in church. Sophia declined going. Saturday night the shoe store stayed open late so it had been a 13-hour day by the time the books had been balanced and the shop closed.

Frieda declined because she was, after all, Swedish Covenant and the children would, of course, go to the Lutheran Church. On one occasion, Boy had overheard her talking to her sister. He had heard her say to Hope, "I don't understand how Sophia could ever have given permission for Boy to go with Richard Urgent to the Catholic Church for that release time training in the ways of the antichrist! I just think it's wrong. We all know the Pope and Catholics are evil!"

After that bit of eavesdropping, he thought, "At least she likes me better if I go to old Reverend Linevold's Lutheran Church!"

Boy remembered how he went with Richard to the Catholic Church on Wednesday mornings. He had asked permission, and his mother had said yes, when he explained how after his friend came back to the school yard from the little church basement after the catechization, all the good Lutheran and Methodist kids would jump on him and beat him at recess .

Boy had thought that was terribly wrong and unfair, so now he went with Richard every Wednesday to learn the Catholic ways. Boy knew there were very few Catholics in town. The church was very small. It wasn't even a church, only a basement. Almost everyone in town was Norwegian and Lutheran and went to the big Lutheran Church. A few went to the Methodist Church, whatever that was. All he knew about Methodists was they had a lady who taught violin. When he had taken lessons from her and had to do a recital at the Methodist Church basement, he had gotten so scared he had thrown up all over their linoleum floor. Aunt Inga had laughed and given him a hug. Sophia had tried to clean him up and comfort him, and Frieda had walked out.

Wednesdays at the Catholic Church he had learned "Hail Mary Full of Grace," the rosary, the proper order of Confession and how never to talk back to the nuns, or even question them. However, he didn't accomplish what he had wanted to, which was to help Richard so he wouldn't get beat up by the other kids. Now what happened was they both were beaten when they came back to the playground.

Anyway, Sunday morning he went to church because Frieda said God would be mad and get him if he didn't. Besides, she said it was a sin against the Third Commandment if he didn't go and already he was full of sin according to her. She said it was in the Bible. He secretly knew, by the look on Frieda's face, that she thought Sophia was sinning, too, by staying home.

This particular Sunday, Boy was very tired. He just wanted to sleep. Every muscle in his body hurt. He was so tired from walking after the pheasants and following Buddy up and down the fields.

Reverend Linevold droned on and on and Boy's eyes kept wanting to fall shut. Then he saw his sister pointing at the pipes on the pipe organ. She was counting them. That seemed more interesting than trying to listen to the preacher, whom he couldn't understand. So he began to point and count. Then Jeanne nudged him in the ribs and said something like the pipes had mouths like the preacher and some of the people. Boy lost track of how many pipes he had counted and they both began to laugh. Next thing they knew, the preacher had stopped talking and everybody in the church, including Miss Olson, the eighth grade history teacher, was looking real stern at him and Jeanne. Then the usher grabbed them each by a shoulder and led them out the door in back.

Thrown out of church! Now what would they do? They started the long walk home. Even though they walked as slowly as they could, they got home before church would have ended. It did not go unnoticed. It would do no good to make excuses. Sophia said little except that she would find out the next day what had happened and then they would all have a little "talk."

Frieda, on the other hand, insisted on hearing the story right away. When they told her how the usher had led them out for counting the pipes on the pipe organ, Frieda began to tell them in a very stern voice how God would be mad at them and would punish them. She also told Boy how bad he was for not behaving "as a gentleman."

When the lecture was over, Boy retreated to the lake. He took Scottie with him and sat and watched the whitecaps on the lake for a long time. When he finished looking at the white-capped waves playing on the lake, he thought, "Frieda's God isn't like the lake and wind at all. He's just against fun!"

Jeanne came running down to the lake. "Mother and Aunt Josephine are going for a ride in the country and want you to go along, but I get to stay home!" Boy headed up to the house. Sure enough Aunt Josephine was there, prim and proper as always, cheeks and lips bright red with lipstick and rouge and makeup.

Aunt Josephine wasn't really an aunt by blood, but had been a life-long friend of Sophia's. Even before Sophia married Lou, she and Jossey had owned a ladies ready-to-wear store together and had lived together in a little cottage on the shores of Lake Minnewaska.

Now Josephine worked with Inga selling women's girdles, corsets, brassieres, and other lingerie. Josephine had never married. She didn't seem to hate men; she just didn't seem interested in them one way or the other. She preferred the company of women.

Boy liked Aunt Josephine partly because mother always seemed happier and more alive and playful when she came to visit. Now Josephine had decided, or maybe Sophia had decided for her, that it was time for her to become more independent. Josephine was going to learn to drive a car and Sophia was going to teach her!

Boy asked if he could bring his gun along and maybe hunt some pheasants if they stopped somewhere. Sophia said, "Yes! That would be a great idea!"

Frieda was going along, just to get out of the house for a little while before she could go to Sunday evening church at the little Swedish Covenant Church. She liked the Sunday evening service because everybody got to pray as long as they wanted, and the preacher always preached a no nonsense sermon about the righteousness of God and how He didn't put up with even little sins. The preacher always made it crystal clear how everybody was responsible for everybody else.

"We are our brother's keeper," he would say, and Frieda would like to repeat it often, it seemed to Boy. It was a great way to be able to justify putting your nose in other people's business, he thought privately.

So they set off on the country back roads north toward Farwell. Sophia was driving, with Jossey close to her on the front seat of the little Lafayette. Boy sat next to the front passenger door. His gun was unloaded and cased, just as Phair would have wanted. He held it upright between his knees. Frieda sat alone in the back seat.

Somewhere in the hills north of Glenwood and just south of Farwell, Sophia stopped the car. She had tired of Jossey's repeated questions of "What's this for?" and "Why are you doing that?" and "Aren't you going too fast? I would never be able or want to drive this fast."

Sophia decided it was time to be more detailed in her instructions about the various gauges, levers and gears in the car. Maybe, she thought, "If Josephine just has more information and I go a little slower, she'll not be so frightened and catch on quicker."

When they had stopped, Boy asked if he could walk the field next to the car. Sophia said "Yes, that's a good idea." She thought to herself, "It will give me more room to show Jossey what I want her to learn."

Boy got out of the car, uncased and loaded his gun, watching where it pointed, just as he had done under Phair's watchful eye the day before. But, today he felt more confident than he had the day before. Maybe it was because he was alone. At any rate he started walking away from the car out into the alfalfa field. He walked about two hundred yards and then turned left, walking toward the fence line.

A hen pheasant erupted from her hiding place right before his feet. He jumped in surprise. But this time, unlike the day before, his instincts responded in smooth motion. The gun came easily to his shoulder. His eye lined up along the barrel, but really not seeing it, seeing only the bird, in liquid motion he followed the flight path and when the lead was just right he squeezed the trigger.

With a loud "bang!" the gun erupted, belching fire and propelling its pellets with true accuracy to catch the bird in flight. The pheasant stopped in full flight, spun, and crumpled. It fell to earth right beside a telephone pole on the edge of the field. He carefully watched the bird fall. He marked its location until he was sure he knew exactly where he would find it. Boy was elated. His first bird ever. Leaving the gun unloaded, as he had been taught, he practically ran to the spot where he had marked the fallen bird.

Things were not going as well back at the car.

When the bird took flight and the gun went off, Sophia and Josephine were still absorbed with the gauges on the dash. The report of the gun's blast brought their heads up as one, just in time to see the pheasant turn and tumble.

Sophia exclaimed in a loud, excited voice, "My God! He got one!"

At this point Frieda could not restrain herself any longer. She felt she had to witness to her faith and her Lord as the preacher had told her to do.

She reached across from her perch in the back seat, slapping Sophia on the side of the head and saying in her loudest, most righteous voice, "You will not curse the Lord!"

At that point, all hell broke loose!

When Boy came back to the car, proudly carrying his pheasant by the neck, he found a full-fledged battle in progress. Sophia was admonishing Frieda, loudly and in no uncertain terms, for slapping her. Putting all religiosity and issues of God's legalistic wrath aside, she informed Frieda, "You do not hit me. You do not hit your employer! I am your employer! Your boss! Do you understand? You obviously do not understand the excitement when a boy gets his first kill. Think about all he went through with Phair and his training."

Frieda, shouting at least as loud as Sophia and with great righteousness, because she knew God was on her side, kept repeating, "You should not take the name of the Lord in vain. He will not hold you guiltless. You should be ashamed of yourself!"

Jossey kept stammering, "Now . . . now . . . now . . . Please now . . . Don't. . . ."

After he had waited a few moments, uncertain what to do, Boy grasped the door handle and opened the door. All three pairs of eyes turned and stared at him. Sophia and Frieda's mouths remained open, but no words flowed forth.

Boy broke the silence. "I got one. I got a pheasant," he announced.

Silence.

Then Josephine, in a soft, quiet, scared voice said, "That's nice."

The ride back to town was silent. Frieda sat stone-faced in the back seat. Sophia's knuckles were white as she squeezed the steering wheel. Jossey sat fidgeting with her hands in her lap.

Boy sat looking straight ahead, cased gun between his knees, proudly displaying the dead pheasant laying in his lap, as they drove south into the deepening dusk of evening.

When they got to town, Boy asked to be let off at Inga and Phair's house so he could show Phair his bird. Without a word Sophia turned the Lafayette down Green Street and stopped. Boy got out. When Phair came to the door, his first words, even before he took the pheasant in hand to look at it, were, "Did you shoot it before sunset?"

"Yes," came Boy's reply.

"Good! Good! You're a good hunter. Now tell me all about it," Phair said. And Boy did.

That night Frieda knew she would enjoy church. She would have a lot to pray for. It would be a good church service. The preacher would be proud of her for how she stood up for her faith and witnessed and all of that.

Josephine would go home to her little apartment above Halvorson's Hardware Store and feel good about being single. She never did learn to drive an automobile.

Sophia hadn't even had a "heart attack" from all the excitement and confrontation. She felt good and vindicated in her role of mother, employer, and friend.

Boy went to bed, his heart full and warm. Phair's praise still rang in his ears. He slept deeper and better that night than he had in a long, long time.

CHICKENS IN THE PARK

The distance from Boy's home by the lake to the shoe store, or to school, or to his friend Herman's house, was always a little over a mile. This distance was covered, round trip, at least two or three times a day, and always on foot or bicycle.

There were two routes that could be followed: the first route you went along the boundary of the County Fairground, then up Main Street, past the International Harvester Garage and the Glenwood Creamery, turned left at the Greek Cafe, past Halvorson's Hardware, and crossed the street in front of the butcher shop to arrive at Sophia's shoe store. It was the more direct way, but boring.

The other route traced the shoreline of the lake past Calahan's dance pavilion, though the city park, past the bandstand, on up the street and past the butchery and cold storage meat locker, past the Pope County Tribune print shop, past Swenson's Hatchery, past Setter's Apothecary and Ice Cream Soda store. A few more feet and you were at Mrs. Mathre's Boston Cafe. A little farther and you went past Bruggness' meat market. Cross Main Street at the corner with the Minton Hotel on one side and Mr. Zappada's Greek restaurant and market on the other and you'll arrive at the shoe store. This was the route Boy took daily. He could dawdle and no one noticed. It was longer, but it wasn't boring. As he walked this path with his white collie one early May morning in t 1940, he arrived at the drop-off point to pick up the papers for his paper route. It was 5 a.m. and both Boy and dog were sleepy as they waited for the Star Journal truck from Minneapolis to rumble around the corner and squeak its worn brakes as it rolled to an uncertain stop behind Mr. Swenson's Lake Country Feed and Chicken hatchery.

This morning the dog's ears perked up as the hatchery door opened and Mr. Swenson emerged with the trays of broken eggs and dead chicks. He carried them out to the trash behind the store. Boy and dog had witnessed this cleansing operation often before. But this day, their attention was drawn to the muffled "peep, peep" of about-to-be abandoned chicks.

"How come you're throwin' 'em away when they ain't dead yet?" Boy asked.

"They's the runts. They're too small. Nobody would buy them. There's no sense feedin' 'em if nobody's going to buy 'em," Mr. Swenson replied. Dog sniffed at them and he didn't think they were too small. Why, he'd eat them right now, given a chance.

"Could I have them?" asked Boy. "Maybe I could feed them and make them grow," he thought to himself.

"Sure. I'll even throw in some corn and oats if you want, but it won't do no good. They'll die in a day or so anyway. They's the runts," Mr. Swenson said.

Boy made arrangements with Mr. Swenson to bring the Red Coaster wagon back to get the chicks and corn and oats once the papers were delivered. The transaction was finished just as the brakes squeaked, bringing the Star Journal truck to a reluctant stop.

The paper route that day was filled with fantasies as Boy's mind pictured large, prize-winning chickens being awarded blue ribbons at the Pope County Fair. What if he fed them and raised them differently? Most chickens received only table scraps or wet and ruined corn, if they got anything other than free range bugs and grass.

Boy had seen an article in the newspaper about the Cargill Company trying to make scientific food for chickens. The article had said that some of Cargill's experimental chickens had grown to four or five pounds. Uncle Will had said one time, when he was bragging about the giant squash and onions that he had grown and now stored with the dill and garlic in the attic of his barn, that he could grow giant chickens if he fed them with powdered buttermilk mixed with ground oats and cracked corn. Boy remembered this, even though his attention that day in Uncle Will's barn attic was mostly captured by watering eyes and thoughts of how he could get away from Will's garlic-laced tobacco breath and the dill and onion odors of the barn attic.

Now that Mr. Swenson had given him the chance, thought Boy, what would happen if he fed these chicks with powdered buttermilk, cracked corn, and ground up oats? Maybe they'd not be runts, but giants. Maybe, just maybe, he could get Mr. Grove to give him the oats left at the bottom of the bin after he had fed his Belgians. Maybe he could get the corn from Mr. Swenson and just maybe he could get the powdered buttermilk from Mr. Kramer at the creamery.

"Sure, kid," said Mr. Kramer, once he'd heard about Boy's project. "You can have all the powdered buttermilk you want." Boy heard them laughing as he left. Clearly, he was the subject of their humor.

Swenson and Grove also agreed to be providers for his project.

When he got home with the peeping chicks and had them safely beneath a warming light in Frieda's sacred basement laundry room, he knew exactly what he was going to do. He would talk to Uncle Julius and convince him that they could make a chicken pen with a floor made of chicken wire that would be one or two inches above the ground. If they made it that way he was pretty sure his prized chickens wouldn't get the croup and other infections that killed so many free-range chicks.

He had already decided during his paper route musings that he would order the medicine to put in the water so the chicks wouldn't die of fever. Now all he had to do was convince his mom that the two dollars for the fancy water trough and the price of the medicine was worth it. He was pretty sure he could do that if only he could keep Frieda from butting in.

Frieda hadn't yet discovered that her sacred laundry room had been violated. Quickly Boy rethought his plan and moved the light bulb and the chicks to the shed alongside the garage. The weasel might get them, but it was worth the risk. Boy was sure the weasel was less vicious than Frieda.

"What's that horrible smell in my laundry?" Frieda demanded just before Sophia walked in the door on her return from the shoe store.

"I don't know," Boy answered.

"Have you brought something down there?" Frieda persisted.

"Hi, Mom!" Boy said, ignoring Frieda.

"Here, let me carry your basket," He said as he grabbed the homemade willow strip basket from Sophia's hand, just as she was about to set it on the kitchen counter. Sophia paused and then a quizzical look crossed her face.

"Hurry on now and wash up for supper. You can tell me what you've been up to and what's on your mind later," Sophia said.

Boy left. He was glad to get out of there before Frieda got started.

Later that night when she sat on the edge of his bunk bed, he told her all about the chicks and the buttermilk and the feed. He told her that he had the chicks under a light bulb in the garage shed and that he had already talked to Mr. Grove, Mr. Swenson, and Mr. Kramer about providing feed and powdered buttermilk.

"Now I understand what your uncle Julius was talking about when he called and said you had talked to him about building a chicken pen and wondered if it was all right with me," Sophia shared.

Sophia looked at Boy and said, "I think it's a good idea."

Privately she thought, "It'll keep him out of trouble." She had often worried about his stubbornness and determination and how to direct it. Maybe this was an answer to her many prayers.

The next morning when the paper route was done, Sophia met Boy at Uncle Julius' and they figured out how to make the pen for the great chicken experiment.

Under the intense scrutiny of Boy and his feeding rituals, the chicks grew and grew. Frieda kept her distance and said nothing. However, she did almost crack when one of the chicks got its wing caught in the net fencing and broke it. The wing got infected and the ever-present flies laid eggs on the torn and broken wing. The little white maggots began to eat the decaying flesh. Frieda watched as Boy cut the broken wing off and cauterized the wound. Ione, nurse and cousin, newly arrived in town for a visit, came upon the chicken surgery just in time. She waylaid Frieda before she could launch into her lecture on the evil that Boy was doing by helping the chick live when God intended it to die.

Ione took her on. She admonished, "God intends this bird to live! The maggots are keeping the wound clean by eating the dead flesh."

"In fact," she continued, "they used to use maggots to cleanse the wounds of soldiers in the great world war. They saved many men from death this way. So, leave Boy alone! He is doing the right thing! This time," she had to add.

Frieda, always ready with her comments, this time shut her mouth. She knew Ione: the nurse, advocate, and rebel. She did not want to go against her. Instead, Frieda said, "Oh. All right." She glowered at Boy and walked back in to the house.

The experiment proved a success. The chickens grew to an unheard-of size. In late September, when Boy gathered up the one with a wing missing and carried it to Bruggness' Meat Market on Main Street, it weighed six and a half pounds.

"My God!" exclaimed Bob Bruggness. "I have never seen such a chicken. Oh My God!"

"Six and a half pounds," was all he kept saying, over and over.

Boy said, "Most of them are bigger, but this one had a problem with her wing. One weighs eight pounds and most of them weigh seven or seven and a half. I don't know how good my scale is."

"Oh my God! What did you feed them?" Bruggness asked.

So, Boy told him about the pen and the food and the medicine he had given them.

"They're pretty good, huh?" Boy concluded.

"Oh my God!" was all Rob Bruggness could say.

Bruggness bought all twenty-six chickens, on the spot, sight unseen. He paid well and still he thought he had stolen them. He paid fifteen cents a pound. No one in the business that he knew of ever paid more than six cents a pound and that was for the finest barnyard chickens, raised on table scraps. A big barnyard chicken weighed two and a half pounds.

In his mind's eye, Rob Bruggness could see the gleam in his wealthy customers' eyes. Mr. Brown, for example, would easily pay twenty or twenty-two cents a pound for the bragging rights of having the biggest chicken on the table.

"Can you get them up here to my store by tomorrow?" Mr. Bruggness asked.

"Sure," murmured Boy in a scared, subdued voice. He didn't rightly know how, but he was pretty sure he could figure it out.

When he left Mr.Bruggness, he went directly to Mr. Swenson.

"Can I borrow some wooden crates to put my chickens in so as I can get them up to Bruggness' market?" Boy timidly asked.

"Sure," Mr. Swenson replied, "just get them back to me by Thursday in good shape. If you break any, it's going to cost you."

"I won't break 'em! And thanks. Thanks a lot!" Boy exclaimed.

Already he was scheming. Four crates. Six chickens to a crate. Two he would squeeze in—somehow. When he went the mile plus from home to Swenson's hatchery to get the crates, it took him two trips with his red Radio Coaster wagon.

"I bet I can get all four of these crates on the wagon," he thought, planning for the next day when he would take the chickens to Bruggness' Market. "One trip and I'm done," Boy said aloud to himself.

However, the easy way destroyed his judgment. When the crates, full of nervous, wiggling chickens, were all stacked on the wagon and secured with a single strand of rope, it looked like a circus-juggling act gone awry. Undaunted, Boy started down the walk. At the end of the walk, he turned left and headed toward the town center. He chose the park route thinking there would be less traffic and it would be a bit smoother, even if it was longer.

By now the chickens were clucking and crowing, and every now and then a head would pop out from between the slats of a crate. When he got to the park, he became aware that he would have to maneuver the wagon over the curb and across the grass. The grass idea didn't bother him, but he wasn't sure how he could negotiate the curb without the wagon tipping over. Just then, as he was wondering about this, Mrs. Benson came along. She had her arms filled with grocery bags and was headed for her apartment in the flats—the low income housing of adjoining, common wall apartments. Mrs. Benson often helped Frieda with the heavier spring and fall cleaning as a way of adding to her meager earnings.

Boy liked her. She was short, roly-poly, full of fun, and had a twinkle in her eye. Life had never gotten her down, although God knows, it should have. Challenges were her specialty. Immediately she saw the problem Boy faced. She put her grocery bags down on Dr. Elder's sidewalk and came across the street to join Boy and the chickens by the park.

"My Goodness! How did you get these crates loaded so high?

Well never mind, let's get you on your way," she exclaimed. "Here—you pull and lift real slow and I'll balance it as you go up and over the curb," she instructed.

Boy pulled and lifted as slowly and carefully as he could while Mrs. Benson, red in the face from exertion, tried to keep the crates of squawking chickens in a vertical line. The wagon and crates creaked, and then miraculously, all four wheels were up on the park grass.

"Well! Not so bad! You take care now," Mrs. Benson said, as she wheeled around and in her rolling gait headed back to get her groceries. Boy waved and watched her for a while and then picked up the tongue of the wagon and began to pull it across the park.

He was daydreaming about all the money he would make as he bumped his way along. That is probably why he didn't see the elevated root of the big elm tree on one side of the wagon and the gopher hole on the other. At any rate, the left wheel of the wagon hit the root at exactly the same moment as the right wheel hit the hole. All of this happened in the couple of milliseconds before the crates and chickens hit the ground in an explosion of lid-popping, feather-scattering confusion.

Freedom! Blessed freedom, clucked the chickens as they headed in all directions. Boy screamed and cried and cursed until all the neighbors were at their doors to see what the ruckus was all about. Chickens and chicken feathers were everywhere. Two of the chickens had already found a roost in the lower branches of a Ladies' Auxiliary Chinese elm tree.

Mr. Nordby, an educator/administrator who lived across the street from the park, was the first on the scene. He tried to help with the great chicken roundup. He took aim on a big yellow Buff Orpington hen. Just as he reached for her she hopped and clucked and flapped her wings. Mr. Nordby, teacher dignity departed, was flat on his belly with his face in the dust. But, like a ball, he bounced back up and was back in the chase after a freedom-loving White Rock rooster. At full speed he swooped in and grabbed the galloping rooster by its neck.

By now the chicken chase had been joined by the neighborly judge, Dr. Elder, and Constable Hanson. Toots Calahan was headed across the park from the lakeside pavilion, ready to join the fray. Mrs. Benson was back from her flat, standing on the sidelines, laughing so hard she doubled over and looked for all the world like a ball with a red face. Soon several others joined her, and they formed a cheering section. Mr. Gross, editor of the County Gazette, chose not to join the chase, but stood, pen in hand, thinking what he could compose for the next issue of the paper.

Someone had called Sophia, who showed up with Inga just as the last chicken was being put back in the crate and the lids were being secured. Mr. Nordby volunteered to get his car. He could get two crates in the trunk. Sophia and Inga took one and Constable Hanson took the other one. Boy was amazed and bewildered when he climbed into the back seat of Sophia's car for the ride to Bruggness' Meat Market. He didn't say a word. He didn't dare. Nobody had scolded him yet, and he wasn't going to blow it if he could help it.

Mr. Bruggness choked as he tried not to laugh. He weighed the chickens and paid Boy for them. Mr. Nordby and Constable Hanson took the crates back to Mr. Swenson's feed store. Boy quietly climbed into the back seat of Sophia's Lafayette, clutching in his hand the money he had just received.

Inga turned around and looked over the headrest on the back seat as Sophia started the car and headed for home, and quietly said, "The good Lord helps them that helps themselves and gets others to help them too."

Later that evening Mrs. Benson knocked on the door. She said with her big smile when Frieda answered the door, "I've brought home the wagon for his self." Sophia, looking over Frieda's shoulder, smiled and winked. Frieda only shook her head. Boy was nowhere to be seen.

GRAPES OF WRATH

When Steinbeck wrote his epic novel, *The Grapes of Wrath*, Boy was not much for reading about dust bowls or recollections of sordid family structures. But, there was an encounter with some grapes of wrath of another kind for Boy, his friend Tucker Benson, Frieda, and some of the other adults of Boy's inner circle.

The summer of 1941 had seen more normal rainfall than most of the summers during the '30s. The lake was beginning to return to a normal level after the severe and prolonged drought of the '30s. The bulrushes that had grown on the lake bottom during the Dust Bowl years were now in four or five feet of water. The members of the Chamber of Commerce, trying to beautify the lake, had fashioned a barge with a sickle bar mounted below the water line so the bulrushes could be cut. The bulrushes would then fill with water and drown. The barge, pulled by an outboard motor boat, looked clumsy. It was laborious, but it worked. The townspeople rejoiced to see the lake come alive again.

The plants also rejoiced at the abundant rain that coaxed them out of their drought-induced dormancy and into once again producing plentiful, succulent fruit. Right at the top of the list of fruit appreciated was the grape. The little, scrawny planting that had looked all but dead, had greened and grown thick entwining vines now had produced large clumps of round-clustered fruit. In late summer, these clusters had turned from green to deep purple.

Frieda was ecstatic. She loved to can and make preserves and stewed tomatoes. But more than anything, she loved the feel of crushing and squeezing juice and skimming skins. As she worked, she told stories of Jesus making water into wine, which she said really wasn't wine, but was grape juice because she was sure Jesus wouldn't drink something with alcohol in it. She told and retold the story of the vineyard and how the man in the Bible had begged his master not to destroy the little grape vines until he had had a chance to put manure on them and make them grow.

She really got into the Bible stories as though she was there herself, she and Jesus making grape juice. Frieda was good though, and her grape juice and grape jelly were the best ever.

It had been several years since there had been grape juice in the fruit cellar at Sophia's house, with the drought and all. But this year, Frieda got really carried away. There was lots of jelly to be sure, but there was even more grape juice. Bottles and bottles of it took up three shelves, fifteen feet long and three bottles deep. Frieda had used up all of Sophia's grapes and then had gone to the neighbors and asked for whatever grapes they weren't going to use. Finally, she had gone to the grocery store and gotten the grapes they weren't able to sell, once they were past their prime.

It had taken over a week near the end of August to bottle and cap all the juice. Now, at the end of September, the shelves were full and the canning was done. The door to the fruit cellar was closed and nobody was to go in there!

The juice and jelly were stored in the cool and dark basement. It was left there to cure and age, waiting for winter days and nights when it would be enjoyed, bringing back memories of warm and gentle summer days.

Around the end of September, Indian summer had descended in earnest. There had been a cold snap and the frost had killed the corn so that it was drying well and waiting to be picked. Then the temperatures rose to eighty degrees with blue skies and gentle breezes, colored leaves and no bugs.

Boy and his friend decided that it was just the right Saturday to go on an adventure and hike into the hills. Boy wanted to show his friend some of the neat places he had found on his solitary disappearances into the hills. Most of the special "secret places" were two or three miles into the farthest hills.

They set off early. They had a lunch Boy had made for them because Frieda had said that she wouldn't be a part of any foolishness, such as wasting of time walking in the hills. The lunch Boy prepared was long on peanut butter sandwiches and cookies and short on fruit, vegetables, and something to drink.

Had Tucker's mother not gone off so early on her day job of cleaning the homes of the rich, she probably would have noticed their nutritional oversights. Or, if it hadn't been Saturday, the long day at the shoe shop, Sophia in her mild perfectionism no doubt would have observed the lunch's shortcomings. As it was, peanut butter and cookies was the lunch *du jour* as they started for the hills at seven.

When they returned at 4 that afternoon, they had had a good time but were dirty and tired and thirsty—very, very thirsty!

"Got anything good to drink—like root beer or lemonade?" Tucker asked. Frieda had gone to town shopping so the house was empty except for the canary that sang from its cage in the living room.

"I don't know," Boy replied. "I don't think so." But, then he remembered all of the shelves of grape juice in the fruit cellar. Certainly it wouldn't hurt to go down and get one of the bottles. Frieda wouldn't ever have to know.

"There's some grape juice in the cellar," Boy offered.

"Well, let's go!" Tucker exclaimed, already on his feet heading for the basement door.

When they got to the fruit cellar, they quietly closed the door behind themselves just in case Frieda came home. It would be best not to turn the light on either, again just in case. Boy grabbed the bottle at the far end of the bottom shelf, the one behind the other two. It wouldn't be noticed. He had remembered to bring a bottle opener from the kitchen just as they began to make their descent to the cellar.

Tucker took the bottle and opener from Boy. After all, he was older by two years and knew how to do these things. When Tucker applied the opener to the bottle cap, it came off surprisingly easy, with a loud "pop!" Then the juice began to squirt and foam up out of the neck of the bottle. The force had been sufficient to blow the cap all the way to the cellar's ceiling.

"Sssssssshhh! We'll get caught!" Boy warned.

Quickly they opened the door and peered out. Not a sound. Just to be sure, Tucker crept up the steps and looked around the door into the kitchen. No one was there. He retreated to the fruit cellar where he found Boy holding the bottle, looking puzzled. There was a stripe of purple juice at the corner of his mouth, which he wiped away with the back of his arm as Tucker opened the cellar door.

"This stuff tastes real good, but kind of funny," Boy said.

"Here, let me try it!" Tucker replied.

The bottle went back and forth between them. At first they tried to analyze why it tasted different from other grape juice Frieda had made and they had drunk. By the second bottle, half of which ended up on the ceiling when the top popped, Boy was venturing that maybe Frieda's stories were right and Jesus had helped her and that's why the grapes tasted different.

Tucker snorted and softly laughed at the idea. When he grabbed the fourth bottle, his elbow knocked another bottle down and it broke all over the floor. Boy looked at his friend and put his finger to his mouth and said, "Ssssshh! Frieda will hear us!"

They drank another bottle of grape juice. About half way through it, Tucker announced, "I don't feel good. I think I'm going to throw up!" Boy looked at him. His eyes didn't focus and his head hurt. Tucker began to retch.

"Let's go upstairs," Boy said.

When Frieda came home, she found the boys in the bathroom. Tucker had his head in the toilet throwing up. Boy was sitting on the edge of the bathtub watching, but not really seeing.

"Oh my!" Frieda exclaimed. "What's wrong?"

"We don't feel so good," Boy replied and began to cry.

"Did you eat something you shouldn't have on your hike?" she asked.

"Just peanut butter sandwiches and cookies."

"What did you have to drink with your sandwiches?" Frieda asked. She remembered the time they got ptomaine poisoning from her homemade root beer.

"Jus' water from the brook," Tucker replied, lifting his head from the toilet bowl. Then he began to retch again.

"Well, I'm going to call Sophia and then the doctor," Frieda said.

She didn't have to call Sophia. Sophia walked in the door before Frieda could get to the phone. There was a quick conference between Sophia and Frieda. They made the decision to call the doctor. Sophia didn't want to wait for Dr. MacIver to come the eight miles from Lowry, so she called Dr. Elder, who lived in town. Sophia didn't particularly like Dr. Elder because rumor was that he drank pretty freely. But THIS was an emergency! These boys might be dying of food poisoning or something.

Dr. Elder was at the house in ten minutes. He quickly examined both boys, right there on the bathroom floor. He shined his little doctor's light into their eyes and ears; he palpated their stomachs, and in the process he smelled their breath.

A smile crept over his face and then, when he had regained his composure, he turned to Sophia and said, "These boys are drunk! Dead drunk!"

Just as he made his diagnosis there was a popping sound, like a firecracker, in the basement just below them, right where the fruit cellar was. Frieda, Sophia and Dr. Elder headed for the basement.

"Oh my God!" Sophia cried when she saw the mess.

Dr. Elder couldn't contain himself any longer and began to laugh out loud. "I'll be damned! Oh my God!" he choked between outbursts of rolling-belly laughter. Frieda was too stunned to even hear her Lord's name being taken in vain.

Dr. Elder leaned on Frieda's shoulder trying to stop his laughing. He turned her so she faced him. "Frieda! You made wine! And they really enjoyed it!" the knowing doctor enthused. Then he softly added, "But will they ever have headaches."

"No! No! I couldn't have!" Frieda cried. "I don't know what happened. I only know I didn't do this! Oh God, Oh

God, tell me I didn't do this!" Then she reflected, "I used a different bottle capper. Mr. Stein gave it to me . . . said his mother used it all the time."

"You made wine!" Dr. Elder repeated. "It probably fermented because the caps weren't tight." As they talked, another bottle exploded.

Sophia just looked dismayed. Yet, there was a smile on her face.

"I couldn't have," Frieda muttered. "I just couldn't have. God will never forgive me! I've brought these boys to ruin. I've made them into drunks!" She began to cry.

Sophia tried to comfort her, but Frieda wouldn't be consoled. Instead, she got a broom and a bucket and a mop and stoically began to clean up.

Dr. Elder asked if he could take some of the bottles of "grape juice" home with him. Sophia invited him to take all he wanted. And he did. Then she went to the phone and called Gilbert, from next door, who liked to drink as well, and asked him to come and get the rest of the bottles. When Sophia got back upstairs, she found the boys still in the bathroom. Boy was asleep in the tub and Tucker was crying that he wanted to go home.

Sophia threw a blanket over Boy, helped Tucker to his feet, and led him to the car. She took him home, not relishing what she would have to tell Mrs. Benson, although she knew that she would probably find it amusing. And she did, as they laughed together. By the time Sophia got home, Frieda had closed herself in her room and didn't answer when Sophia knocked on the door. Sophia opened it just a crack and peered in. There was Frieda on her knees, by the bed, praying.

Sophia overhead her saying, "Please forgive me! I know I led your children astray, but please, please don't put a stone about my neck."

Sophia quietly closed the door, went to find Boy, and put him to bed.

THE HARVEST

In 1942 and 1943, most able-bodied men of rural west-central Minnesota, as well as other places in the United States, were off to the humid jungles of the Pacific or the gritty air of North African deserts to fight in the second great war of the century.

Back home, the crops still needed planting, cultivating, and harvesting. So, the old men and young boys were recruited to the farms to get it done. Electricity had not yet come to Grey Eagle, the childhood farm home of Boy's father, nor had indoor plumbing, combines, nor rubber-tired tractors. Harvest time consisted of a gathered community following a box-like tin contraption mounted on steel wheels and pulled by a smoking, wheezing, coal-fueled steam engine. The machine they followed was called a threshing machine, and they were called the threshing crew. This core community of leftover men and boys moved from farm to farm, losing and adding new faces at each stop. They had to get the wheat, oats, barley and flax off the fields so that these commodities could be converted into food and drink, oil and clothes.

This motley collection of men and boys, women and girls, was a community that did a task they held in common while they shared a life in common. This task and life in common knit and wove the community together for good or ill. The Mossman farm at Grey Eagle was home to this community in the late summer of '42 and '43. It was the same as it had been all the years since 1880 when it had been settled by Beal and Ann Eliza Mossman. Boy had been to the farm of his father and his Scots ancestors many times in his early years, but when his father died, Lou's portion of the farm was left to Sophia, and she needed to protect her widow's share.

Boy and Jeanne had played at the farm and knew Lou's sister-in-law and brother, Aunt Gertie and Uncle Fred, well. Boy had been there at harvest time before and had gone to the fields with Aunt Gertie morning and afternoon with sandwiches and drink for the sweating, tired men. But in 1942, as an almost eleven-year-old, he was asked to take a team and a wagon, like the men, so that he could collect the bundles of wheat, oats and flax. He was to haul them from the field to the feeder belt of the steam-driven threshing machine. Each farm had to provide a certain amount of manpower because of the war, and Boy was now a part of it. Fortunately, Boy was big for his age.

He didn't see what he was being asked to do as a duty. He was as elated as a peacock. A rite of passage had been accomplished, or so he thought. He no longer would ride with Aunt Gertie in the old, rusted Ford pick-up to bring morning and afternoon food and drink to the men in the fields. He would drive a team! Maude and Bert, the big bay Belgians, would do as he told them! He hoped. He would sit at table, breakfast, noon, and supper with the men. And he would drink his coffee, laced with milk, from a saucer, just like the men.

The night before the harvest began, Boy didn't sleep. The day before, his mother had driven him the twenty-eight miles from home by Lake Minnewaska to the farm. That evening he had watched as the Community gathered. It had progressed like a parade of machine and engine, teams and wagons, trucks and cars—down the gravel road. Like an undulating prehistoric monster, it had slowly turned its laboring body, entering the farm and finding the gate to the field where it would await the feast of grains beginning on the morrow.

Suddenly, Boy had become scared and shy. He went to the barn where Uncle Fred had shown him the stalls where he kept Maude and Bert and where the harness hung upon the wall. He looked at the horses. Then he stared. God, they were BIG! He didn't have any idea how he would get the harnesses on them. They made his Morgan horse look tiny. Boy looked about but Uncle Fred was nowhere to be seen. He had retired to the hayloft with his bottle, out of Gertie's sight.

Alvin's voice rang out. "Pretty big, huh, kid? Here, let me show you how that harness goes. You know, this is a dandy team. They won't give you any trouble, but I'll help you hitch them in the morning, if you want."

Boy's eyes were wide. Alvin's words were like chocolate on ice cream. Oh, yes. He wanted Alvin's help. He wanted it badly. Saviors come in all descriptions. The odor and the shine of manure on Alvin's boots did not dull the gifts of grace and care.

The next day broke clear and warm; it was seventy degrees at six a.m. When Boy got to the barn, Alvin was already there, true to his word. He had his team already hitched, and they stood patiently munching hay. Alvin turned his attention to helping Boy get his team out of their stalls and cross-tethered in the aisle. He reached up and got the harnesses down and put them on the horses' backs.

Then he stepped back. He didn't want to do the work for Boy; he just wanted to help him learn. This was good, for in the days that followed when Alvin gave him a compliment, Boy felt that it was real because he had let Boy struggle on his own until he succeeded.

Maude and Bert stood patiently and waited. Boy thought they smiled at his clumsy attempts to get them yoked and to fasten the linchpin to the wagon. Nineteen forty-two was a good year. A good harvest. A good community of men and women. Humor ran high. People helped each other. Under Alvin's watchful eye, Boy worked and learned. Boy probably loaded only one wagon for every three of Alvin's, and Boy's were perhaps only half full, but never once did Alvin put Boy down. Instead, Alvin would come up to him and say things like, "Maybe if you would do it more like this, it would go a little better."

Alvin taught Boy many little things about the team, the wagon, and the load. He taught him how to pitch the bundles and how to put them on the belt so that they would smoothly enter the hungry mouth of the great machine and not choke its throat. Alvin taught Boy how to balance a load and how to position his team and wagon at the thresher. Most importantly, Alvin helped Boy learn how to get on with the other men. Sometimes when the other men would begin to get on Boy with their jokes and ridicule, Alvin would intervene and change the subject. Alvin was respected by the other men even though he was different from them. He had time for kids—even as a bachelor farmer.

When Boy was the last one in from the fields, even as the sun sank low and touched the fence line at the horizon of the western farm beyond, Alvin was there to help him pitch his bundles on the endless track that provided the grains to the gray machine. In the dusk they would unhitch their teams together and give them food and drink, then go feed themselves and find a place to sleep the night away.

That year things went well. Lou's sister-in-law Aunt Kate was Uncle Frank's widow and part owner. Even Uncle Fred was happy. The grain was clean and brought a good price, and the great gray machine had not broken down, so overhead was low. The week ended in celebration and the community of threshers moved on to the next farm to begin once again to function with a life and task in common. Each time the thresher and its crew moved, there were some new and different players.

The harvest of '43 was a different story. On the surface, things appeared about the same as the previous year. The community gathered in the same way with the same parade of men, machines, and horses. They came down the same gravel roads and set up in the same fields. The same whistle blasted its same mournful cry when the large steam engine was belted and yoked to the threshing machine, signaling that all was ready for the morning and the beginning of the harvest. There the similarities ended.

When Boy looked for his friend, Alvin, one of the women told him that Alvin had died after being struck by lightening while trying to get his horses in from the pasture before the June storm could unleashed its full fury. Boy stood alone, numb and blinded by tears. He felt scared and empty and lonely. Inwardly he knew that apart from whatever else he felt, he would have to find another teacher, another man to help him learn more about this business of the harvest.

He went to the barn where Maude and Bert were stabled. There he found Joe, whom he recognized from the year before. Boy had never liked Joe, but he knew that Joe was a good farmer and a professional thresher who went with the machine from farm to farm.

"Will you help me get the harness down so I can oil it?" Boy softly asked.

Joe glared at him for a few moments, then he exploded. "What the hell, kid, can't you pull your own? God-damned little shits like you oughtn't be here anyway. All you do is get in the way and slow things down. Why don't you just stay home and play with the girls?" Then he walked out, snapping a lead strap at Maude who snorted and flinched.

Boy was humiliated and even more scared than ever. He went to the house where he was staying and headed up to the room over the kitchen. He flopped down on his bunk. He would not go down for supper, and eventually his tears put him to sleep.

The next day the harvest at the Mossman farm was to begin. Boy overslept a bit in the gray and misty dawn. It had rained off and on throughout the night. Quickly Boy got up, slapped some water from the basin in the commode on his face, and hurried off toward the barn. He had not undressed the night before.

Boy slipped in the wet grass and mud a few times on his way to the barn. Once he fell. He burst through the barn doors and into the center aisle. Some men were gathered there, already drinking beer. They laughed when they saw Boy's muddy clothes and realized he was trying to get his horses out of their stall so he could harness them.

"What you goin' to do? Wash the grain? Are you so stupid you don't know you can't thresh on a day like this? You must be the most dumbest piece of shit in the world, kid!" Joe, the ring leader and spokesman for the group, berated Boy. The men laughed.

Again, Boy was humiliated. He wanted to hide. He left the barn and walked up the path past the house, where some of the men were eating, and past the chicken house, the ice house and the outhouse, and up into the old apple orchard. There he sat and thought. Talking to himself and throwing wormy apples at a rusty can by the fence, he thought, "I must have done something wrong. But I don't know what. I don't know why they're mad at me."

Quite awhile later, Boy went back to the barn. The men had left. He opened the stall doors and lead Maude and Bert to the aisle so he could brush them. He tried to talk to them. They listened, heads cocked to one side and nuzzling his armpit with their soft noses, but they weren't much help.

That day the beer flowed freely. A couple of fights broke out among the men over women and who said what about somebody's girlfriend. All the fights seemed to be over women, Boy guessed. Nobody talked to Boy. He went to look for Uncle Fred to ask some questions about the job he had to do, but Fred had left for Grey Eagle to buy some liquor. Later in the day, when Boy finally did find Fred, he was snoring in the hayloft and smelled of booze and body odor.

Finally, at the end of the day, just as it touched the horizon before it set, the sun emerged beneath the clouds like a big orange ball. It was a harbinger that there would be a clear day of work tomorrow.

In the morning, Boy was up early and already had Maude and Bert out of their stalls in the center alley of the barn when some of the other men began to arrive. One of the men grabbed his horses by the halter and pulled them into the alley beside Maude and Bert, yelling at Boy "to get the hell out of the way!" Others joined in saying, "Hey, kid, there's men here to get work done!"

Another man grabbed a pitchfork and swatted Boy across the back and poked at Boy's horses. He was screaming, "You're too fuckin' dumb to get them horses harnessed. It'll take you all day, you little son of a bitch, so get out of the way!"

By the time the men left with their teams harnessed, Maude and Bert were jittery and Boy was crying. He was devastated, and he was mad as hell. Boy got the harness on and his team hitched to the wagon in record time—for him.

But in the field things did not go well. Boy worked hard without a break all morning, and all he had to show for his effort was two partial loads. The grain bundles were heavy and still soggy from the rain the day before. But the biggest problem was that Boy, left on his own without experienced coaching, wasn't getting his wagon in the right position. Besides, Boy's mind would drift away and he would fantasize about what he would like to do to the men who had berated him. He had trouble concentrating. And nobody talked to him.

When Boy had finally gotten his second load to the feeder belt, the great gray machine had broken down. The cause of the breakdown was simple to determine. The grain was dirty. Somebody had put the wrong screens in for the flax that was being harvested. Some of the men blamed Fred for trying to cheat them. They believed he was trying to get bushels of grain to weigh more in his fields where the books were kept so he would be paid before the other's were docked for dirty grain at the Grey Eagle Elevator. There was shouting among the men and a shoving match broke out.

The crew stopped for lunch. The men at table were surly and sullenly silent. Boy wondered where the humor, camaraderie and good spirit of the previous year had gone. On the third load, in early afternoon, Boy felt the load shift. As the wagon tipped, and even as he was jumping clear so not to be pinned, Boy realized he had forgotten what Alvin had taught him the year before. Alvin had told him, then showed him, how to balance a load so this wouldn't happen.

But he had forgotten. He had been too preoccupied with worrying about why the men didn't like him and about his anger at them for their meanness and ridicule.

Maude and Bert stumbled. They regained their balance by pulling against each other to help one another keep from falling. Once they were solidly on their feet, they stood tangled in the traces. They snorted, fear visible in their eyes, but stood patiently waiting for Boy. The tongue of the wagon was broken and the axle was broken beyond repair.

Boy pulled the linchpin that fastened the horses to the wagon and then led Maude and Bert to safety a distance away. As he did so, he reached into his pocket for the carrots he had put there. He gave them each one, scratched behind their ears, and softly said, "It'll be OK." But it wasn't!

He turned to find himself face to face with Mike, one of the other meaner, more-outspoken men. Boy could feel and smell his hot and foul breath.

"What the fuck's the matter with you—you stupid little bastard!" he bellowed.

"Don't ya know a fuckin' thing about how to load a wagon? Get the hell outa here and take those glue factory plugs with you!"

"Damn kid! Too dumb to let live," he muttered as he walked away.

Boy left the field. He put Maude and Bert in their stalls and gave them each an extra portion of oats. He whispered, "It's not your fault." He left the barn and tried to find Fred, but Fred was drunk and still loudly arguing with his accusers about the grain. Obviously, nobody had told him about the accident, or he hadn't listened if they had.

Boy found Aunt Emmy. She put her arm around him and listened to him as he expressed his hurt and fear and anger. She wiped his tears, and he felt he'd been rescued. The next day half the men and teams were gone. The threshing machine needed to move to the next farm in order to stay on schedule. At the Mossman farm much of the grain still stood in shocks about the field. Ripened grain is not very forgiving and doesn't wait for anyone, and so it spoiled.

Sophia helped Boy pack and they rode the twenty-eight miles home in silence. There was no harvest celebration. Boy was still a boy and wondered if he even wanted to be a man.

THE FEVER

As summer drew to a close, the dog days of August began to shorten and give way to cooler evenings and crisper mornings. These subtle signals were harbingers that filled the air with hints of seasons yet to come. Autumn was being heralded by the flocking of blackbirds, the gathering of Monarch butterflies, and the dulling of the Robin's breast.

Fall and the hunting season would soon begin. This alone raised Boy's spirits, particularly this year because he could look forward with unbridled anticipation to the coming hunt. The previous year had filled him with trepidation as the hunting season approached. His health had threatened yet another precious thing that gave his young life definition.

In late April '44 he had come down with a sore throat and a fever. At first Frieda had discounted it as just a cold or spring doldrums brought on by a long winter and a boring school year that seemed never to end. In fact, there was suspicion in Frieda's tone of voice as she talked to Sophia that this might be Boy's ploy to get out of school for a few days in order to make summer vacation come sooner.

However, the next day, when Boy's fever hit 104.5 degrees and he was complaining that he was having trouble breathing and that his ankles, knees, feet, and wrists really hurt, Sophia decided to call Dr. MacIver. The doctor came from his home and office in Lowry and looked at Boy's throat, knees, and hands. He drew some blood to take to Dr. Elder's office lab in town and then rolled up his sleeves. With Frieda's help, he undressed Boy and lifted him into a tub of tepid water to try to bring the fever down.

The diagnosis came back. Rheumatic fever! Boy's knees, ankles, feet, and wrists swelled until the skin cracked and bled. Total bed rest was the prescription. Boy saw a worried Dr. MacIver talking to Sophia, so he listened as hard as he could.

"He may have heart damage. Sometimes that can be so bad that he might live awhile, but most kids who have heart damage don't live long. The valves give out and the child dies," the doctor explained. "I'm sorry to have to tell you this, Sophia. You've had so many hard things in your life, but I don't want you to be surprised by another tragedy," he said sympathetically.

Boy heard Sophia crying. He heard Frieda chime in, "The Lord never gives one more than one can bear. He must be testing you or punishing you for some reason."

The next day Frieda announced that her sister, Greta, had come home on furlough from the mission in Zimbabwe, Africa. Frieda said that she would be taking a few months off to be with Greta. She said she was sorry she would be gone with Boy sick and all. But after all, he was twelve and big enough to take care of himself. Frieda said she was sure he would be better soon, and besides, God would take care of him. Frieda concluded, "Greta needs me. She has been working hard to save the natives."

Sophia was distraught. Didn't Frieda understand she needed her here? She wasn't sure what she would do. Dr. MacIver had said that if Boy were to have any chance of recovery, without serious heart damage, he would have to be on strict bed rest. He wasn't even to get up to go to the bathroom. This meant many things, Sophia knew, and none of them would be easy to figure out.

Leaving the store would not be a problem. Caroline, the farm girl she trained to fit and sell shoes, was a good and reliable worker. She could cover for an hour or so without any problem. Besides, Sophia knew she would call her fussier customers, like Mrs. Wollan, and ask them to come in when she would be there. Also, Inga's ready-to-wear women's store was directly in front of the shoe store. Inga's larger store faced Main Street, and Sophia's store faced the Glenwood Avenue side. A short hallway that went past the beauty parlor that Uncle Phair managed connected the two stores. Inga would be glad to solve any major problems that might come up.

No. The problem was that it was 1944 and the war raged in Europe and the Pacific. Bus load after bus load of young men, and even men in their forties, left for Fort Snelling daily from in front of the Minton Hotel. Later they would leave Fort Snelling for some hellhole in the Gilbert Islands or the deserts of North Africa. Each week, news of the dead or wounded would come back to the quiet confines of the little town by the lake. Sophia's customers and friends were the parents, aunts, uncles, sisters, and cousins of these men.

Gasoline rationing was on. How could Sophia ask the townspeople to understand why she had to use more gas to drive back and forth the mile from home to the store just to check on Boy or to empty his bed pan? Inwardly, Sophia seethed over Frieda's selfish timing. She could have waited, at least until they knew if Boy would make it. Now, on top of everything else, Sophia felt she would be embarrassed by her apparently extravagant use of gasoline.

"Well," she thought, "I will just have to do what I have to do. Being alone to parent is hard enough without this added burden of illness."

Another problem she faced was figuring out what to do with Boy's goats. Those goats were Boy's prized possessions, even though they were his sister's thorns in the flesh. He had gotten the nanny, Snowflake, from his ne'er-do-well Uncle Fred. Fred had not even asked her before he showed up with the goat in the back seat of the car. The goat had been pregnant and Fred was anxious to get rid of it, so he made a big show of being generous by giving it to Boy. Why Lou had to have such a brother was beyond Sophia's comprehension.

Boy had taken to the goat immediately. A few days later, when the twin kids were born, Sophia herself melted and had to admit that they were cute. She did, however, see just more expense and more to take care of, as if they didn't have enough already.

God, she hated her life! It would be so much easier if there had never been a Lou or children. If only she could have remained director of her own destiny. God, she hated God!

The sun was now setting and the twilight was full. Sophia still sat and mulled things over and over. She would have to go in and talk to Boy about getting rid of the goats. She knew she would hide her feelings. She would sit by his bed. She would appear calm but she would feel the waves of nausea from the stench of his cracked and oozing skin. She knew Boy would cry and carry on. He always loved everything so deeply. He loved those goats. He loved her. He had loved Lou, even more than she knew. He loved beauty.

He loved Phair. He just loved. Every loss was such a big thing to him.

Couldn't he see how hard her life was? Couldn't he make it a little easier for her by just accepting what had to be without feeling anything? Damn him! Damn this whole thing called life! The whole damn thing could tear one's heart out. Maybe that's why her heart gave her all the pain and problems.

"Damn this body of mine!" she said in a whisper to herself. "Where's my fun? Where's my satisfaction?" She was remembering the happy times with Lou, the dancing, the lovemaking, the traveling, the working, the quiet times of holding. A smile crossed her face. What if Frieda, poor, hunchbacked Frieda, could see inside her mind and soul? What if she could hear her hate? What if she could read her naughty thoughts? "Well, the good thing is," she said aloud, "Frieda will be gone a few months and I won't have to deal with her holy drivel! Boy will get along. He always has—if he lives. If he dies. . . ." She didn't want to think about that.

Her hand turned the doorknob and she entered the bungalow. Jeanne and Frieda greeted her. They had things to say and tell, but she walked on by and into Boy's room. He lay there swollen and pale. Naked. He couldn't stand the pain caused by the weight of pajamas or a sheet on his swollen limbs. Tomorrow Uncle Julius would come by with a frame he had built to hold the sheets like a tent above Boy.

Sophia sat by the bed and began, "You know we have to sell the goats."

"Nooo," Boy's response was frail but determined. He began to cry.

Sophia continued, "Jeanne can't take care of them. You know how much she hated it when you would get her up at 4 a.m. every day to hold Snowflake's legs down so she wouldn't kick the bucket over while you milked her. Jeanne just couldn't take care of the goats all by herself. She hates those goats.

"She hates how they smell and rub against her. She only got up to help you because she loves you. The same reason she got up to help you with the trap line and the muskrats." Sophia's voice had changed. She now sounded firm and a little irritated, although Boy said nothing.

"Besides," Sophia continued, "Frieda is leaving for a few weeks and I need Jeanne to do your job of cleaning the store each morning and to try and help me take care of you. I'll call that goat man in Eagle Bend tomorrow and see if he'll come and get the goats. Let's see, his name, I think, is Mr. Thompson."

Sophia got up from the bed, walked out and quietly closed the door.

Boy continued to softly cry.

He lay there in the dark and remembered the fun he had with Snowflake. She had been a source of money too! Dr. MacIver had been excited when Boy had gotten the goats. He had said that goat's milk was the one source of help for his ulcer patients. He said they would easily pay twenty-five cents a quart for good, clean goat's milk. And that was a lot more than the seven cents a quart they paid for cow's milk.

Dr. MacIver had then given Boy the names of his ulcer patients. Boy contacted them and a number of them bought his milk. He had delivered the milk every day after school. Of course, he had had to give Jeanne five cents a quart for every one he sold. But still he made some money.

A smile came to his face when he remembered how he and Jeanne had taught and helped the goats to get on the garage roof so they could scamper to the top and slide down the other side into the garden. The goal was for the goats to eat the string beans that Sophia had insisted he grow. The goats achieved the goal. It had taken Sophia a long time to figure out why there had never been any string beans brought to the table. Secretly, Boy wondered if Frieda hadn't spied on him and told Sophia what was going on.

He remembered how angry Aunt Martha had gotten and how Aunt Inga had laughed when he named the female twin kid born on George Washington's birthday, "Martha." The male twin, "George," had died at birth.

He remembered. Now they would be gone. He cried himself to sleep. When the goats were sold a few days later, and Mr. Thompson drove down from Eagle Bend to get them, Boy watched out the window from his bed as they were taken from the little shed he had built for them behind the house.

He remembered looking out that same window into the blizzard of Armistice Day, 1940. The shed was only 30 yards behind the house, but he couldn't see it that day because of the snow and the blowing snow. It was a total whiteout. He went back and recalled wondering if his precious goats were alive. He wondered what had happened to his two prize ducks and the four chickens he had kept when the others had been sent to market. That day he knew he would have to go out there and get them or they most certainly would freeze. If he could get to them, he would take them to the basement, the half where the schoolteachers didn't live.

Sophia agreed. They had to be brought in. Frieda protested that it would be better that the goats, chickens, and ducks died rather than to send Boy out into the teeth of the blizzard. But then, Frieda had never liked the goats anyway. Boy had wondered if she thought this was God's way of getting rid of them.

One of the problems in getting to the shed was that

the storm had piled ten-foot high snowdrifts all around the house as it swept with fury off the lake. The doors were snowed shut! After studying the situation for a time, Sophia decided to tie a cord to Boy's belt so that if he lost direction in the blinding show, he could follow the string back to the house. Next was trying to figure out a strategy to get him out of the house since the doors were of no use.

It was decided to lower him out of the dinette casement windows, which were higher than all the other windows and slightly above the snowdrift. Boy climbed up on the dining room table and then onto the window ledge, opened the window, and put his feet and legs out. His feet could just touch the top of the snowdrift. He felt confident that he could walk on top of the snow out to the shed and then lead the goats and carry the ducks and chickens back to the house. He was sure the snow would be packed hard enough for such a trek because he had heard his uncles talk about storms like this before and how the drifts got to be hard like concrete.

Boy pushed off from the window ledge, plan and direction firmly in mind. Unfortunately, the snow next to the house was soft and not wind-packed, because the house itself had sheltered the snow from the fury of the wind, so his plans sank out of sight just as he did. Eight feet down! Snow in front, snow behind, and snow above.

He scrambled and climbed and finally got on top of the drifts. Unfortunately, he had lost his sense of direction. Which way to go? He knew that if he went the wrong way, he would head straight out onto the lake and into eight miles of nothing. Then he remembered the cord Sophia had tied to his belt. He saw the direction it led back to the house.

While the snow kept him from seeing the house, and he couldn't see the shed, he knew where he needed to go and where the shed had to be—he hoped.

Like a blind man he set out. The wind took his breath away, but he kept plodding along. When he ran into the forked Box Elder tree that held the tree house, he knew he was going the right way. While the bump and cut on his head left little drops of red on the white snow and a throbbing in his head, he felt reassured. He knew he wasn't lost.

He almost missed the shed, however, because it was buried up to its roof. Only Snowflake's bleating voice guided him to her scrunched-up body, squeezed in by the snow, just under the top of the shed roof. She licked his face with a thankful sloppy kiss when he grabbed her collar and began to pull her out.

When he had her out, he dug down in the snow and "unburied" the ducks and chickens and put them on top of the snow with the two kid goats, Tom and Jerry. They looked a bit worse for wear, but all were alive. Next he tied the end of the clothesline rope he had brought along to the roof's pinnacle. It would guide him back to get Tom and Jerry and the ducks and chickens. He would not leave Maynard, the mallard, nor Randolph, the Rock Island rooster, to die in the blizzard.

Then he picked up Snowflake and put her over his shoulders, two feet hanging down on either side, and began the laborious trek back to the house. Once at the house, Snowflake was carried down the stairs and into the laundry room. Somehow, however, she didn't seem to appreciate this change of venue. Her mild bleating turned to a loud and raucous "Maaaaaaaa."

Boy made three more trips into the snowy oblivion. The clothesline guided him back to the shed and then back again to the house.

On the second trip, he brought out Tom and Jerry, the

twin bucks born to Snowflake. Their voices added volume and roundness to the tones their mother emitted. On the third trip, he brought the ducks. Maynard was under one arm and Mildred under the other. Both seemed to welcome the warmer climes, but their quacks voiced their protest to the weather gods for creating such an overture to winter.

Finally, Randolph, the Red Rock rooster, and his three golden Buff Orpington lady friends, were gathered into a pillowcase and brought to join the basement chorus. The blizzard, the goat, and the avian jam session went well into the evening. When the reverie didn't abate by 10:00 p.m., Miss Swenson, the more aggressive of the two schoolmarms who had rented the basement apartment on the other side of the plasterboard wall separating them from Snowflake, Tom, Jerry, Maynard, Rudolph, and the Buff Orpington sisters, came stalking upstairs to talk to Sophia about her poor screening of the new tenants.

Sophia merely replied, "We couldn't let them freeze out there."

Frieda, however, chimed in, "But they really don't belong in the house, especially not in my laundry!" Frieda's statement was all the encouragement Miss Swenson needed to go into her lengthy lecture on cleanliness and unpleasant odors. It was true—the goats did seem more interested in eating the Fels Naptha soap than in washing with it. The laundry tubs were great for swimming it seemed, at least from watching Mildred and Maynard, but toilet training was not in their repertoire.

Sophia conceded that Miss Swanson and Miss Larson certainly had a point, but the blizzard was not yet done. The animals would stay within and there was no reason for anyone to leave. Boy would stay in the basement with the animals. They seemed less noisy when he was there.

Besides, he could pick up their droppings and try to control the odors by disposing of them as soon as possible. Beyond that, they would all just have to make the best of it.

The blizzard lasted two more days. When the sun finally came out and lit up the ice crystal sun dogs to the right and left of the sun's bright and brilliant face, which was trying to pierce the subzero air, Swenson and Larson had had it! Their moods and faces were as frigid as the air. They paraded up the stairs, each with a suitcase in hand and out the back door. Boy thought they were a funny sight as they struggled, flopped, and flapped their way around, over, and through the eight- to ten-foot drifts of crystal blue snow on their way to the street that would take them to town.

Sophia looked somber, wondering what their story would do to her ability to rent the basement room ever again. Boy, however, applauded the goats and ducks and chickens for getting rid of the schoolmarms. He had never liked them anyway.

Frieda fussed and fumed about the mess her laundry room was in. She seemed sure that God was punishing her for some shortcoming, but she knew not what. She talked about the goat God had given to Abraham to sacrifice instead of Isaac. Her way of telling the story seemed to imply that now God appeared to be sacrificing her instead of the goat. She never did mention Noah and the ark.

Returning to the present, Boy put his head back on the pillow. He smiled weakly to himself, even as he cried softly as Mr. Thompson's truck and the goats drove away. Summer wore on. May became June and June became July. The summer routines were established. Sophia would go to work but would return home at midday or call if she was too busy. Occasionally, Aunt Inga or Jenny would stop in on their way to or from an errand. Often Jeanne was around unless she was helping at the store or visiting Jeanie Kayrol. But there were many hours when Boy was alone and bored. Boredom led to rule-breaking. The rule was that he was not to get out of bed! His knees, ankles, feet, and wrists were still swollen, especially on the left side.

One day after tiring of listening to the radio soaps of Ma Perkins, "brought to you by Oxydal," and Jack Armstrong, the All-American Boy, "brought to you by Wheaties, the Breakfast of Champions," and Captain Midnight and Buck Rogers, he decided that if Buck Rogers could explore space he could explore the outer reaches beyond the confines of his bedroom prison.

But how? The pain in his legs, especially the left one, still brought tears to his eyes whenever he moved it or put pressure of any kind on it. He simply couldn't walk! Then he remembered. There was the ottoman, the oversized footstool, by the big brown overstuffed mohair chair in the living room. If he somehow could get that into his room, he could maybe slide out of bed and put his left knee on it and push with his right foot, like a scooter. He was sure it would work.

But how could he get the ottoman into the bedroom without drawing attention to his plan? He knew his plan would never be approved by his jailers named Sophia and Dr. MacIver. That evening the gods smiled on him. Elizabeth, cousin Paul, Phair and Inga, Sophia and Jeanne all crowded into the bedroom for a visit.

Carpe diem. Boy seized the moment. He suggested that instead of bringing in the big chair that took up so much room, why not bring in the ottoman that would take less room? In fact, maybe it could be kept there. Just for visitors. It would take less effort than always having to have to move chairs in and out. Sophia thought it was a great idea. Boy smiled to himself. The next day, when Sophia, taking Jeanne along, headed for the store, the stage was set. He could see the garage from his bedroom window. He watched the '41 Buick drive away.

By this time Sophia felt secure that Boy would follow all of Dr. MacIver's rules. However, this day, as soon as the Buick Special left the alley and turned the corner heading down the street toward town, Boy was already squirming toward the edge of the bed.

Problem one was that the ottoman was across the room in the corner. Never mind. Undaunted and foolish, Boy eased himself over the edge of the bed. At this point, two things happened at once. Nausea swept over him like an ocean wave. His head began to spin. He had not been perpendicular in more than two months. The second thing happened when his left foot hit the floor. Pain shot like a rocket from his foot, up his leg and out the top of his head. The result was dramatic. There was a loud, resounding crash. Boy landed unceremoniously halfway under the bed and lay like a crumpled rag doll. When the pain began to subside and his head cleared a bit, he thought, "Maybe this break for freedom wasn't such a good idea after all."

But now that he was here, he reasoned, "It will be easier to go for the ottoman than to try to get back into bed." Next, he discovered the source of the crash that had accompanied his fall. Under the bed with him was the empty bedpan and the walking cane that had been left so he could hook and pull the phone or bedside table into reach. The bedpan and its emptied contents were a definite and nauseating negative, and certainly of little use and hard to explain later on. The cane, however, was another matter. It could be used to extend his reach. If he lay on his belly, he could extend the cane, hook the ottoman, and pull it to him. Using both hands, and gritting his teeth against the pain in his legs and wrists, Boy began to slowly push the cane in the direction of the coveted ottoman. He moved it an inch at a time, sometimes moving on a trail of tears, sometimes following the roar of profanity along the highway of liberation.

Then, success! He hooked the leg of the ottoman and slowly drew it to him. He stroked it with the gentleness usually reserved for a prized and treasured dog. It would be his loyal servant. He would try to figure out how to explain away the odor and empty, dented bedpan later.

But now he had to figure out how to get his left knee onto the ottoman so he could use it as a scooter. His right leg was less painful and less swollen than the left, so that would be the pushing leg. Slowly he began to raise himself. One more inch and he would be there. But then the ottoman slipped and he was on his face with his nose pressed into the hardwood floor. A trickle of blood ran from one nostril as profanity flowed from his lips. With the cane he pulled the footstool back to his side. This time he held the bed as he raised himself.

Success! He was now in position and all in one piece, albeit a little dizzy. A warm tide of pride swept over him as a silent prayer of thanks escaped from his lips. The freedom of the house was at hand at last. He started off, out the bedroom door and down the corridor. He pushed himself slowly with his stiff and weak right leg as he cautiously balanced himself on his left knee atop the little stool.

The door to the left, off the corridor, led to the kitchen. Once inside the kitchen, he was amazed at how much better the air smelled. The queasy, sick-to-his-stomach feeling had left. He made the grand circle, through the dinette and into the living room, stopping a moment to play the scale on the piano, then moving on into Frieda's vacant room and back into the corridor. Just then the phone rang!

He panicked! Then he remembered that the caller wouldn't know that he answered it here in the corridor rather than in the bedroom. He let it ring twice more. Then he answered it, disguising his voice to sound sleepy. "Hello."

"Were you sleeping?" his mother's voice sounded from the receiver.

"Ah, ya . . . I guess," he lied.

"Well, I'm just calling to see how you are and if you would like me to bring some ice cream. Jeanne and I will be home in about an hour and a half. You be a good boy and stay in bed. As if you had any option not to," she laughed.

"Sure," he said.

He smiled as he clicked the receiver back into its cradle. Then he headed back into the kitchen to begin the circle one more time. He remembered all the times he and his sister raced around this circle. Sometimes Jeanne would chase him to whack him on the head for some comment or deed of mischief. Or sometimes he would try to catch her for similar acts of love.

The most memorable cruise around the circle was the Saturday morning when they had devised a game of putting bread in the toaster by the French windows on the dinette table. They pushed the bread down and ran to see how many times they could make the circle before the bread popped up! When it popped they pushed it down again, and again, and again, and again. The bread turned from white to brown to deep dark brown to black. Smoke rose from the toaster and billowed out the open window. Still they ran the wonderful circle.

And then they heard the sirens. Two minutes later, the big red fire engine pulled up in front of the little bungalow. A minute later, Mr. Haugen, banker and volunteer fireman, grabbed the little toaster by its cord-like tail and doused it with the fire hose. Two more minutes and Sophia drove up, having been alerted at the shoe store by Mable, the telephone operator. It took Sophia only a moment to assess the situation, then her angry face turned almost as dark as the burned toast.

Quietly Boy and Jeanne sought cover beneath the bunk beds in their bedroom. But Sophia's objective was to find Frieda, who it turned out was in the backyard, hanging wash on the line. She was singing hymns as loudly as she could and was oblivious to the fires of hell burning in the front of the house. Frieda may not have heard the wrath of God, but she heard the wrath of Sophia that day.

Boy's journey was but a snail's pace this day as he made the circle, but still it was a satisfying step toward freedom. He was safely back in bed in the smelly room by the time Jeanne and Sophia returned to check on him. The climb back into bed had not been easy, but still it was a lot easier than trying to come up with a good story as to why the bedpan had ended up under the bed.

When he finished telling it, he wasn't so sure that his story about the dog knocking the bedpan down had been all that believable, especially since the dog was in the yard and Sophia thought she remembered letting him out. Sophia's raised eyebrows and skeptical look had told him that she really didn't believe him. But she said nothing.

Later that night, Boy told his sister what he had done and how the bedpan was the casualty of his adventure. Then he swore her to secrecy! She crossed her heart and pledged on her Girl Scout's honor that she would never tell his secret. Boy believed her.

Day after day the little ottoman carried Boy around the house, always returning him to the bed before Sophia returned to make her rounds to check on him. Slowly the swelling subsided in his knees and wrists and ankles. One day in late July, Dr. MacIver suggested that Boy could begin to try to get out of bed. "I think I'll have you sit in a chair for only a few minutes at a time to begin with," the good doctor said.

"You'll be very weak from all the time you've been in bed. You'll probably not be able to tolerate very much at first, but don't get discouraged. Your strength will come back. Whatever you do, don't try to get up by yourself. Be sure someone is here to help you. I'll check on you in a few days."

Having made his speech, Dr. MacIver turned to leave. As he exited the door, Jeanne and Boy looked at each other and began to laugh.

Sophia, who had been listening and watching, looked puzzled but dismissed the laughing as merely happiness that now Boy could really feel that he was on the way to recovery. She, too, was glad and happy that Jeanne seemed pleased as well.

In reality, things are not always as they seem to be, especially if one observes only the obvious and does not look for patterns. Had Sophia looked for patterns, she would have realized that in the past weeks, Jeanne had always found some way to control the times when she and her mother left the store for home and Jeanne had always made a phone call just before leaving. Perhaps then Sophia would have understood the laughter as an expression of relief over not being caught for violating Dr. MacIver's bed rest rules.

When the doctor made his house call a few days later, Boy was already walking around the house with the assistance of two canes. The good doctor was amazed. His look of amazement soon turned to one of shock, then of anger as Boy told him about his foray into the yard earlier that morning.

Quickly MacIver produced a stethoscope, firmly commanded Boy to lie down, and listened to his heart. He listened and listened. Then with a sigh and a slight sagging of his shoulders, he announced that he couldn't find anything wrong, except a slight murmur. Nonetheless, he felt compelled to give a little talk about how his orders were always to be followed and how Boy was lucky that his outdoor adventure had not led to serious consequences.

He warned Boy, with Sophia listening to his orders, that Boy was not to go outside again until he made another house call in a few days. If Boy followed his instructions and everything looked good, then he might give permission to spend a few minutes outside when the sun was out and the weather was warm.

When Dr. MacIver had gone, Sophia sat down next to Boy and asked him, "Have you been up before?"

She had sensed his confidence and strength. Also she listened to her intuition and this time it told her that all was not as it seemed.

"Yes," Boy said, in a very quiet voice.

"I thought so. Quite a few times, right?" Sophia asked.

"Yes," he replied, his voice barely audible.

Sophia sat there for a few moments. Then, thoughtfully, she said, "Well, we won't tell Dr. MacIver. He so wants you to get well and he may not understand."

When the doctor returned two days later, he asked, "Were you a good boy? Did you follow my orders?"

Boy said nothing. He chose not to tell him of his stroll down to the lake the day before, nor of the climb into the tree house the day before that. Instead, Boy merely smiled.

MacIver was quick to interpret the smile as acquiescence

to his superior wisdom, and said, "Good! You see, it's better this way. You just follow my orders and all will be OK. You will get well this way."

Jeanne, who was in the room and had been Boy's regular companion on his journeys to the outer lands, began to laugh, then quickly changed it to a cough. MacIver looked at Jeanne and asked, "Are you coming down with a cold? Here, let me look at your throat."

"No, I'll be OK." Jeanne responded.

"We don't want you to get sick like Boy," the doctor replied.

But Jeanne persisted in her resistance to any medical exploration and MacIver acquiesced. As Dr. MacIver prepared to leave, he said to Boy and Sophia, "I have one prescription I want you to take each day. You have to get the weight back on that you lost if you're going to get your strength back. My records show that you went from 150 pounds to just under 100. So, I want you to go up to Setter's Drug Store, every day, and have a malted milk. I will tell Mr. Setter that this is a prescription. He is to report to me if you fail to come and get your medicine. Now remember, you must get a ride. You cannot walk. It's a whole mile up there. Am I understood?"

Inwardly, Boy was delighted. He had never heard of a prescription like this before. Outwardly, he said nothing, but merely nodded his head politely. When MacIver had left and Sophia had driven away to return to the store, Boy and his sister set off on their walk to Setter's Drug Store for the first dose of his medicine, which he would share with Jeanne.

The daily walks along the lake, past the park, in front of the judge's house and Dr. Elder's house, around the corner and into the apothecary-smelling drug store were sheer delight.

Jeanne was his sister, but she was also his friend, self-appointed teacher, tormentor, and protagonist. Without her, life would have been dull. They knew, as though from the beginning of time, how to cry together, fight together, tease and laugh together. Yet their views of their little world and the people who moved in and out of their town and their lives often were seen so differently that it seemed like Boy and Jeanne grew up in different towns, in different valleys, but of the same mother at the same time.

Sometimes Boy made the journey to the apothecary with its marble-topped, iron-legged tables by himself. Once inside the doors of Setter's, the medicinal smells became synonymous with the sweet taste of a Black Cow or a malted milk. Boy's weight came back and Dr. MacIver smiled.

AMENDS

In late August, just after Boy's thirteenth birthday, Sophia announced that they would be taking a trip "down to Minneapolis."

This was unusual. The Great War had forced gas rationing and you could use up almost a full month's allotment on such a trip, even on the more generous "B" card. Such a trip was three hundred miles. Further, it was strange and extravagant, for it was not the time of year to go to market to buy shoes for the store for an upcoming season. The shoes for the winter season already had been purchased and the lines and fashions for the spring were not yet out.

Boy's look of curiosity prompted Sophia to continue. "Dr. MacIver says you should be seen by a heart specialist just to be sure there is no damage caused by the fever. Uncle Phair will go with us. He wants to know firsthand if you'll have permission to hunt this fall."

Boy said nothing but felt the familiar knot of fear begin to swell. What if the doctor said he couldn't hunt? It felt worse than death. It was the one thing he was good at. His classmates already treated him with scorn because he was quiet and a loner. He only had two best friends, and he didn't have a real dad. He knew he generally didn't fit in. He was ridiculed for using big words and always trying things that other kids didn't. He was envied for driving the car long before he was old enough for a license; he was ridiculed for playing the violin; he was teased and scoffed at for driving race horses and running a trap line; he was rejected and beaten for befriending Richard, who was Catholic; he was laughed at for his solo camping in the hills; he was scorned for working in his mother's store.

But, when it came to hunting, he was accepted by the in gang, the football players and the popular ones. The superintendent's son and even the girls accepted him. When it came to hunting, he was the king. Their ridicule was silenced and their questions and awe were apparent.

After all, had he not hunted with the great Jimmy Robinson? Had not his picture and the story appeared that glorious October day in 1943 in all the syndicated newspapers telling of his hunting prowess as he guided Jimmy and the three furloughed wounded war heroes. It was the war veterans' first hunt since 1939. The hunt, of course, occurred under the critical eye and tutelage of Uncle Phair who had instigated and initiated the whole thing as a way of honoring the country's veterans who liked to hunt. But, nonetheless, Boy had done his part.

But now, maybe, some doctor in Minneapolis would say he couldn't ever hunt again.

When Sophia and Jeanne had finished eating and gone their various ways, Boy slipped out the door and began walking toward the hills. After awhile he stopped and sat by his favorite tree by the little brook he knew so well. Quietly he began to cry. Then he began to curse. His mind filled with all the fear and hurt and shattered hopes his life had taught him to believe would come. Time passed and he lay down to watch the dying evening sun reflect off the clouds.

It was dark when he got up and brushed the leaves and twigs from his clothes and started the trek home. When he got home no one greeted him. They were in the living room listening to "Fiber Mcgee and Molly." Boy went to his room and lay down, not bothering to undress. He had noticed that Sophia had already packed his bag. Then he felt Sophia shake him. She whispered, "Time to get up! We've got to get started. You have to take a bath and brush your teeth. We wouldn't want the doctor to think you're a stick in the mud."

Boy bathed and dressed, and then the long trip started. First stop was to pick up Phair. He sat beside Sophia in the front seat. Boy and Jeanne sat in the back of the '41 Buick. Four hours later, they were on Fremont Avenue in Minneapolis, in front of Frank and Iris Horn's house. These were old friends of Sophia's who had become surrogate aunt and uncle to Boy and Jeanne from the time of their births.

Jeanne bolted from the car and ran to the door; she wanted to see her favorite uncle. Pleasantries were exchanged and arrangements made for the night's lodging. Then Sophia, Phair and Boy were back in the car headed for the Medical Arts Building downtown and the rendezvous with the doctor. Boy said nothing. He watched everything. He was scared, but he had decided no doctor, anywhere, even in this Godforsaken city, could force him not to hunt. It wouldn't matter what the doctor said.

The elevator was cramped but fast as it whisked them to the ninth floor. A short wait and they were ushered out of the big reception area by an overweight nurse in her heavily starched white uniform with the funny little triangular hat perched atop her head. They were guided into a little office with an opaque window in the door. Printed on the glass were the words: Dr. Haroldson: Specialist in Rheumatics and Heart Disease.

In due time, the doctor, with graying hair at the temples and a cultivated serious look that wrinkled his brow and clenched his jaw, appeared. He shook hands with Sophia and Phair and said, "How are we today?" to Boy.

Boy started to answer; he wanted to tell him he didn't want to be there, and no matter what the doctor said it couldn't keep him from hunting. But he didn't get a chance, for already he was being told to undress and put on a funny backwards gown. The embarrassment of stripping in front of all the people kept him speechless. Then the doctor and nurse were hooking him up with many wires that they fastened to his chest and arms and legs. The machine was turned on, and as it whined and wheezed, it made funny lines on a paper it spewed from its innards.

Next, the serious, stone-faced doctor was pressing a cold instrument with tubes that led from his ears to Boy's chest. Boy had had this done to him before by Dr. MacIver, but this doctor listened a long time. He told Boy to take a deep breath and then listened some more. Then he listened to his back. Boy was told to put on a robe and was led out into the hall where he was told to run up three flights of steps and come back; the doctor wanted to listen again. Again, they hooked him to wires and again the machine whined and wheezed and again it spewed out paper with funny lines that went up and down.

Finally, Boy was told to dress and go to the waiting room. The nurse would come and get him when the doctor was ready. Boy waited and waited. He worried as he thought about what the doctor would say and how he would reply. Again he decided no doctor nor machine would tell him what he would or would not do. After an eternity in the waiting room, while the doctor studied the paper from his machine and talked to Sophia and Phair, the starched nurse with the triangular hat came to get him. "The doctor will see you now and tell you what he has found," the nurse said.

Boy, Sophia and Phair followed her into the doctor's inner office with the opaque glass in the door. Doctor Haroldson invited them to sit, but Phair preferred to stand. He held his round straw hat in both hands. The doctor began, "You're a lucky boy. There is really no major heart damage. There is just a bit of a murmur where the valve leaks a bit but it should heal, I would think." Doctor Haroldson continued, "You will have to take it very easy for some time yet–just to be sure. And of course will have to have a heart examination and checkup every year and. . . ."

Before he could continue Boy interrupted, "Can I hunt this fall?"

"Oh, I would think you could on warm, clear days if you don't walk too far," the doctor responded.

"But what about ducks?" Boy demanded

"Oh no! Never ducks. Maybe never again. That would be way too cold and wet. We must never, ever, have you get cold and chilled!" Doctor Haroldson responded in a most serious voice.

"Damn you! Damn you! God damn you!" Boy screamed.

He tried to kick at the doctor. Phair grabbed him by the arm and hauled him through the fancy door into the hall. Once outside the office and away from where the doctor could overhear, Phair shook Boy and said, "That is not how you behave! I thought I taught you how to deal with hard times and things. I thought I taught you how to stay in control. I thought I taught you how to be a gentleman! Now you will go back in and apologize to the good doctor who is trying to help you." With that, Phair opened the glass door with the doctor's profile clearly visible.

Boy stood before the doctor. For a long time he said nothing. He just shuffled from one foot to the other. Then he stammered, "I'm—I'm sorry. I—I just want to hunt. Ducks. With my uncle here."

"Is there any way Boy could hunt ducks?" Phair asked.

"If he stayed completely dry and warm and got ten hours of sleep. I think then it would be all right," Dr. Haroldson gently replied.

And then he added, "I don't think that's possible from what I know of duck hunting."

"Thank you. I'm sorry for Boy's outburst," Phair responded. He opened the door for Sophia and, as he did, Boy said nothing, but took the doctor's extended hand, shook it and looked him in the eye.

Once back in the hall outside the doctor's office, Phair touched Boy's shoulder and said, "Now we'll go to Corrie's Sporting Goods and buy the warmest, driest clothes we can find. You will be with me in the duck blind come opening!"

Boy was with Phair in the blind that September–he and Phair and Buddy, the American water spaniel. As they sat under blue, warm skies, Phair talked of getting Boy a dog of his own that he could train and hunt with for years to come. Together they decided March would be a good time to get the dog, for then they would have all summer to get him ready to hunt in the fall. Hours and hours, interrupted only occasionally by a lone duck enjoying the "bluebird" weather, were spent trying to decide what kind of dog they would get. Finally, the decision was made. It would be a Springer Spaniel and his name would be Lucky Jim.

Once the decision was finalized, Phair began to lecture. Boy would have to learn to stay in control. He could not lose his temper no matter how long it took the dog to learn certain tasks. Phair would help Boy, but it was up to Boy to learn the lessons of self-control, or else he could never teach the dog. Long after the fall hunt ended, the lessons continued.

Phair was a kindly but exacting teacher, and Boy was an eager student and a quick study.

By early spring, Boy's health was robust once again. The fever was forever gone and only a slight murmur of his heart whispered of Phair's healing love. March came. Lucky Jim was to arrive by train on the twenty-third. He was coming from Marshfield, Wisconsin. On the twenty-second of March, 1945, the spaniel was loaded on the train for the trip to Glenwood. He was on his way to his new home.

Phair, on that same day, at 69 years of age, died of a stroke.

COMING OF AGE

It was July 1945. The temperature was ninety-six degrees. He was hot and his hands were sweaty. He had his bottom planted firmly on one step and his feet planted two steps below. He struggled as he cursed under his breath. Slowly, the steel wheel moved. A step. He shifted his position to the next step up and started over. He was scared to death that his hand might slip and he might drop the wheel. If it slipped from his grasp it would roll down the steps and through the plate glass window and out onto Main Street. He would lose his job, and he would be scored as a failure and a disgrace, just as he was during threshing at the farm two years before.

He was thirteen years old, almost fourteen, with his first real job. He was working at something that was not a kid's job, or a farm job at his uncle's place, or a paper route, or a job for his mother or aunt. He was working for Mr. Husaby, owner of the county's largest farm implement store. Farmers were bringing in tractors by the droves to have their wheels converted from steel to rubber tires. The old front steel wheels were to be stored in the attic of the garage. Storing them was Boy's job.

He had to get the steel wheels up the stairs! Each one weighed between one hundred fifty and two hundred pounds. He was not about to ask for help. Neither was he about to admit that perhaps this endeavor was beyond his capability. This was a time of passage. He was out to prove himself a man. He didn't quite know what all that meant, but he knew that he was entering "manhood," as they called it.

Three weeks before he had awakened in the middle of the night. There had been a strong sensation in his loins. He felt hard and uncomfortable. A pressure and pain radiated up and down his genitals. Then, there had been the feeling of release, a feeling of liquid warmth creeping down his thighs. He moaned in his sleep, not aware, in conscious mind, what it was that he was dreaming; he was only vaguely aware that he had been dreaming. He knew the dream had been pleasant. It seemed to have been about her, the young woman who had shown herself to them when he was a boy of nine.

In the morning, when he awakened, he was embarrassed. There was a gooey, sticky spot on the sheet and top covers. He feared what Frieda would say in judgment when she got the bedding for the wash. He didn't know what excuse he might make. That worried him. He usually knew what he might say to her, but this was new to him.

He knew from what boys had said in the locker room that he had ejaculated and exploded his "angel hair" for all to see. Semen, his biology teacher called it, the stuff that could make babies, had come out of his body. But now he only wished that he could remember the dream. He knew that is what had triggered the eruption. It must have been a good one. It was pleasant and wonderful he thought secretly to himself. He could still feel the warmth radiating from his pelvis.

He got up and went down to the basement and the large shower stall located there. Washing in the warmth of the water, he watched his penis grow. Again he felt the pressure, pain, desire and pleasure. He looked and that which had hung so soft and lifeless throughout his life, now stood pointed toward the ceiling, hard and large and with a life of its own.

He slowly pulled the foreskin back. He was glad he was not circumcised. The sensations were almost painful in their intensity as he moved the skin back and forth, back and forth. Soon there was the eruption of silky, sticky fluid. This time he felt the whole sensation. This time he saw the young woman in his mind. He knew again the beauty of her curves and her breasts and body.

It was the young woman he had encountered next door in the circus tent his uncle had put up in his back yard several years before as a way of showing some kind of love for his son. Boy was nine that year. He and four or five other boys, all eight- and nine-year-olds, had gone to the tent. There they were playing cowboys or war or something. They had homemade rubber guns and were shooting rubber bands at each other when a young woman of sixteen who lived on the edge of town walked in on them. She had not been invited. Once in the tent she talked to them for awhile and then asked if they had ever seen a grown woman naked. They said nothing, but just sat there while she went to the tent's opening and pulled the flaps down. Then she proceeded to take off her clothes—all of them.

This was the first time Boy had seen a fully developed woman's body naked—totally naked. Her beauty mesmerized him—the hair between her legs, the swelling fullness of her breasts, the round and sensuous fullness of her body.

She had invited the children to touch her. She said she wanted them to touch her. Now, in his mind's eye, standing in the shower, it all came back to him. He was back in the tent. He remembered that the reverie had lasted for all of four or five minutes before the tent flap opened and there stood Aunt Elizabeth yelling, screaming at the child-woman and at the boys too.

Boy thought all hell had broken loose, and it had. They all ran in every direction. Where the girl went or how she got dressed Boy didn't know. Where the other boys went, he didn't know either. He did know that because it was his aunt who found them, his mother was called home from the store. He remembered standing, shame-faced and trembling before her as she scolded him about his immorality. He remembered he promised her that never again would he look at a woman or touch her beauty.

But, in his heart, the promise that he made was that he would not get caught again. He could still feel the touch of the young woman's hands on his belly and his privates. She was a vision of beauty he would never forget. A vision, he believed, created by the goddess.

Now the heat and sounds in the store below jolted him back into real time. He realized that he had moved to the top of the steps in Husaby's Garage. He had not lost his grip on the steel wheel he was struggling to put away. He had a sense of satisfaction, a sense of strength, a sense of the fact that now, now—now he was becoming strong enough to claim the role of a man.

He didn't really know what that meant. He did know that in the years since the encounter in the tent, when the locker room boys bragged about what they had done to Larry Fremont's sister the Saturday night of the senior prom, that he was different from other boys.

He felt no titillating joy but only shame for them when he recalled the description of their exploits. He would come later to know that the Fremont girl had been gang-raped at the party at her home. One after another of Boy's friends had entered her bedroom. They saw her in her nudity. They put themselves inside her. When she whimpered and cried that this was not what she wanted, they didn't stop, they only laughed. Years later the word abuse, of the worst sort, would describe what she had been subjected to.

Larry Fremont, his friend, died of a fall while seeking to capture pigeons from their nests on the steeple of the local Lutheran Church. Larry's sister, only a year older at fourteen, had been looking for someone to care for her, to know her pain and caress it all away. Her father had died tragically two years before. Her mother was seldom home. She wanted someone to be with her, to wipe her tears not to use her, then brag and leave her. She sought companionship, but instead had been used for some kind of group masturbation by self-centered boys. Then she was alone and shamed, an object of derision, a conquest for locker room bragging rights.

Boy knew that he was different! The story made him sick and did not fit the memory in his mind's eye of the woman in the tent.

He knew it when he would go to the lake with his boat to fish for supper for his sister and mother, as he lay on the bottom of the boat and felt the rocking and watched the clouds roll by. Long before the first urging of his sex he had fantasized again about what she looked like in all her parts and what it would be like to be loved and to love, to be valued by a woman so beautiful. What would it be like to be truly seen by such a one?

Lines of poetry would come to his mind, almost as though given by the gods or goddess. Then, he would dismiss them, for he knew he would be thought a weirdo and a sissy if he wrote them on paper so that someone else might see them. As he reveled in his private world of fantasy and dream, he would see himself running alongside her on the beach or defending her or . . . but then he would be rudely returned to real time by the sound of a nearby boat, or by his dog rocking the boat as he shifted his position.

No, from what he could tell, he really wasn't like other boys. They had fathers—fathers to talk to. They had brothers—brothers to wrestle and just be around. Older brothers to learn from. All he had was a sister. He wondered what she could possibly know about being a man. His only brother was older by two years but had died three days after birth. What if Boy's father hadn't died? His dreams and fantasies began once more. He had never known what a brother was, or what a brother could tell him. His two close friends, both older than he, never talked about their experiences of sex and feelings and growing up. He didn't know how he would find out what it was to be a man.

As he drifted in that twilight zone, not quite asleep and not quite awake, he pondered many things. Secretly, he wondered if he had been wrong the day he had helped the child, Julie.

Julie was five years old and had wandered into the wild peat bog two blocks from her mother's house. Three teenaged boys had found her there, stripped her and tied her with her legs apart. She was hidden in a wild cucumber patch surrounded by mosquitoes biting her arms, legs, eyelids, and private parts. The boys probed her with their fingers, penises, and sticks. She cried and bled. Then they left her hurt and bound. They ran for fear when her cries attracted attention, thinking someone would come and they would be caught. They were cowards to the core, Boy thought. Were all men cowards? He didn't like that thought at all, but what if it was true?

Boy had heard her cries. He followed them into the shadows of the peat bog. There he found her. Boy cut her free, wrapped her in his shirt, and brought her home, a block away from the bog. Her mother almost killed the messenger, until the young girl cried through her sobs and tears, "Stop! He is the one who found me. He made the others run away. He brought me home!"

By now the little girl's mother had taken her from his arms. She cried for her child as she called the doctor. Then she turned to Boy. "Thank you," she said quietly, now composed. "Do you want some milk and cookies?"

Boy had felt good that day. He was ten. But he was shaken and he wondered about himself. Perhaps he was too soft, a sissy, not like other boys. Maybe he should have entered into their fun, but he felt it was so wrong to hurt someone. Maybe what he had done was right, and they were wrong. He just didn't know!

When he had told Uncle Phair about what he had done, Phair praised him, but then Phair was also thought to be different. Uncle Gil had said that Phair liked men and was "queer."

Boy just didn't know what it would mean to be a man.

Boy did know, as he sat breathing hard and staring at the wheel, safely in its resting place on the attic floor, that he felt a sense of pride and strength he had not known before. He had done it! He had not lost his grip. The monster wheel had not rolled down the steps, through the window and out to Main Street. He really had done it! He wondered if the other boys could have done as well.

Somehow he had demonstrated a certain kind of control, a certain kind of strength, of which he had not been aware. He didn't know how that all played out either in the business of being a man.

Others seemed more athletic than he was, and certainly they seemed to be more popular. He had seen them in the showers after gym. Several had more body hair and were bigger "down there" than he was. They bragged of their exploits, of "making it," and of what they'd done to the girls. He didn't want to share in their bragging. He got teased and got called a 'faggot' and a 'virgin,' but he knew it would be worse if he told them of his poetry and his visions of beauty and his sense of awe at a sunrise or the mystic marvel of a woman's rounded body.

He wondered if he wasn't stronger in his mind and body and deeper in his thoughts. After all, Mr. Husaby had hired him, even though he knew that at least two other boys, football players, had applied. At that moment, he heard Mr. Husaby's voice behind him asking, "You all right?"

"Ah . . . ah sure," Boy replied. Then he slowly turned and headed down the stairs for the next wheel. He rolled the next wheel to the foot of the steps. Slowly he sat and, as before, braced himself and began the long journey up.

Halfway up, he paused. His hands were sweaty and his shirt soaked. He was breathing hard. He looked down and there was the plate glass window in all its glory. And, on the window was the drawing of the familiar Husaby roadrunner cartoon painted in colorful, chalky paint. As Boy rested, he recalled the first encounter he had with Mr. and Mrs. Jake Husaby.

It had happened four years before. The Husabys were proud of their national record for sales of International Farmall tractors. They had hired an artist to paint the road-runner on the window. It was their symbol of fast service and cunning quickness to assure their present and future customers of quick, creative service for the farm equipment purchased.

Mrs. Husaby, in particular, was proud of the outcome. After all, it had been her idea. Mr. Husaby had been more direct.

He had argued, "Why not just say what we mean and have him paint 'Quick, dependable service'?"

But he had lost to his more persuasive partner, who had argued that a "picture is worth a thousand words" and that "people's attention is more likely to be captured by a flashy picture than by just plain stuffy words."

The roadrunner was Eleanor Husaby's pride and joy!

The afternoon after the painting was finished, Boy and his friend Gordon had walked by the Husaby Garage. They had tested the painting and found that if they ran their fingers along the glass, the chalky paint would erase and they could make their own creative marks on the profile of the roadrunner. Later that evening they had come back to further pursue their creative artistic endeavors. The roadrunner, indeed, was taking on a different character when all of a sudden there was a heavy hand laid on each of their shoulders. When they slowly turned, sweat forming on their foreheads, they were looking directly into the unsmiling face of George, the local constable and lifelong friend and classmate of Jake Husaby.

He didn't use words like "creative" and "artistic" to describe what the boys had done; he used words like "vandalism" and "destructive." He then informed them that he would tell Boy's mother and Gordon's father, who was the superintendent of the local schools.

"Oh, God," Boy silently prayed. He did not want his mother to hear of this. He feared the wooden spoon and her ensuing "heart attacks" more than the wrath of God or anything else that he could think of. So, he pleaded with George not to tell his mother. He asked if he couldn't please talk to Mr. and Mrs. Husaby.

Constable George thought a moment and said, "All right." George piled them into the police car and took them to the Husaby mansion, as it was called by the locals.

George told Jake and Eleanor what the boys had done. They stood, like criminals, on the bear rug, beneath the mounted deer head, staring into the two stone faces of the Husabys.

Boy thought, "Maybe this wasn't such a good idea after all."

Eleanor spoke first. "I am ashamed of you! Do you have any idea how horribly bad you have been? You are very nasty boys." The shaming went on and on. She said some more, but Boy could not remember what it was. Gordon stood staring at his feet, probably counting his toes to be sure all ten were there.

Eventually, Mr. Husaby intervened. He asked Boy and Gordon, "What are you going to do? What do you think would be fair? How are you going to pay us back? That painting cost a lot of money. What do you think your punishment should be?"

Gordon said nothing, but he looked like he wanted to die, or turn invisible, or at least run.

Boy finally spoke. "Well . . . sir," he paused and then continued, "maybe we could sweep the floors and wash the windows that aren't painted—sometime—after school. Until you think we have done enough. Until you think we've paid you what you need."

Mr. Husaby looked at the ten-year-old. He looked a long time, at least a minute or two, or an eternity. Then he said, "Not bad. I will expect you here tomorrow, right after school."

Eleanor Husaby started to say something more. She was still angry. But Jake held up his hand in a gesture of silence.

She opened her mouth and then closed it, realizing the boys had gotten her point.

The summer after Boy had turned thirteen, when he was almost fourteen, he had come back to Mr. Husaby and asked if he had another job. Mr. Husaby said he was looking for a stock boy but had a couple of other older boys whom he was going to talk to. Two days later he called the shoe store and asked Sophia if Boy was there. He had a job for him

That afternoon, when Boy came to the garage, Jake Husaby seemed to absently survey Boy. "Hmmm," he said. "We have these old front steel tractor wheels that need to get stored in the attic. They're pretty heavy. You think you're strong enough to get them up there?"

"Sure," Boy answered, with more confidence than he felt. Boy was large for his age and trying to get stronger. He had, after all, managed all right with Harry Bell's race horses. He knew how to take responsibility. He had shown that over and over at the shoe store. Phair had complimented him often when they hunted and fished, and Phair was a perfectionist. Boy wanted to forget the harvest experience of last year. He had worked ever since he was seven, and he was kind of proud of that.

"Sure, I can get them up there," he said, only now with more, perhaps ill-founded, confidence of a child fantasizing he was a 'manm. The first wheel had almost proven that he was over his head. He hadn't been all that sure he would get it up the steps, but he did.

Now his reverie was broken and his breathing returned to normal. He continued to struggle up the steps with the second wheel. By day's end his body ached in every joint and muscle, but he had five wheels safely deposited in the attic. He smiled through the sweat and grime streaked across his face as he stopped and looked at his accomplishment before heading down the steps.

"Coming back tomorrow?" Jake Husaby's voice greeted him as he headed for the door.

"Sure," Boy responded. "I'll be here at seven."

"Haven't had enough yet, huh?" Jake's resonant deep voice seemed to chide.

"I'll be here at seven, after I've cleaned Mom's store," Boy said as he disappeared out the door. True to his word, at seven the next morning he was back again. There were more steel wheels to maneuver up the steps to the resting place they would have till the garage burned to the ground fifteen years later.

Mr. Husaby had been watching him, restraining the pleasure from his face. But he had not missed the thoughtful strategy Boy had developed to ease the task of moving the wheels up the 24 steps.

Late in the day, Jake Husaby came to Boy and said, "Tomorrow I want you here early. You'll learn a new job. Ray will teach you how to do inventory in the parts supply department. We'll get someone else to move the wheels."

"Didn't I . . . I do it right?" Boy stammered.

"No. No. You did just fine. I'm promoting you, for God's sake," Husaby retorted. "Jesus! I thought you'd know that!"

Boy looked down, embarrassed, but the warmth in his chest radiated throughout his entire body.

At first the new inventory job was interesting. He learned a lot about the bolts and nuts and doodads it took to keep a tractor or a thresher running. But soon it became routine and then it got downright boring. One afternoon in the boredom of the back stacks of bolts and nuts, the image and picture of her returned—the young woman from the tent. Warmth radiated from his genitals; the familiar swelling happened and there was the pleasing pressure in his crotch against his jeans.

"How you doin'? Hope you're not too bored," boomed Mr. Husaby in his deep, rich voice.

"So this is where he's been keeping you," followed the lilting voice of Eleanor Husaby.

Boy's face turned beet red. He hoped they couldn't read his mind. God, he hoped they couldn't. How did these adults always find him and manage to surprise him? When you get older it must be part of nature to learn how to sneak up on kids. Maybe like growing a beard or breasts, he thought.

"You look real hot, all red and all," Jack commented. "You got a fever?"

"Maybe you ought to take a break and get some fresh air," Eleanor chimed in.

"No, I'll be OK" Boy stammered.

"How about some water anyway," Mrs. Husaby continued.

"I have a better idea," said Mr. Husaby. "Joe, you know my runner, is sick today, and we have to get Anderson's tractor. It's been down for two days already. Think you can handle the job?"

Boy's eyes got large when he realized what Jake Husaby was suggesting. He was pretty sure that Mr. Husaby knew that he had been driving Aunt Inga's Essex and then the Oldsmobile for four years now. He was pretty sure everybody in town knew, including the constable, but nobody would say anything if he didn't hit anybody or anything. And he hadn't—yet.

Boy answered in a voice tinged with fear and so soft it was hardly audible. "Sure, Mr. Husaby, I can do it."

"What?"

"Yeah, I'll get the tractor! I'll get right on it!" Boy's voice sounded loud and strong.

It took only a heartbeat or two to get behind the steering wheel of Husaby's 1936 two-ton, flatbed International Harvester truck. He turned the key, pushed the starter to the floor, and the engine roared. There was a grinding of metal on metal as he forced the gearshift into reverse. He slowly, carefully backed away from the garage under the watchful, critical eye of Eleanor. Then he shifted into forward and headed out of town; five miles south lay the Anderson farm.

As he bounced along the dusty back roads heading for the Anderson's, Boy's mind wandered back to the image of her, picking up where he'd left off before the Husabys walked in. He saw her in all her naked glory. He let his daydream wander for a moment, and then he got scared when the lumbering truck kicked gravel on the shoulder of the road. It reminded him to pay attention before he hit the ditch.

"Back to reality," he began to ponder. He couldn't figure out how all this fit together, how the newfound strength of his body fit with the stirrings in his loins. And how did that fit with the trust the Husabys showed him? And how did that fit with the shame he felt, and how did that fit with the pleasure and fun and dreams of her? And how did that fit with responsibility and work and respect, and how did that fit with friends and bosses and relatives and on and on. It felt like his brain was bumping as hard as the truck.

Self-doubt mingled with self-consciousness and mingled with his self-confidence, mingled with . . . and now he just passed the drive to the Anderson farm and he knew they had seen him. As he turned and headed back to the tree-lined drive leading past the fields into the farmstead, he knew that all these questions and all the ways that they related had something to do with being a man, with becoming a man. But what? Somehow, it had something to do with using one's body for pleasure and work and caring and . . . and . . . loving. Somehow it had something to do with learning to respect someone else and to live up to your word. Somehow it had something to do with trust and fairness and doing a good job. Somehow it had to do with that whole, funny, crazy mix of things. Somehow it had to do with learning to overcome loneliness and to move through life in a way that was . . . in a way that was something . . . he just didn't know what. What were the expectations, anyway?

"Damn that chicken!"

"Hey, watch out for my chickens," Mrs. Anderson's voice rang out.

Damn! He'd almost hit her scrawny chicken and almost hit the chicken house too.

"Damn! Damn! Damn!" he muttered to himself.

"You have to watch where you're going," Aletta Anderson scolded.

His calm was returning. "Yes, M'am," Boy responded. "I'm here to get your tractor."

When the tractor was secured to the bed of the truck, he followed the back roads back to the garage. There was a pride in his chest as he looked in the mirror and saw the tractor. Today he was a man. He sensed it in his heart. But what was a man? He still didn't know. He only knew that who he was yesterday, and a week ago, and the month before, he would never be again. Boyhood was gone.

SWAN

Turning off of State Highway 55, he began his descent into the valley following the Soo Hill Trail. Once past the Glenwood city limits, he headed directly for Inga's Ladies' Ready-To-Wear Store on Main Street. His 1939 Willys van was loaded with trunks of fine fur coats that he would display for Inga in the hope that she would buy some on consignment to sell to her more wealthy customers in this west central Minnesota town. The war was now over and wealth would start to come back again. His business should certainly start to pick up. Boy watched from the door at the rear of Sophia's adjoining shoe store as the trunks were unloaded onto the dolly, then opened, with the coats hung on racks to best display their sheen and beauty.

Sophia finished with her customer, left the shoes in boxes for Boy to reassemble and put away, and went to warmly greet and welcome S.P. Glemaker. "I had no idea you had a sales trip planned up here for this fall," Sophia said.

Inga interrupted, "He just called this morning and said he would be going on a selling trip and would be here late this afternoon and so here he is."

Sophia wondered, "How long will you stay and where else are you going on your trip?"

Finally S.P. responded, still smiling broadly and looking from Sophia to Inga and back to Sophia. "I'll be here for a few days; this is a slow time of the year at the store. People just don't want to believe winter is coming. So I thought I would come and see if there was anything I could interest Inga in from my fall line of coats. I just needed to get out of St. Paul for a while, what with Alma's illness and death and all." He paused. "This is the only stop I'll make on this trip."

Memories flooded back for Sophia as they always did whenever she saw S.P. again, even if it had been years since the time before. S.P. Glemaker was the kindest, most generous employer she had ever had. She had gone to St. Paul right after she had returned from homesteading in Montana. Her health had returned and she wanted to get on with her life. She had gone to his fur store looking for work, and he had hired her as a sales person.

Domestic things and men really didn't interest her much. She really didn't want to have children, at least not then. She had tried the social service work at the orphanage and failed. She had tried the helping professions, but they seemed more abusive than helping—people trying to control kids and other people and punishing them if they didn't behave. Even though she had a degree in social service, work in the field had broken her heart and health once, and she didn't want that to happen again. "Maybe I was just too soft and emphatic," she wondered. She doubted that. She liked to make hard decisions and could be a firm, intelligent and informed person regardless of what the business was. She had tested this as she homesteaded in the Missouri River bottoms in Montana.

She liked to sell new ideas, and she was good at it. She could both see and sense the things to say and to do that would bring others to her point of view. She had the pleasing personality to open hearts and to make it happen. But what she felt about the social service field was the same she felt about nursing, which she had also studied for a short time at the La Crosse Lutheran Hospital; it was too messy. She felt there was something better to do than empty bed pans and deal with other people's shit.

Sophia was drawn to the business world like metal to a magnet. It was 1918 when she had returned to Minnesota from Montana. On her return she had gone to stay with her friends, Iris and Frank Horn, in Minneapolis. Frank Horn was a powerful lawyer and bank officer for the First National Bank, and Iris loved the role of socialite that his position afforded her. Iris and Frank had been childhood sweethearts and had come up from impoverished backgrounds together and much preferred affluence.

As they talked that first evening of Sophia's return, Iris had gone on and on about this lovely fur coat she had bought from this fine gentleman in St. Paul. This was the third coat she had bought from him. Frank and Sophia spent the whole evening listening to Irene's recitations about what she had learned from "the fur man" as she waited for her coat to be fitted and then altered in the factory above the sales room on Sixth Street in St. Paul.

The proprietor of the store was named Swan Pearson Glemaker. He and his older brother, John, had come from Sweden. John had come first. He had answered an ad in the paper in the Glemakra Valley where they lived. It said there were endless opportunities for a prosperous life in Minnesota in the new world. "Become an entrepreneur in the fruit and vegetable business, selling to the large market of St. Paul," the ad said.

John had immediately booked passage on the ship designated in the ad. The ship would take him to New York, and then he would travel by rail to St. Paul. The night before John left, he and Swan had talked late into the night about how Swan should join him when he had made all of this wealth. John promised he would send money back for Swan to come over on the next ship leaving Sweden. The excitement that night ran like a high tide between them.

A few days after John's ship had sailed, Swan decided he wouldn't or couldn't wait any longer. He would take his savings and book his own passage. He took all the money he had saved. He had told Iris that he was sure he would find John when he got to Minnesota, wherever that was. Minnesota couldn't be that big, and besides, he would sell himself to the same employer that John had. The ad had said that for there to be a reduced fare, they would have to work for this man for a year. He would provide board and room. It shouldn't be too hard. Swan's excitement stayed as high as eagles can fly. The year working in the vegetable fields would give him time to save some money and to learn English.

This was how Swan, like John and countless others, entered the slave labor market. When Swan got to Minnesota and to a farm near Lindstrom in Chisago County, he found that the room provided was in the barn. The board consisted of porridge, side pork, and occasionally bread. Cheap wine was available or else you could drink water. The days would begin at five and end at dusk.

Once a week they would load the produce they had harvested onto a solid-tired truck and take it to the Farmers Market in lower town St. Paul. These days would begin at two in order to be at the market by five. The produce market was right next to the raw fur market where the bundled pelts of beaver, seal, rabbit, muskrat, otter, mink and marten were brought by the trappers to be sold to the coat, hat and mitten manufacturers in St. Paul. The majority of the pelts sold remained in St. Paul since it was a center for the fur industry.

John and Swan struck up an acquaintance with the buyers and the managers of the fur companies located nearby. They got to know a man from the Harris Coat Company, which was the largest manufacturer of fine fur coats. Soon they were offered jobs, if they could leave the employ of the farmer for whom they worked

Again, excitement ran high. They went to talk to the farmer who employed them and were informed when they asked to quit, that not only could they not leave, but they could not leave at the end of the year, either. Obviously they had not read the fine print that said that they had agreed to pay $5 a week for room and board, while their wage was $2 per week for their labor. They would need to continue working for him while trying to work off their debt, even though it was getting larger by the week.

All the fine print had been in English. It had also said that they would pay 20 percent interest on the money they owed for the ship passage when they came from Sweden. The farmer informed them, "You could, of course, find somewhere else to live if you can, but most folks around here would think you'd be trespassing or a runaway." He added, "Also, most people around here charge $7 per week for board and room." He laughed and walked away.

At first John and Swan felt devastated. They were, in fact, slaves, and would never be free. At night, when they were alone, they began whispering to one another. They devised a plan of how they would run away the next time they rode the truck that took the produce to market.

At four that market day morning, when the truck rumbled around the corner coming off of Jackson Street and Wacouta heading for the market, John and Swan silently stepped over the other sleeping workers and past the dozing crew master. They jumped off the end of the truck and disappeared into the shadows to wait until the Harris Coat Company opened for the day.

True to his word, the manager at Harris Coat gave them jobs. Both young men proved themselves to be industrious, creative artists in the design and manufacture of fine fur coats. Within a year, John was promoted to the cutting table and Swan to the design room. John and Swan took a new last name as a kind of protection if the farmer were to come looking for them. They were now known as the Glemaker boys, having taken the name of the valley where they lived in Sweden. John continued to use his first name because it was common, but Swan feared that his name would soon be recognized, so he resorted to using his initials. He had kept as his middle name the family name of Pearson, and now he introduced himself as S.P.

"S.P. Glemaker here, may I help you?"

S.P. was only twenty-one when he came to Lindstrom. At twenty-two he was one of the youngest people working in the design department of the Harris Coat and Garment Company. The supervisor liked S.P. and was quick to support him and to sing his praises to the company's owner. As a result, the young man quickly developed trust and admiration for the man he worked beneath. Even as he was naive and inexperienced, S.P. was also innately and intuitively creative. He was blessed with the eye of the artist, both for the beautiful and the practical.

It only mildly surprised his supervisor when, in quick succession, S.P. told him of a prototype of a mitten and a coat he had designed. He explained he had made them in the late evening hours after the factory had closed. The mittens had been cut and sewn so that the seal fur was to the inside, providing warmth for the wearer's hand. The stitching was rolled and waterproofed and the exposed skin side had been rubbed with mink fat.The supervisor was ecstatic. In this north country, where the unforgiving cold was enhanced by long nights and short days and where the sun, if it got up at all, was sleepy and of little use in stoking the fires to generate the energy for survival, the seal fur mittens would be very marketable. It was the "season of cracking ice" as the Indians called it. Fingers froze as fast as the eye could blink.

S.P.'s mittens were like a gift from the gods.

The supervisor knew how profitable these mittens could be. He pondered how he could wrest the prototype from S.P. He wanted to present it to the company owner as his own.

The same day as he thought about this, S.P. produced another package. This one was larger and contained a full-length coat. The coat looked like all the other coats that the Harris Company produced. S.P. deliberately opened the coat and laid it on the table. Then he proceeded to unbutton the little buttons all along the sides until he could whip out the lining made of northern rabbit skin. He had designed a coat for all seasons. A coat with a removable lining!

The supervisor let out a slow whistle. Now he was unable to contain his excitement and enthusiasm. He tucked the mittens and the coat under one arm and grabbed S.P. with his other hand and headed for Mr. Harris's office. He babbled all the way to the top floor about how valuable these inventions were and how much money they would make and how he would help S.P. get the patents for them. He instructed S.P. that he would go in first and talk to Mr. Harris and convince him of the brilliance of these innovative designs.

Then he, personally, would help get all the papers for the patents drawn up. S.P. should wait in the outer office.

Two hours later, Mr. Harris and the supervisor came out. They were joking and smiling. They didn't stop to say anything to S.P., who wondered why Mr. Harris never even recognized him, and why the supervisor didn't introduce him, and why he had motioned to him to remain silent and stay seated.

Mr. Harris shook hands with the supervisor and left.

The supervisor came over to S.P. and showed him the official looking papers that started with the words "U. S. Patent." When S.P. questioned why they were signed only by the supervisor and Mr. Harris—and if he shouldn't also sign them–the manager said it wasn't necessary, it was only a formality.

"You will be duly rewarded, S.P.," the supervisor told him. But he never was. The patents had been stolen.

The patent came out with the supervisor's name. Exclusive rights of manufacture had been given to the Harris Company for the next twenty-five years. The night that all this became public, John and S.P. and their half-sister, Hilma, newly arrived from Sweden, sat up half the night and talked. John and S.P. expressed their anger and hurt. Now they had been taken twice. It was time to quit trusting and taking men at their word.

John and S.P. had saved some money in the three years they had worked for Harris. Hilma had brought a fairly substantial bankroll with her from Sweden.

By dawn's light it was decided that they would start their own coat manufacturing and sales company. They would design and make fine coats for those with an eye for the beautiful. The white bear of Sweden would be the protector and symbol of the Glemaker Fur Company. The company that would last for the next fifty-two years was born that night. S.P. and John never darkened the door of The Harris Coat Company again.

The first fur store and coat factory was small. There was a small sales room on the second floor and two rooms on the third floor. One of the rooms was used for designing and cutting the furs to make the coats. The other room was for sewing. The store was located in Lowertown, not far from the Harris Company. In spite of its obscure location, the carriage trade found Glemaker.

S.P. and John were good at sales and promotion. They were low key, soft spoken and imbued with honesty and integrity. Their customers felt like a part of the creative team. Their business prospered and their customers became their friends.

Edith, newly arrived from Sweden, was hired to keep the books. John or S.P. often met the Swedish immigrant boys and girls, men and women at the train station before they were hustled off to the fruit and vegetable farms. They were hired to cut and sew and sweep up remnants. Soon the upstairs factory quarters were too small. They moved the operation to 14 West Sixth Street. Here they leased a building with a spacious sales floor on street level. Edith's domain was the business office on the Mezzanine. There was summer storage in the basement and a packaging room and loading dock just behind the sales area. The factory was on the second floor, with separate areas for design and cutting and sewing and fitting.

This complex, with its elegant display windows, was right next door to the Garrick Opera House on St. Peter Street, where the fur store was located in 1918 when Sophia came to town looking for work and was introduced to S.P. by Iris Horn.

By this time S.P. was married and had three small children, Aida, Paul and Lois. His children were important to him, as were his vows. He was a pillar of the Swedish Covenant Church. His ethics were impeccable. He did not want to be like those who had enslaved him and stolen from him.

His marriage, however, was not a happy one and loneliness often overwhelmed him, and he lived on the edge of depression. He would immerse himself in work and in pleasing his customers. His life as an artist, a salesman, and a business man brought him much pleasure and satisfaction, but the gulf between his private life and his business life was great.

When Sophia walked in the door that day, he knew in an instant, with an artist's intuition, that he loved her. He knew it from that very first moment. He would tell her thirty years later.

When Iris introduced Sophia, S.P. didn't let on what he was feeling, even though the motion of his emotion was rumbling in his head like an earthquake. Instead, he listened to her stories about the orphanage and the time in Montana and how she wanted a job. He stayed focused and was taken by her competence as well as her beauty. In the end, he offered to teach her how to be a businesswoman.

She was hired and began to learn the special art of customer satisfaction. These skills she would practice the rest of her life. The next two years were packed with learning, both about business and about life. As her mentor, S.P. taught her not only about sales, but merchandising and market analysis and how to know your customers and finances and all the rest. As they worked together she came to know he liked her, but never once did he let on that he was in love with her. His pious Christian belief had taught him how to suffer in stoic silence.

Many years later, S.P. told Boy one night as they talked in S.P.'s hospital room just two weeks before he died, how much he loved Boy's mother and how he wished Boy was his real son.

In the years Sophia worked for S.P., Sophia lived with austere Aunt Jen Houseman on Summit Avenue. Here she learned all the tactics of grace and elegance of the wealthy. She was schooled under the watchful and angry eye of her mother's older sister, who had married an architect, one of several brothers from a wealthy Irish family. Aunt Jen's husband had died at forty-four and left her a millionaire. She chose to live alone with power and wealth, demanding subservience from stranger, friend, and family alike.

Here Sophia acquired a regal status that modified and broadened her abilities and outlook so that she was comfortably able to relate, with equal grace, to the prince or pauper she met in daily life. S.P. liked and admired Sophia's ability to understand and accept people from all walks of life. The same general nature was his, and both of them had found it born in the cauldron of oppression and depression.

After two years, Sophia left Glemaker Furs in St. Paul and went to Glenwood to live with Josephine on the shores of Lake Minnewaska. They opened a ladies' ready-to-wear store together. There she could apply all that she had learned from S.P. Sophia and Josephine had a solid and loving relationship both in work and in personal life. Sophia, however, was restless. She craved the woman to man conversations she had learned to enjoy with S.P.

When Lou "of the Grey Eagle Mossmans" came to visit on his stops between his sales trips to the wheat fields of

Idaho, Alberta, and North Dakota where he sold International Harvester farm equipment, Sophia was delighted. She looked forward to his visits and their conversations. Lou loved to dance and joke with Josephine, but his poetic heart craved spending as many hours talking to Sophia as he could.

S.P. learned of Sophia's engagement to Lou from Hilma, who had kept in touch with her. After a ten year engagement, Lou and Sophia married. Hilma helped plan the wedding. S.P. would not attend. Even his Swedish stoicism could not mask the pain and loss he felt.

Now ten years had passed since Lou had died and thirty years since Sophia had worked for him. S.P.'s oldest daughter, Aida, had died of lung disease. He had thought he couldn't recover from that. His wife, Alma, had berated him for his softness of heart and his tears. When she became ill, her anger had become controlling, like a storm. She took her vengeance out on S.P. Secretly, he wished her dead. He knew Sophia was a widow; he never lost touch with all of the places her life had taken her.

Then Alma died.The six-month wait–for reasons of propriety–before he made his trip to Glenwood and Sophia's presence seemed like an eternity. Now, as he stood watching Sophia and talking to Inga, he thought, "Perhaps there is a real God of grace at that."

The day S.P. arrived, he suggested that he take Sophia and Jeanne and Boy to the high school football game that was being played on the local field. Sophia protested. They would need to eat first. There wouldn't be time after she balanced the books and closed the store. S.P. must be tired from his trip.

Jeanne listened to her mother ramble on. She was preoccupied with the gifts that S.P. had brought for her and Boy.

Now he was inviting them all to go to a football game. She hoped her mother wouldn't skew it. Usually no one asked her to go to the games except Jeanie Calahan. She had never been to a game with a dad type, who really seemed to like her, and not just because he wanted to tease her or pinch her developing body, like Uncle Will or Uncle Gil when they were drunk.

"Can't we go? Please?" Jeanne pleaded.

Boy said nothing. He didn't know who this man was and why he wanted to be with his mother and his sister. He was fourteen years old and they had gotten along just fine for ten years without some gray-haired do-gooder coming around. Besides, nobody had ever acted like this around his mom.

Boy wondered why his mom had let this man go on about how much he liked being there. He had never seen anybody bring her gifts before when it wasn't her birthday or Christmas. Nor had anybody ever shown up with neat stuff for him or Jeanne either. He felt again the smooth rosewood handle of the jackknife in his pocket.

Aunt Elizabeth, Sophia's youngest sister and business partner, interrupted his thoughts. "Sophia, why don't you go? I'll close the store and bring the books and money pouch to your house this evening, or else I can have it here in the morning when you open up."

S.P. was quick to add, "I already talked to Hannah Mathre over at the Boston Cafe and she will serve us early. I ordered special steaks for all of us."

Sophia shrugged, "Oh all right, I guess you've got me surrounded. Football it is."

At the game, they all sat together in the bleachers on the east side of the field. It had taken them a while to get there. After S.P. had parked Sophia's Buick, barely missing both the car in front and the one behind, Sophia had gotten out and introduced S.P. to a couple of teachers who were friends and customers, Miss Olson and Miss Johnsrude. Boy tried to hide. He had a history with both of them. Besides, he was angry and wanted more time to think and plot against this man. He knew he could drive better than this old Romeo who could hardly park the car. After all, he had been driving since he was nine and hadn't hit anything yet!

When they got to their seats, S.P. had bought pop and candy for everyone.He tried to talk to Boy, but Boy would have none of it. Only "Yes sir," "No sir," "I don't know," "I guess so," were his responses.

S.P. soon turned his attention to Jeanne. She chatted on and on about this player and that player and this cheerleader and that cheerleader.

Boy said nothing, but thought, "What is she trying to do? Besides, what does she know about the players, anyway? The only one she recognizes is Donny Granton and that's because she would like to go out with him." He mused, "But he won't ask her, even though he's tall enough for her."

After awhile, Boy wandered off; he didn't want to be a part of this anymore. Besides, the game was boring. Towards the end of the game he came back, but then he couldn't find his mother or Mr. Glemaker or Jeanne. They had all disappeared.

Later he found Jeanne talking to Jeanie K. and Sally. Jeanne told him that S.P. and Sophia had gone to the car shortly after half time. The boy started for the car. When he got there, S.P. and Sophia were sitting close together in the front seat. They were talking and laughing. Boy opened the door and got in the back seat. This was a place he was not accustomed to and he didn't like it. He always sat in the front seat, next to his mom. S.P. and Sophia, sensing his anger and discomfort, moved apart.

"Who won the game?" S.P. asked.

"I don't know," Boy replied.

"Did you have fun?" queried S.P.

"I suppose," Boy muttered.

"When Jeanne comes, do you want to go to Setter's Drug and get an ice cream soda?" S.P. asked.

Boy shrugged. He thought, "Mom must of told him how much I liked malts and sodas, or else why would he bring it up?"

When Jeanne got back, they went to the drug store. Jeanne and Sophia and S.P. laughed and talked. Boy said nothing. S.P. said goodnight and hugged Sophia close and long when they dropped him off at the Minton Hotel. S.P. patted Jeanne on the cheek. Boy huddled in the corner of the back seat.

"See you tomorrow," S.P. called. Boy said nothing but seethed inside.

Saturday, Boy was up early before the others got up. He went to the barn and fed Nancy, the horse Sophia had gotten him in partial payment for Lou's land that she had sold. When he was angry at his mother he called it his Dad's land, not hers.

So now she was getting rid of Boy as well. He wondered what she would take in partial payment for him. Nancy nuzzled his hand and nibbled at his cheek. He felt the softness of her muzzle and the tears began to trickle from his eyes. He kicked the stall, screamed, and cursed. Nancy jumped, her ears flattened, her haunches quivering. Boy threw his arms around her and talked to her in a gentle tone. He told her about the game last night and how alone he felt. She settled down and playfully pushed him with her nose. He got the point and gave her oats and headed for the store to clean it for the long day's work.

Sophia showed up to work, smiling and happy. She told Elizabeth and Caroline all about the night before and how much fun she had. When Boy returned from the back room, he overheard Sophia whispering to Elizabeth about how she thought Boy had been upset because she had given S.P. so much attention.

Elizabeth was saying, "Oh he'll get over it, just give him a little time. You go on and have some fun, you deserve it."

Boy thought, "No, she doesn't. She has treated me like a man in all respects and now she is getting rid of me."

Throughout the day S.P. kept showing up in the shoe store whenever he had a break from selling coats. He always tried to talk to Boy as well as Sophia, even though Boy did nothing to make the conversation easy. On one of the breaks he brought some candy and gave Boy money for a movie that night since the store would be open late. He might just as well go out and have some fun.

Boy said "thanks" and took the money and candy. That night after the movie, Boy walked the block and a half back to the shoe store, expecting to find Sophia closing the store and balancing the books. He could get a ride home and all would be back to normal.

When he opened the door, Caroline was just closing the books.

"Where is my mom?" Boy asked.

"She left with Mr. Glemaker about two hours ago," Caroline answered. "Business was slow tonight so they went out to eat, I guess," Caroline continued.

Boy said nothing, but turned and left. The mile walk home was long and lonely.

S.P. made the one hundred and fifty mile trip from St. Paul to Glenwood five times in the next six weeks. He got only three traffic tickets, which was good for him, Aunt Inga revealed. He got one for not stopping at a stop sign, one for speeding, and one for driving on the wrong side of the road. Friday afternoons at the shoe store, Sophia became more fidgety as the day got later.

Boy spent more time with Jeanne in the back room talking and playing. He would get scolded for not getting the shoes restocked more quickly or for keeping the customers waiting while he found a particular size or style. Usually Sophia was patient with him and taught him well how to measure feet properly and how to politely cater to the whims and worries of fussy customers, fearful that a bad fitting would leave their smelly feet deformed. But, not on Friday afternoons, when S.P. was haunting the highways on his way to Glenwood to court the widow Sophia. You could box the tension with the shoes.

It seemed the whole store, including Caroline, Inga and Elizabeth, not to mention Sophia, breathed a collective sigh of relief when S.P.'s Graham Paige arrived undented and under its own power.

Often Boy would try to disappear before the grand arrival. He would head for the fairgrounds and the horse barns. There he would find Harry Bell. While grooming Harry's pacer, "Friend Joe," he would tell Harry how he wished his mom wouldn't see S.P.

Harry always listened and then would say, "Well, you know, she may be lonesome. It's been a long time since your dad died and us older folks sometimes get lonely; you'll know when you get older." Harry always looked sad at those times. Once Boy saw a tear roll down his check. Harry quickly looked away and pretended to cough. But Boy thought he was probably remembering his daughter who had died, killed by a drunk who had missed a curve coming home from the prom.

The town folks had come to Harry's support. They commiserated with him, "Poor Harry! To lose her in the prime of life. She was the most beautiful girl around." Harry's life had never been the same since. But Harry knew of pain, and Boy knew he knew of loss and love. He recalled how he had first met Harry, and Harry had become first his teacher, and then his friend.

When Boy was eleven years old, Harry Bell was sixty-three. Harry had two race horses that he stabled at the Pope County Fairgrounds. Boy had a little Morgan horse, a mare, also stabled there. He had acquired the little Morgan because his mother had to sell the land at Little Birch Lake in order to help support Boy and Jeanne and herself through the lean years of the Great Depression. The man who bought the land couldn't come up with all the cash, so he gave the Morgan horse in partial payment. Now Boy needed a mentor to help him learn about horses and their training.

When Boy first came to the barn at the fairgrounds and met Harry, he looked sad. Boy was shy and a bit scared as he stood by the box stall where his two-year-old Morgan mare munched some oats and hay. Harry came over to where he stood.

"Fine horse you got, my boy. But maybe you should feed her oats or hay at a time, but not together, so she won't founder." The first lessons had begun.

Harry had been a wealthy and powerful man at one time. He had investments and property and was a good and shrewd businessman, or so they said. He and his wife, whom he cherished, had one daughter. As their daughter had grown to young womanhood, she was thought by all standards to be of exceptional beauty and talent.

But now Harry was down on his luck. First the stock market had crashed, and all of Harry's investments were wiped out. Then his wife was taken seriously ill. There was a question whether she would live or die. She did recover but completely lost her hearing. So now she stayed within their little flat and Harry was her only contact with the outside world.

One night, two years before the Morgan mare and Boy came to the barn, Harry's daughter, then nineteen, had gone to the prom. Her date got drunk, rolled the car, and she was killed.

Now Harry drove a cab to make ends meet. He retreated to the private world of the barns where he kept his horses. Friend Joe and The G Patch, grandson of the great pacer and trotter Dan Patch, were the recipients of all of Harry's tears and love.

He was a man looking for a son to love and teach. Boy was looking for a teacher and a dad to care. In the months and years that followed, Harry helped Boy with the Morgan mare, and also taught him how to fit a harness, and then how to sit a harness racing sulky and how to drive a race. Behind Harry's trotter, The G Patch, Boy would become the youngest driver on the racing circuit.

However, first Boy had to learn some things about horses and animals in general, and some basic life lessons. Harry had agreed to train and work with a one-year-old stallion horse, a spirited animal who knew what he wanted. Soon after the stallion came to live at the barn, Harry asked Boy to put a halter on him and teach him to lead. Boy jumped at the chance. He was eager to impress his newfound friend and teacher.

It had rained the night before, so the barnyard was muddy, except for where the rocks protruded. First Boy had to get the halter on the stallion. This, he thought, was his chance to show the stallion who was boss. He grabbed him roughly by the ear and pulled the halter over his head. The stallion stamped his feet as Boy tried to get it buckled. The stallion also managed to stomp Boy's toe. In his pain, Boy jerked the lead rope with a vengeance. Boy cursed and struck the young horse in the face. Boy was going to show him who was in charge.

Boy would break him to the halter and the rope. The stallion had other ideas. He took off across the pasture. Boy hung on to the rope for dear life. He simply would not look bad in Harry's eyes. Within five feet Boy lost his balance, but still the rope remained firmly in his grasp. The young horse was running with Boy dragging behind. He bumped and bounced across the pasture, through the puddles, across the rocks and over the horse droppings. Shit took on a new meaning in his mind and life that day! Finally the stallion stopped, snorting and pawing at the ground. Boy stood up, muddy, dirty, bleeding, battered and bruised. He went up to the stallion and looked him in the face.

Tears streaming down his face, Boy screamed some profanity and whacked him across his nose with the knotted end of the lead rope. This horse would learn who was boss. Boy was going to break him! Again, the stallion would have none of it. They took off once more, back across the pasture. Once again, Boy plowed the muddy puddles with his nose and scraped and cut what little skin was yet unbruised.

This time when the stallion stopped, Harry, who had been watching the whole charade, came up to where Boy stood with tears rolling down his muddy, bloody, bruised cheeks.

Harry's gentle voice broke through Boy's embarrassment and pain.

"Son, just take a shorter hold on the rope and talk real quiet in his ear while you lead him in a circle. Sometimes, I'll scratch the ear while I do this. That way you have control and are in charge, and he'll settle down and know you like him. You see, you never break a horse . . . or anything in life, I guess. You get so much further if you gentle horses. If you walk and talk quiet and easy, things tend to go a whole lot better." Harry walked back into the barn to tend Friend Joe, his pacing horse.

On another day Boy was exercising Dandy Dan, a burned out, standard breed racer that belonged to Inga Marvin, who also stabled her horses at the track barns. As he was getting ready to mount, Harry walked over to him and said in his raspy, low voice:

"You know, son, this horse is used to racing, so if you were to turn him to go counterclockwise around the track, he'd think you were taking him out to race. You wouldn't be able to control him 'cause he's a rubber neck. You know what that means?"

"No, sir," Boy replied.

"Well, it means that when you rein him in to slow or stop him, he pays no attention, but will only lay his head back in your lap and keep on going at full tilt." Harry paused to let that sink in and to be sure he had Boy's attention. "When that happens, what you do is reach down and grab his upper lip real tight and give it a real good twist." Harry took hold of Dandy's upper lip to demonstrate what he meant, but he didn't twist. Even so, Dandy came to full attention.

Harry chuckled. "See, he's had that done before. It makes him pay attention and know who's boss." Harry watched as Boy rode off and up to the track. He turned clockwise. After four times around the half-mile oval track at a brisk canter, Boy decided to rein him in and head for the barn. Dandy had other ideas. When Boy pulled back on the reins, Dandy laid his head back and went into overdrive. Even at a full gallop Boy was able to hold the reins in with his left hand and reach to grab the horse's upper lip and give it a mighty twist, just as Harry had instructed. Dandy Dan immediately got the message and the rest of the trip back to the barn was, "I get it—you're the boss."

Harry had been watching the whole thing. When Boy and horse got back to the barn, he smiled and gave a slight nod of his head toward Boy, chuckled and said, "See, it works, doesn't it?"

"Yes, sir," boy mumbled as he slid from the saddle to the ground.

Now coming back from his musings, Boy again turned his attention to Friend Joe. When Friend Joe was groomed and exercised and Boy had bedded Nancy, the little Morgan mare, he headed for home.

The kitchen was warm and the lights were bright. Sophia was cooking and singing softly to herself. Jeanne and S.P. were playing Scrabble in the living room. They were laughing. Boy headed for the basement where he could beat the punching bag. After awhile, S.P. came down.

"I have something for you," S.P. said.

"What?" Boy snapped back.

"It's out in the trunk of my car. Wanna help me get it?" S.P. asked.

Boy didn't reply, but silently followed S.P. out the back door. From the trunk of the Graham Paige, S.P. produced a brand-new Army saddle.

"Here. Do you think Nancy will like this? I saw you trying to ride her bareback the other day. She kind of liked to trick you, shifting her weight from one side to the other so that you would fall to the ground. So I thought the saddle might help."

Boy was embarrassed. He had hoped no one would see the problem he was having getting up on the horse. He particularly hoped no one had seen nor heard how mad he had gotten at Nancy for her playful ways of putting him on the ground by shifting her weight from one side to the other just as Boy was throwing his leg over her back. When he was on the ground she would look at him, almost as though she were smiling.

Now the worst of his nightmares was true: S.P. had seen the whole thing.

Boy looked at the ground. He took the saddle when S.P. handed it to him but didn't let on that he liked it. He said nothing.

S.P. left to go back to St. Paul and write his daily love letters to Sophia, and Sophia called a family meeting.

"What do you think of Mr. Glemaker?" She began.

"Oh, I like him, I like him!" Jeanne responded. "I like him a lot. He's so much fun. So kind."

Boy was silent. He kept looking at the floor. He kept kicking at some imaginary spot just in front of the big toe on his right foot.

"What do you think of S.P.?" she asked him. Sophia's look was direct and persistent.

Boy looked up and her eyes caught his. He looked away, but the scar from the sledding accident two years previous left the answer etched in his forehead and his face.

"Well?" Sophia insisted.

"I don't want him here. I wish he would go away."

"But he's real nice and kind to you. Why don't you like him? He could make our lives so much easier," Sophia went on.

Boy pouted. Still he said nothing.

Jeanne chimed in, "Yes, yes, let him stay."

"He wants to marry us," Sophia said. "And he is a good man. I think we could make him happy. And I think he could be good for you," she said, looking at Boy.

Nothing. Stare at the floor. Say nothing.

S.P. continued his weekly trips to Glenwood. His courting and kindness increased. As he got to know Sophia and Jeanne and Boy his gifts of love and care deepened and broadened.

He learned that Boy loved to target practice and had fantasies of becoming an Olympic champion in match competition. So one weekend he came with a long box and gave it to Boy. In the box was a Model 52 Winchester .22, the kind used by Olympians in competition.

Boy's eyes almost fell out of his head they became so large and wide as he looked into the box at the special gift, yet he said nothing. He simply took the precious rifle.

That night he cried into his pillow. He had never known such love and kindness, nor had he ever known anyone who knew him as well as S.P. did.

In January, Sophia went to Minneapolis supposedly on a buying trip for the shoe store. The vendors of the spring and summer lines of shoes were at the Radisson Hotel in Minneapolis. But interestingly, Sophia, Jeanne and Boy stayed at the St. Francis Hotel on Seventh Street in St. Paul, just around the corner from the Glemaker Fur Company.

The last time, two years before, they stayed at the St. Francis Hotel and it had been very hard for the boy. It was 1944 and they had been in town to clean and close Aunt Jen Houseman's Mansion on Summit Avenue. It was a month after her death. Boy had slept with Sophia in the Blue Room. He had awakened. In terror. She was fondling him. He pretended to sleep. Yet the next day he was angry and agitated. She said he was just upset by Aunt Jen's death and tired from trying to clean and close the house. She said they should spend the next night at the St. Francis Hotel.

Boy didn't sleep. Nor did he again for several nights.

This time was different. S.P. drove Sophia and the children to Minneapolis for the shoe buying. Boy had his own room and not only did S.P. pay the bill for the hotel room, but the goal of the stay was comfort not escape. S.P. drove the first day, but after that, Sophia announced that she would be more relaxed if she and the children took the cab. Besides, it would save S.P. time, and, just maybe, an accident!

When they returned by train to Glenwood, the wedding date had been set for May. Sophia now affectionately called him Clem and not S.P. But in late February, Sophia had some second thoughts. Boy still did not like S.P. Clem, who was fifteen years her senior. And while at seventy he was robust and energetic and had a clean bill of health from Dr. Charlie Hensel, he still was much older than she.

But not in years and years had she had so much attention and felt so loved and cherished. It was like her every wish was his desire, and each day his knowing how to love and what to do increased. Should she stay? Or should she leave this ancient man of love, this strange and different answer to her prayer? Sophia knew that in her prayers she should have told God how old she wanted him to be and not just how she wanted him to be.

The indecision tore at her heart.

The stress put her back in bed with yet another one of her "heart attacks." The first glimmer of appreciation for S.P. came to Boy when it seemed that it was S.P. who mysteriously caused the heart attack this time and not Boy.

Dr. MacIver, friend, doctor, and mentor through many life events, sat by Sophia's bed. He confronted her. "You have got to make up your mind. If you don't, you'll kill yourself. And I can't do a thing about it. This old Jewish-looking man that's come to call on you is a gift from God. You ought to consider what he brings to you and the children. You ought to consider it very seriously! If you want him to leave, just tell him to leave. However, if you want him to stay, tell him you'll marry him. He's going to love you either way. You're a strong woman. You know how to live alone, but it might be more fun to have a companion who loves you. But make up your mind and get on with it."

Dr. MacIver finished his speech. He got up. With a slight bow and nod of his head, he said good night and left. Sophia, her heart no longer racing, got up and went to the kitchen. She fixed a cup of tea and put some brandy in it, "for medicinal purposes."

She called Boy and Jeanne to come to the living room. The early spring sun was just setting over the lake outside the plate glass window. The ice was not yet out, but the gray-black of the honeycomb melting of the lake's icy covering reflected the thaw of her intent and the conscious knowing within her heart that transformation was at hand. A new season of life and of the heart was about to begin.

Sophia designated Jeanne to carry the note she had written to the Reverend Mr. Quilt. Jeanne made the long walk past the lake, past Mrs. Benson's flat, past the fair-grounds, around the corner, past the shoe store, and past the school to stand at the large, foreboding oak door of the Lutheran parsonage. She knocked, timidly. This was scary. She didn't know what to expect, after all, he was a minister. The door opened.

"Is, is Reverend Quilt home?"

"Yes, won't you come in Jeanne?" the attractive woman invited.

"Good," thought Jeanne. "This must be Mrs. Quilt, and at least she knows who I am."

Reverend Quilt appeared. He was young, relaxed, easy. "I'm sure glad it's not the old Reverend Mr. Linevold," thought Jeanne. Still her throat was dry and her voice squeaked when she began to speak.

"My mother wants me to give you this note," she said waving the piece of paper in front of his face. "She wants to ask if you would marry her a week from Saturday. I mean, if you would marry her and Mr. Glemaker. They want to get married here. It will be only the family coming. Me, my brother, Aunt Elizabeth, Aunt Inga, Mr. Glemaker's sister, Hilma, his sons Erik and Edress, his daughter Louise and Waldo, and. . . . Oh yes, I forgot, maybe Uncle Gil will come if he isn't drunk."

Jeanne handed Reverend Quilt the note. He opened it and read:

Dear Reverend Mr. Quilt, Mr. Glemaker and I would be very honored and pleased if you would perform our wedding on Saturday, May 20. To put your mind at ease, while this is the second marriage for each of us, neither of us has been divorced. As you have been told, I believe, my husband, Lou, died ten years ago, and Mr. Glemaker's first wife of many years died a bit over a year ago. We feel this is the right course of action for us. We will continue to make our home here in Glenwood for my children's sake, but Mr. Glemaker will stay in St. Paul during the week so he can run his business.

So if you feel this is all right in your eyes and God's, we would like to be married on May 20 at eleven in the morning at the parsonage. It will be only a very small wedding with immediate family present: We will have a meal and reception following at the lodge on Lake Le Homme Dieu at Alexandria. You and Mrs. Quill, of course, are invited to attend.

Please send your reply home with my daughter Jeanne. Thank you and may God bless you.

Sincerely,

Sophia Lee Mossman

Reverend Quilt refolded the note and invited Jeanne to sit down in the formal living room. She did, sitting on the edge of the Queen Anne chair surrounded by shelves of leather bound books. They were classics, like *The Iliad* and Shakespeare and weighty books about God.

After awhile Mrs. Quilt reappeared carrying a glass of red raspberry Kool-Aid, which she gave to Jeanne. Later still, the Reverend Quilt came back in and greeted Jeanne. "I hope I didn't take too long, but here is a note you can give to your mother. He continued, "How do you feel about your mother marrying Mr. Glemaker?"

Jeanne replied, "Oh I love it! He's so nice. It will be just so great."

"Good," responded the reverend. "This note tells your mother that I will be more than happy to do the wedding."

Jeanne took the envelope, thanked them for the refreshment and backed on out the door. At the end of the sidewalk, by the street, she began to run and dance her way home.

The Reverend never asked about Boy's feelings.

May 20 dawned clear and bright. The day was warm for mid-May in central Minnesota. The air was heavy with the scent of lilacs in first bloom.

S.P. stood on the shore looking out across Lake Minnewaska. There was a gentle breeze. The waves were coming in. Each wave carried one part of the message of his soul. Wave by wave, just like the waves of love that swept over him as he thought of Sophia. Just like the waves of gratitude to God—a God of grace when he thought of being married to her, when he thought of having her as a part of his life and of being a part of her life and family. Just like the waves of joy and peace that swept through him as he thought of Jeanne how she adored him. He stood for a long time and watched.

Boy, on the other hand, stood before a mirror, trying to struggle with a tie that matched the uncomfortable suit Sophia had bought for him. Boy resented the tie and suit. They seemed to be as awkward and strange, restrictive and disruptive, as his mother's marrying this man.

The morning had been like a party. Elizabeth had come over from next door to help Sophia dress. She had brought a corsage of carnations, only to discover that S.P. already had given Sophia an orchid bought from Holm and Olson's, the elite florists in St. Paul. Mr. Olson, S.P.'s friend of many years, had picked it out himself. Elizabeth looked embarrassed. But Sophia said it was just right. She would wear the carnations over her right breast and the orchid over her left breast.

The new love from S.P. would not replace the old love that had helped her and healed her all these years since Lou's death. Boy heard her say that. So why did he feel replaced? He headed for the lake. The others wouldn't miss him. They were laughing and talking and having fun. They were warm and easy. He felt cold and icy inside.

Boy thought about what his mother had said to Elizabeth. Then he thought about his aunt, something he didn't do very often, because Uncle Gil would get in the way of his thoughts. He didn't like Uncle Gil, but he didn't know why. Now as he stood by the lake wishing the waves would wash his pain away this dislike of Uncle Gil puzzled him.

After all, uncle or not, Gil, like Harry Bell, had been given more than his share of pain to bear. He had grown up in South Dakota on the edge of the Nakota tribal reservation and had seen, and knew, the heartache of prejudice and discrimination. Boy knew the story of how he had gone off to be a doughboy in the Great War, had his leg injured in an accident, and gotten TB of the bone. The doctors had saved the leg but had had to stiffen the knee so now he walked forever with a limp, dragging that leg along. He had been dealt a lot of hardship. Life had bruised him. Scarred him. Stained him.

Boy should have found kinship with him, but he didn't. Boy should have liked him, but he couldn't see past the bottle, the alcohol with which he tried to drown his pain. When Uncle Gil was sober he really tried. He had taken Boy fishing and offered to take him hunting. He had been generous, not just to Boy, but to Al and Bob, giving them affordable housing in his apartments. His generosity reached out to many others—when he was sober. But when he was drunk. . . . Boy shuddered. It wasn't the wind that chilled him, but his thoughts. Why was he thinking of this now? He didn't know. Right now, there was so much he didn't know.

Years later, Boy would look back and remember these inner battles that he watched and others fought and sometimes won and sometimes lost. Then he would recall, with shame, that he had not had the wisdom then to reflect on the life and pain of Gil and others. He was caught up only in his own pain. If he could have thought that marriage day beside the lake that it was at least, in part, because of Gil's struggle to drown his pain, and Elizabeth's witnessing of it which birthed her strength and compassion, that was the blessing given to Sophia and to him as part of her family. If only— perhaps life has an abundance of if-onlys.

He heard the whistle that Sophia kept by the door to summon him home. It was time for his life to change. It was time to go to the parsonage.

Standing in the formal living room, surrounded by the leather-bound books, it was hard to tell who was more awkward, the Reverend Quilt, the bride and groom, or the attendants. They all seemed a bit out of place. They all seemed a bit unsure of how to proceed.

The bride and groom stood directly before Reverend Quilt, Sophia looking squarely at the reverend with her best business-like gaze. S.P. was looking directly at Sophia with a soft, almost teary-eyed countenance. S.P.'s children, Erik and Louise, stood to his right. Jeanne and Boy stood to Sophia's left. Exactly behind the two, as though closing off any avenue of retreat, were sisters Elizabeth and Inga.

"Do you take this man to be. . . ." The Reverend Quilt droned on.

Boy fidgeted, shifting his weight from one foot to the other. He was uncomfortable, not really hearing the words of the preacher, but at the same time hearing them. He was more lost in his own thoughts which tumbled over each other like rocks coming down a hillside.

Rocks and stones! Like anger and hate. Like wondering how they got to this place. Resentment of his mother. Abandonment. Feeling as though he was tumbling with the rocks. Not sure. Tumbling with the rocks. Not sure. And then there came the "Amen."

They filed out the parsonage doors. They said their thanks and smiled their awkward smiles of embarrassment or appreciation. They got into the cars and headed north toward Alexandria, Lake Le Homme Dieu. The party. The reception.

It was shortly after noon when they arrived at the lodge. The day remained warm and beautiful and the scent of lilacs filled the air. They were ushered into the beautiful, rustic lodge. The wedding party was well-anticipated. The tables were set with fine crystal and linen tablecloths and napkins. The champagne was ready. Sophia and S.P. were at the head table. The rest of the party was there and seated. On one side were S.P.'s relatives and on the other, Boy, Jeanne, and Sophia's family.

In the endless loud talking and conversation, Boy felt lost and lonely.

When the meal was finished and the cake was cut, toasts were offered. Even Jeanne was mentioned!

And outside, it was obvious even to the casual observer that Uncle Gil had not only the champagne but liberal portions of his own private stock. He was feeling no pain nor inhibition. He was a bit more talkative than the others. He cornered Waldo, S.P.'s son-in-law, outside between the lodge and a landscaping bush. He began by saying, "That man sure looks Jewish, doesn't he? Long hooked nose. I knew that Sophia would find herself something like that. I never could trust those old Jews. Look at him! Just look at him! You can tell. Narrow eyes, pointy. You know, he's going to cheat somebody. I bet he's cheating her. I bet he's just taking advantage of her. An old fart like that. What's he doing, anyway?"

Gil slurred on.

Finally Waldo had had all he could take. He interrupted.

"I beg your pardon. This gentleman is my-father-in law. He is Swedish. I know him well. He is very fine. He is just right for Sophia, and he certainly loves the children and talks often of them, especially Jeanne. I would like you to mind your manners and your tongue, if you please."

Gil glared at Waldo in anger and rage. What right did this man, this little man, this outsider, have to talk to him in this way? He stalked off by himself. When Boy saw him next he was sitting by the rear tire of his car.

Meanwhile, on the other side of the lodge, the wedding party was having a grand time. The beauty of the day, the beauty of the people and the beauty of the moment all conspired to celebrate love. Erik produced some expensive Cuban cigars he had been given and had saved in anticipation of this occasion. There was one for his father and one for himself. He offered one to Waldo, who took it and cradled it in his hands like a prize. He also offered one to the preacher, who took it but didn't smoke it.

He looked around for Gil. He had brought one for Gil as well. Finally, he and S.P. found Gilbert by the car. Gil grumpily took the cigar and lit it. He inhaled. Then he exhaled a large, yellow, white, smelly cloud of smoke back in S.P.'s face.

He said, "I suppose congratulations are in order."

S.P. smiled gently but said nothing. S.P. had his secret. He had overheard the conversation between Gil and Waldo. He had been standing behind some lilac bushes on the corner of the lodge conversing with Erik. S.P. had turned to go and talk to Waldo and Gil. That's when he overheard their conversation.

S.P. had thought privately to himself, "If he only knew. He really doesn't know. I came from Sweden. I came to people of my own nationality. I came supposedly to help harvest crops. As a boy, I was treated by them as though I was a slave. I was imprisoned. When I ran away, I was taken in by some Jewish merchants. They valued me and what I had. They befriended me, loved me, supported me, and helped me get started. They led me to this point in time—to this happiest moment of my life—to this greatest gift that God could give—to Sophia!"

Now, he thought, as he stood there in silence, "Had it not been for the Jewish people, I never would have met Sophia. I never would have been in business when she walked in my door. I never would have seen her loveliness. I never would have come to this point, all these years later, where I could ask her to be my partner. None of this would have happened had it not been for the Jews who helped me escape from my own people and helped me become who I have become. If only he knew. He doesn't know, nor will he ever."

The words tumbled in S.P.'s head like a mixture of hail and raindrops. Words like moisture caught in the updraft. Frozen. Dropped with thundering force to the ground of being. His inner heart was warm and cold. Hard and soft. Gentle and tough. All mixed together.

Lost in his thoughts, S.P. felt Sophia's hand touch his shoulder. "Come now. Let's go. We have our reservation at

Sunset Beach Resort," Sophia quietly coaxed. "Let's get on with it. Let's get into something a bit more comfortable." So they left. Sophia stepped into the living room where S.P. was waiting for her after she had changed from her wedding suit for the trip out to the resort for their honeymoon. S.P. stared. She looked radiant, absolutely beautiful. She was. She was more beautiful than Boy ever remembered. There was a peace and softness in her face and a twinkle in her eye. The lines of worry were gone—at least for now.

S.P. began to blush. He began to fidget and blurted out. "You are the most beautiful person I have ever seen, Sophia. You are everything God could ever dream—or create of beauty."

Boy heard this. He kept his eyes glued to the floor. He agreed with S.P. She was beautiful—mind, body, spirit. But still he wondered why this ancient man was in her life. Why? Why was it that things had to change in this way?

Sophia gave some last-minute instructions to Jeanne and Boy telling them to obey Frieda. She was here only for these few days while Sophia and S.P. vacationed at the Sunset Beach resort. Then they left, driving the four and one half miles out of town, east around the north end of the lake to the Sunset Beach Hotel.

Boy went out with his dog. As he wandered, he thought, "Why don't I go out to the resort with them? I can leave tomorrow. I can ride my bike. I can be there in a couple of hours. That way I can at least hear what they're saying and I can be a part of this and not rejected."

He began to form his plan—what he would explain to Frieda, how he would get out of the house. That night he slept little. He was restless, tossing and turning. Finally he got up at four, went out, and walked along the shore of the lake. He watched as the sun came up over the hills to the east. He watched as the town began to glisten in the new day's light as the shadows retreated out over the lake. He heard the birds sing their new song. He felt the mist in the air sting his face and chill his body. The mist and the early sun mixed to form a soft light, like the light within his mind forming a fuzzy picture of what he was to do. He returned to the house. He had breakfast with Jeanne and Frieda.

Frieda suggested chores and work he had to do, but the boy retorted with, "I have planned a bike trip for today. I will do the chores when I get home," he said. "Besides, my friends will miss me if I don't join them," he lied.

Finally, Frieda reluctantly agreed that he could take two hours to be with his friends, but then he would be expected to do his work when he got home. Also, she was sure she could think of other things for him to do. "A lazy mind and idle hands lead to evil thoughts and evil ways," she advised, unasked.

Boy went to the garage, got his bike and rode off in the direction of his friend's home. When he was out of sight of his house and Frieda, he circled back and headed for Sunset Beach Hotel.

Two hours later, when he arrived at the hotel, he went to the reception desk and asked what cabin Mr. Glemaker and Sophia Lee were in. The woman behind the desk smiled at him and said, "You mean Mr. and Mrs. Glemaker."

Boy replied, "No. I mean Mr. Glemaker and Sophia Mossman. She's my mother."

"Yes, I know," the woman replied. "She's very lucky to have Mr. Glemaker in her life. He's a good man. I own one of his fur coats."

"So what!" Boy thought, but said nothing.

The silence was awkward. Finally the woman asked,

"Are they expecting you?"

"Oh yes," Boy replied. "I'm sure they are."

"They're in cabin 201 C. You go out this door and turn right. Go to the first path to the left. It's the fourth building, the first cabin past the recreation building."

He went out the door, took his bike and wheeled it around and walked slowly in the direction the woman at the desk had indicated. He parked his bike. He wondered if this was such a good idea after all. What if they got mad at him? What if they just refused to come to the door? He timidly knocked at the door. He felt like he had been here before—maybe when he was very little. He felt sick to his stomach.

S.P. answered the door. "Oh my! Here you are! How did you get here?"

Boy pointed to his bike, which lay against a tree.

Sophia's voice sounded from the dim light within the cabin, "Who is it?"

"Why, it's Boy. He's come to see us. He rode his bike all the way out here. Just to see us. Just to say hello."

Boy blurted out, "No. I've come to stay. I want to be here. I don't want to be at home with Frieda! I don't want to be with Frieda! I don't like her! I don't want to be at the house. I want to be with you."

Sophia looked embarrassed. She looked at S.P. and said, "He was supposed to be with Frieda. He was supposed to stay home."

S.P. turned, sensing the urgency in Boy's voice, and replied, "Oh Sophia. Can't we have him stay—at least for awhile? It's such a nice day. He and I could take a walk. Maybe we could do something. Maybe we could all three play Scrabble or some other game. Or maybe he could swim. I can understand that he doesn't want to be with Frieda and

Jeanne. After all, he is a boy and he misses you, and he probably doesn't like me much either—right now."

He turned to Boy and said, "I hope that changes." Boy thought that somehow this man, who was the enemy, was taking his side. Somehow . . . this was all very confusing to Boy.

The silence was deafening. Then Sophia said to S.P., "Well, if it's all right with you, I think it would be very wonderful, very fine if he could stay."

She, too, sensed Boy's hurt and had known all along of his animosity toward her developing love for this old man. She knew that he was afraid that he would lose her love. Boy didn't know her heart was big enough to love them both. Perhaps to even love him more because she would have more energy as she wouldn't have to do everything that her life required all by herself. She knew of Boy's anger and fear. She knew it focused on S.P. and she wasn't sure how she would bridge the gap between the two of them. She felt caught in the middle.

But here S.P. was, taking it over, sensing, helping to bridge the gap.

S.P. grabbed a jacket. "Come on, Boy! Let's go." They headed out. They walked along the paths of the resort. They walked by the lake. They walked out on the pier. They looked at the very expensive Chris Craft speedboats tied to the pier. They said almost nothing, but walked together.

Boy watched from the corner of his eye. He saw the kind, relaxed expression on the old man's face.Still he tried to stay angry. He tried to rekindle the fire of rage within his belly. "What right does this man have to be around?" Boy thought.

But it was as though a gentle rain was falling on the fire—not enough to put it out, but enough to raise some steam that blurred the edges of the picture. Meanwhile, clouds had covered the sun, and rain was beginning to fall, so they headed back toward the cabin. When they entered the cabin, they found Sophia reading.

S.P. suggested it was time to get a bite to eat, so maybe they should go to the main lodge. They ate. The rain was still falling when they came back to the cabin. Obviously, Boy could not ride his bike home in the rain, S.P. observed. Why not stay a while longer. Besides, there were games to be played! Boy's choice.

While he decided, S.P. showed him some card tricks. Sophia sat to the side and smiled. She admired the patience and accepting way that S.P. approached Boy. He didn't scold or blame him for his anger and disrespectful ways. He seemed to know of the pain and fear within Boy's heart.

The rain stopped. The sun was a bright orange ball, kissing the horizon across the lake, as it called an ending to the day. What was left of the clouds scudded away toward the east. Sophia said to Boy, "Well now, it's time for you to head on home."

S.P. intervened again. "Oh, let him stay. We can make a bunk for him here in the corner of the room. He doesn't have to go back just yet. He doesn't have to ride back in the dark. He can go back in the morning—if he wants. Besides, Frieda would probably be really upset with him if he came home now. I'll go call Frieda and let her know he's here and will stay the night with us. If that's all right with you, Sophia." S.P. left the cabin and headed for the lodge to make a difficult phone call to an angry Frieda.

Boy and Sophia looked at each other. "He's a good man and he likes you. I hope you'll give him a chance," Sophia said.

Boy said nothing. But, he stayed that night. He spent time with his mother the next day when S.P. made an excuse to go on an errand somewhere. Later in the day he spent some time with S.P. who rented golf clubs and they played golf, with S.P. as the teacher-coach and Boy as the eager learner. They didn't talk much to one another. But they did play together.

Boy stayed that night. S.P. called Frieda again. This time she scolded him for being too soft on Boy. The next day they checked out. S.P. loaded Boy's bicycle on the back of the Graham Paige and tied it in place. The three of them drove back from the honeymoon.

The summer of 1946 was hot and busy. The house on Lake Shore Drive was transformed. A whole wing housing a master bedroom and a den was added on. Boy now had Sophia's old room and all its painful memories. It was as though the walls themselves echoed her many "heart attacks" and the pain of his rheumatic fever oozed from the paint itself. Jeanne had the room down the hall, the room that had been Frieda's.

The materials for the master wing had been chosen with care. S.P. had picked each board himself at the Shaw Lumber Company, owned by his friend in St. Paul, and hauled the one-hundred-fifty miles to the picturesque site. One window looked out over the lake to witness its mysterious moods. The opposite window looked to the hills, rising in power, guarding the valley.

It was as though he was building a temple to honor his beloved. It was as though he could not do enough for Sophia.

It was as though he could not be attentive enough.

It was as though he could not be close enough to her.

Always the question was the same: " What would you

like, Sophia?"

When she answered, the hunt was on to find the finest materials available. Mr. Shaw had contacts from Georgia to the Olympic Peninsula in Washington, from California to Maine. S.P. did not let him rest until he had found the exact treasure to fulfill the wish expressed.

Ted Barsness, the contractor who had built the house originally, skimping at every corner so that Sophia could have a house at all, now was told to spare no cost. He relished the task. His days began at sunrise and ended when the sun sank into the lake bathing the sky with magical gold and orange and purple. In August, the wing was complete. In September, the little fireplace glowed and the embers' soft light highlighted the contented smiles on Sophia's and S.P.'s faces.

Each week S.P. still had to make the trek back to his business in St. Paul. On Sunday afternoons the good-byes got longer and harder. Boy noticed the familiar tear in S.P.'s eye as he would break the embrace and head for the Graham-Paige. Sophia was more quiet. She seemed to lose herself more in her shoe business. She seemed more distracted and Boy felt even more isolated and closed out.

Again, the flames of rage were kindled and focused on S.P. The bitterness had not yet melted in Boy's heart. Late September, on a Saturday morning, Boy went to the den to start a fire in the fireplace, to take the chill from the air. As he rose from his task of lighting the kindling, he heard soft voices, more like whimperings coming from the master bedroom on the other side of the door. He pushed the door open and watched as S.P. and Sophia held each other in an embrace. Caught in the throes of passion, they did not see him.

Boy closed the door and went outside and cried. His place in Sophia's life had changed and he could not understand what all of that meant. His tears expressed confusion more than grief. For beneath the flames of rage, he tasted cool, life-giving water. Here was the father-friend he had always wanted. Yet the war within his soul still raged. On one side was the warmth and kindness, the generosity and love and patience that S.P. had shown him. On the other side of the battle line was anger, the bitterness and the rancor that he felt for this man who had taken a special place in his mother's life.

Sometimes it's harder to get what you want than to do without. He had honed the skills to live as a loner, different from others in thought and style, without support. He hadn't yet learned how to open his heart to another.

At times like this, he felt himself to be a raw, oozing wound, a victim of a battle, a casualty of war. The war hidden in Boy's inner being went unnoticed. The only thing noticed was his increased isolation from the family. The hours spent at the barn lengthened. The rides he and the Morgan mare took into the hills increased in frequency and hours as he searched for peace and armor for protection of his soul.

Then, the other shoe fell: the announcement came that the commute from St. Paul to Glenwood was too arduous, too strenuous, too life-sapping. They would sell the house in Glenwood. They would sell the shoe store. They would sell the Morgan mare and move to St. Paul. They would sell Boy's life as he had known it.

He would be torn now from the only place, the only security he had ever known. He would be torn away from Aunt Inga, the woman he knew had loved him. He would be torn away from the land, even from the grave of Uncle Phair. He would be torn up like a tree, a sapling pulled out by the roots and put in a soil, a climate that was strange and different and unknown. He would be placed in the city, a place without barns, a place without hills, without lakes lashed by wild prairie winds creating white-tipped waves, without a place to run and hide and be when the loneliness became overwhelming.

He would be torn from the very roots of who he knew himself to be and taken to a place that was strange, like a distant land. He recalled some of the Bible stories Miss Myrtle Jenison had taught in Sunday School. He recalled a guy named Moses who wandered in the wilderness, and another guy named Joseph who had been sold out by his brothers and hustled off to Egypt. Well! Boy was now being carted off to a different kind of Egypt!

"Mothers, brothers, what's the difference?" he thought with anger and bitterness filling his heart. Plans for the move emerged. The house was placed on the market. The store was placed on the market. It wasn't long before interested buyers showed up. The Andersons bought the shoe store. Dr. Placcard, a young doctor fresh out of medical school, a new partner in the practice that had belonged to Dr. Elder before his tragic, deadly, hunting accident, bought the house.

Boy and Sophia talked about what to do with the Morgan mare and the fancy sleigh. Finally, it was decided to give them both to Dr. MacIver who had befriended both Boy and Sophia. Dr. MacIver would give the mare to his son and the cutter sleigh to a museum.

The vestiges of who Boy was and how he had been in the world were being cast aside one by one. Sold. Sold and taken to a strange and distant place where he would be devoid of his uniqueness. He saw it as a kind of slavery. The cold that blanketed his soul felt like a snowstorm that could easily freeze his core of being. Real blizzards, he had survived. The storms that churned the lake, he had survived. The loneliness of the hills, he had overcome. But now he wasn't sure.

In the dark and quietness of night he tried to deal with his fear of the unknown. He was not very successful. Nightmares were the ponies he rode now. Fear, as always, and so with Boy, birthed anger. Sparks of rage moldered deep within. Rage, that mixture of fear and anger, without target and direction, searched only for the obvious to consume. The day came. S.P. asked Boy for his help to transport some of the clothes and other more delicate furnishings to St. Paul. They would take the old Willys Jeep vanette truck. They would leave early in the morning in order to arrive at the house on Lincoln Avenue ahead of the movers. The plan was that they could unload the Willys and have the delicate pieces put away before the heavy, clumsy pieces were carried in.

Boy and S.P. got into the truck around five. S.P. drove, such as his driving was. He first sang softly to himself, then began to try to carry on a conversation with Boy. But Boy was sullen and angry. Already filled with rage, he felt a final indignity of having to help with the move and ride with S.P. to the strange and foreign city. He didn't know what was in store. He didn't know who he would meet or even if he would have any friends. He didn't know the school, except that Breck was a military school where, someone had said, they sent rich, spoiled boys who couldn't get along at other schools. He knew he wasn't rich. He didn't feel spoiled. He could get along at his old school just fine.

They traveled along Highway 55. S.P. kept trying to get a conversation going. "You know the reason you're getting the chance to go to Breck is because your Aunt Inga took a large portion of the money she got from Aunt Jen Houseman's will and put it aside so you could go there. It's a good school. They say that almost 100 percent of those who graduate qualify for college. Besides, Inga thought it would be really good for you because they have horses there and they have a cavalry. She wants you to be happy and feel at home. You'll be one up because of all your experience with the Morgan and racing horses and all," he concluded.

Silence.

Undaunted, S.P. continued. "You'll fit right in. You may even be able to become an Officer because of your experience. That would be pretty special and unusual, what with only two years of high school left. I understand that most of those who become officers have been there all four years."

Silence.

"I think you have every reason to feel good about this." S.P.'s Swedish accent was becoming heavier as he became more tense and uncomfortable with Boy's silence. "You know, you have a wonderful Aunt Inga. A wonderful family that loves you."

Boy was beyond being reassured or cheered up.

S.P. continued. "Your mother had another of her heart attacks. These are caused by stress, Dr. MacIver says. I have this good friend, a wonderful doctor who teaches at the University. His name is Charlie Hensel. I know he could help her. He's a wise and brilliant man. I am sure with your encouragement your mother would go to see him, especially if I made the appointment and went with her. You could probably go, too, if you wanted. I think she would probably get well. At least I think he could help her, if anybody can. You want her to live, don't you?"

S.P. was obviously trying too hard and getting nowhere.

Silence. They continued driving.

Then, for no apparent reason, the explosion happened. An explosion like a plane engulfed in a ball of fire in the sky, but this explosion was in Boy's head and heart. It was an explosion of his very soul.

With an almost animal-like sound in his voice, Boy lurched from his passenger side of the van and grabbed the steering wheel. At the same moment he struck S.P. in the face and pushed his shoulder. The vanette swerved, hitting the edge of the roadway. It bounced and headed down into the ditch. The van did not tip. The ditch was wide and filled with water. The truck stopped. Its engine coughed and died. Mud and water oozed through the cracks around the doors and began to fill the passenger compartment. The snub nose of the little van was stuck deeply in the mud and water. The cargo hold of the truck was still above the water line so the prized antiques, along with the dog, stayed dry and safe.

S.P. was pale. He looked aghast. His countenance registered fear and shock and understanding. He had known the destructive power of rage born of prejudice before. Nonetheless, his body trembled and his hands shook as he sat, white-knuckled, grasping the steering wheel.

S.P. turned toward Boy, who sat with water now around his waist, unable to believe what he had done. He heard S.P. say in a loud, tense voice, "We are going to get out of this truck. We are going to get someone to help us get out of this ditch, and you and I are going to have a talk!"

Had it not been for the danger and the gravity of the situation, it probably would have seemed a bit humorous.

S.P.'s Swedish accent had returned full force. His anger and sternness got lost in the accent. Man and Boy were sitting waist-deep in water and mud, and the dog was barking a joyous bark of liberation from the dry confines of the rear of the truck. But, Boy did not lose awareness of the seriousness of the situation. His attention had been captured and his delusion was about to unravel.

They got out of the truck and scrambled up the bank toward the field by the side of the road. Boy tried to stand, but his knees buckled and he went down. He stood again and again he went down. His whole body was shaking and his teeth chattered so he couldn't talk. Finally, he just sat down, put his head in his hands and sobbed. Boy felt S.P.'s arm around his shoulder and his hand holding Boy's head close against his cheek.

Minutes passed, and with time Boy's composure returned. S.P. grabbed Boy's hands in his and turned Boy so he looked him in the eye. "You could have killed us both. Is that what you wanted? If you had killed us, your mother would have had the worst losses of her life, and heaven knows she has had many losses. But to lose you, and I think to lose me"—he paused—"I think would be the worst. She loves you and I will never take your place in her heart and life. Not that I would ever want to. I do love your mother and everything about her, more deeply than God will ever even know. I want to be with her and to help her. I want to be with you and Jeanne. I want to help you all. I want the best for all of us."

"What you don't know, because you're blind yourself, is that your mother's love is big enough for us both. I don't want us to be competitors for her love and attention. I don't want you to make us competitors, because then we both lose, and so does she. And now you could have killed us both with your anger and rage. Why am I the enemy? What about me makes me the enemy?"

Boy pulled on the grass and sat staring into space. He felt the cold wetness of his shoes and pants. His body trembled, perhaps from cold, or perhaps from the piercing path of truth that S.P.'s words had cut into his consciousness and being. He didn't know how to honestly answer the question. He didn't know how S.P. was the enemy, so he said nothing. They sat in silence. S.P. took his shirt off and put it over Boy's shoulders.

Boy looked up and saw the man's aging body, his sagging chest, his no longer firm-muscled arms, but somehow it no longer bothered him. This man looked strong! S.P.'s voice cut the silence. "Talk to me. Talk to me! We'll get nowhere, you and I, if you stay inside that shell of silence."

Still silence.

S.P. continued, "You know God uses us to help each other, but He doesn't like secrecy and silence. That's why He gave us voices and language so we can tell what we think and feel. He tells us that there's nothing so bad we can't talk about it."

His Swedish Covenant piety couldn't leave God out of this, Boy thought. Boy's thoughts now turned in that direction. God never had answered his prayers. Where is this God of grace?

And then, like a glacier moving, slowly calving, dropping its thick shelf of ice into the warming sea, Boy began to melt. His soul, his heart within his being, began to warm and thaw. To Boy's credit, he was willing to seize the moment to be taught. Carpe diem! The crystal clear water of the glacier began to form. It was only a trickle, but it was a beginning. Some of the roots of prejudice had been gouged away in the grinding movement of the glacier.

Boy began to sob again, but this time, not from fear. Tears of many years rolled down his cheeks. Rage turned to fear, turned to sadness. His shoulders shook. He didn't know when S.P. had embraced him. He didn't know how long they had sat on the bank. He didn't know when the tow truck had come and begun to pull the van from the mud. He only knew that his life felt like it was being pulled from the mud. Somehow this moment, this man, was filling the void deep within him—a void that had been cold and empty a long, long time.

This man whom he had feared, this man whom he had made his enemy, was now the agent of discovery for what Boy had wanted for so long.

They sat there a long time. Neither paid much attention to the men with the tow truck who seemed embarrassed by what was happening between Boy and S.P. Slowly the vanette was pulled back to the road, and water ran from its doors. The men dried the spark plugs and finally, after several tries, got it started.

S.P. got his shirt back from Boy, put it on, and waded back across the ditch. He produced a water soaked billfold and paid the men with "laundered" money. S.P. and Boy got in the van. S.P. said, "Let's get something to eat and then we'll go on home."

Boy smiled and nodded in agreement.

When the move was finally complete and they were living on Lincoln Avenue in St. Paul, Boy began his job of driving the delivery truck for S.P.'s fur store. This had been arranged long before the move was made. At first Boy had felt privately excited about this new responsibility, but now that the reality was here and he drove the truck out of the narrow little alley between the fur store and the opera house, he wondered about the wisdom of having agreed to this. He was pleased that S.P. trusted him. He was pleased to be a part of the business, even as his mother was. But he was scared to death. He didn't know the city and never had seen so many cars before.

Now, for the first time though, he felt he had a father, a real father, married to his mom. Uncle Phair had been like a father. So had Harry Bell, but now he had a father married to his mother. For the first time he felt a sense of trust that this man would not go away.

Trust was what was needed in the days that lay ahead.

The summer, what was left of it, was spent repainting the Glemaker Great White Bear signs that advertised the fur store. They were located in a wide perimeter about the metropolitan area. Boldly he would set out each morning with his ladder, bucket and brushes. By ten most mornings he was on a phone calling back, asking S.P. to tell him where he was and where he had to go.

When late August arrived, and the delivery of the coats began, he knew the outer perimeter, but he didn't know the city. Later, after school began, he would arrive at the store to do his deliveries. If he was lucky, he would be home again at ten, having gotten lost only three or four times. Each time he got misplaced he would call. S.P. would kindly and patiently ask him to describe where he was and then would give him directions.

The night he was delivering coats to the officer's wives in Fort Snelling, Boy found himself coming to the end of the street of officer's houses. He could see just across the grassy area a broad, wide highway that seemed to be going in the same direction he wanted to go. He bumped the truck across the grass onto the smooth cement highway, shifted gears, and was just getting up to speed when the extra bright headlights came directly at him. At just the last moment, the roar of the plane hit his ears as the giant bird lifted and just barely cleared the truck. He was on the runway for the Wold-Chamberlain Field airport. When he called home he could barely speak and his pants were wet. S.P. merely laughed and told him where he was and never to go cross-country again, no matter how attractive the other side appeared to be.

BRECK CAVALRY

At seven in the morning, Boy stood on the corner of Cretin and Lincoln Avenues. This September Monday in 1947 was clear and not very cold, but boy was shaking. Outwardly, he was not cold, but inside he was frozen. Besides, his innards were like Jell-O or the leaves on a quaking aspen tree.

The previous week had been one of frenzied activity. The reality of school starting in this place, as foreign to him as Egypt was for an exiled Moses, was about to begin. Sophia had driven the Graham-Paige and she and Boy had found the Maurice L. Rothchild & Company haberdashers located on Robert at 7th Street in St. Paul.

Here Boy had been outfitted in the blue-gray uniform of Breck Military Academy, the Breck School for Boys. There were two pair of blue-gray pants, two bluish-gray dress shirts, two black ties, an Eisenhower jacket with cap, a dress hat with visor and Breck insignia, a pair of shiny black shoes, and a full length, black overcoat, military-style, of course. It had been decided that Boy would join the Breck Cavalry because of his love and knowledge of horses, so he was also outfitted with a pair of jodhpurs and almost knee-high shiny black leather riding boots. When all of the fitting had been done and the articles that did not need alteration or hemming neatly piled to be carried away when they left the store, the very polite haberdasher turned to Boy and Sophia and asked, "Is there anything else I can do for you? Do you have any questions?"

Before Sophia could reply, Boy blurted out, "What about uniform underwear? Do I have to wear that, too?"

With that, Sophia took Boy by the arm, turned him and pointed him toward the pile of clothes and said, in a tone not to be questioned, "Pick those up. We are done here for now."

Turning to the salesman, who was now blushing, she said "Thank you very much for all your help. We will be back to pick up the alterations on Saturday." They left the store.

While St. Paul, Minnesota, didn't look much like Egypt, it definitely felt that way to Boy. There were no hills behind his house into which he could escape. He was surrounded by foreboding institutions. St. Paul Seminary, with its fledgling black-garbed Catholic priests marching single file about the grounds with prayer books in hand, flanked his house to the west at 2128 Lincoln Avenue. St. Thomas College and Military Academy, with uniformed cadets, closed up the north. Things had gotten much better between S.P. and Boy, and Boy was adjusting to, and yes, sometimes even enjoying the Cities. Yet, he still felt trapped. Now the trap was about to be sprung.

The uniform, finally on, and the necktie, tied in the proper manner, felt awkward and more like a straight jacket than anything else. He didn't want to go to that school on Como Avenue with its austere Haupt Hall guarding the entrance from Como Avenue and the main building of classrooms, dorm rooms, and commons overlooking the parade grounds and athletic fields.

Boy would have run, if he had had somewhere to run. In fact, he was just thinking about it when the blue and white bus with "Breck School" written on the side rumbled around the corner and squeaked to a clumsy stop. The door swung open and driver Mike Uram peered down from his command post at the steering wheel. Boy's eyes fixed on Mr. Uram's hand that rested on the steering wheel. It was missing a finger. Boy's fantasy took off. Maybe that's how they disciplined the students and people who worked at Breck.

Mike's firm voice, laced with knowing acceptance, broke through Boys' vale of self-generated fear. "Well, get in. I'm not going to bite you. We haven't got all day." Boy got into the bus for the ride that would begin a major change in his growth from Boy to man.

In 1938, forty- six-year-old Chester H. DesRochers came west from Maryland, where he had been an assistant headmaster at the Episcopal-affiliated McDonough School, to become headmaster of Breck, another Episcopal-affiliated school. He brought with him three definitive interests and resources. First he was ambitious, creative and very modern in his ideas of 'schooling'. Second, his wife, Beula DesRochers, was an excellent administrator and translator of the creative into forms of practicality. And third, he had a passionate love of horses. Under Headmaster DesRocher's leadership and because of good luck, Breck grew both physically and in student population by leaps and bounds.

For example, by 1941 Breck had expanded by 36 acres and had added a main building named for DesRochers predecessor, Charles Edgar Haupt, along with a three-story dormitory and high school building, complete with kitchen and dinning facilities. Also added were a bus garage and horse stables. The student body had expanded from 30-40 students to 249.

In order to foster the teaching of discipline at Breck, DesRochers in 1942 invited Major L. L. Cunningham of Notre Dame University to accept an appointment as dean of boys. Part of Cunningham's job was to establish a Breck military training program. . . . The military training became mandatory in 1943 and would remain for another 16 years.

Military training at Breck, directed by the school's own staff, was less rigid than the programs directed by Army officers at other schools.

—Telling Our Story: Life At Breck School 1886-2000

The bus bounced its way down Cretin Avenue, crossing Summit Avenue, turning left on River Boulevard, and then immediately turned right on to Exeter Place, grinding to a stop. The door opened, and in climbed Dockman, a freshly scrubbed freshman, replete in uniform and looking just as scared as Boy felt.Dockman sat down and the bus rumbled on. Boy's thoughts, if that's what they were, bumped and ground in harmony with the bus' protesting engine.

He had heard all about the discipline and the life values the school was supposed to furnish. But all it provided for Boy, as far as his thoughts could figure, was a springboard for fear and a ripping of the fabric of freedom from his previous life. Men would be yelling orders and classmates would be making fun of him. After all, they were city boys and he was a country boy. They were good athletes, no doubt, and he only knew about horses and hunting.

The only military man he knew was Uncle Gil and he hated him. Oh, he had heard the stories about his grandfather and the Civil War. He loved the stories and the man in them, but he had never known his grandfather. Grandfather Lie had been dead five years before Boy was even born. "So if these men and classmates were anything like Uncle Gil," he thought, "I'm in for a long two years of humiliation and rejection, if I don't die before it's over."

Starting in 1946, Breck's commandant was Lorand Andabazy, a colorful Hungarian-born war hero who had won silver and bronze stars in the U. S. Army and earlier starred at the Ballet Russe de Monte Carlo.

"You've got the precision fine, but they march like a bunch of ballet dancers," a Fort Snelling reviewer once commented to Andabazy. Breck's military training had a deeply serious side and intent, as well: to prepare students for the possibility of going to war. By 1942, 52 students had left school to become active members of the U. S. armed forces.

—Telling Our Story: Life At Breck School 1886-2000

Boy didn't know the intricate history of this place that he was being "sentenced" to attend. He had heard that it was a place for bad boys, but he didn't think he was that "bad." He had heard that it was a school that his Great Aunt Jen Houseman had loved and supported because of her friendship with Mr. Edgar Haupt. He had heard this from his Aunt Inga, whom he adored, but he thought she was a bit off on this one. When he visited Aunt Jen at her Summit Avenue mansion, all she ever did, if she talked to him at all, was to yell at him and tell Sophia that he was undisciplined and she should not have spared the switch so much.

Boy didn't like Great Aunt Jen very much, so he didn't think he would like this Breck place or these people she liked very much either.

However, Boy did know that it was because of the generosity of this great aunt and the money she had given to Aunt Inga to see to it that Boy went to Breck. Thanks to Great Aunt Jen, he was in this predicament, or as others said, had been given this opportunity. Big deal! "If this is opportunity," he thought, "Please don't knock again!"

The bus came to a stop alongside Haupt Hall, to the accompaniment of the screeching brakes. The bi-fold door opened. Boy had come to the conclusion that he would be as quiet as he could be and try to become invisible.

He would say only, "Yes, sir," and "No, sir," and nothing more. In spite of himself, as he stepped from the bus and looked across the parade grounds and football field and beyond to the horse stable where the horses were being groomed, he could not help himself when he smiled.

At that moment, this guy in boots with sergeant stripes came up to him and said, "I'm Jack. Jack Leonard. You want to join the cavalry?"

"You don't want to join that bunch of Mounted Meatballs," a voice called out.

"Yeah—you don't want to join them! They're just a bunch of losers who can't figure out their right foot from their left, so they let the glue plugs do it for them," someone else chimed in.

"Shut up!" Leonard's voice boomed, "You're just a bunch of jealous wimps!"

"That's enough, boys!" a firm but quiet voice said.

They all turned and there stood Captain Harry Smith, commandant of Breck School. Faces turned red, and everybody scattered to some other place each needed urgently to reach. Boy fell in behind Jack Leonard. It seemed the safest place to be.

The cavalry at Breck was established in the spring of 1944. Under the leadership of Headmaster Chester DesRochers and Captain Harry Smith, it would become part of the Reserve Officers Training Program (ROTC) at Breck. However, it was because of the patience, expertise and tutelage of Cavalry Master Philippe Verbrugghen that the cavalry took shape and became a common, but unique, sight on the campus and on the paths paralleling the campus boundaries.

According to the *Breck Bugle*, the student newspaper, issue of January 21, 1944:

> *"A cavalry troop will be organized as soon as the weather permits. Men who are interested may see Mr. Verbrugghen. Distinctive insignia will be worn by the troop. Breck is the only school in the northwest with a Calvary troop."*

On June 1, 1944, the *Breck Bugle* reported:

> *"Cavalry Master, Mr. Phillipe C. Verbrugghen is the instructor in charge of the riding classes at Breck. A small-statured, quiet man, he wields an influence about the school which is far greater than his modesty would allow him to suppose. Besides his riding-master duties, he takes charge of some of the*

smaller boys' athletic periods, and has a reputation for doing many voluntary services, for the little boys and for other people, which are well beyond the line of duty only. And he sings out a lusty and effective 'Ho!' when he is commanding his brand-new Cavalry Troop, mounted upon his beloved steed. He is a son of the late Henry Verbrugghen, a famous conductor of the Minneapolis Symphony Orchestra."

Later that afternoon during his first day at Breck, Boy got up the courage to ask the verbose and gregarious Sergeant Jack Leonard, "Where do I go to join the cavalry?" Jack looked at him for several moments and smiling what was to become a familiar, knowing, smirky smile, pushed his cap back on his head and said, "So you want to join the 'four legged follies.' I didn't think you were that dumb, but since you are, just come with me after classes today and we'll get you set up."

Boy didn't know what all of that meant, but he was soon to find out. Somehow he knew, that a life long friendship had started in that moment.

> *"For eight months of the school year that patient group of equestrians known as the Breck Cavalry has been the brunt of sarcastic jibes by the rest of the Corps. Its members grin and shrug slightly when some would-be humorist inquires about the latest dope on Breck's 'mounted meatballs' or 'four legged follies.' Yet when the government inspection and final-day parade roll around, it is this polished outfit which steals the spotlight and wins many favorable comments for the school."*
>
> —From the 1948 Breck yearbook, *The Mustang*

Following Jack Leonard across the parade grounds, Boy's nostrils caught the oh-so-sweet aroma of horse manure wafting on the crisp, westerly fall breeze. The country boy was home again. Boy looked up to see the stable directly before them. He had been looking down, lost in his thoughts on a day that had not gone all that badly. It was as though he had succeeded at becoming invisible. Nobody had asked his name. Nobody had yelled at him. Nobody had criticized him. It had been a good day!

Jack's voice cut through his foggy consciousness, "Mr. Verbrugghen, this here is Frank; he just started at Breck today and says he wants to be in the cavalry. He's nuts, but that's what he says he wants to do."

Mr. Verbrugghen looked Boy over very carefully for what seemed an eternity. Finally he spoke, "You'll need permission from your parents. We require that of those who ride," he said.

Boy fumbled in his uniform jacket pocket and produced a neatly typed note. He handed it to the very trim Verbrugghen, who studied it for a bit, looked up and asked, "Sophia Glemaker is your mother?"

"Yes, sir." Boy responded at the same moment that Jack exploded, "You son of a gun—you didn't tell me you had already figured on joining, before we even met this morning."

Boy felt like saying, "You didn't ask—you were too busy talking," but he said nothing.

Verbrugghen broke the silence by turning to one of the other cadets and said, "Get this boy a horse to ride."

The cadet, a kind of cocky-looking lad, said, "Sure Mr. Verbrugghen—ah—I mean, yes, sir," and then he disappeared into the barn.

In due time, Cadet Rob Bartter—who was to become a good friend later—appeared leading a rangy bay horse, not unlike some of the standard breed racing horses Boy had worked with back in Glenwood. Behind the cadet, whose name Boy had yet to learn, was a small group of other cadets. They appeared ready to ride, but were showing a great deal of interest and curiosity in this new, quiet, shy kid from the country.

Boy said nothing, but was puzzled over what all the interest was about. It was almost like he was or was about to become an object of something—maybe a joke—or maybe an example of what to or what not to do. Or . . . Boy didn't know what.

Bartter handed the bay's reins to Boy and said, "Here. Why don't you get on?"

Boy thought he detected a kind of snicker from the others but took the reins and said, "Thanks."

Boy noticed the others watching him intently. One of them yelled, "You know you mount from the left."

Boy replied, "Yes, I know. I've ridden quite a bit, but never in an English saddle." Now, there was an audible snicker from the group.

Boy turned the horse in an inner circle, watching the horse closely, as Harry Bell had so carefully taught him. Boy liked the horse. He was a gelding and seemed lively. He liked the splash of white that went the entire length of his face, from muzzle to forehead. The second time Boy turned the horse he paid attention to the tack. The bridle and martingale seemed to fit right. Stirrups looked to be about the right length. It all seemed to be in order, except he wanted to check that saddle cinch. While he didn't know much, if anything, about English saddles, he knew that any kind of cinch that held the saddle to the horse's back had to be very tight or it would be disastrous. He also knew the oldest trick in the book was to give a tenderfoot a horse saddled with a loose cinch and then watch the fun as the rider would slide beneath the horse.

More than one rainy afternoon had been spent at the horse barns by the race track in Glenwood listening to the old timers tell stories about novices who had been tricked. Boy had laughed with the best of them, for he was not considered a novice. In fact, at thirteen, fourteen, and fifteen, he had been the youngest sulky driver on the local racing circuit out in the west-central part of the state.

And now he studied his horse. He knew the cinch was loose and had been deliberately left that way. He said nothing. Instead, he took Blaze around in one more inner circle, and then stretched him out by gently pulling on the reins so the horse moved his front hooves forward a little while keeping his rear hooves in place. Boy stepped to the side, loosened the cinch knot, pulled the cinch tight with all his strength, and let the horse blow all the air out. Before he could take more air in, Boy heave-hoed on the cinch one more time. Blaze grunted while Boy secured the cinch knot. When Boy looked up from his task, he saw a slightly dejected bunch of fellow cadets and a slight smile on Mr. Verbrugghen's face just before he gave the instruction for everybody to get their horses and mount up.

"No other school in the Twin Cities had anything like a riding program, and DesRochers made the most of it, using the stables to recruit students even before they were built. We were driving home—we'd just been looking over the campus," recalled Margaret Sherry, DesRocher's daughter, "when Dad

pulled into a gas station. A boy was trudging through his newspaper route. Dad jumped out of the car, ran up to him, and said, 'How would you like to go to a school with horses?' "

—From the 1948 Breck yearbook, *The Mustang*

Boy stepped to Blaze's left shoulder and placed his left foot in the stirrup. Firmly holding the rein, he grasped the saddle and swung up into it as though he had been riding English all his life. Nobody saw the look of worry leave Boy's face, nor did they hear the sigh of relief escape Boy's lips. They now were all too busy getting themselves positioned so as not to be tardy when the cadet commander ordered, "Forward ho, walk your horses!"

Maybe they did not want to hear from Sergeant Jack Leonard enforcing his lieutenant's commands. All of these maneuvers were done under Verbrugghen's ever-watchful and scrutinizing eye.

"The [riding] program attracted to Breck one of its most entertaining teachers, Phillipe Verbrugghen, son of the noted orchestra conductor Henry Verbrugghen, who had spent five years on a cattle ranch in the Australian outback."

—From the 1948 Breck yearbook, *The Mustang*

At the front of the column rode the lieutenant, followed by the sergeant. Boy rode somewhere toward the last half of the column. He felt uncomfortable. He felt he was being watched. He even suspected he saw some of the cadets surreptitiously turn slightly in their saddles to look at him, being careful not to be caught by the watchful Mr. Verbrugghen, who rode at the rear of the column.

Boy thought, "I must be getting paranoid. They can't be watching me. Why would they ever want to watch me? They had their little joke with the cinch and all." Still, he felt the nervous energy that, he would learn much later in life, was triggered by his precognitive intuition.

Boy was so preoccupied with all his rambling thoughts and weird suspicions that he almost missed hearing the command, "Canter your horses."

The horse in front of him began to canter and the horse behind him seemed to urge him on. Abruptly Boy came out of his mental mastication. He spurred his horse to close the gap before him. Blaze responded by going into overdrive. He not only went to a canter but to full throttle and into a gallop. Boy pulled on the reins and leaned back in the saddle to slow him down.

To no avail! Blaze was a rubber neck. Instead of slowing, he merely laid his head further and further back until basically it rested in Boy's lap. Boy was mildly aware of the laughter of some of the cadets around him. They knew that this would happen. Boy didn't pay much attention. He had his hands full or, one might say, his lap full. Boy had encountered such a horse only one other time and his mentor, Harry Bell, had told him what to do. The instructions all came back in a moment—in Harry's voice and at a full gallop.

"Boy," said Harry's voice from within Boy's brain, "you grab that fleshy part of the muzzle of your horse. You grab it as hard and tight as you can, and then you twist it. You twist that muzzle as hard as you can. Your horse won't like it," Harry's raspy voice sounded in Boy's brain, "but he will understand that you are the boss and it's in his best interest to do what you say."

Boy reached down and grabbed Blaze's muzzle and his upper lip, and oh, God how he twisted! "God, thank you," Boy muttered under his breath as Blaze immediately became obedient, just as Harry had said.

Once back in the column, which had come to a halt, with Boy and Blaze in their proper place, Boy looked around. He felt scared and embarrassed. He had blown his first ride. He probably had flunked out of the cavalry. He probably had embarrassed the other cadets, for they all were looking down and away from him.

He was probably the last to hear Mr. Verbrugghen ride up along side him."Are you all right?" Mr. Verbrugghen asked in a very gentle, but concerned voice.

"Yes, ah sure. Ah, sir. I mean, yes, sir," Boy responded.

"You shouldn't have been on that horse. Whoever put you on it should have known it's a rubber neck," said Mr. Verbrugghen.

Boy, without thinking and being unfamiliar with the ways of military discipline, interrupted. "It's all right, sir, I like the horse. It's like one I used to ride back home—ah—I mean, where I used to live." Now Boy was embarrassed. He knew his face had turned red and he knew he had to be in trouble for his impertinence.

Mr. Verbrugghen ignored the boy's red face and instead asked, "Where did you learn that move you put on that horse? That was just the right thing to do."

"You aren't mad at me?" Boy blurted out.

"Of course not!" Mr. Verbrugghen responded.

"I learned it from my friend, Harry Bell. He taught me all about horses, how to sit a sulky, what to do, you know."

"Sure. Sure, I know all about how important a friend who teaches is. I know," Verbrugghen gently responded.

And with that he turned and called to the lieutenant, "Take them back to the barn." And so they did.

When the troop was unsaddling, a few of the cadets came up to Boy and said, "Nice job," or something like that.

Boy mumbled, "Thanks," or something like that.

What he felt was more important, however. He had never felt included or accepted by peers in this same way before. He felt warm, as though he belonged somewhere. He was afraid that they would change their minds and all the warmth would go away. But, this moment was here—now. How did this day ever get so turned around? Where was it Breck School started? How was it he ever got here?

He couldn't remember anymore. He just was glad he was here. Then Jack Leonard's voice jarred him back, "Let's get the hell out of here and go find some girls!"

THE JOURNEY

The first year away from the beloved hills and lake of his childhood made Boy feel as though he was completely lost most of the time. His few close friends at Breck, especially the cavalry, and on the Immanuel Lutheran Church basketball team, formed the nucleus of his community, the place where he felt accepted. Slowly, he was broadening his circle of friends, but it was taking time. Basketball, both the junior varsity team at Breck and the church league helped him gain confidence. Boy was not a good basketball player, far from it. In fact, he spent most of his time nursing a broken finger or two and a broken nose (six times in two years) because of his clumsiness and lack of coordination. But, somehow, his teammates still encouraged him and would get the ball to him in the center when he could get open. Boy couldn't understand why they kept him around, but he was glad they did. When Boy asked his friend Jack Leonard, "Why do they keep me around?" Jack blew it off and said, "Because you're ugly."

That was as good an explanation as any Boy thought.

Saturday morning, June 5, 1949, the phone rang in the house on Lincoln Avenue. "Hello," Jeanne said trying to catch her breath, "Yes, he's here somewhere. Just hold, I'll find him." Yelling over her shoulder so Boy could hear in his room at the top of the stairs, "Aunt Inga is on the phone and wants to talk to you."

"I'll be right down. Don't let her hang up!" Boy replied and took the stairs two at a time on the way down.

Spring had come that year in mid-April and none too soon. The basketball season ended in March and was celebrated with a party at Boy's house after the final game. It was a gala affair that had lasted until after midnight. At two a.m., Boy awakened with a terrible stomach ache. He got up, barely making it to the bathroom before throwing up all the hot dogs and party goodies he had eaten. Just as he finished cleaning the floor, Sophia surprised him. Adults always did that to him at the worst possible times.

"Are you all right?" she asked.

Damn! He had awakened her. Somehow he didn't care, he felt so awful. When he turned to look at her she exclaimed, "Oh my," and knelt beside him before he could speak. "Let me take your temperature. You look like you're burning up."

"Get the thermometer, Clem," Sophia said to S.P. who came upstairs after he was awakened by Sophia getting out of their bed. He was still pulling on his bathrobe. As S.P. disappeared on his appointed mission, Boy again scrambled to the toilet to retch and heave.

Sophia took command. S.P. was about to start back up the stairs with the thermometer when Sophia called out "Forget the thermometer. Call Doctor Henson!"

Boy passed out.

In a fog, with his eyes unable to focus, Boy heard Doctor Henson say, "Were the boys drinking at the party tonight?"

Sophia answered, but Boy drifted off and didn't hear her reply. Then Doctor Henson's powerful voice broke through the fevered fog once more, "Then it's gotta be appendicitis—probably ruptured or close to it judging by his fever. It's 105.5. I'm calling the ambulance to take him to Miller Hospital. I'll call Doctor Baker, he's a good surgeon for this kind of thing. He can meet us at the hospital."

Boy slipped beneath the fog once more. In a dreamlike state he found himself in places he had never actually been before but now was there again. A siren pierced the silence; the face of a little boy pressed against a window pane, staring into nothing, or was he staring at dead people? In his dream, he didn't know.

The siren sounded far away, yet surrounded him with sounds and swirling colors of yellow, green, red and black—very black. He thought he felt an arm beneath his shoulders and a hand upon his head. Was it something imagined or was it real? The siren stopped and the motion stopped. All that remained was the retching in his stomach and the taste of bile in his mouth.

A light as white and bright as a noon-day sun was above him. Then blackness enveloped him and the whole world about him went dark. When he awakened, tubes ran from his stomach; tubes ran into his arms; tubes ran into his nose; tubes were everywhere. His eyes slowly focused on familiar faces peering down. There was Sophia, and S.P., Ione, and Jeanne. Had they died too? But perhaps he wasn't dead. Boy wasn't sure. The pain in his gut could never be from heaven, at least not the heaven he had learned about. Perhaps he was in hell!

A lilting voice said, "He's awake now. He'll be fine, just a little nauseated and groggy. He just needs to rest. Go get a bite to eat. I'll get the head nurse to give him something so he will be more comfortable when you return."

Boy drifted off to never-never land once more.The next days were filled with pain and strain. He dreamed of the ruptured appendix and four feet of small intestine filled with toxic peritonitis that Doctor Baker had removed and shown to him in a glass beaker. When Boy tried to move he was sure the stitches would shatter and his stomach would explode. The student nurse with the lilting voice coaxed Boy, coerced, teased and tormented him into sitting, standing and walking. Boy cursed her, "Why the hell don't you leave me alone? I don't want to walk!" She laughed at him and teased him some more.

Ten days after the surgery Boy left the hospital, and that same night he had a date with the student nurse with the lilting voice. They walked, hand in hand, on Seventh Street, turned on Wabasha, and walked to Sixth Street where they stopped for a hamburger at Mickey's Diner.

They held hands across the table and she asked him, "Do you want a cigarette?" Boy answered, "I don't smoke."

"Oh, come on now, just try one," she teased.

Boy didn't want to appear juvenile to her so he took one from the pack she pushed toward him, saying, "OK."

Big mistake! He coughed and his eyes watered. She laughed at him, perhaps more deeply than he knew in that moment. He was anything but debonair, but he thought he was.

When Boy called for a second date, she said, "I had fun, but you're not my type. I don't want to see you any more."

Boy experienced another blow to the stomach, if that's where the seat of the ego is. At least that's where the stitches hurt as he cried himself to sleep that night. All he got as a gift from the student nurse was the habit of smoking.

But spring came and with it there was preparation for graduation. The days were full of anticipation and trepidation. Graduation would happen on June 10, and the idea of that left Boy with feelings of nostalgia.

Boy felt a strong urge to reconnect with his roots in Glenwood, as part of letting go the last of his past life in order to launch into whatever his future would hold. Boy's mind, both conscious and in dreams, often was filled with visions of the rolling green hills and the lake of blue water, with the white caps dancing on it. He needed to say goodbye if ever he was to graduate and say hello to the new map of his life to come.

Boy wanted to see his friend David Ree. He needed, once more, to sleep in the bed in the little room in Aunt Inga's house. He wanted, once again, to row the old leaky cedar strip boat on the lake of his childhood. He would walk the shores of the lake and hike the hills which had nurtured him.

Boy asked S.P., "Can I take the Buick to go to Glenwood. I'll only be gone two days—until Sunday."

"Sure, be careful," S.P. replied. "Just don't run over any more stop signs."

S.P., it seemed, always reminded him of the foibles in his life. Boy was ashamed of the $600.00 damage done to the Buick when he had not stopped quickly enough, hitting the car in front, and pushing it over the "bobby" semaphore in the center of the street. The car in front was not damaged, only the Buick was. Worst of all, it left the family to travel about in the panel truck that belonged to the fur store. It took four weeks of Boy's earnings, the penalty for the four weeks it took, to repair the Buick.

Boy hung his head and said to the floor, "I'll be careful."

When Boy called Aunt Inga, she was pleased that he would visit. He called his friend David Ree, who had been Boy's closest friend before Boy left to live in St. Paul.

"David! I'm coming up to Glenwood. Can we get together? I really want to see you. This graduation thing is really bugging me. I feel scared or like we're getting old or something."

"Yes, I would like that. When are you coming?" David asked.

"Friday. My step-dad said I could use the Buick, if I don't hit any more stop signs."

David was timid, introverted and reflective like Boy, but there the similarities stopped. Boy was adventuresome; David liked to blend in. Boy was tall, lanky and slow of foot. David was short, compact and fast. David was a star on the football team because of his speed and coordination. His fleetness of foot won him a reputation. He would always run for daylight and away from whoever was chasing him or trying to tackle him. Sometimes he ran the wrong way and scored points for the opposing team. David redefined the phrase "he runs scared."

On the drive to Glenwood, Boy reminisced. He remembered the day he, David, and another friend, Dick Deal, went fishing. They were casting for bass. David was in the bow of the boat, Dick in the stern, and Boy was in the center. All had agreed not to cast "side arm" so not to endanger one another with their lures, replete with treble hooks. This day Dick forgot. With a mighty swing of his arm, the tip of his rod whipping back, then forward, he released the hold his finger had on the line just in time to send the lure with its treble hook directly into the back of Boy's left knee. Two of the trebles caught and tangled in

Boy's pant leg, the third penetrated the back of his knee, embedding the point deep within, the hook's barb firmly encamped behind the knee's tendon.

Boy howled, Dick went pale and sat down. David froze in time, sitting woodenly on his perch in the boat's bow. Boy was first to grasp the meaning of the moment. "What the hell are you doing?" Boy demanded.

He could not move his leg without making the situation worse. If he moved, the hooks embedded in his pants merely forced the hooks in his knee to move in deeper. Boy would have to cut the pant leg off to stabilize the situation.

"Give me your knife!" Boy had yelled at Dick. Dick fumbled in his pocket, opened it and handed it, blade first, to Boy. Boy merely said, "jeez," took the knife, cut the pant leg off and then cut the hooks free from the material. No longer hidden by the pant leg, blood was clearly visible running down Boy's leg.

David, from his ringside seat in the bow, moaned, "Noo—I hate blood!" Then he fainted and fell out of the boat.

"Jeez!" Boy said, looking up from his damaged leg. "Well, let's fish him out."

But Dick already had reached over the boat's gunnel and had a hold on David's shirt. After David recovered, Dick rowed the boat to the beach in front of the hospital, which was conveniently located along the lake shore. David, fully revived and avoiding anything to do with blood, volunteered to run up to the hospital to get a doctor to come and remove the hooks from Boy's leg.

When all was said and done, Boy and David remained closest friends. The only real casualty of the day was David's fishing pole, which fell out of the boat with him and remained forever in its watery grave. Boy smiled to himself and urged the aging Buick to go faster; he wanted to see David.

David lived with his parents in the same low-income flats by the lake that housed Mrs. Benson and her family on the end opposite David's family. Harry Bell and his wife Mildred lived in one of the middle flats. Thus the flats, in effect, had housed many of Boy's most important support community. Now Boy was returning to say farewell to those who were left. Harry had died. Mrs. Benson and her family had moved after her oldest son, Reynold, had been killed when his B-17 bomber was shot down on an air raid over Germany in 1945. Only David and his family remained.

As Boy drove he wondered, what would he say? What would he feel?

His first stop was at Aunt Inga's little brown-gray stucco house on Green Street. Inga had seen him coming so she was out the door and moving toward the car before it was even fully stopped. Inga had a plan. She couldn't wait to tell Boy about it. The words tumbled out so fast Boy couldn't quite comprehend what she was saying.

"Slow down. Slow down!" Boy said, "You want to take a trip west to visit Uncle Rudy and the remaining friends that you and Uncle Phair knew from years ago?"

"Yes, yes," Inga said, "and I want this to be your graduation present. I've bought a new Buick Super. It's black—jet black! I bought it just for this trip. I've got maps we can look at tonight. I've invited your friend David to go with us. He said he could come over tonight so we can do the planning."

Boy badly needed to pee. He stood on one leg and then the other as Inga rambled on. Finally Inga noticed his discomfort and said, "Well—we can talk more later. Now go and make yourself comfortable."

As Boy disappeared into the house to find the bathroom he had heard Inga say to herself, "Well the good Lord certainly does help them that help themselves."

So plans for the trip were made. The next night Boy and David lay on their backs on the long dock in front of the Lakeside Pavilion. They were looking at the star studded sky as they fantasized and talked late into the night. They smoked Kool cigarettes and assumed airs far removed from their real selves.

It was June 5th, and Boy loped down the stairs at his house on Lincoln Avenue, worried in his heart that something had happened and Aunt Inga had changed her mind about the trip.

"Hello," he wheezed anxiously.

"What's the matter?" Inga asked. "You sound out of breath."

"I'm OK," Boy replied.

"Good—I just wanted to tell you the latest. I'll be down to St. Paul on the ninth, then your graduation is on the tenth and you'll probably need a couple days to recuperate from the parties, so we'll pack your things on the twelfth and drive up here, get David, and plan to leave about ten a.m. on the thirteenth. Sound OK to you?" Inga asked.

Boy didn't even have to think as he said, "Yes, Ma'am, it sure does."

"Good! Then I'll see you in just a few days." Inga hung up the phone and was gone.

Graduation went without a hitch. It was a spit-and-polish affair in full military regalia. Boy even snuck out of the reception after the ceremony to go across the parade grounds to the horse barn so he could nuzzle his horse, Blaze, one last time as he said farewell.

June 12th dawned bright and sunny. Sophia joined Inga and Boy for the trip to Glenwood where she would say good-bye and *bon voyage* and then return to St. Paul by train.

That evening, after a dinner of fish at Aunt Elizabeth's house, Elizabeth and Sophia supposedly took Boy and David to run an errand before returning them to Inga's for a night's sleep. It turned out the errand was to get them aside, away from Inga, to give them firm instructions regarding the trip.

Sophia began. "Under no circumstance," she said to the boys, "will you let Inga drive." She continued, "One of the main reasons the two of you are along on this trip is to drive so that Inga gets to make this journey to see our brother Rudy and some of her other friends and relatives along the way without endangering her life. Am I clear? Inga does not get to drive. Is that understood?"

"Yes, Mrs. Glemaker," David said with a tremor in his voice, like the fear of the Lord had just struck him.

"Sure," said Boy.

Elizabeth added, although she perhaps didn't need to, "Boy, you in particular know what a poor driver Inga is. Why, she'll drive on the wrong side of the road as easily as on the right, and this new Buick is more powerful than anything she's ever driven before. She might think she can do things with it that she can't. Besides, Inga doesn't see that well anymore."

Then, Sophia picked up the baton in this relay of instruction as Boy and David shifted uncomfortably in the back seat of Elizabeth's Chevrolet.

"Inga will try to convince you that it is her car after all and she should share the driving with you. She's pretty headstrong, but you will just have to say no! Can you do that?" Sophia demanded.

"I think so," Boy said, answering for the two of them while David fidgeted.

" 'I think so' is not good enough!" Sophia pressed.

"Sure, we'll keep her from driving!" Boy said with more confidence than he felt.

"Good. Now let's get you boys a good night's sleep."

They drove back to Inga's house, where Boy and David went to get some restless sleep, waiting for the morning. At nine a.m. on June 13th, they were on their way. Boy was driving; Inga, beside him, was riding "shotgun." David was in the back seat where he began to sing the refrain that they would, singularly or together, sing off tune and with variations, for the next four weeks. David had bought the sheet music and brought it with him.

Baby, it's cold outside.
The weather outside is frightful,
but the fire is so delightful,
and since we've no place to go,
let it snow, let it snow, let it snow.

The black Buick Super headed north on Highway 29. While the Super was not the battleship of the Buick line, it was the heavy cruiser. Four holes along the hood signified its powers. Comfort was at its maximum. One could drive forever and never know fatigue, Boy thought.

They reached Alexandria, seventeen miles north of Glenwood, in what seemed like moments; then they turned west on Highway 52. ". . .*and the fire is so delightful, let it. . .*" One p.m. Fargo, North Dakota. The entourage was out of Minnesota.

Inga turned to Boy and asked, "Do you want to see the house where you lived when your father died?"

"No, let's just keep going." Boy replied.

"Are you hungry yet?" Inga asked.

"No," David replied between verses of "*Baby It's Cold Outside*" and answering for both he and Boy, "We can eat in Valley City."

Still heading west, the miles rolled on by and soon they were in Valley City. They had a bit of lunch at Don's Truck Stop and filled the tank with gas. They were ready to start again.

"How far are we going to drive today?" Boy asked Inga.

"I thought we would try to make it to Bismarck," Inga replied.

"Good by me," David chimed in as he started to climb into the back seat.

"I'll drive now," Inga announced in a definitive tone.

"No, that's all right, Aunt Inga, I'm not tired," Boy replied.

"I will drive," Inga insisted, "It is my car. I want to drive and, besides, I'm tired of riding."

David got out of the back seat but kept looking at the ground, shifting nervously from foot to foot, then taking a step back away from where the confrontation was happening.

"I really don't want you to drive, Aunt Inga," Boy stammered.

"Well, I'm going to drive and that's all there is to it!" Inga declared. "You get in the back and let David ride in front with me. I'm only going to drive to Jamestown. It's only twenty-five miles, then one of you can drive again," Inga finished her announcement.

Silence! End of Discussion! Defeat!

"But *baby it's cold outside . . .*" The tune was flatter than ever. It should have been an omen. Twenty-three miles west of Valley City—five miles east of Jamestown, the slick black Buick passed under a railroad trestle, gaining on the car ahead. A curve in the road half a mile farther concealed any view of oncoming traffic, but Inga never slowed, never hesitated as she pulled into the left-hand lane to pass the slower car. Oops—not enough room. Inga swerved back to the right, the Buick's right rear bumper hooking the front left fender of the car she had tried to pass. Boy was thrown from the rear seat to the floor. He heard and then felt his rib crack as he landed on the potato chip tin. David had turned his head to look back to see what they had hit and his forehead hit and scraped along the right side window of the Buick as it plowed, almost head on, into the truck in the east-bound lane. Everything happened so fast, but as it unfolded before them, it was almost slow motion.

Airborne, the black Buick hit the far ditch, bounced—once, twice—then skidded to a stop thirty yards into a wheat field. The Buick's horn was stuck, blaring a mournful, ear-shattering noise. The hood, bent back, stood straight up. People from other cars were running into the wheat field.

Boy untangled himself from the potato chips and crushed tin and clambered out the left rear door. He was in a total daze. He didn't bother to see how Inga or David were doing, but instead went to check the oil. Eventually, he grudgingly yielded the oil dipstick to a kindly stranger who had pulled the horn wires. The stranger gently, but firmly, guided the stupefied, shock-numbed lad to a place where he could sit undisturbed.

David came limping toward Boy, rubbing his arm, a cut and an abrasion clearly visible on his forehead. He looked bewildered and confused. He sat down beside Boy. "Wow," was all he said.

Boy muttered, over and over, "It's all my fault—it's all my fault."

Vaguely they became aware of an ambulance arriving, siren blaring. They watched, without comprehension, as Inga was carried on a gurney and slid into the ambulance through its yawning rear door. The ambulance left.

Boy and David watched a patrolman come to where they were sitting. He said something they didn't understand. Gently, he reached down and helped them up and then guided them back across the ditch and into the patrol car.

When they got to the hospital in Jamestown, the shock was wearing off and both Boy and David were aware of the pain pulsating through their bodies. Boy's rib cage was taped with numerous layers of wide adhesive tape. David got stitches and a patch on the cut and glass burn on his forehead. The doctor then wrapped his ankle tightly with an adhesive bandage.

Boy spoke for the first time, "I want . . . I want to see my Aunt Inga."

David and Boy were ushered into her room where a doctor and several nurses were busy fussing over her.

The doctor turned to them and said, "Your aunt will have to stay over night, but she was lucky—no real serious damage. As you can see, she has a bump on her forehead that will give her a couple of black eyes in a day or two. Also, she fractured her forearm but, again as you can see, we got that set and in a cast that she'll have to wear for a few weeks."

"How long?" Boy interrupted.

"About six or seven weeks, I imagine," replied the doctor. "But besides that, her only other injuries are a bruised thigh and a twisted ankle. She'll limp for awhile, but no big deal. She'll be good as new in a few weeks," he concluded. The doctor smiled at them, turned, and left the room.

Boy and David were crestfallen. This news hurt more than the bumps and bruises they sported. The trip of their lifetime had lasted all of one day and ended in a wheat field just east of Jamestown, North Dakota.

Now Inga interrupted their séance of self-pity. Her voice

was a bit weak and husky, but her words were firm and clear. "I've called back to Glenwood and Mr. Haas at the Buick garage has another Buick Super waiting for you to pick up tomorrow. It's the exact mate to the one I just smashed. The nurse told me that there is a train that leaves tonight at nine o'clock. You two will be on it!" Inga commanded. "You can buy your tickets straight through but you'll have to change trains in Fargo. You'll catch the Winnipeg Flyer on the Soo Line. It'll take you to Glenwood by five tomorrow morning. Shouldn't be a problem—do you think?" She looked at the boys, waiting for a reply.

Boy and David, mouths dropped open, just nodded and stared at her wide-eyed. They saw her more like a queen perched on her throne than an injured woman lying in bed.

"One more thing," Inga continued to her young knights in waiting. "I don't want you talking to anybody but Mr. Haas at the Buick garage. I swore him to silence. I know he'll keep his mouth shut because I owe him some money now and he owes me some from before when he bought some dresses from my store for his wife. I don't want anyone else to know about our little escapade. I especially don't want Elizabeth or Sophia to get wind of the fact that I was driving. They told you not to let me drive, didn't they?" Inga asked looking at Boy and David.

Boy nodded and murmured, "Yes ma'am."

"I thought so," Inga acknowledged.

"Now get on your way. Get on down to the station—you've got a train to catch. I'll be out of here and ready to go when you get back."

It was a brave act, but Boy could see the pain and weariness etched in Inga's bruised and battered face as they left the room.

That night as David and Boy sat on the depot platform waiting for the east bound Empire Builder the western sky, with Venus cradled by the crescent moon in the after-glow of the sun's departure, was a scene of beauty neither boy had ever known in his life.

In Glenwood the clandestine caper came off without a hitch. Mr. Haas met the east bound Winnipeg Flyer at 5:30 a.m. Boy and David wheezed and limped their way, descending from the train and along the platform, to hide in the early morning shadows cast by the depot building. Soon the Buick man appeared on the platform and the boys were hustled to his waiting car and then down into Glenwood. Once at the garage, Mr. Haas was full of questions and instructions. "Is Mrs. Phair really OK?" he asked.

"Oh yes, fine. Just a little bruised and tired from the ordeal," Boy lied.

"Good. Here are the papers. The registration is in order, I believe, and I put on a set of dealer's plates. They should get you back to Jamestown where you can get the ones from the other car and put them on. Any other details, Inga can take care of when you come back. Oh yes—one more thing. I called Matt Benett about the insurance and he has transferred it. You can tell Inga I don't think her secret got out because I think I convinced Matt that she had sold the other car in Jamestown. I hope there won't be any trouble," the Buick man paused, but quickly went on, "You boys sure you're all right to drive?"

Boy sucked air once more and the look on his face said he didn't feel too good. David tried to keep the right side of his face hidden so his blackened eye wasn't visible. "Oh yes—we're just fine. Just a little tired from the train ride, you know," Boy tried to seem upbeat, but failed miserably.

There was a long pause as Mr. Haas looked the boys over carefully.

"Well, you probably want to get going and I want to get home for breakfast," Mr. Haas said. What he probably thought was "God, I hope these kids don't smash this one, too!"

"Remember now, this here is a brand new car, got only five miles on it, so you're going to have to drive it real slow—not over forty for the first three hundred miles. Then you can speed it up a bit, but not over fifty, and try not to drive all at one speed. Vary it a bit; they break in better that way." He paused, "Well—take care now. Good luck. And be careful!"

Mr. Haas turned and started toward his car, but then called over his shoulder, "Greet Inga from me. Tell her not to worry. No one saw us and I won't tell anyone where the green Buick went."

Boy drove and David sang as the Buick, this time green, once again headed north, up the Northern Pacific hill on Highway 29 and on to Alexandria where they would again turn west for the drive to Jamestown.

David crooned and Boy chimed in, *"Baby it's cold outside—the weather outside is frightful, but you are so delightful, lettuce grow, lettuce grow, lettuce grow."*

It was only 6:45 a.m. After the first half hour, while David slept and Boy drove, the Buick rolled on at sixty miles per-hour. After an hour and a half, Boy slept and David drove. Now the Buick crept at forty, but the singing was much better and created less pain for singer and audience alike.

At five p.m., the city limit sign of Jamestown came into view. David remembered how to find the hospital and there was Inga, sitting with a paper bag of her things and medicines. She looked God awful! Both her eyes were black and with her white hair and flushed red cheeks she looked like a raccoon. Her left foot was in a brace and her left arm was in a cast. Still she smiled and waved with her good arm. "Anybody see you git outta Dodge?" she chortled.

"Nope—no one," Boy responded.

"Good. Then we're free as birds. Let's go eat and find a place to stay the night." Then Inga spotted the green Buick. "Nice car, but I liked the dented one better."

At eight a.m., the Buick with its cargo of three rolled west. Inga was glad to ride shotgun never uttering another word about wanting to drive.

The chorus of Inga and David singing "Baby It's Cold Outside" was lost in the whistling of the wind blowing clean, warm June air through the open windows. When they had stopped at seven for breakfast, Inga asked the truck stop cook to pack some sandwiches for a picnic lunch. Early noon found the Buick on the shores of the Missouri River at Mandan. The picnic was good.

In late afternoon, the Buick cruised through Medora, keeping a lookout for remnants of Teddy Roosevelt, as it made a short loop through the Badlands.Then it was back to Highway 52 heading west; by now Inga was fading fast. It was obvious that the vagabonds would not make it to Glendive, Montana, this day.

"Let's stop pretty soon," Boy said.

"Good Idea," David agreed.

"I think we're just about at the Montana border. There is the town called Beach just before we get into Montana," Inga said, trying to look at the map, but her glasses had been broken in the accident. They decided to see if the little town of Beach on the North Dakota / Montana border would have accommodations.

How Beach, North Dakota, got its name is thoroughly a mystery. There isn't any water, much less an ocean, for more than a thousand miles in any direction. Beach did have a hotel—a two-story, wood-framed, unpainted clapboard, bathroom-at-the-end-of-the-hall building. Any port at day's end would do and Inga was at the zombie point on the exhaustion scale. While her spirit and smile never wavered, her sixty-six year old body was struggling to overcome the blows it had taken in the crash.

On the other hand, Boy and David had reached the point of ridiculous irrationality and hilarity in their fatigue. The endorphins released by their fatigue and singing had numbed their brains and dulled their pains. The whiskered front-desk man at the Beach Ritz was also numbed, but by Johnny Walker. Inga helped him out by writing the names in the hotel registry. It was her last valiant effort of the day.

"Whiskers" threw the keys on the counter and with a sweeping gesture of his arm announced, "Yer shrooms char tchew-o-one and tchew-o-tchew. Thur up shtairs." Then he looked at Inga, Boy, and David with a blank, toothless smile just before his chin dropped to his chest and his head bumped down to the counter in a swoon of alcoholic bliss.

It was half an hour later, Inga already in bed and gently snoring in Room 201, when Boy and David spotted the coiled rope beneath the window in their Room 202. The sign above the rope read: "For Emergency Use Only." It didn't take David and Boy long to decide that they had an emergency. They quickly uncoiled the rope and threw it out the window. Promptly David announced, "I'm scared. I don't want to go down and break my other leg."

Boy replied, "Oh come on—we won't get hurt. Besides, we're only one floor up."

"OK, I guess," David said with tired resignation.

Boy went out the window first. His ribs hurt but he managed to rappel down the unpainted wall. David hesitated, but then followed and landed at the bottom with a big smile on his face.

Inside, at the front desk, they shook "Whiskers" awake and announced, "We want to check into Room 202."

"I shink churs shomebody in thare," Whiskers announced, looking confused, rumpled and puzzled.

"Yes," said Boy, "It's us, but we still want to check in, just to be sure."

"OK. Shears shome keys," Whiskers said as he pushed a second set of keys across the counter. The keys were for Room 206.Boy grabbed the keys and he and David headed up the stairs trying to control their laughter.

Again it was out the window, down the wall, and back to Whiskers, who was once more asleep at the desk.

"We want to check into Room 202," Boy said, still trying to keep from laughing. David was coughing in an attempt to mask his laughter. Whiskers looked up, opened his eyes, closed them again and scrunched his face, opened his eyes again, shook his head and blankly stared at the boys.

He stood up, rocked back and forth and from side to side, finally he slurred, "Jeez—thers a whole bunch of pee . . . pee . . . folksh already shup ther." He paused, squinted, and shook his head. "I shink one ov shem ish ewe . . . shay are you my nephew?" Then Whisker's body slumped once more, and as he folded into the chair his head thumped on the desk. Whiskers was gone for the night.

David and Boy were laughing so hard as they bumped and scraped up the wooden stairs that they awakened Inga, who looked out of her door and asked, "What's going on?"

"You don't want to know," Boy replied. "We're just going to bed—we'll tell you in the morning."

And so they did—until Inga's blackened, yellowing, greening bruised eyes ran with tears of laughter. The next day, spirits and bodies refreshed, the entourage entered the Big Sky country or Montana. They headed north to Wolf Point then west again, but now on Highway 2 to Nashua.

Nashua was the little town where many years before Rudy and Martin, owners of the general store, Boy's Uncles-to-Be, had brought their sister, Boy's mother, Sophia to seek a cure for tuberculosis. For Boy, it was where his mother, Sophia, had homesteaded on the Missouri River bottoms. It was the place where the Indians had befriended her and helped her heal. It was the source of the stories of their many kindnesses to Sophia as told by her to her children. It was from this place and from the Indians who had lived here that Sophia received the gift of the little gun which Boy so cherished now.

Of course now, so-called progress had consumed the teepee village and the little homestead cabin under many feet of water, water of the manmade lake formed by the Fort Peck Dam. Still, Boy wanted to go as close as possible to the site. He wanted to feel the energy if he could. He wanted to try to imagine what Sophia's life had been like when she had lived there so many years before.

"Aunt Inga, can we drive over to the dam, kinda where mom's cabin used to be?" Boy asked.

Inga agreed. They drove in silence to the Fort Peck dam. But there was nothing to see except massive boulders, rip-rapping against potential flood waters. The boulders were ugly and they created sunbathing surfaces for hundreds of appreciative rattlesnakes.

Often progress and developers destroy the sacred so that all that's left is memories, which must live by being cherished and shared. Boy mused, "Perhaps the rattlesnakes are protecting the remnants of my family's memories."

The next stop was Shelby, Montana. Inga wanted to visit relatives of some relations of somebody. Boy and David weren't interested, so they crooned, *"Baby, It's cold outside . . . relatives are frightful, but the land is so delightful. . ."*

Inga's visits to relatives completed, they went north to Sweetgrass on the Canadian border. A distance into Canada, a ferry carried the Buick and its inhabitants across the Bow River to an Alberta prairie road that ended in the yard of a ranch belonging to some long-time friends of Inga's. The traveling party would rest at this oasis for a few days, preparing themselves to encounter the majesty and beauty of Lake Louise and Banff in the Canadian Rockies.

Healing happened quickly now. Boy discovered that a pain worse than a cracked rib came when David declared it was time to remove the adhesive plaster bandage from Boy's torso. Boy screamed "Ouch!" and David laughed.

Inga's eyes, no longer puffy, had exchanged their shades of black for brighter yellows and greens. David still looked like a pirate with a patch above his eye, but his limp was gone and his fleetness of foot returned which took him out of Boy's reach when he tried to retaliate for the bandage stripping.

Inga's friends were generous folks and welcomed the party with genuine hospitality. The meal the first night was to be a feast of beefsteak, raised and butchered right at the ranch by Ted himself. "Do you want to come with me to fetch the steaks? We have to cut them off the sides of beef that are hanging and curing in the slaughter barn," Ted asked Boy and David.

"Sure," they answered in unison.

Once inside the slaughter barn, they followed Ted up

the ladder to the loft. There hung two magnificent sides of Black Angus beef—covered with little white maggots!

Ted took his knife out and began to scrape the maggots off.

"Disgusting!" yelled David and bolted back down the ladder and away from the barn. As he left, his face looked a ghastly white.

"What's the matter with him? He got a weak stomach?" Ted asked as his knife sliced through the maggot free side of beef, removing the beautiful steaks that would be their supper.

Boy watched, fascinated, and replied, "Oh David? He'll be all right. He just doesn't like the sight of blood." Boy was remembering the fishhook, the boat, and David fainting.

The steaks that night were the best Boy, Inga and David had ever eaten. The Black Angus had been raised on virginal Canadian prairie grass and cured to tender perfection under the expertise of Ted's watchful eye and the industry of the maggots in the slaughter-house loft. Eleanor, Ted's wife, cooked the steaks to gourmet quality and served them with homemade bread and butter and home-canned corn.

Matching the perfection of the food was the brilliance of the stories and the depth of love shared among Inga, Eleanor and Ted. David and Boy sat and listened. Old and new friends alike, it mattered not, joined in the sharing that went on into the night when tiredness finally caused them to surrender. The boys climbed yet another ladder, this one to the bunk-room where they slept.

The days passed quickly as did the miles and the beauty of the Rockies. The harmony with *"Baby it's cold outside. . ."* didn't improve. After traveling to Lake Louise and Banff and crossing the spine of the Rockies at the sixteen hundred meter Vermillion Pass, the entourage dropped southward. On this part of the journey, Boy and David learned that the only paved road in western Canada in 1949 had been built by the United States government. It was the first mile they traveled into Canada north of the Sweetgrass crossing. Some said this paved mile of road was a United States' gesture of goodwill toward Canada. Others said it was an attempt by the United States as a role model. Still others firmly believed it was because the U. S. engineers got lost and didn't know where the border was.

Gravel roads made the going slow, the singing louder, and the beauty of the land more appreciated. Just inside Canada, north of Spokane, Washington, Inga and her brood came to the small towns of Nelson, Rossland, and Trail, British Columbia. Getting to this trilogy of towns was one of Inga's goals. It was here that Phair's first family still lived. From here he left to manage the plush hotels for the Canadian Pacific Railroad. He left because he found he could no longer live the lie of pretending to be heterosexual, when deep inside he knew he wasn't.

His daughter still lived here. Phair had never seen his grandchildren. Boy knew, from conversations he and Phair had before his uncle died, how deeply pained his conflicted soul had been. Inga knew this also. Now it was the time to heal old wounds. Inga wanted to find his daughter and her family and tell them of the beauty, integrity, and honesty of the man they had never known.

Their welcome was warm, and when Inga, Boy, and David left to begin their journey back to Minnesota, it was with a deeper and broader understanding of what family really meant.

Spokane, Washington: Uncle Rudy and his second wife, Christine, had settled there. Rudy and Martin had lived a long time in the West. Martin had died, but his family still lived, scattered throughout the West. The stop in Spokane to visit Rudy and Christine would be another very special reconnection for Boy with part of his mother's history.

For Inga it had particular meaning. She was "stitching" the family together. It was her secret agenda for the journey. It was what drove her to overcome all the obstacles that had presented themselves. She wanted Boy to know, feel and see where each of the remnants of the family lived, how the land affected them and how they, in turn, cared for the land where they lived.

They stopped and found "family" in Spokane, in Missoula, in Bozeman. Each stop brought late-night listening. During the days on the road, the miles were filled with stories and reminiscing.

"Baby it's warm outside and you are so delightful . . . let it blow . . . let it blow. . . ." From Bozeman, they went south to Yellowstone National Park. They dared not return home without having been faithful to Old Faithful. At this point, the journey was beginning to wear. They had been on the road for more than three and a half weeks and were hitting that emotional wall that John Steinbeck talked about, where you know the journey is over even though you're still miles and miles from home.

"The boredom inside is frightful, but you are still delightful . . . let us roll . . . let us roll . . . let us roll. . ."

Escaping from Yellowstone, the plan was to make it to Billings where the travelers would get a good night's sleep before heading east with renewed vigor and great resolve. Alas, hotel workers were on strike in Billings. When Inga asked the innkeeper about accommodations, the response was, "yes they would provide accommodations—on the sixth floor. But," the hotel clerk politely informed them, "you will have to carry your own suitcases up and make your own beds. No, you cannot use the elevator. You must understand. The elevator operator is one of the people on strike and we don't want to anger anyone or the strike will go longer."

"You got to be kidding!" Boy blurted out.

"Can't you see this lady is hurt?" David exploded.

After some intensely persuasive conversation, the clerk recanted and agreed to take Inga up in the elevator. The boys caught him several times staring at Inga's cast and the fading yellow and green mask about her eyes.

The innkeeper quickly checked his melting resolve, however: "I will give only the lady a lift in the elevator. The boys will have to take the stairs. I'm sorry, but the lady has a medical emergency and you boys don't." He turned and walked into his office and shut the door.

Boy and David lugged the luggage up the stairs, vowing never to return to Billings. They fell exhausted into bed.

The following day they reached Belle Fourche. At least they had made it into South Dakota. The next day was a long, hot day of driving, but they arrived in Watertown. *"South Dak—ota is frightful and we were once delightful . . . let us go . . . let us go . . . let us go. . ."* Not only were the words taking a beating and the song changing, but the oppressive heat was drying their throats and the notes, bad as they had been, were getting worse. They were sticking in every key but the right one.

Boy wanted to see the Methodist hospital in Watertown where he had been born, but it had burned down and was a total loss, along with all the birth records, including his. Perhaps there was a message in that. Maybe he didn't really have an identity at all. "Who knows what the gods intend," mused Boy—"the journey's final day . . . onward, resolutely onward, to Madison on Minnesota's western border . . . onward to Montevideo . . . then northward, past the duck slough near Lake Emily, a place of memory upon memory, of one hunt and then another with Uncle Phair."

The little town of Starbuck appeared in front and as quickly disappeared in the rear view mirror. The Buick skirted the northern shore of Lake Minnewaska and entered Glenwood. At Inga's little stucco house on Green Street, Elizabeth observed to Inga, "I thought your Buick was black."

The doors opened, Boy climbed out of the driver's side and David exited the rear seat. Inga only smiled and tried to hide her cast from her younger sister's view.

ENDINGS

In the years following the move to St.Paul, the trust and humor between S.P. and Boy had grown and strengthened. Experience had piled upon experience. There had been two vacations on the North Shore of Lake Superior that included fishing on the open water for large lake trout, shooting bear that ravaged the garbage behind the cabin, golfing, but never beating S.P., who had more energy than most people half his age.

When time came to apply for college and to figure out the finances, S.P. was there. Boy was encouraged in his dream to go to medical training. S.P. and Sophia were frequent visitors at the college and at the breaks, always willing to open their home to parties and friends. When Boy needed a car to go back and forth from the college in Iowa to St. Paul, S.P. was there to help him find and buy his '47 Chevy. Always the approach and attitude were the same: praise, encouragement and help. If Boy was doing something wrong, which wasn't all that seldom, S.P.'s intervention was, "Maybe if you did it more like this it would work better, or you would get along better."

In the spring of Boy's junior year, S.P. and Sophia decided to retire. Paul, S.P.'s biological son, didn't want to buy the fur business. This was a major disappointment to S.P. and meant that the business was closed after fifty-two years. The merchandise was sold. As the going-out-of-business sale went on, Boy noticed each time he came home that S.P. looked older and more tired.

On one of the trips home, Boy brought with him the girl he hoped to marry. Nothing was said, but S.P. seemed to sense it. He took Norma aside and pleaded, "Please take care of Boy. He's very special to me."

This was a hard burden to put on someone, but S.P. was not thinking of that; he only wanted to be sure that Boy would not return to loneliness. The week following the store's actual closing, S.P. was diagnosed with advanced prostate cancer. He was seventy-six.

It seemed incredulous. He was a man of great vitality, a man who had played golf and beaten Boy with great regularity. The cancer had invaded his bones. He was dying. Years later, Boy would come to know that type of cancer well, and the part of the body it invades. He would learn that a man's prostate and a woman's ovaries are the sites where the body wisdom stores its issues of identity—what it means to be a person, a man or a woman, and who that particular man or woman is.

S.P. had always been an artist and a businessman. He had always been there for his customers. That was who he was. Now the business was gone and his identity was eaten up.

The impending loss would be great, not only for Boy and family, but for the community. S.P. had preached in church on numerous occasions and had done more than an adequate job for the vacationing pastor. He had been there for neighbor and family, strong enough to do whatever was needed. He had been the agent of transformation for Sophia's health when he had, true to his word, convinced her to see Dr. Charlie Hensel. Boy rememberd how he and S.P. had sat in the office when Dr. Hensel had completed all his tests, and in his loud and bear-like voice had said to Sophia, "Lady one day you will die, but you will never die of a heart attack. Unfortunately, doctors have scared you into illness. Now it's time to put your fear aside. You have a husband, a son and a daughter who need you. Go and have fun with them."

True to his word, Sophia died fourteen years later, ten years after S.P. died, but not of a heart attack. Her heart was strong.

But now S.P. was dying, and there was no agent for his transformation.

The plans he and Sophia had made to travel to Sweden and Norway were not to be experienced. The plans to have more time with one another were not to be. The two months at home while going to outpatient radiation treatment didn't even slow the disease. The pain became too intense and Dr. Hensel admitted him to Miller Hospital, knowing that he would not leave alive. S.P. needed special care. He was weak and drifted in and out of consciousness.

He was a patient in the same hospital where Dr. Hensel had helped Boy get a nursing orderly job as part of his preparation for medical school. Boy worked as a surgical orderly, a psych orderly, and a general duty orderly. This broad-based, practical training helped Boy understand the rigors of human suffering and the field of help he was intending to enter.

For twenty-three days after S.P. was admitted, Boy would work an eight-hour shift, then go to S.P.'s room and sit. He would "special" S.P. for eight hours, making sure that everything was done to keep this man comfortable. Boy attended to his medications, turned him in bed, sat and listened when he wanted to talk, emptied his bed pans, checked on his catheters and his fluid output, and did whatever else was needed.

When the shift was finished, usually around midnight or sometimes 7 a.m., Boy would go to the orderly staff room to sleep a bit before starting all over again. It was during these days with S.P. that there was much conversation when the pain was in remission. S.P. shared stories of his youth. He told of his early days, newly arrived from Sweden. He told of his inventions and of the beginning of the fur store. He told of falling in love with Sophia. He told Boy, as in a litany, as though in a sacred confession, all of his deepest feelings, sad and happy, trusting and doubting. He would end some of the sessions by apologizing to the boy for boring him with stories. Boy always protested against this apology.

On the twenty-third day of the hospital stay, S.P. seemed stable and stronger. He and Sophia, who had been a constant companion each day in the hospital, encouraged Boy to take an evening off. Boy would go to a movie with a friend. Adrian had called him many times and Boy refused to leave the hospital. This time, Boy was still reluctant to go, but on reflection, thought that perhaps S. P. and Sophia wanted and needed time alone, so he left.

As he left the hospital, Jeanne came in headed for S.P.'s room. She, too, spent as many hours of each day with S.P. as possible. If S.P. and Sophia wanted time alone they would just have to tell Jeanne to leave, but Boy felt good that S.P. would not be alone.

Boy and his friend went out to eat, went to the movie, and when they returned, there was a call waiting for Boy from the nursing station at Miller Hospital. S.P. had drifted into a coma. Could Boy come right away?

The last words S.P. had spoken were, "Where's Boy? I want him here. Please ask him to come."

Boy made the trip across the city to the hospital in record time. When he came into the dimly lit hospital room, S.P.'s breathing was labored. The family was standing around the bed. The death vigil was in full progress. The doctor had been there, examined S.P. and said it was a matter of only hours.

Boy stood toward the end of the bed, off to the side. Sophia came and took his arm. She pulled him to the side of the bed."Clem wants you," she whispered.

Boy moved to the head of the bed and put his hand on S.P.'s shoulder. He stood there a long time. The breathing became more erratic, shallow. Then S.P. opened his eyes and whispered something. Jeanne, Sophia, Boy, and S.P.'s daughter, Louise, all looked at each other. They couldn't hear. They couldn't understand. Boy leaned down and put his arm around S.P. and his ear by S.P.'s mouth, trying to hear the words. Softly and with difficulty S.P. spoke them again.

"Take care of them."

He gasped and breathed his last. He was gone.

With the gentleness he had learned from this fine man, Boy drew his hand across S.P.'s eyes, and they were closed one last time.

EPILOGUE

Sophia Lie Mossman Glemaker died June 4, 1962, but not from tuberculosis or some other lung disease. Nor did she die of "heart disease" caused by Boy, as Frieda led him to believe would happen. She died after a valiant, year-long struggle with pancreatic cancer.

For Sophia to go gently into death's long goodnight would have been too out of character for this strong-minded, compassionate, wise, independent woman, so she did not. Instead, she continued in her caring until the very moment of her death. What briefly follows are some vignettes and quotes from her last days and hours before she passed, and even from the moment she stepped into the next world.

Said to Boy and Jeanne when the pain medications she was on were making her mind confused and wander the final week she lived, "Oh, God! I don't want to sound like Inga when her mind wanders because of her hardened arteries. I want you to be able to understand me."

Again, said to Jeanne and Boy, "Don't let the doctors make any heroic efforts to keep me alive. If I live, I want to live. If I die, it's OK. God and I are friends."

Said to Boy at the hospital one day when Jeanne wasn't around: "I just looked in the mirror and this cancer has me looking godawful. Don't let Jeanne come in and see me. She is a woman and shouldn't see how ugly I have become!"

Told to Boy as he lay beside her and cradled her in his arms on Sunday, June 4, 1962, at the hospital, the morning before she died. She recalled all the events that happened before Boy's birth, as well as when he was very young, before Lou's death. Sophia told stories and Boy listened for four hours. When it came time to leave, Boy said, "I'll come back." Sophia responded: "This is the last time we will see each other." Boy said, "I know."

That evening, at eight o'clock, Jeanne went to Sophia's hospital room and saw that she was in distress. Jeanne went to get the nurse to help. When they returned, Sophia had died. She made the journey by herself, in her own time.

COMMENTS FROM BOY

Boy finally found his name. He tried Frank, the name his uncle used. It didn't fit. It felt too staid for his risking, loud, outspoken style. He settled on James, one of the Sons of Thunder, as Holy Scripture describes.

And, becoming a man has never been easy, but in recent times it has been like navigating a rudderless ship on an angry sea. The model of a warrior as a goal for masculine identity needs to be discarded because of the machismo that comes with the warrior image. Hopefully this identity for males will come to a place in human history where it is no longer valued for it leads to racism, sexism, rage of all kinds, anti-choice, exploitation, domestic violence, and, worst of all, war. These spin-offs of the masculine brain operating in isolation from the feminine are undesirable traits in an overcrowded and overcrowding world. Yet they continue, unbridled, even to the point of using war as a strategy to control oil and other world currencies in this new environment of globalization.

Further, these spin-offs create a confusion of spirituality with sadism and brutality. Witness this confusion. Millions of people flocked to theaters to see *The Passion of Christ* believing they would see something spiritual, and instead watched hours of unbridled torture and brutality. Is this what makes a spiritual happening? Does whoever gets the most wealth or power win? Does whoever inflicts the most fear, pain and death dominate?

The world can no longer tolerate the dominance of this masculine brain approach. Now, as at no time in the past, we, as a human race and as a living planet, must look to the power emanating from the inclusion of the primordial feminine for our survival.

Unfortunately, it seems that we are still lost in the sinking sand of the exclusive masculine, where the linear brain still functions in intracranial isolation. This deluded consciousness is socially linked with the other masculine isolates, which form a narcissistic political power base that makes decisions that in turn trap the whole world culture in its delusion.

Within Boy's family, both nuclear and extended, different members entered a quest to find a new way of being and thinking that was not based on conquest and competition, but rather on cooperation and compassion. What I have attempted to bring to the reader through this book about Boy is how the process to become a new being unfolded.

How did this happen?

What spawned Boy and led him down a different path of survival and being, out into a world that demanded its men become strong, inclusive beings of compassion, sensitivity, courage, adventure and tolerance, integrated with all life forms?

Were Boy's grandparents the real progenitors of a new way of becoming man, or perhaps person?

Perhaps the impetus is embedded in the metaphor of grandfather Lee during the Civil War, hunting for food and safe passage after escaping Andersonville prison and then heading back to the North. A hunt necessitated in order that he and his comrade might survive. He found the path of survival because he spoke a common language with the women who took him in and protected him from death as he hunted for a way home, as told in the "The Gun."

Or was it Grandfather's parents or his parent's parents that, if we searched hard enough, would provide the model for being in harmony with the earth and its creation? Mutations of a social structure happen rarely, surely not as often as they do in a biological structure, but almost always in response to a need for survival.

For example, in "The Gun," the grandfather, Andrew B. and grandmother, Ann Elise—"Lizzy"—were deeply committed to the idea of equity and equality between the sexes and with all races. This commitment was birthed by both family and war experiences.

In a similar way in the second chapter, Grandfather Mossman (Beal Turner), struggled to learn about compassion and acceptance in his encounters with his wife Ann Eliza and his daughter, Emmy, as she insisted on choosing the path for her own life.

Yet, it seems that we, collectively, as world citizens, have not yet provided good models for becoming a man or a *liberated* woman, so the struggle is played out in private, individual ways and in selected families. Perhaps Boy was privileged to be born into a family that engaged in such cosmic struggles.

It is my belief that the model that could lead in a new direction is the archetype of the Hunter with its deity the goddess Diana. I have come to this belief through my encounters with Boy's uncle, Jasper Phair (Inga's husband), who was Boy's father surrogate and whom you met in the "Swimming Lesson," the "Pheasant Hunt," and "Amends." Perhaps it also became evident in the story "Swan" where you met S.P. Glemaker, Boy's stepfather and early mentor.

My hope is to find a paradigm that will permit us to incorporate the feminine into the decision-making and life fabric of our world, without losing the firm ruggedness of the masculine. Both archetypes, affirmed within the psyche of each individual, are necessary for the survival of humanity.

Sadly this direction, this idea of the hunt, has not been incorporated or even understood as having embedded in it a model for parenting and for growing *boys and girls* into men and women that can hunt for truths of all kinds, for minds, for bodies, and for souls. Unfortunately, the idea "to hunt" is still culturally thought of as excessively masculine. It is, I fear, thought of in the usual way as killing, of the total domination of the life of another living thing.

But in the manner of the archetype, to hunt, meant one should be open and vulnerable to the prey, in order that the prey would sacrifice its power so that all of life might grow, emerge and benefit. The roles of prey and predator in this archetype are in constant, dynamic relationship to one another—the prey becoming predator and the predator becoming prey of another, incorporating both masculine and feminine. In a metaphoric way this can apply to new thoughts, paradigms, and inventions as well as to the struggles for survival in the biological world. In this dance of dynamism the evolution and balance of life emerges.

Such a paradoxical paradigm demands a broader understanding of the feminine and thus the deity of the hunt, Diana, the goddess. In Boy's hunt for identity, the goddess is embodied in the person of Sophia, mother of Boy, who quietly leads Boy in the direction of compassion, sensitivity, responsibility, creativity, courage and adventure.

Boy's journey is similar to the journey of hunting that many women have had to take, out of necessity, during the last half of the last century in a quest to overthrow the tyranny of oppression in education, the work place, abusive relationships and politics. It was a journey that Sophia herself had to take, as a way out of a life-threatening illness and too, out of poverty, after Lou's death.

It was a hunt for health that led her into the unusual experience of homesteading in a place where she was helped by the kindness of people of a different and unfamiliar culture, as told in "The Gun."

It seems as though *all journeys* and searches for new paradigms of being are birthed in pain and in a *role model* vacuum, but within the framework of the goddess gender.

NOTES

Sophia's family consisted of Mother, Father and ten siblings. Below are Boy's maternal grandparents and the aunts and uncles important to this book.

Boy's Maternal Grandfather:

Andres (Andrew) Bjornson Lie, who was born in Nordre Aurdal, Norway, in 1840 and came to the United States in 1861. On April 2, 1862, he became a soldier in Company D of the 13th Wisconsin Regiment and fought in the Civil War, being honorably discharged April 6, 1865. In his civilian life he was a carpenter and a farmer.

Boy's Maternal Grandmother:

Anne Elise Nelson, who was born in Kristiania, Norway, in 1851 and in 1862 immigrated to Wisconsin. She later moved near St. Paul and then on to Pope County. In 1870 she and Anders were married. They had twelve children.

The important siblings in this book are:

Julius Lie: Born September 25,1871, died 1951
Magnus Lie: Born April 8,1877, died 1954
Martin Lie: Born April 7,1879, died 1948
Inga Lie Just: Born June 9, 1883, died 1965
Cora Alvina Lie: Born March 28,1885, died 1907

Rudolph Lie: Born April 11,1887, died 1959
Matty Lie Bungate: Born December 21, 1888. died 1972
Elizabeth Lie Stilton: Born November 24, 1894, died 1988

Lou's family consisted of Mother, Father and five siblings. Below are Boy's paternal grandparents and the aunts and uncles important to this book.

Boy's Paternal Grandfather;

Beal Turner Mossman, who was born June 12, 1836 in Coshocton County, Ohio. In 1850 he moved with his parents to Coesse, Indiana.

Boy's Paternal Grandmother:

Ann Eliza Truax, who was born May 29,1840 in St. Paris, Ohio. She and Beal were married June 9,1861. On April 1,1880, they moved with their family to an 800 acre farm homestead on the north east shore of Little Birch lake in Todd County near Grey Eagle, Minnesota, where Louis Marshall, Boy's father was born.

The siblings important in this book are:

Emmy Evaline: Born May 2, 1867, died March 6. 1958
James Francis: Born March 9, 1871,died 1940
Isaac Jay: Born February 7, 1873, died 1922
Fredrick Turner: Born March 24, 1878, died 1972
Louis Marshall: Born October 24, 1885, died January 19, 1936

By the time Boy was born in 1931, all of his grandparents had died, as had several of his aunts and uncles. It should be noted that Boy's family "lost" a whole generation, inasmuch as two generations in his lineage had children well into their forties and even early fifties.

Boy's maternal grandfather was born in 1840 and his maternal grandmother in 1851. Sophia was born in 1891 when her mother was 40 and her father was 51. Sophia was 40 when Boy was born.

Boy's paternal grandfather was born in 1836 and his paternal grandmother was born in 1840. Louis was born in 1885 when his mother was 45 and his father was 49. Louis, born in 1885, was 45 when Boy was born.

Other significant facts and people.

The name *Sophia* is used because it means "her wisdom." It was her wisdom that helped Boy survive and learn as he grew to have an identity of his own.

Swan Pearson Glemaker was Sophia's second husband. She affectionately called him "Clem"; he introduced himself with his initials "S.P." S.P. was born March 1876, died June 1952; S.P. and Sophia were married May 1946.

Gilbert Stilton was Elizabeth Lie's husband (she was Sophia's sister).

Josephine Smith was Sophia's friend and business partner. After Sophia married Lou, Josephine worked with Inga, Sophia's sister, in her Ladies Ready-to-Wear Store on Main Street in Glenwood.

Jasper Phair was Sophia's sister's (Inga) husband. They married late and had no children though Jaspar became a father to Boy after Lou's death. Jasper taught Boy to hunt, fish and swim. Inga "rescued" Boy often.

Frieda became Boy's and Jeanne's nanny because Sophia needed help caring for her four- and five-year-old children. After Sophia was widowed the first time, she moved to Glenwood and went into business in women's shoes. Sophia searched diligently and finally found Frieda, who became part of the family for eight years.

Aunt Jen Houseman was Sophia's aunt on her mother's side of the family. She married young, to a brilliant architect named William Houseman. By age forty-four William was a millionaire. He suddenly died and left Jen Houseman a very wealthy but austere woman who lauded it over everyone, but still "did good" by her relatives.

George Ostby was the chief of police in Fargo, North Dakota, during the years that Sophia and Lou lived there. He became a friend of the family and was particularly helpful during times of crisis.

James Gilbert was Emmy's first husband.
He died March 1886.

Robert Miller was Emmy's second husband. He died about 1890, two years after he and Emmy were married.

William DeLaurier was Emmy's third husband. He died in 1953, five years before Emmy's death in 1958.

These stories are characterizations of events from the lives of Boy's people and from his own life. These happenings both shaped him and warped him at the same time.

ABOUT THE AUTHOR

Counselor. Pastor. Hunter. Sundanced with Lakota. Harness Racer. Writer. Dog sledder. It's true that James Mossman has, at one time or another, been all of the above. Yet labels are hardly adequate to tell the story of this eclectic soul, this incredibly learned man whose values were forged in another time, whose impact has transcended all barriers, whose life has been lived on his own terms. For all of this, countless folks give thanks.

> *"Neither of us has any doubt that, without his counsel, we would not be married today," writes a former client. "Our marriage survived, flourished actually. We have both been to other counselors in the past and have never met anyone who feels "safer" than Mr. Mossman."*
>
> *"With James I feel so much less alone, less isolated," writes another. "This is what I think James brings to people who come*

to know him—in the book, in his sessions, at the dinner table, out fishing, in the car."

Born in Glenwood, MN, Mossman was raised in the hardscrabble existence of the Depression. Surviving the untimely death of his father and his mother's epic struggle to raise two children on her own, Mossman went on to race harness horses, write poetry, study overseas, and compile a stellar list of credentials: Ordained clergyman; Licensed Independent Clinical Social Worker; Clinical Pastoral Education Supervisor; Sexual Health Therapist; Chief Operations Officer; Chaplain. For those who know him, perhaps just one label really fits—friend.

"Individuals, couples and families have come to you with their wounds and pain," writes Joanne Negstad of Lutheran Social Services. "Through their relationships with you, they have discovered hope and healing. You have ministered to so many on their spiritual journey."

"James has this quiet and effective way of gaining perspective on difficult issues," writes Lutheran pastor Susan Peterson. From corporate titans to the Native American Community, from the forgotten streets of Miami to the north woods of Minnesota, James Mossman has been there. He has listened. They have learned. And together, we have all lived a little bit better than before.

You are welcome to contact James F. Mossman at:
jfmossman@comcast.net.